Robert Burns, John George Dow

Selections from the Poems of Robert Burns

Robert Burns, John George Dow

Selections from the Poems of Robert Burns

ISBN/EAN: 9783744763509

Printed in Europe, USA, Canada, Australia, Japan

Cover: Foto ©Andreas Hilbeck / pixelio.de

More available books at **www.hansebooks.com**

SELECTIONS

FROM THE

POEMS OF ROBERT BURNS

EDITED

WITH INTRODUCTION, NOTES, AND VOCABULARY

BY

JOHN G. DOW, M.A.

LATE INSTRUCTOR IN ENGLISH IN THE UNIVERSITY OF WISCONSIN

BOSTON, U.S.A.
GINN & COMPANY, PUBLISHERS
The Athenæum Press
1898

PREFACE.

THE present volume was intended by the editor, the late Professor John G. Dow, to furnish such a selection from the poems of Burns as should, in moderate compass, fully illustrate the character and the range of his genius. In the Introduction it was Professor Dow's first purpose to consider Burns as a poet, and accordingly, after a brief biographical sketch, he passed over to a purely literary discussion. The reader will find a chapter on the obligations of Burns to his predecessors, another on his attitude toward nature, and so on. He will, however, discover no trace of that liking for moral dissection which has too often diverted critics from matters more immediately pertinent. The sections on language, the notes, and the glossary, will, it is hoped, afford the reader all the assistance needed to make the poems completely intelligible.

Professor Dow died suddenly January 21, 1897. His manuscript was to all intents and purposes complete, but it had not received his final revision. The editors of the Athenæum Press Series regard themselves as fortunate in securing, for the purpose of such a revision, the services of William Allan Neilson, Ph.D. (Harvard), a graduate of the University of Edinburgh and a close student of Burns.

G. L. K.
C. T. W.

JULY 1, 1898.

CONTENTS.

CONTENTS.

INTRODUCTION.

I. OUTLINE OF THE LIFE OF BURNS.

ROBERT BURNS was born on the 25th of January, 1759; he was the eldest of a family of seven, and knew hardship and poverty from his earliest years. His father, William Burnes, a type of Scottish peasant not yet extinct, was industrious, temperate, intelligent, strong-willed, and deeply religious. At the time of the poet's birth William Burnes was a crofter; he rented and farmed seven acres of land near the banks of the Doon, about two miles from the town of Ayr, and occupied a two-roomed house, built of stone and clay with his own hands, hard by the kirk of Alloway. This was Burns's home for the first seven years of his life. At the age of six he was sent to school under John Murdoch, an excellent young teacher, whom the villagers of Alloway clubbed together to employ for a small recompense. In 1776, William Burnes, ambitious to do well by his children and to keep them under his own eye instead of sending them out into service,[1] rented the neighboring farm of Mount Oliphant with borrowed money. Robert and his brother Gilbert continued to go to school at Alloway, but on Murdoch's retirement in 1768, when Robert was but nine years old, their regular schooling came to an end. The substance of Burns's education was derived from the careful instruction of his father and from his own reading;[2] this was

[1] *Cotter's Saturday Night.* 20, note.
[2] See Gen. Introd., p. xxxix.

supplemented by one quarter at Dalrymple parish school in 1772, a few weeks at Ayr Academy in 1773, during which he revised his English and learned some French, and part of the summer of 1776 at Kirkoswald, where he began to study surveying, had his trigonometry overset by a girl, and became acquainted with the ways of smugglers. The constant companionship of his father was of the utmost importance to his intellectual growth. Apart from regular instruction during the winter evenings, the mature experience of William Burnes in matters both intellectual and practical, his clear and sure insight into men and things, his stubborn integrity, and his lifelong and heroic but hopeless struggle to beat poverty with independence, passed like rich seed into the mind of his son, and became at once the ethic and the material of poetry.[1] In those early years, too, the boy's imagination was fed from the store of ballads, songs, and legends which his mother knew, and from the fairy tales of an old domestic, Betty Davidson.[2] In other respects the home was governed by a profoundly religious sentiment, though not darkened by the Calvinistic bigotry then prevalent in Scotland. But poverty gripped the family very hard. The farm was "a ruinous bargain," the good landlord died, the pinch of debt came, and they fell into the hands of a merciless factor.[3] Then began for Burns the "unceasing moil of a galley-slave."[4] His father, who had married late, was beginning to age and to feel the effects of early hardship. At fifteen the son was doing a man's work, and at sixteen he was the chief laborer on the farm. The strain on his undeveloped system was so great and the living so poor that even his unusually powerful physique suffered, and he

[1] See esp. *The Twa Dogs, C. S. N.,* and *Man was Made to Mourn.*
[2] See *To the Deil,* 63, note.
[3] See *The Twa Dogs,* 96, note.
[4] Autobiographical letter to Dr. Moore.

became the subject of chronic fainting fits and melancholia. About this time he began to fall in love and make his first efforts in poesy. In 1776, too, "in absolute defiance of his father's commands," he attended a dancing school, and, out of an ungainly, shy, and pious lad he rapidly developed into a social favorite and a gallant, who, besides his own amours, was "in the secret of half the loves of the parish."[1] In 1777 the family removed to Lochlea, another poor farm, about ten miles northeast of Mount Oliphant. Here they continued the same laborious struggle with poverty for seven years longer, until, under excessive toil and a burden of litigation, the father broke down, and in 1784 was "saved from the horrors of a jail" by the kindly intervention of death. During these years Burns dabbled in verse, but showed little productive power. From the bondage of the farm he variously sought relief in the social relaxation of a Bachelors' Club, which he founded, in the boon companionship of Freemasonry,[2] and in a disastrous attempt to enter on the business of a flax-dresser. This last venture took him to Irvine, where he met the young sailor to whose influence he attributes the demoralization of his respect for the seventh commandment. At the same time he proposed marriage to Ellison Begbie and was refused.[3] In Irvine, too, he first became acquainted with the poems of Robert Fergusson, who made him "string his wildly sounding lyre with emulating vigor." Returning to Lochlea, he began to keep a Commonplace Book, copy out his compositions, and study the criticism of verse. He was coming to see that poetry was his proper vocation, and henceforth his history may be traced in his writings. On his father's death, he and Gilbert, by putting in a claim for arrears of wages, saved from the general ruin

---

[1] Autob. letter to Dr. Moore.
[2] See *To the Deil*, 73, note.
[3] See *Mary Morison*, notes.

as much as enabled them to rent and stock the farm of Mossgiel. At Whitsunday, 1784, the family removed to their new scene of trial, and very soon thereafter the poet met his fate, Jean Armour.[1] Towards the close of the same year he incurred kirk-censure, and began his series of satires on the Auld Licht clergy.[2] These satires won for him a local renown, which encouraged him to great poetical activity during the next two years. But two successive crop failures and disgust with his miserable lot, aggravated by the result of his intimacy with Jean, their irregular marriage and her parents' attempt to annul the bond, made him resolve to quit Scotland. The publication of his collected poems with a view to raising his passage money and the sudden fame which resulted "overthrew all his schemes by opening new prospects to his poetic ambition." In November, 1786, he went to Edinburgh, then a considerable literary centre, and carried all classes by storm with the brilliance and force of his personality. In 1787 he published a new and enlarged edition of his poems, from which he cleared as much money as enabled him to give his brother on Mossgiel £200 and stock a farm for himself in Dumfriesshire. This was Ellisland, a wretched choice, to which, after a regular marriage, he brought his wife Jean in December, 1788. To eke out a living, he secured a post on the excise,[3] and in 1791, his farming being again a failure, he abandoned Ellisland and removed with his family to the town of Dumfries. Since 1788 he had been writing songs for Johnson's *Scots Musical Museum*, and in 1792 he undertook work of the same kind for George Thomson's collection.[4] He regarded this as a patriotic work, for which he would accept

---

[1] See *Ep. to Davie*, 108, note.

[2] See *Ep. W. S.*, *H. F.*, and *Ep. McM.*, notes, and Introd., pp. lxx–lxxv.

[3] See *To Dr. Blacklock*, notes.   [4] See *Bonie Lesley*, note.

no payment, and this employment in the service of his country's muse kept his spirit bright to the last. But the hope had been stricken out of his life, his excise work was both odious and exacting, cronies gathered round him and toping worshippers who thirsted to be able to say they had drunk a glass with Burns, and henceforth his course was down. Under repeated assaults his health broke, he sank into a consumption, and on the 21st of July, 1796, in family circumstances of the acutest misery, the stormy soul passed into its rest.[1]

II. THE SCOTTISH TONGUE.[2]

Lowland Scotch, the language used by Burns, and still living as a *patois* throughout the south and east of Scotland, traces its descent from the Northumbrian dialect of Old English. By the Danish settlement of Northumbria during the 9th century, the Angles who inhabited Lothian and Tweeddale were cut off from close connection with the southern kingdom, and, after much conflict during the 10th century, their territory passed by regular cession under the sway of Kenneth, king of the Celtic Scots, who engaged that "the people of those parts should retain their ancient customs and their Anglian speech." Students of Shakspere's *Macbeth* are familiar with the revolution which transformed this Celtic kingdom of Scotland into one whose language, manners, and interests were Anglian. Malcolm Canmore, the successor of Macbeth, besides having spent his youth at the Anglo-Norman court of Edward the Confessor, brought

[1] The episodes of Mary Campbell and Mrs. Maclehose are related in the Notes. See *To Mary, Highland Mary, To Mary in Heaven, Ae Fond Kiss.*

[2] For further study of this subject, see *The Dialect of the Southern Counties of Scotland*, by Dr. J. A. H. Murray, pub. for the Philological Society, London, 1873.

with him a powerful Saxon influence in his wife Margaret, sister of the Ætheling.. During his reign (1058–93) a strong Anglo-Saxon policy was maintained, refugees from the harrying of Northumbria were sheltered and encouraged, the nobility was reformed by the granting of estates to southern exiles who became personally bound to the throne, and the church was organized anew on a southern plan by Queen Margaret. Their sons and successors continued to identify themselves with the Anglian interest, and during the next two hundred years, under the combined influence of court, nobility, and church, the Anglian population and the Anglian tongue spread northwards round the eastern shore through Southeast Perthshire, Angus, the Mearns, Aberdeenshire, and Elgin, as far as the Moray Firth, and westwards till they covered all the country south of the Clyde except the wilds of Galloway.

In the language of Burns we have Lowland Scotch, it is true, only after it has been subjected to a long process of accommodation to later English forms and usages ; but even in Burns it is easy to trace the dominant assertion of the Scandinavian family likeness which differentiates the Anglian dialects of the north from the Saxon dialects of the south, and especially the Norse characteristics which differentiate Scotch Anglian from the Anglian spoken south of the Scotch frontier.[1] The Anglian tongue was not Scandinavian, but West-Germanic at base. From the first the Angles bore a strong kinship of both race and language with the Scandinavians, and later their speech acquired an additional impress of Scandinavian influence from the Danish and Norse settlement of Northumbria. The greater conspicuousness of the Scandinavian element in Lowland Scotch is due partly to the fact that the more northerly province, lying somewhat out of the way of influences that operated in Eng-

---

[1] But cf. Dr. Murray, *Dialect of So. Counties*, p. 24.

land, was better adapted to preserve the original words and forms, and partly to distinct Scandinavian infusion operating freely on a language already closely akin. Both during and after the Danish invasions of England, great portions of Scotland were settled by immigrants direct from Norway. They poured round the north and down the west coast, settling the Orkney and Shetland Islands, Caithness and the Hebrides, established themselves on the fiords of Argyleshire, the coast of Ireland, and the Isle of Man, and crossed thence to the lands about the Clyde and the Solway Firth. The physical aspect of the people and certain peculiarities of their dialect would also indicate a distinct Norwegian impress on the mixed Anglo-Celtic population of Angus and the Mearns. The extent to which they mingled with the Angles of Lothian is less evident; there they met with a more numerous kindred from Jutland, Friesland, and the lower reaches of the Elbe, and were readily absorbed. These direct accessions of Scandinavian influence were further augmented by the severity of the Norman Conquest on the north of England, which drove many Norwegians and Danes, who had there become domesticated, to cross into a refuge open to them beyond the Cheviots. This graft of Danish stock may account for certain Danish words and forms in Lowland Scotch, but the Scandinavian influence on Scotland was mainly Norse.

While the Anglian tongue was spreading in Scotland it suffered some modification from its contact with the retiring Celtic. This modifying influence mainly affected the pronunciation, but it also brought an appreciable influx of Celtic vocables; it did not affect Anglian grammar. The spread of Anglian was in great measure due to the adoption of it by those whose mother tongue was Gaelic or Cymric, and whose organs of speech, being habituated to the Celtic sounds, preserved some peculiarities of utterance which influenced the forms of words,[1] just as French words became modified in form when they became current in the unaccustomed mouths of the English during the 13th and 14th centuries. This condition of things was also favorable to the importation of Celtic vocables into the Lowland speech, and, although the true power of the Celtic race lies in the spiritual and emotional elements it has contributed to the Teutonic genius through racial intermixture, this incidental component of Lowland Scotch is large enough to be worthy of a more detailed consideration than it has yet received.[2]

A slight infusion of Dutch which we find may have come with the Flemish settlers who were encouraged by the family of Malcolm Canmore.[3] But the next considerable influence which affected the Lowland Scotch tongue was that of France. This French influence ran in two currents, one by way of England, the other direct from France. The former began with the introduction of Normal feudalism and culture north of the Tweed during the 12th and 13th centuries, and then the Scotch language took color from the Normanized civilization of which it was the medium. During the 14th and 15th centuries the same current passed northward, mainly by the channel of Chaucer's poetry, and the court language and literature of Scotland received, though in a more mechanical way, much of the enrichment that French

---

[1] See Dr. Murray's *Dialect of So. Counties*, pp. 51–54.

[2] As it is, the number is considerable and includes words not merely " relating to Celtic institutions and customs." The following are taken entirely from the text: airt, bog, bogle(?), brat, brock, caird, cairn, clachan, claivers, coggie(?), craig (crag), cranreuch, creel, crummock, downans, duan, filabeg, glen, gowan, garten, ingle, kebbock, knaggié, laddie, lag, linn, lum, neuk, pownie, scroggie, skelp, sonsie, spleuchan, spunk, tocher, usquebeagh. There may be others.

[3] Examples which occur in the text are : heckle, mutchkin, naig.

had given to English. To what extent this influence affected the language of the common people it is of course impossible to say. The second of the currents above mentioned began during the reign of William the Lion (1165–1215). The royal alliance which this king formed with France became an hereditary friendship. Alike during the long Scotch struggle for independence and during the Hundred Years' War waged by England for possession of the French crown, France and Scotland were traditional friends and allies, and both saw in England their natural enemy. This alliance was superseded by the union of the Scotch and English crowns in 1603, but the friendly tradition still survived, and even as late as the 18th century the Stuarts looked to France for aid in their attempt to recover the English crown.

During this long period Scottish civilization became saturated with influences from France. In the 13th and 14th centuries, Scotch students flocked to the University of Paris; in the 15th, Scotch universities were founded on the French model; in the 16th, Scotch law was reorganized according to French jurisprudence, and the Scotch kirk and Scotch theology were constituted according to the principles and creed of the French reformer. In these and other ways French influence dominated Scottish national life, and this dominant influence showed itself especially in a drenching of the Scotch language with words, forms, shades of meaning, accents, and even grammatical solecisms, drawn from and copied after the French. This French element in Lowland Scotch, however, was different from the French element in Middle English; in the former case there was not the same chemical combination of the two tongues that there was in the latter, but only a mechanical intermixture, which, in course of time, permitted a great deal of this uncombined matter to be removed by the filtration which time effects.

Much, however, passed into the current stream of the language inherited by Burns.[1]

III. SCOTCH LITERATURE BEFORE BURNS.

After the Anglian district south of the Tweed was consolidated with the English kingdom, the vernacular spoken there began to sink into the position of a vulgar dialect. Literature in England developed in another form of the language, the Midland, and the literature of the Anglian tongue was finally restricted to southern Scotland. There it found a national field, with a national audience and national inspiration, and flourished vigorously under the fostering care of court and clergy and learned laymen. But the Reformation and the Revival of Classical Scholarship gave this young literature its deathblow by, first of all, diverting the channels of literary expression, and, secondly, by exhausting the intellect and fretting the temper of the nation with theological and presbyterial polemics. When the New Learning spread northwards, the Scottish scholars were seized with the passion for classical erudition, which made men all over Europe look with contempt on the still crude European tongues

[1] Dr. Murray (*Dialect of So. Counties*, pp. 58, 59) gives a long list of words, many of them extremely barbaric, used by writers of the 16th century. The following is a partial list of words and forms from the present text : aiver, baillie, bawsent, bonie, breef, brisket, cartes, causey, certes, chimla, corbie, core, curchie, curple, daintie, dool, douce, fash, fause, faut, fawsont, feat, fen, fracas, gree, grushie, gizz, gusty, hurcheon, kimmer, leal, limmer, lyart, manteels, marled, mavis, mell, merle, mischanter, plack, pley, plenish, poortith, pouch, proves, ratton, saunt, scow'r, seizin, souple, sowther, spairge, spence, stank, sten, stoure, sucker, tassie, tester, virl, vauntie. Note also such accents as envý, deposíte, complaisánce, mantéel ; the vocalizing of *l* in words like faut, fause, and the prevalence of the French u-sound, as in sure, dule, loot, and ou-sound, as in court, doubt, pow'r, which are pronounced coort, doot, poor.

and court the majestic beauty of Latin. When we recollect that Scotland was but a small and not a populous kingdom, we may realize how severe was the blow to the vernacular Scotch when the greatest genius of the country of that age, George Buchanan, elected to write almost entirely in Latin. Side by side with Latin scholarship were the English proclivities of Knox and his followers. Knox still essayed to write Scotch, but he Anglicized his diction as much as he Anglicized his politics. He represents the beginning of that tendency which was by and by to make English the language of education and literature in Scotland, the language of polite society, and even the "dress" language of the farmer and the artisan. So much was Scotch neglected by the Reformers that no complete vernacular translation of the Bible was produced, and one of the last who wrote the old language in its purity was Ninian Winzet, Knox's Catholic antagonist.

The union of the crowns in 1603 and the transference of the royal seat from Edinburgh to London reduced Scotland to an appendage of England, and removed one of the most powerful factors in the cultivation of a national literature;— the fostering tutelage of the court. But the union did more: coming as it did immediately after the Reformation, it left the country entirely in the hands of the exponents of Calvinistic theology, who cared nothing for literature. The air was filled with strife of the petty schismatic kind, and the mind of the country was eaten into by the corrosive action of a fiercely argumentative creed. Altogether, it was a bitter and unlovely time, which was raised out of its littleness, without losing any of its bitter and unlovely qualities, first by the roar of civil war and that stubborn Scotch devotion to the house of Stuart, and later by the terrors of religious persecution. The tendency to write for English audiences continued to grow in fashion, but the old vein of vernacular literature ceased to be worked, except in an incidental way by the writers of popular songs and ballads;[1] this field offered the only relief which a highly musical and poetical people found from the chills of presbyterial rigor. With the Revolution of 1688 and the stable government of William III came a promise of better days; but the current of tendency was now more than ever for a closer union with England. Political intrigue accomplished what the armies of the Plantagenet had failed to do, and in 1707 the independent Scottish Parliament sitting in Edinburgh was merged in that which met at Westminster. The last symbol of nationality was gone; only the national sentiment remained; and Scotland became a mere province of the southern kingdom. The decay of the language is sufficiently indicated by the total disappearance of Scotch prose and the complete ascendency of the King James version of the Bible. A national literature, in the strict sense, was forevermore an impossibility for Scotland.

During the 18th century, however, under the privileges granted by the Revolution and the Act of Settlement, literature had an opportunity of reviving. The Parliamentary Union destroyed all that was left of Scottish nationality except the spirit of patriotism that was later to give Burns a hot blast of inspiration, but the closer union with England made it easier for Scottish talent to rise on English lines, and lingering patriotic sentiment and that home love which grows warmer under real or fancied injury served to awake anew the vernacular strain in verse. Education prospered in the four universities and in the parochial schools. Literary society was cultivated in Edinburgh in close imitation of the club life of London. English periodicals, like the *Spectator*, found a ready audience in the northern capital. The correctness and intellectual quality of the school of

---

[1] These are mentioned later in the chapter on Scottish Song.

Pope were as diligently studied in the north as they were in the south, and the later English development into watery sentimentalism was faithfully reflected by northern imitators. The great body of literature produced in Scotland and by Scottish writers who went to London was in the English tongue, and, despite a few qualities that give it a northern individuality, was as thoroughly English of the 18th century as though there had been no division between the two countries.[1] The qualities that distinguish this northern contribution to English literature and entitle it to special regard in respect of its Scottish origin are a closer touch with physical nature and a richer vein of romanticism, both of which qualities make Scotland appear as the pioneer of the twofold development that later produced Wordsworth and Coleridge.

Alongside of this Scotch-English literature was the Scotch revival, which culminated in the work of Burns. This revival took a double growth, and shaped itself, on the one hand, into the literature of pure song, and on the other into a less special poetic literature, of which Ramsay and Fergusson are the chief representatives. These two lines lead us, the one to Burns's songs, the other to his poems. In both respects it is of importance, not merely in its connection with Burns, but in its general relation to the history of English poetry. For both in song and in poem it shows that the so-called "return to nature" was never necessary in Scotland, because Scotland had never departed from nature. When English poetry was presenting its most artificial appearance, this Scottish muse had all the buxomness of country life and the freshness of the early morn. There was neither stilted

---

[1] Prose writers like Hume and Robertson have nothing to distinguish them from their English brethren beyond an occasional Scotticism in diction. In poetry Thomson, Blair, Home, Falconer, Beattie, and Macpherson rank as English writers.

artificiality of conception nor cold artificiality of expression; both thought and language were simple, sensuous, and, if not always passionate, always rich in feeling. This was the true tradition inherited by Burns. It was this which fed his genius and gave him power as the first great " natural " poet of the new era. But the literature of this Scotch revival was a different product from the earlier literature of the 14th, 15th, and 16th centuries. It was different in national quality, because the Scotland which it represented was no longer a nation. It was different in its audience and appeal, because those to whom it addressed itself either were more and more becoming Anglicized in their education, speech, manners, and sentiment, or belonged to a class socially inferior, who had little education, few political rights, and small public interest. It was different also in its language. The vernacular as a literary vehicle had so long lain in desuetude that the writers who now sought to revive its use for literary purposes applied themselves, not to the diction and vocabulary of the old masters, but to the living speech of the common people. There was still the older tradition, be it granted, but this fresh application to the vernacular in its living use among the lower and country classes introduced into literature, for the first time, a broader element, which we do not find in Barbour, but which had existed all along as part of the living vulgar tongue.

Both phases of this revival are represented in a book which appeared at the beginning of the century, James Watson's *Choice Collection of Comic and Serious Scots Poems* (Edin., 1706-9-11). Omitting song literature for the present, we find the most considerable name in the collection to be William Hamilton, of Gilbertfield (died 1750), a writer associated as affectionately in his own life as he is in the verse of Burns with Allan Ramsay. In Watson's collection was that poem of his, *The Death and Dying Words of Bonie*

Heck, a Famous Greyhound, which furnished Burns a model for the *Death and Dying Words of Poor Mailie, a Pet Yowe.* In 1719 he and Ramsay interchanged a poetical correspondence that again served as example and model for Burns's *Epistles;* and in 1722 he produced that abridgment of Blind Harry's *Wallace* which passed into the common stall edition, and so fired Burns's youthful patriotism. But the two poets of this Scotch revival who are of greatest importance, both as regards their own work and in their influence on Burns, are Ramsay and Fergusson.

Allan Ramsay (1686–1758) was a poor Lanarkshire boy who received his entire education at the parish school of Crawfordmoor. At the age of fifteen he was apprenticed to a wigmaker in Edinburgh. By-and-by he acquired substance, began business for himself, became a favorite member of the Easy Club, developed a literary vein, wrote and published verses, and presently passed from the industry of wigmaking to that of bookselling, — an admirable type of the long-headed, "canny" Scot, a man born to thrive, eminently mundane and full of glee, with an overmastering relish for humor of the broader kind, but temperate and shrewd, with a strict eye to business and with no disturbing passion or imagination. He picked up literature at the Easy as an incidental to his wigmaking craft, continued it as an incidental to the bookselling business, which was his mainstay, and, having earned both fame and a competency, dropped it altogether, with a quarter of a century of good life still before him. His first efforts were issued in the form of leaflets, which he sold for a few pence each. For some years he worked the neglected vein of the older Scotch literature, and in 1724 the fruit of his researches came out in the *Evergreen.* This was a "collection of Scots Poems wrote by the ingenious before 1600," taken chiefly from the Bannatyne MS.,[1] and including many poems of a later date

---

[1] See p. xxxii, note.

than 1600. In 1724–27 he brought out the first three parts of the *Tea-table Miscellany*, a mixed collection of old and new songs, both English and Scotch, and by authors of both nations. In 1725 appeared the single work by which he is now universally remembered, the pastoral drama of *The Gentle Shepherd*.[1]

The scope of Ramsay's influence may be measured by the fact that the *Tea-table Miscellany* ran through twelve editions in a few years. The *Evergreen, The Gentle Shepherd*, and other works of his were only less popular. At home he was caressed by the nobility, and his shop in the Lucken-booths, with its conspicuous heads of Drummond and Jonson, was a favorite rendezvous for the wits of the capital. Among the people at large he was the acknowledged prince of living poets. His fame spread beyond Scotland, and editions of his works were printed in London and Dublin in 1731 and 1733. He had an extensive correspondence with contemporary men of letters, and critics praised his *Gentle Shepherd* as the best pastoral that had been written since Theocritus. His significance in relation to Burns is that he prepared the way for his greater successor, and by the impetus he gave to the cultivation of vernacular verse, by the success he achieved in reviving and popularizing the old native strains, by the education he gave the public in appreciating a literature strange to English and Anglicized taste, and by the frank and natural quality of his original compositions he practically made the swift and triumphant popularity of Burns possible.[2]

---

[1] In 1716 he edited the old poem, *Christ's Kirk on the Green*, with an additional canto added; in 1718 he republished it with another original canto. After *The Gentle Shepherd* he published another volume of poems in 1728, and in 1730 a book of *Fables*. Then, with remarkable wisdom for a popular poet, he ceased to write. Edition used: Works, 3 vols., Fullerton & Co., Edin. and Lond., 1848.

[2] For his work in pure song, see pp. xxxvi–xxxvii.

In language, too, he set Burns the example of employing both Scotch and English in his poems, using the former altogether in his most natural and spontaneous efforts, and reserving the latter for occasions of artificial dignity or serious elevation of thought.   In only one poem of consequence [1] does he attempt a higher flight on the humble pinions of the vernacular.   His English poems are not of high merit, and he wisely preferred the field where his talent lay.   But in doing this he had to antagonize the literary fashion of the day and brave the public criticism of literary censors.   But in Ramsay's case, as later in the case of Burns, there was an ulterior advantage accruing to his use of the homely dialect which he heard spoken about him : both in this way remained truer to nature, and they anticipated the change in poetic diction commonly associated with the name of Wordsworth.[2]

[1] *The Vision*, printed in the *Evergreen*, with a misleading title, which deceived Scott, and a note that it was " compylit in Latin be a most lernit clerk in time of our hairship and oppression, anno 1300, and translatit in 1524."

[2] A humble pupil of Ramsay, whose work also touches that of Burns at a single point, is Alexander Ross (1699–1784), a poor schoolmaster of Forfarshire, who whiled away the *ennui* of country pedagogy by writing verses that brought him a parochial fame.   At the age of sixty-seven he went to Aberdeen, taking with him the MS. of *Helenore, or the Fortunate Shepherdess*, and there met Beattie of *Minstrel* fame, who praised the poem and introduced it and its author to public notice.   The poem opens with an address to his muse, whose name Scota furnished Burns with the idea of Coila :

> Come, Scota, thou that ance upon a day
> Garr'd Allan Ramsay's hungry heart-strings play
> The merriest sangs that ever yet were sung.

Ross likewise composed some merry songs that help to carry on the lyric tradition to Burns : *Woo'd an' Marritan' a'*, *The Rock an' the Wee Pickle Tow*, and others.

· Robert Fergusson (1750–74), in a limited sense the heir of Ramsay, is of greater consequence as the immediate fore-runner and generously acknowledged master of Burns. Son of a poor Edinburgh clerk, born frail alike in body and in will, but with a quick, warm heart, a fine spirit of mirth and mockery, Fergusson's rare abilities soon revealed genius. He was fortunate in a university education, but by his father's death and his mother's poverty he was immediately forced to undertake the dismal drudgery of a lawyer's clerk. He was assailed by fate within him and fate without, and having no reserve of either moral or physical strength, lacking, too, a friend to stand by him in his hour of need, he sought to forget his poor home and his aching fingers in the glee of the clubhouse, dissipated somewhat, sank into broken health, then into remorse and religious melancholy, and finally passed to a swift and distressing end in a public insane asylum. In judging his work it is well to remember that he was barely twenty-four when he died, and that his three brief years of productive effort were much broken by the waste that comes of conviviality. From 1771 he contributed numerous poems to *Ruddiman's Weekly Magazine or Edinburgh Amusement;* in 1773 he collected and published these in a volume. The volume contained nine Scotch poems, including *The Daft Days, Braid Claith*, and *Hallow Fair;* the rest were English. In his later compositions he culti-vated the Scotch vein by preference, and was only coming to a realization of his powers when the blight fell upon him.

Inheriting the Scotch tradition which Ramsay had once more popularized, and the public which Ramsay had awak-ened, Fergusson likewise inherited the elder poet's "spunk o' glee," the broad fun and sly satire which were so accept-able to his audience, and that love of nature which brings a waft of country air into his city poems. . His genius, singularly void of passion, and immature in all except a precocious tone of reflective wisdom, is that of the townsman born and bred who loves and misses the country. His subjects are drawn mainly from city and suburban life ; he paints the humors of Auld Reekie and hits off her characters with deft good nature, banters the lords and advocates of the Session, satirically moralizes on the respectability of the citizen's broadcloth, preaches to his fellow clubmen, with mock gravity, on the virtues of cold water, wakens the ghosts that haunt the Canongate, and collogues with plain-stanes and causey on the High Street. But he gladly listens to the song of the gowdspink, his eye catches the butterfly in the thoroughfare, and he passes in fancy to the rustic joys of the farmer's ingle. His style of treatment is humorous, pathetic, and moralistic. In these and other respects his relation to Burns is so close that it would almost seem as if his entire equipment, his humor, satire, and sagacity, his sympathy with nature and his warm humanity, his vivid sight of his object, even his diction and versification, had been transplanted into the richer soil of Burns's mind, and flourished there anew.

IV. SCOTTISH SONG AND MUSIC BEFORE BURNS.

Scottish Song was the direct outcome of Scottish Music, and, especially in the work of Burns, was directly inspired and regulated by its musical source. Mainly Celtic in its origin, but developed in the lowlands, this music has peculiarities that give it a distinct place in musical history. The old Celtic scale, in which the most ancient melodies were composed, had only five notes; it was our modern diatonic scale minus the fourth and seventh. A familiar example of it is the melody of *Auld Lang Syne.* A slight examination will show how readily this scale lends itself to the production of minor strains and what may be called minor effects in a major key ; and this is one reason why so many, even of humorous, Scotch songs have a touch of that pathos which is akin to melancholy. The strain is not one of grief or sadness ; it is simply the spirit of the hills, where the very cries of the birds are lonely, bringing down to the social fields of the " laigh country " the solitariness of mountain life. Of a part with this general effect is the particular effect of the frequently incomplete melodic ending, which leaves the listener in suspense and gives a touch of exquisite idealism to the close. One of the best examples is *The Brume o' the Cowdenknowes.*[1]

The influence of church music very early filled the gaps in this scale, and one of the early popular instruments was the pipe or recorder, which played the scale of C major without accidentals. Even this offered little scope for modulation, and the ingenuity and melodic skill of the early Scotch composers are well shown in their adaptation of the older kind of melodies to the new scale, and the production of expressive effects corresponding to changes of key. In this respect James I of Scotland, one of the most distinguished improvers of Scotch music, was renowned in the early Italian schools as the inventor of " a new music, mournful and plaintive, different from all others."[2] With the improvement of the violin came another development of the popular music. The pipe was still a favorite instrument, and, as we see from Satan's performance in *Tam o' Shanter*, was equally fitted for the rendering of the liveliest measures ; but the violin had more to do with the growth and spread of those folk melodies which finally gave birth to the songs of Burns.

---

[1] For further treatment of the subject, see Grove's *Dict. of Music*, art. " Scotch Music."

[2] " Una nuova musica, lamentevole e mesta, differente da tutte le altre " : Tassoni, *Pensieri Diversi*, ed. by A. Barbarigo, Venice, 1665, bk. x, ch. xxiii, p. 406. For further references, see D. Irving, *Hist. of Scottish Poetry*, p. 158, note.

The fiddle was *par excellence* the instrument that stirred the native blood; it was also the instrument that for nearly two hundred years fought the kirk single handed and came out victorious, and it was the only instrument Burns used in tuning his genius to the melodies he enshrined in poetry.

These melodies were transmitted from place to place and from generation to generation mainly by ear, and in this way they grew. The plowman in the field or the maid among the cows will whistle or sing a half-caught strain until the air completes itself. But the air will be apt to take some little turn from the singer's mood or temper, and then it is no longer the same; it has assumed a different color, sentiment, and individuality; it has become a different song, demanding different words. Melodies, too, among a musical people, are readily caught when words are lost, and the song, carried away into another glen or haugh, hums itself in the popular mind, until by-and-by it shapes itself into words that embody its changed sentiment. It is easy, for instance, to detect modifications of the same strain in the opening measures of *Och Hey Johnnie Lad*, *Corn Rigs*, and *Auld Lang Syne*, whose finished melodies have grown widely apart. A better illustration is *Lady Cassilis' Lilt*. In this old melody we can see the source of the plaintive strains of *The Bonie House o' Airlie* and *A Wee Bird Cam to Our Ha' Door*; a different modulation of the same air gives us *Hey Tutti Taitie*, whose tenderness appears in *The Land o' the Leal*; and with only a slight change of accent this pathos is transformed into the martial bravery of *Scots Wha Hae*. But, though the ancient melodies were thus changed at the hands of an unskilled people, their original construction indicates that they were the work of artists in melodic composition. And no doubt the fact that they suffered modification from the country people who sang them is partly the reason why they are so rich in feeling. They have gathered to themselves the unspoken humor and pathos of we know not how many lives, and as we listen to them we seem to hear the voices of generations of dead singers come trembling to us across the centuries with a laugh or a sob.

From very early times there was a national heritage of words to these national melodies. We have little evidence of their character beyond what is furnished in a few titles mentioned in stray places, like *The Tale of Cockelbie's Sow.*[1] But the number referred to even as early as the 15th century indicates a considerable body of floating folk songs that grew up and scattered themselves as the ballads did without any recognized authorship.[2] The 16th century produced a curious book, *Ane Compendious Buik of Godlie Psalms and Spiritual Sangs* (1570), in which the Reformers, feeling themselves powerless against the art of folk-music, sought to catch the populace by singing " psalms to hornpipes." Like the Salvation Army of the present day, they took over the popular songs, titles and all, and only altered the words so far as to make them suit the religious purpose for which they were designed. These religious travesties serve the double purpose of preserving the titles and first lines of many of the most popular ditties of the day, and of indicating the desperate shifts to which the kirk was driven to circumvent the devil and counteract the Satanic influence of popular song. But anything like mirth, even under a religious guise, was alien to the spirit of the old Scotch Presbyterians; and especially during the 17th century, in addition to the long and bloody struggle with Episcopacy, the gloom of the Covenant hung heavy over bonnie Scotland.[3]

Yet even during that austere and bitter time, when men

[1] Printed in Laing's *Select Remains of the Ancient Popular Poetry of Scotland.* 4°. Edin., 1822.

[2] See Introd. to *Songs of Scotland.* Lond., 1871.

[3] *The Complaynte of Scotland* (1549) gives the names of thirty-seven songs which the shepherds sing to the author in his dream. About 1555

were shedding their blood for a creed that choked all earthly inspiration and a church that stifled the mirth of children, the natural genius of the people found relief in country songs that form a respectable prelude to the "melodious bursts" that fill the 18th century. The first work of the century, indeed, was the collection and publication of these,[1] many of which formed the crude material of the later efforts of Ramsay and Burns. As nearly all of them were, owing to kirk influence over the press, transmitted by oral tradition or in unaccredited broadsheets, very few names of authors have been preserved. We have, among others, Sir Robert Aytoun, who may have written one version of *Auld Lang Syne;* Lady Grizel Baillie, whose ballad *Were na my Heart Licht I Wad Die* so pathetically appealed to Burns in his dark days at Dumfries ; and the Semples of Beltrees, of whom Francis is credited with the authorship of *Maggie Lauder, Fy Let us a' to the Bridal,* and others. These are names socially and politically conspicuous, but the major part of the 17th century songs are anonymous, — a fact which Burns lamented when he came to work this field. A few songs like *Muirland Willie, Tak your Auld Cloak about ye,*[2] *Waly, Waly up the Bank,* and the Scotch *Barbara Allan*

Sir Richard Maitland compiled a collection of Scotch poetry, from which Pinkerton, the antiquary, in 1786 published an excerpt. In 1568 George Bannatyne, fleeing from the plague, retired to a country house and wrote out in MS. the most valuable collection of old Scottish poetry which we possess ; this was the collection from which Ramsay drew material for the *Evergreen.* In 1579, by order of the Legislature, minstrels were classed as vagabonds.

[1] The chief MS. collections of the 17th century are the Skene collection, airs with titles of words sung (1630-40), and the Straloch MS. (1627-29). The Aberdeen *Cantus,* a collection of about fifty songs with music, of which, however, only half a dozen were Scotch, was published at Aberdeen in 1666.

[2] Shakspere's *Othello,* Act ii, sc. 3, shows that a version of this song was known in England as early as 1611.

carried on the ballad type imitated by Burns in *Tam Glen* and *Last May a Braw Wooer.* Many furnished Burns both a subject and a model; *e.g., Gala Water, Wanderin Willie, Auld Rob Morris, My Jo, Janet, O Gin my Love Were Yon Red Rose.* Others, like *Katherine Ogie, Saw ye Johnie Comin, Will ye Go to the Yowe Buchts Marion,* merely handed down old melodies which Burns worked to better effect. A few, like *Annie Laurie* and *Leader Haughs an' Yarrow,* passed into other hands, and a large number were left untouched, or served only as fertilizers of the lyric soil, and gradually disappeared. The song writers of the 17th century seem to have been loath to acknowledge and care for their literary offspring, perhaps from the stigma of vagabondage that was laid upon the minstrels, perhaps for the reason that may be guessed from the opening lines of the *Silly Auld Man,* a song of the reign of Charles II:

> I am a puir silly auld man
> An' hirplin ower a tree,
> Yet fain fain kiss wad I
> Gin the kirk wad let me be.

The kirk had good excuse for seeking to regulate the popular Scottish muse of this time. Whether from innate wickedness or from a natural defiance of presbyterial severity, the muse walked abroad in a shockingly high-kilted fashion, and kicked up her heels in a way that seems deliberately intended to flout the "unco guid." Many songs were written which appear to have had nothing but licentiousness for their motive, while others had nothing to recommend them but low buffoonery. This prevalent coarseness and vulgarity of the earlier song literature, modified though it was by the inexpert hand of Ramsay, should be remembered when we come to think of Burns's work, not merely in its conversion of brick into marble, but in the strictly ethical respect of purification. Burns knew this song literature thoroughly, and it is a marvel that his hand, steeped as it was in this compound, should have been so little, like the dyer's, subdued to what it worked in.

During the 18th century fresh impulse was given to the cultivation of Scottish song by the Jacobite enthusiasm, by the work of Allan Ramsay, and by the fashionable taste for Scotch music.

The Jacobite minstrelsy continued the tradition of the English cavaliers. The Whig Revolution and the final exclusion of the Stuarts from the throne provoked in Scotland the liveliest indignation and derision, and flooded the country with a tide of popular song in which the sense of injury blends bitterly with devotion to the "richtfu' king." The songs are for the most part anonymous, orphaned waifs of the passionate semi-Celtic Scottish heart, and, though not as a rule marked by fine poetic genius, are brimful of life. They sound every note of tenderness, fidelity, hope, courage, pride, defiance, and scorn, and their high-hearted victorious loyalty, which not even Culloden could subdue, is poignant with satirical humor. They group themselves into three classes round the three struggles of 1689, 1715, and 1745. The second group contains two notable songs, the fine burst of indignant loyalty known as *Lady Keith's Lament*, and that masterpiece of patriotic rough-handling, *A Wee Wee German Lairdie*, of which the very title is a vesicating blister. The country was far more deeply stirred by the rising of the '45 and the romance of "bonnie Prince Charlie." Though it was chiefly the clans who acted in the fray, the cannie lowlanders joined in the triumph while it lasted and made the land ring with songs in honor of the "young Chevalier."[1] They greeted him with *O but Ye 've Been Lang o' Comin*, and *Welcome Royal Charlie;* mocked the Englishmen in *Hey Johnie Cope* and *Up an' Rin Awa Hawley;* donned the white

---

[1] See Hogg's *Jacobite Minstrelsy.*

cockade and sang *Charlie He's my Darling* and a hundred
more ; and, when all was lost, they comforted their "bonie
hielant laddie" by sending the butcher Cumberland to hell and
describing Satan "in a neuk rivin sticks to roast the duke."

Ramsay's song work is of two kinds, original and editorial,
and most of it appeared in the *Tea-table Miscellany* (see p.
xxvi).   His original songs, including those in *The Gentle
Shepherd*, are never striking for their intrinsic merit; the
only ones that have held their place are *Lochaber no More*,
The Lass o' Patie's Mill, and *The Yellow-haired Laddie*, and
these chiefly on account of the fine melodies to which they
are set.   Ramsay is kindly and droll, but neither his joy nor
his sorrow is rapturous or deep ; he has none of the passion
requisite in a lyrist.   Even love with him has a good deal of
the proverbial Scot's "canny lang-headedness."   It has none
of the fine idealism and passionate abandon of that portrayed
by Burns.[1]   Yet Ramsay was greatly inspired by Scottish
music.   He wrote many of his songs to the traditional melodies, and gave the names of the old airs to which his new
words were to be sung.[2]   His less original, but more fruitful
work consisted in collecting old songs and presenting these
in a dress suited to his time.   While, however, he preserved
many of the songs and airs that afterwards inspired Burns,
he took great liberty with his material.   We cannot know
the extent to which he carried his retouchings and rehabili-
tations.   He gives about twenty songs that are presumably
old, and of the hundred or so that claim to be original many

---

[1] A typical example is his treatment of the pathetic story of Bessie
Bell and Mary Gray, two maidens of Perth, who withdrew from the
plague and " biggit a bower an' theikit it ower wi' rashes," and died and
were buried there.   Ramsay gave the legend a comic turn by making
both the sweethearts of one man who could not make up his mind
which to choose.   Compare also his *Auld Lang Syne* and *Corn Rigs*
with those of Burns.

[2] In 1726 he published a volume of these airs.

are based on songs of which he preserved at least the motive. A good example of the latter class is *The Last Time I Cam ower the Muir*, in which he preserves only the first line of an old song and composes the rest to suit that line, — a plan both commended and followed by Burns. When we consider the license assumed by the old Scottish muse, we need not violently regret the curb Ramsay put upon her tongue. It is improbable that he suppressed anything of real value, and as it was he left scope enough. What he certainly accomplished in the four volumes of his *Miscellany* was to preserve even in lines and titles much that would otherwise have been lost, to foster the love of song throughout the country, and not only to prepare the way, but to leave a rich body of inspiration for his greater successor.[1] From the time of Ramsay to Burns the vernacular continued to be cultivated by a multitude of writers, the extent of whose work can be estimated only by referring to the literature of the subject. The song writers[2] came from all classes, — every grade of the nobility and gentry, the learned professions (including even stray clergymen), the crafts and industries, and even the vagabond classes. Likewise, a great body of anonymous song literature was spread abroad, some idea of which may be gathered from Herd's collections of 1770 and 1776.

[1] Ramsay tells us that about thirty songs of the *Miscellany* were by friends of his, — Robert Crawford, Hamilton of Bangour, Hamilton of Gilbertfield (see p. xxiv), and others. Most of these wrote in English or Anglicized Scotch. Crawford's Scotch is thin, but his *Bush Aboon Traquhair* became a popular favorite, and his *Doun the Burn Davie* was reworked by Burns.

[2] Conspicuous among them are the Duke of Argyle, Sir Henry Erskine, Lady Ann Barnard, Mrs. Cockburn, Miss Jane Elliott, Rev. John Skinner, Dr. Blacklock, Pinkerton the antiquary, the poets Mallet, Ross, Home, and others, Dugald Graham the town crier of Glasgow, Tibbie Pagan the shebeener, and Jean Glover the vagabond.

Finally, song production was immensely stimulated by the passion for the Scottish folk melodies that swept over both Scotland and England in the 18th century. Since the middle of the 17th century Scottish airs had become so popular in England that London literary hacks made it a business to manufacture imitations, spurious in both words and music. One of the leading spirits in this enterprise was D'Urfey, the playwright (a favorite of the merry monarch), who in his later life published a collection in six volumes.[1] In Scotland the national melodies began to be published, both with and without words, from the beginning of the century. The earliest collection which contained words was Wm. Thomson's *Orpheus Caledonius* (1725–33). Then followed a steady run of similar works[2] down to the publication of Johnson's *Musical Museum*, the first volume of which appeared in 1787, and Thomson's more aristocratic collection, to both of which Burns contributed his best work in Scottish song.

V. BURNS'S WORK IN ITS RELATION TO THE PAST.

(a) *His Poems.*

The sources and models that most influenced Burns were those of his own country and his own century. The earlier

---

[1] *Wit and Mirth, or Pills to Purge Melancholy* (London, 1719–20: reprinted in facsimile 1872). In 1651 there had also appeared in London John Playford's *Dancing Master*, which, along with a few genuine Scottish airs, contained some very clever imitations that were adopted north of the Tweed, and had good sets of words written to them; *e.g.*, *The Deil Cam Fiddlin thro' the Toun* and *The Deuk's Dang o'er My Daddie* (both by Burns). In 1700 Henry Playford published *A Collection of Original Scottish Tunes (Full of the Highland Humors) for the Violin : being the first of this kind yet printed.* The first edition of *Pills to Purge Melancholy*, edited by H. Playford, had been published in 1699.

[2] Note especially James Oswald's collections (1740–42), which were used by Burns.

Scottish literature affected him scarcely at all, except as it embodied and transmitted the national sentiment, language, and tradition.   His patriotic enthusiasm took him back to the times of Wallace and Bruce ; but he had not read Barbour's *Bruce*, though the spirit that produced it he distilled into *Scots Wha Hae*, and his acquaintance with Henry the Minstrel's *Wallace* was made through the modernized and weakened version of Hamilton of Gilbertfield.   Of the poets and prose writers of the 15th and 16th centuries he knew nothing, though here again he presents strong affinities with Dunbar ; nor did the extensive ballad literature have any appreciable influence on the development of his genius. This limitation applies equally to English literature.   Beyond a fair knowledge of Shakspere and Milton he drew all that influenced his work from the century in which he lived.

In English literature of the 18th century, however, he was well read, and it affected him in a far deeper degree than is generally allowed.   The books he read may have been few, but they were select, and his assimilative power multiplied tenfold the significance of those he did read.   Even from his schoolbook he imbibed a literary love for Addison, and before he appeared as an author his reading embraced (besides Scotch literature) a set of Queen Anne letters, on which he painfully modeled his epistolary style ; the poetry of Pope, Thomson, Shenstone, Beattie, Collins, Gray, Goldsmith, Macpherson, and Churchill ; the prose of Addison, Steele, and Johnson ; some of the novels of Richardson, Sterne, Smollett, and Mackenzie ; the *Mirror* and *Lounger* of his own day ; and some technical works on Agriculture, Mental Philosophy, Scripture History, and Original Sin. To these add the thorough acquaintance with the Bible that used to be required of every respectable Scottish youth and an enthusiastic study of a collection of songs on which he carefully whetted his critical perceptions as well as tuned his imagination. The sum total, when we consider the fact that he "drew blood from everything he read," gives a literary education which renders it a mere affectation to speak of his "untutored muse."

In estimating its influence on his mind and work we must keep before us the character of 18th century literature, — its classicism and its sentimentality. In its earlier age it was a dry and intellectual literature, given to the study of correctness and permitting no exuberance of either thought or diction, affecting " wit," or intellectual sparkle, but possessing little sense of the humor that is kin to pathos; having a lively fancy, as illustrated in *The Rape of the Lock*, but little of that penetrative power which unites fancy to the profoundest emotions of the heart; an aristocratic product, a literature of fashionable city life and the life of the provincial gentry, in which the poor had no figure, and mere rustic simplicity was held to be "low." Supervening on this in the second age of the century was a veneer of sentiment, which was its nearest approach to genuine feeling; it was as if the appeal to reason and intellect had been overdone, and emotion, so long held in check, sought relief in "tears of sensibility." This affected and sometimes whimpering sentimentality explains the *furore* created by Sterne and the extravagant reputation of Mackenzie.

Apart from the special mention Burns gives to many of the 18th century writers,[1] stray echoes of these may be heard from time to time in his verse, as when he adapts a stanza of Gray's,[2] a line of Pope's,[3] a couplet of Goldsmith's,[4] or a thought of Young's[5]; and in a general way the artificial char-

---

[1] *E.g.*, in the *Ep. to Lapraik, to McMath, The Vision*, etc.
[2] *C. S. N.*, 14–17.
[3] *C. S. N.*, 129, 157.
[4] *C. S. N.*, 156.
[5] *To a M.D.*, 51.

acter of the century may be traced in an occasional note of mere rhetoric,[1] or again in the stilted gait of his English heroics. The artificiality and classicism of the school of Pope do not, however, affect him so much as the sentimentality of the succeeding age, which appealed strongly to his sensitive and undisciplined nature. He was especially fond of Sterne's *Sentimental Journey*, and he absurdly overrated Mackenzie's *Man of Feeling*. In *The Vision* he regrets that he is not master of the "bosom-melting throe of Shenstone's art" and cannot "pour the moving flow" of Gray, whereas, in fact, the emotions excited by these masters were only titillations, compared with which his own were earthquakes. He brought into this fashionable age the stormy sincerity and passions of a new era, and he never approached nearer to insincerity than when he adopted the affectations of the literary *beau monde* he had come to supersede.

Of a part with this 18th century influence are his frequent excursions into the English tongue. Both Ramsay and Fergusson served as examples for an intermixture of English with Scotch. But the wide range of his own culture and preparation also inclined him towards the use of English ; the undivided authority of literary criticism pointed in the same direction ; and he himself seemed to feel that the fashionable English writers were somehow a degree above him and his homely dialect. English had for him something of decorum and dignity that did not sit easily on the rustic Scotch. Hence, when he wrote English, it was with a view to assuming a certain elevation of tone and dignity of manner. In *The Cotter's Saturday Night* he is both serious and dignified, but it is still a familiar dignity, and the Scotch ele-

---

[1] *E.g.*, "doitit Lear," "Labour sair," "droopin Care," and "dark Despair," all in a single stanza of *Scotch Drink*. Cf. the introduction of abstractions like Hospitality, Benevolence, Learning, and Worth at the close of *The Brigs of Ayr*.

ment is not on the whole prominent. In *The Vision* he naturally assumes the English tone when the sentiment becomes elevated. In such lyrics as *Afton Water* and *To Mary in Heaven* he shows mastery even of pure English ; but on the whole English was to him a book language, and his English work is of comparatively little account beside his Scotch. Whenever he writes completely at his ease, he uses the language that comes nearest his heart ; and when he draws very close to his subject with familiar affection,[1] or when he introduces humor or mockery,[2] the Scotch is richest and strongest.

As a counteractive to this artificial and cramping influence may be set the partial acquaintance he had with Shakspere and Milton and his reading of Macpherson's *Ossian;* but his chief source of "natural" inspiration was the Scottish literature of his own century. Previous sections have shown how the ground was prepared for him in this respect, and he repeatedly mentions, with the most generous regard, his accepted Scottish masters.[3] But his relation to them is not merely that of a later poet's regard for more or less eminent forerunners in the same line. He takes their poems whenever it suits his purpose, appropriates their subjects, their motive ideas, their forms of verse, their inventive detail, and even their diction. In actual borrowing and imitation his derived work exceeds that of any other great English author except Shakspere. Of his poems hardly any except his two masterpieces, *The Jolly Beggars* and *Tam o' Shanter*, is original in the sense that the first idea and form of it sprung from his own brain ; and even the latter of these is not strictly entitled to claim this originality. His *Epistles* are

---

[1] Cf. *On Scaring Water-fowl* with the openings of *A Winter Night* and *The Brigs of Ayr.*

[2] Cf. *My Nanie, O* with *O Tibbie, I Hae Seen the Day.*

[3] See *Ep. W. S.*, 11, and *Ep. L.* (I).

nearly all modeled on the rhyming correspondence of Ramsay and Hamilton of Gilbertfield. *Puir Mailie* borrows from the same Hamilton's *Bonie Heck*, and *Mailie's Elegy* from Skinner's *Ewie wi' the Crookit Horn.* *Halloween* is based on a poem of the same name by John Mayne; *Man was Made to Mourn* on an old Scottish elegy, *The Life and Age of Man; Tam Samson's Elegy* on Robert Sempill's *Death of Habbie Simson.* From Fergusson, whom he most audaciously utilizes, he draws both the idea and the form of *The Cotter's Saturday Night, The Holy Fair, Scotch Drink, The Brigs of Ayr, A Winter Night,* and indirectly much more than these (see Notes). He did not, indeed, require to learn of Fergusson his "boast of independence," nor his "livid hatred of hypocrisy"; but his study of Fergusson fed his temper in both of these directions, and showed him how they could be turned to poetic account. From him, too, he may be said to have first learned to apply his splendid common sense, and to blend with it his inevitable humor; from him, perhaps, his first lessons in seeing the human aspects of inanimate nature and the brute creation; and from him certainly the deft art with which he makes his favorite stanza ring like the crack of a whip. When, at twenty-three, he gave up poetry altogether for a time, it was "meeting with Fergusson's poems" that made him "string anew his wildly sounding lyre with emulating vigor." Apart from individual cases of imitation and borrowing, a general comparison will show how thoroughly he saturated his mind with the work of his more precocious master, and it will show further how little his originality suffers from a frank acknowledgment of his debt. These points, however, affect only the poems of Burns; in his songs he has a hemisphere of poetic dominion never visited by Fergusson at all.[1]

His debt to Ramsay is only less great, though far less

[1] See notes on *C. S. N., H. F., B. A., Sc. Dr., W. N.*

conspicuous. Ramsay was first in the field, and much of what Ramsay transmitted to Burns he transmitted by way of Fergusson. But Burns studied Ramsay long before he received from Fergusson his second quickening, and he continued to be a student of Ramsay long after he had laid Fergusson aside ; Ramsay's indirect influence is visible as early as *Poor Mailie's Elegy*, and it is well marked as late as *Tam o' Shanter*. This influence frequently shows itself in isolated lines that are borrowed entire or adapted ; elsewhere in verse forms, especially in the difficult measures of the *Epistle to Davie* and *A Dream;* or again in bits of invention that are adopted and reworked, as in the use he makes of Ramsay's specter and attendant sprites in *The Vision*. Less specially it shows itself in the tone and general character of his familiar epistles, many of which are as carefully modeled on those of Ramsay as his descriptive sketches are on Fergusson. It appears most of all in a licentiousness that makes a deal of his powerful work unfit to be quoted. Allan Ramsay showed an astute insight into human nature, as well as a keen eye for the sale of his books, when under their innocent titles he smuggled the spirit of the English Restoration into a country that had long been surfeited with formal sanctity. In this respect he found in Burns a pupil only too apt, and Ramsay's influence more than any other single cause accounts for certain features of *The Jolly Beggars*, *Holy Willie's Prayer*, *The Ordination*, and many of Burns's minor pieces.

(b) *His Songs.*

In his songs the roots of his genius are even more deeply imbedded in the past. Jacobitism (see p. xxxv), which survived as a romantic inspiration far into the present century, was in the time of Burns still bound up with living recollections. In his case it not merely furnished material for poetic practice, but was part and parcel of his real sentiment. In an age and country that had not yet become democratic enough to look elsewhere than to a royal family for its fountain head of -patriotism, the poet turned with contempt from the unpoetical house of Hanover to the royal Stuarts, all of whom had befriended poetry, many of whom had themselves been poets, and whose lives had from the first been marked with tragic and romantic destiny. " Except when my passions are heated," he says, " my Jacobitism is merely by way of *vive la bagatelle* " ; but in both prose and verse he has left ample record of this sentiment. His tour in the highlands warmed this sentiment to a keener glow, which found expression in numerous songs. His visit to Culloden produced *The Lovely Lass of Inverness;* strains of Jacobite music shaped themselves in his mind to *The Battle of Sheriffmuir, Whare Hae ye Been Sae Braw Lad,* and *There'll Never be Peace till Jamie Comes Hame;* and the same inspiration gave us *Macpherson's Farewell, The Highland Widow's Lament, Fareweel to a' our Scottish Fame,* and (if it is his) Scott's favorite, *It Was a' for our Richtfu' King.*

His chief stimulus in song production, however, was Scottish folk-music. With this inspiration he diverted Johnson's *Musical Museum* from its original purpose of a mixed popular collection into purely Scottish channels, and made it, if not the " standard text-book of Scottish song for all time," at least a work with something of the quality and permanence of a classic. The object of this and of Thomson's more genteel collection was first of all musical; they sought to give to a public already formed a full and representative body of the Scottish melodies, supplied with words that could be sung in the concert hall and drawing-room, as well as in the cottage or on the hayfield. Although much had been done by Ramsay and others, the popular melodies were still far more numerous than the versions to which they could be sung; many of the fine airs that were floating among the people had words either silly or indecorous. And, further, owing to the fact that melodies persist while words change, "many of the Scots airs had outlived their own and perhaps many subsequent sets of verses except a single name or phrase or sometimes one or two lines simply to distinguish the tunes by."[1] It was Burns's task to collect these scattered fragments of Scottish song, and transmit them to Johnson and to Thomson with suitable words, either picked up or composed by himself. The slight acquaintance he had with the violin enabled him to gather and save many melodies, often from the singing of old women and country girls at their work. In Thomson's collection they suffered from their setting by the German composers, Haydn, Beethoven, Pleyel, and others, who wrote the arrangements; but Burns's correspondence with Thomson shows how jealously he sought to guard the melodies in their quaint native originality. "Whatever Mr. Pleyel does, let him not alter one iota of the original Scottish airs." The words, too, wherever these were in harmony with the sentiment of the music, he transmitted in their integrity. But where the words were incomplete or weak or indecent, he worked out a version that would "say" the song.

Even in his earliest songs he adopted the custom followed in his later life, of making the song grow out of the melody. Thus his songs sing themselves. This melodious quality is more than literary, and sometimes it is combined with a partial neglect of pure literary excellences; it belongs to that range of art where music and poetry occupy common ground. He thus describes his method of composition: "Until I am complete master of a tune in my own singing (such as it is), I can never compose to it. My way is: I consider the

----

[1] Cromek's *Reliques of Robert Burns*, p. 131. Philadelphia, 1809.

poetic sentiment corresponding to my idea of the musical expression, then choose my theme, begin one stanza, and when that is composed, which is generally the most difficult part of the business, I walk out, sit down now and then, look out for objects of nature around me that are in unison and harmony . . . humming every now and then the air with the verses I have composed. When I feel my muse beginning to jade, I retire to the solitary fireside of my study, and there commit my effusions to paper, swinging at intervals on the hind legs of my elbow chair by way of calling forth my own critical strictures."[1] Elsewhere he writes: "These old Scottish airs are so nobly sentimental that, when one would compose to them, to 'sowthe the tune,' as our Scotch phrase is, over and over is the readiest way to catch the inspiration."[2] From first to last he thus composed his songs in an element of music of the finest and simplest emotional quality, and that is one reason why his songs are emotionally so rich.[3]

By far the greater number of the songs which bear his name are only modifications of older songs that had long been current. But that this work of rescue is little second in importance to his original work is sufficiently indicated by such recoveries and improvements as *Ca the Yowes, Duncan Gray, Gala Water,* and *Auld Lang Syne.* These *rifacimenti* range from trivial verbal alterations to songs in which he merely preserves a chorus or the title and a line or two. From his MS. notes to the first four volumes of Johnson's *Museum*[4] and his letters to Thomson, we see that he was thoroughly versed in the history of Scottish song, and that

[1] Letter to Thomson, September, 1793.

[2] *Comm. Pl. Bk.*, September, 1784, under *Montgomerie's Peggy.*

[3] Further reference to this subject in detail is made in the notes. See also the Thomson correspondence.

[4] Collected and printed by Cromek in his *Reliques.*

he regarded this upon which he was engaged as a national work involving the honor of his native land. Every scrap of song that he could find giving any indication or possibility of genius he treasured and turned to account ; and to Johnson he expressed himself as ready to " beg, borrow, or steal " for the furtherance of his patriotic object. " The chorus is old, the rest is mine " ; " music good, verses just above contempt " ; " such a beautiful air to such execrable verses " ; " where old titles convey any idea at all, it is usually in the spirit of the air " ; " insipid stuff, but I will not alter except where I myself at least think I can amend " ; " I have adopted the two first two lines and am going on with the song on a new plan," — these few quotations at random show his attitude towards his material and his method of working it. A reading of his correspondence with Thomson will show further that he rescued and altered not as an antiquary, but with the instinct of a poet. It is needless to emphasize the fact that his improvements, in point of genius, far transcend all that he improved upon ; it is more important to notice that this clarification of genius, and not the "inspired scavenger " kind of work frequently credited to him, constitutes the purification he gave to Scottish song. Having saved those floating strands of lyric genius, he incorporated them into the warp and woof of his own composition, and they are as truly his as the Arthurian idylls are Tennyson's. What he did was to redeem the old as well as to reinspire the new, to concentrate a national enthusiasm within himself, to give coherence and body to it, and to reanimate, impersonate, and glorify the lyric genius of his race and country.

His purely original work was likewise, first of all, inspired by the music of his fatherland. One of his best, the bacchanalian *Willie Brewed a Peck o' Maut,* was composed without this inspiration ; likewise the passionate rhetoric of *A Man's a Man for a' That.* But we know how the music of *The*

Wren's Nest thrilled him as he wrote *O Wert Thou in the Cauld Blast*, and how the old strains of *Katherine Ogie* lent their pathos to *Highland Mary;* we can hear the reel time in *O Tibbie, I Hae Seen the Day* and the martial beat of *Hey Tuttie Taitie* in *Scots Wha Hae;* the wild notes of *Macpherson's Rant* give their fire to the *Farewell,* and the lilt of *Daintie Davie* rings in every line of *Rantin Rovin Robin.* The list might be indefinitely extended, and the subject offers a far deeper satisfaction than the mere gratification of curiosity. Those who see in the songs of Scotland only pleasant little ditties, to which they might listen with the same amusement as to negro minstrelsy on a banjo, are ignorant of the fact that Burns has converted these melodies into the most passionate, most tender, most humorous interpretations of the fundamental emotions of the human heart. To the fact that Burns had one of the most vigorous and penetrating intellects ever given to men, add that the melodies which he interpreted came to him laden with the griefs, joys, and humors of several centuries of national life, add the lyric genius of the interpreter and the trembling passion of his heart, and Scottish song in his hands begins to throw off its local or provincial interest, and to assume the value of a κτῆμα ἐς ἀεί, a human possession for all time.

It is true that he has dealt with the subject of love more conspicuously than with any other. But, to say nothing of the superb excellence of his love songs merely as such, it should be noted that the passion of love scarcely ever stands alone as a source of interest. In many it is adventitious and subordinate, and the song takes its quality from a totally different source, — from its martial heroism in *Go Fetch to me a Pint of Wine,* its heart-breaking pathos in *Bonie Doon,* its brisk and winning audacity in *O for Ane-and-twenty, Tam,* its pastoral quietness in *Ca the Yowes,* its arch humor in *Duncan Gray,* its chivalry of pure respect in *The Banks of the*

Devon, its feminine roguishness in *Last May a Braw Wooer*, its unearthly consecration in *To Mary in Heaven.* In these and many more the range is scarcely limited at all by the fact that they have love for their text. He had a theory, happily not adhered to, that love and wine were the exclusive themes of song, but the preponderance of his love songs is merely due to the fact that he was so much more of a human being than most; they come from the overflowing fullness of his animal life in the best sense of that word.

But though we set aside his love songs altogether, he would still be the author of *Auld Lang Syne*, that universal consecration of friendship ; of *John Anderson my Jo*, in which he has equally for all time consecrated the long devotion of wedded life; of *A Man's a Man for a' That*, in which he has crystallized the spirit of democratic manhood ; of *Scots Wha Hae*, which gives in a burning drop the quintessence of the struggle for independence that created Scotland; of *Macpherson's Farewell*, which immortalizes while it interprets the baffled spirit of the outlaw ; of *Rantin Rovin Robin*, the paragon of birthday songs, and *Willie Brewed a Peck o' Maut*, which makes bacchanalian good-fellowship sublime. We should still have the fireside charm of *Contented wi' Little*, the breath of the hills in *My Heart 's in the Highlands*, the bitterness of exile in *The Bonie Banks of Ayr*, the national defiance of *Does Haughty Gaul Invasion Threat*, the droll bickering of *My Spouse Nancy*, the homely peace of *Bessie and her Spinnin Wheel*, the motherly playfulness of *Hey Baloo my Sweet Wee Donald*, the "green pleasures and gray grief" of premature old age in *The Auld Man*, the heroism of *Kenmure*, the fun of *The Weary Pund o' Tow*, the quaintly tragic trepidations of *What Will I do gin my Hoggie Die.* These and many others, into which the passion of love in its limited sense does not enter at all, show a many-sidedness of genius nowhere approached in the songs of any other writer.

VI. BURNS'S WORK IN GENERAL.

More directly as regards the substance and quality of Burns's work and its position in the historic development of English literature, its distinctive marks are those that signify the rise of the new poetry which reached its culminating points in Wordsworth and Byron, — a return to natural subjects and a new sincerity in the treatment of them. In neither of these respects was this literature new to Scotland except in so far as the magnitude of Burns's genius made it so. But both subject and treatment were so novel to English litera-ture that on receipt of a volume of Cowper's poems, written almost contemporaneously with Burns's earlier work, Benjamin Franklin was so impressed with the "something new" in them that he read the poems a second time. As matter and treatment cannot well be separated in any great work, what is said on these subjects is here arranged under a classification of the former, which fairly covers the range of the poet's material: (1) Nature inanimate; (2) Nature animate; (3) Man; (4) The Deil; (5) God. Thereafter a few remarks are added on the Art and Ethic of his work.

(a) *Nature inanimate.*

Though Burns was reared in close neighborhood with the mountains and the sea, these enter but little into the substance of his poetry. In *The Vision* (l. 133) he speaks of the delight he had as a boy in listening to the dash of the waves on the "sounding shore"; but only once does the sea give him an image of rare imaginative beauty:

> The pale moon is setting behind the white wave,
> And time is setting wi' me, O.

In general, the sea is to him, as to the popular Scottish mind, associated with separation and exile. It gives the sad refrain "owre the sea" to his poem *On a Scotch Bard*, written in anticipation of severing all his dearest ties, and in *Auld Lang Syne* friendship is knit closer by the thought that "seas between us braid hae roared." In respect of this dearth of sea atmosphere, we must remember that Burns was still a landsman, whose interests were fundamentally those of a pastoral and agricultural people ; and in later life the sea was to him but the harvesting ground of the smugglers, whose occupation touched him on a side other than his poetic. Here, likewise, his poetic inheritance weighed upon him ; there was no sea tradition in Scottish, as there was in English, literature, nor was the sea associated with the achievement of Scottish nationality.

Similarly, the "mountains wild" of Scotia hold themselves aloof from the nearest purpose of his heart and the warmest atmosphere of his verse. He sees them "toss'd to the skies," the sun "gilds their distant brow," he "wanders on their heathy tops." But his hills are not the wild mountains of the north; they are the neighborly heights of the lowlands, that feed the sheep and send down the streams on whose banks he loves to rove. The north hills furnish him an element of the romance that belongs to the clans and Charlie, and he can sing like a clansman :

> My heart 's in the highlands, my heart is not here.

But the mountains, like the sea, are for him symbols of solitude and alienation ; they are beyond his most intimate range, because they are not closely associated with the humanity that is the ultimate theme of his song.

His attitude towards nature is well illustrated in his treatment of the wind. In its softer moods he sometimes, though rarely, draws upon it with fine skill for pictorial effect, as in the *Lament of Queen Mary :*

> Nae mair to me the autumn winds
> Wave o'er the yellow corn.

But he excels in describing a storm, partly because it appealed to his tempestuous nature, partly because it awakened his livelier sympathy with the suffering animals. We recognize the mastery of stroke in *Tam o' Shanter:*

> The wind blew as 't wad blawn its last,
> The rattlin showers rose on the blast;

and in the *Epistle to W. S.:*

> Even winter wild has charms for me,
> When winds rave through the naked tree,
> Or blindin drifts wild-furious flee,
> Darkening the day.

This sympathy with nature in her wilder moods is the essence of his youthful poem, *Winter, a Dirge;* it gives the point of departure in *A Winter Night,* and it recurs again and again in both poems and songs as a source of animation, even where he only applies it indirectly by way of contrasted imagery. No better description of a winter storm was ever written than that in the opening stanzas of *A Winter Night;* but there, as elsewhere, the passion of the storm wakens a strain of a different kind :

> Listenin the doors an' winnocks rattle,
> I thought me on the ourie cattle,
> Or silly sheep wha bide this brattle
> O' winter war,
> An' through the drift, deep-lairin, sprattle
> Beneath a scaur.

And the threnody of the " winter wind " becomes a descant on " man's ingratitude."

This is the tonic note of his treatment of inanimate nature. Much as he loved nature, and wholesomely as he drew from her sweetest springs of health, her inanimate beauties never alone served to satisfy his human need. Unlike Thomson, he is never purely descriptive, unless we except a few short passages like the "spate" in *The Brigs of Ayr* and the "burnie" in *Halloween;* he has always an ulterior and more vital interest, — animate nature and humanity. Thus, in *The Woods of Drumlanrig* and *Bruar Water*, both of which took their occasion from a nobleman's "barbarian" disregard of natural beauty, he gives both woods and stream a human personality, and makes the interest extend to the trouts, birds, hares, lovers, and the "wee white cot aboon the mill." So the mountain daisy becomes for him the emblem of a betrayed maidenhood and of his own blighted hopes. Incidental descriptions are merely backgrounds for something animate and human, or serve as decoration for a canvas in which the prime interest is a living one. The songs all have their origin in some human interest, and when the descriptive element is most prominent, as in *My Nanie's Awa,* or *Again Rejoicing Nature Sees*, the description is presented not for its own sake, but as an offset to human emotion.

Still, though humanity comes first and nature second in Burns, his love of nature is none the less intimate and sure on that account. Amid all his fleeting and disappointing loves this is the one love that is always sure, the one source of healing that never disappoints. That he mentions her only incidentally shows a finer feeling for her worth and a surer sense of her comfort than if he went philandering after her on set purpose to admire ; and, though expressed admiration of nature is only an incidental in his verse, it was no mere incidental, but an inborn habit of soul in his nature. Even as an incidental, it is so uniformly present that it amounts to a universal element. His mind is always full of natural beauty, always in touch with nature's refreshing power. He cannot speak to his Deil without finding room to adorn his address with flashes of natural description that make pictures in themselves. Even the bacchanalian revel of *The Jolly Beggars* begins: "When lyart leaves bestrew the yird," and through the haze of tobacco smoke and the fumes of whisky punch we catch blinks of sunshine and whiffs of the sweet field breeze. In his first *Epistle to Davie* he finely sets forth his trust in nature's healing influence, where he anticipates beggary as his fate; in the songs this love of nature tingles with a rapture only short of his love for woman.[1]

Burns has none of the later Wordsworthian "philosophy," but he shows a sympathy with inanimate nature and a fresh delight in her beauties not excelled by Wordsworth. The chief features of his treatment of nature are its closeness and intensity; when he writes of the mountain daisy, it is like a mother caressing her dying child. But there is also a newness that gives his poetic interpretation of nature an historic value. Before his day the minor Scots poets had habitually treated the theme, but only in a provincial way. In England another Scotsman, Thomson, had shown how nature can be turned to poetic account, but the "landscape glow" of Thomson still represents something lifeless and inconversable. In English poetry nature had been out of fashion for a hundred years before Burns came. Cowper, his contemporary, began to see nature as a living thing, and added the interest in humanity; but Cowper was first of all a student of books, and his love of nature, human though it is, reflects the mild and philosophic disposition of the book-loving man. Burns was first of all bred in the school of country life. From his boyhood love of nature was a passion in him, as it was later in Wordsworth. In his verse it became a rapture. Such an attitude towards nature is in our own day a common experience; it was not so in the third quarter of last century, when Burns began to write. Nature worship was then unknown alike as a poetic cult and

[1] See *Ep. D.*, 43-52; cf. also *The V.*, 126 ff.; and *Ep. W. S.*, 67 ff.

as a popular fashion. It was Burns who first felt and expressed the love of nature as a real joy, and in his verse this humanized love first appears as a living passion in English poetry.

(b) *Nature animate.*

So closely allied to his love of physical nature as often to form part of it is his sympathy with the lower animals. But the animals, both wild and domestic, belong more to the living humanity that commands his ultimate interest, and his treatment of them forms no merely incidental portion of his work. Here we have his love for nature specialized, and the result is individual poems, like *Poor Mailie, Mailie's Elegy, Auld Mare Maggie, My Hoggie, Water-fowl on Loch Turit,* the *Mouse,* and the *Wounded Hare.* In these the fullness of his own animal life overflows, and his spirits and affection go with it.

His domestic animals are to Burns among his dear and intimate friends, all the dearer by reason of their dependence and dumb ways. They cease to be part of his farm stock, and become poor relations whom he loves and social companions who can enter into his feelings and hold converse with him. *Auld Mare Maggie* is the record of a lifetime of good-comradeship with his horse. He had known her as a foal in the pasture and watched her tricky ways. She had pranced with pride as she bore home his bonnie young wife. She had been to all the markets with him and carried him home when in his cups. With him she had won racing honors from all the roadsters of the countryside. She had plowed with him, carted with him, given him foals of her breed, shared all his troubles, and now, when they have worn to crazy age together, he brings her a New Year's handsel, and promises he will reserve a pasture for her, that they may still "toyte about wi' ane anither." Sympathy of this kind is closely akin to humor. To this sympathy add a touch of drollery, and you find Burns personating them to the life, and becoming a sheep with Mailie and a dog with Luath and Cæsar. Not only does Mailie, in the *Elegy*, descry him a long half-mile away, run to meet him with kindly bleat, and trot by his side through all the town, but in the *Death and Dying Words* he assumes her individuality, interprets her sheep sense, gives her offspring the best of lessons in good sheep behavior, laments the state of her master's purse, and with her dying breath bequeaths to honest Hughoc that precious gift, her "blether." The subject matter of *The Twa Dogs* is less brute than human, but its interpretation of Scottish peasant life is primarily set in an interpretation of canine life which is so sympathetic that the dogs never lose their identity; they are dogs from first to last, from the manner of their sitting down[1] to their rising up. They are dogs in their point of view even to such details as their reference to the whipper-in as "it," and to bull fighting as "fechtin' wi' nowt," or the canine sympathy with which Luath says:

> My heart has been sae fain to see them
> That I for joy hae barkit wi' them.

In his treatment of wild animals Burns is equally sympathetic and tender ; but here the brutalities of sport, which he always denounced, and the severities of nature, which man cannot help, deepened his humor to indignation and pity. The song birds, of course, belong to his lyric joy, and throughout his poetry we hear the carol of lark and linnet, the robin's pensive warble,[2] the " wild-whistling blackbird," the " mellow mavis' e'enin sang." Poems and songs alike thrill with the happy voices of nature's wild choristers.

[1] See Burns's first reading and subsequent alteration.
[2] See note on *Bruar Water*, l. 47.

Even cries not in themselves musical become for him sounds of joy and expressions of nature's happiness. "I never hear the loud solitary whistle of the curlew in a summer noon or the wild mixing cadence of a troop of gray plovers in an autumnal morning without feeling an elevation of soul like the enthusiasm of devotion or poetry."[1]   The other side to this sunny gladness of natural love is his pity for their sufferings when their own mother's heart seems to freeze towards them.   Then in the stormy winter night he thinks of the silly sheep and the ourie cattle, and the words come like tears of infinite compassion.

> Ilk happin bird, wee helpless thing,
> That in the merry months o' spring
> Delighted me to hear thee sing.
> What comes o' thee?
> Whare wilt thou cower thy chitterin wing
> An' close thy ee?

Then, while "pitiless the tempest beats," he has pity even for the beasts and birds of prey. This womanly tenderness, which is always combined with masculine strength, takes a still keener expression when it is touched by the thought of human wantonness and cruelty.   Burns has frequently delivered himself on the subject of field sports;[2] but when he sees the waterfowl on Loch Turit rise and fly from his mere presence, and the poor mouse run in panic from the gaudsman who pursues it "wi' murd'rin pattle," his tenderness is at once irradiated by the reflection that these are his "fellow-creatures," and he their "earth-born companion and fellow-mortal."

If he had a suggestion of this strain of sentiment from any one, it was from Sterne ; no previous poet had expressed

[1] Letter to Mrs. Dunlop, Jan. 1, 1789.

[2] See *August Song to Peggy*, lines *On a Wounded Hare*, and the opening passage of *The Brigs of Ayr*.

it. But the firm strength and healthy grace of Burns's feeling, compared with Sterne's bibbering lament over the ass,[1] again mark the advent of a new era ; here again the genuineness of his poetry shows itself. He offers none of the vague rhapsodies of a bleeding heart. He describes what he sees and what he feels. The hare he laments was one he saw limping past him ; he heard the shot fired and threatened to throw the wretch who fired it into the Nith. The mouse was one he turned up with the plow ; he saw it run and saved its life. Mailie was his own "pet yowe," to whom the accident happened ; he saw her "warstlin i' the ditch." Luath was his own dog, who talked with him and who knew what he said. His feelings, whether of tenderness, joy, sorrow, or indignation, are always real and always intense. This close and loving sympathy with the lower animals found its first poetic expression in Burns and his contemporary Cowper, and it has never been so finely and amply expressed since.

(c) *Man.*

As a man Burns thought nothing human alien to him. Like every wise artist, he handles by preference the material with which he is most intimate. But his secondary range includes every phase of humanity that comes under his notice, from the ragamuffins at Poosie Nansie's to the king upon the throne. It is a mistake to speak of his poetry as if its horizon were limited to that of the Scottish peasant. Personally, he mixed on terms of intimacy with all classes. He numbered among his friends many leaders in the world of fashion, both in letters and in society, members of the bench and bar, clergy of the New Light, members of Parliament, and representatives of the dramatic stage, and in the

[1] *Tristram Shandy*, bk. vii, ch. xxxii.

broader field of political life he joined hands with Washington across the Atlantic and the French Revolutionaries across the channel. All of these interests appear in his work side by side with his pictures of the Scottish peasantry, and provoke verses that are instinct with character and animation and personal contact. Apart from his familiar epistles, of which he has given us more than any other poet except Horace, he has left scores of epigrams, epitaphs, and squibs that are merely the discharge of his superabundant electricity when it comes into contact with anything human.

Burns believed with Pope that "the proper study of mankind is man." But here the agreement ceases. The "man" of Pope's line must, by birth, breeding, or sympathy, be an aristocrat, something of a wit, a townsman, and *habitué* of the coffeehouses and *salons;* no other kind of man was of important interest. Burns's man, who is "a man for a' that," is of the democracy that revolted against privilege and accomplished the revolution. Burns himself was of the democracy, and all his treatment of humanity takes its tone and color from his democratic point of view. His father belonged to the unprivileged and suffering classes, and was harassed to the grave under the aristocratic institution of British landlordism. The poet himself was always poor. In his youth and early manhood he was only an overworked plowman, "half-mad, half-fed, half-sarkit." He was never anything more than a "little farmer." His latter days were spent in "searchin auld wives' barrels,"—following an occupation that bore a worse social stigma than that of a policeman. His aristocratic experiences in Edinburgh and elsewhere were only episodes in his life. Knowing his own genius and having tasted of its power, knowing, too, by cruel experience, the hardships and sorrows of the poor, he very early contracted a jealousy of wealth and social distinction which, in his later years, became inveterate. During his second winter in the capital, when the roses were now dead leaves and thorns, this jealousy was embittered into scorn and hate ; and, when he returned two years later, the picture he gives of himself and of his reflections amid the pomp of Princes Street is curiously like that of Langland five hundred years before in the Strand of London.[1] This *Piers Plowman* element of his character is deeply marked in his writings, especially in his prose, but he was saved from its warping influences by his sanguine temperament, his elastic joy in living, his humor, and his faith in human goodness.

British class distinction, then, is not merely one of the influences that affected Burns's view of life : it is the social groundwork on which his poems are built. This was not so much a distinction between rich and poor as between aristocracy and plebs, — a distinction then so implicitly accepted as a fundamental part of human destiny that even Burns regards it as inexorable. It is true he denies the rationality and justice of it, and his attitude towards it, even in his early poems, is a kind of rebellious uneasiness and resentment. In *Man Was Made to Mourn*, looking sadly on the fields " where hundreds labor to support a haughty lordling's pride," he asks, in angry mood :

> If I 'm designed yon lordling's slave —
> By nature's law designed —
> Why was an independent wish
> E'er planted in my mind ?"

But he sees no remedy except in death.[2] He is no apostle of the rebellion which expresses itself in lawlessness and disorder. He looks clean through the guises of distinction, and king, queen, and royal family in *A Dream*, and the

[1] See letter to Mrs. Dunlop, Mar. 4, 1789. Cf. *Piers Plowman's Vision.*   [2] Cf. *Ep. to Davie*, ll. 16 ff.

aristocratic leaders of the nation in his *Earnest Cry and Prayer* cease to be "personages," and become men and women whom he levels to their rank as human beings by right of his common humanity. But this intuitive process must not be confounded with political or social leveling. The disillusionment he brings is not that of political radicalism, but of sheer human nature. He professed to learn from Lord Daer "to meet with unconcern one rank as well 's another"; but, although to him "the rank was but the guinea's stamp" and "the man the gowd," he never proposed to abolish the stamp and reduce society to the bullion of humanity. Social distinction never enhanced a person's value in his eyes, but he accepted aristocracy, squirearchy, and gentry in general as part of the social economy which produced the cotter, and which, while he did not defend it, he had too strong sense impotently to attack.

Compare *A Dream* with another poem, in which he reaches to the opposite pole of British distinction, *The Jolly Beggars.* The poem is a work of divination by which he lays bare the human heart of the vagabond, as in the other he pierces to the quick of royal humanity. In it the claims of rank disappear, and his assertion of human freedom presents itself in a way that startles. We are introduced to the kitchen of Poosie Nansie's public house, where round the fire on an early winter night there are met seven or eight tramps of all shades and both sexes, who drink their superfluous money, pawn their clothes for more, and make the rafters shake with revelry in celebration of their defiant liberties.

> A fig for those by law protected !
>   Liberty 's a glorious feast;
> Courts for cowards were erected,
>   Churches built to please the priest.
>
> What is title ? what is treasure ?
>   What is reputation's care ?

> If we lead a life of pleasure,
>   'T is no matter how or where.
>
> Life is all a variorum,
>   We regard not how it goes;
> Let them cant about decorum
>   Who have characters to lose.

Here we are not merely outside the range of social distinctions: we are even outside the range of social restraint and the simple regimen of the ten commandments. But, wild as the scene is, we are down on the bed rock of human nature.

But the great body of his work is not only surrounded by an atmosphere of Scottish rural life, it is made up of scenes and studies in the lives and manners of the Scottish peasantry from the peasant's point of view. *The Twa Dogs*, a poem drawn direct from what he saw on his father's farm, is a picture of the two sides of British country life. It is not "the old controversy between the rich and the poor."[1] It rests on the sharp aristocratic distinction between a privileged landed gentry and an unprivileged yeomanry and peasantry, who still maintain much of the mediæval distinction between Norman baron and Saxon hind. Unless this is understood the point of the poem is missed. The side which Cæsar portrays is what Burns knew by every ache in his soul and body. He had worked with "the unceasing moil of a galley slave" to make up the "racked rent." The laird's whipper-in, "wee blastit wonner," had many a time ridden full cry hunting the fox over his father's crops, with the hunters at his heels. His pride had often been stung to see how the gentry would "gang as saucy by poor folk as I wad by a stinkin brock." The scene described in lines 93–100 is taken from one of the experiences that drove his father to the grave a broken man. His secondary descrip-

---

[1] Shairp's *Burns* (*Eng. Men of Letters*), p. 191.

tions of "gentry's life in common," their follies, vices, and *ennui*, are taken from current belief amongst his own class. If this side alone were portrayed, the poem would be a moral satire, as bitter and realistic as portions of *Piers Plowman*. It takes a sweeter and more ideal complexion from the pictures drawn by Luath of the cotters' fireside joys, their harvest homes, and new-year merry makings, their village politics, their thriving children, their blink of rest. Underneath their unlovely toil and semi-starvation he recognizes the ethical beauty of their lives. But neither is Luath's idealism divorced from what is real. He, too, is keenly realistic in his detail of the cotter "howkin in a sheugh," the "smytrie o' wee duddie weans," the "twalpennie worth o' nappie," the "luntin pipe an' sneeshin mill," the "wee touch langer an' they maun starve o' cauld an' hunger." But over it all he sheds the soft light of human love, and a new ethical strength is felt when he says that

> Buirdly chiels an' clever hizzies
> Are bred in sic a way as this is.

In *The Twa Dogs* he accepts the division in social life, and, seeing the futility of kicking against the pricks, he softens the severity of the contrast by the sunshine of human affection. In *The Cotter's Saturday Night* and in *Halloween* we have pictures of the same rural life, into which the disturbing influence of class distinction does not enter. There he forgets there is such a thing as social inequality, and describes the peasantry in the quiet dignity and devotion of their cottage homes and in the innocent mirth of their rustic festivals. *The Holy Fair* describes a country gathering of another and less innocent kind, while it shows up a different side of Scotch religion. In the *Haggis* and *Scotch Drink* he gives a poetic celebration and something of national glory to the countryman's food and liquor. In the *Deil* he touches

off rustic superstitions regarding the fourth person of the
Scottish godhead.   In general, his poetry is a reflex of the
country life of Scotland in all its beauty and ugliness, its
mingled faith and superstition, piety and irreverence, sobriety
and drunkenness, integrity and hypocrisy, and from its
strength and lifelike truth in this it takes its primary value.

But in three respects his treatment of life rises out of
this provincial atmosphere, — its patriotic and national tone,
its universal quality, and its look towards the future. Patriotism is never merely provincial, and no poetry was ever more
intensely patriotic than that of Burns. Patriotic in that it
gathers up the traditions and elements of Scottish national
life and character, it is still more so in the fire of national
pride with which the poet himself is aglow. He is a national,
not a local, poet, and, although his Scotland is a thing of the
past, his poetry will endure, not as a provincial product, but
as a national monument. Secondly, his poetry has that
which makes it appeal as directly to Americans and foreign-
tongued Europeans as to Scotsmen. Shining through the
local and particular, there is always the universal element
which we find in the men and women of Shakspere's dramas.
His men and women are, first of all, human beings; only
in a secondary sense are they peasants of Ayrshire. We
miss, it is true, those fine forms of nobility which Shakspere
found it easier to create because he had them always
before his eyes. Burns, too, missed them; hence much of
his warfare with the time that was "out of joint." But, such
as it is, his material is the permanent substance of human
nature, and his treatment is so free from the intellectual
astigmatism which constitutes provinciality that, next to
Shakspere, he is, perhaps, the most intimately known foreign
poet in Germany. But, thirdly, Burns was beyond the atmosphere of provincial humanity, in that both as man and poet
he embodied the germinal ideas of the new democracy which

was to be the most active force in the life and literature of the succeeding age, — individual right and human brotherhood. His actual politics count for little. Singing in the morning twilight of modern times, he had no clear perception of political liberty and political equality based on the above ideas; he had no "theory of government." But his imagination anticipated the time when these principles would dominate all political life and transfigure the nations of the world. His political sympathies, which sprung from his feeling for the pain of life among the unprivileged toilers, belong to his recognition and assertion of the claims of human worth and the nobility that is alike unauthenticated and unabashed by rank. His poetry gave these claims irresistible utterance. It was a voice straight from the democracy, speaking for the democracy with unexampled directness, energy, and pride ; and in this, not less than in his poetic interpretation of nature and his sympathy with the lower animals, he was the pioneer of a new *renaissance.*

(d) *The Deil.*

In Burns's treatment of the supernatural we find a similar freshness and originality. Twice he introduces figures that appear like veritable apparitions, — Coila, in *The Vision*, and Death, in *Dr. Hornbook*, — and a comparison of these will show where his strength lies. We are prepared for both, in the first case by the poet's reverie, in the second by his assumed condition. In both cases, as soon as the visitant is observed the illusion of the supernatural disappears. Both apparitions are flesh and blood ghosts. We are beyond the world of mere illusion and in the presence of beings that have the reality which belonged to similar creations of the Hellenic mind. Coila is quite a corporeal Scotch lassie. Death is fearfully real in his gaunt length, with his thin shanks and " fient a wame," his implements and his beard and the fit of temper in which he " nearhand cowps." But Death is a creation of humor, and therein lies its superiority. The serious and the supernatural do not seem to accord in Burns's mind. Even the fine poetic illusion of the fairies dancing on the " infant ice " under the brigs of Ayr passes away among capitalized abstractions. And Burns is less at home among " spirits of health " than among "goblins damned." Death himself has an element of *diablerie* in his composition, and, apart from the above, the supernatural in his work is wholly devilish in its origin and wholly humorous in its character.

The reason is that for him the supernatural was inseparably associated with the teachings of the Scotch theology which he did so much to discredit and wipe out, especially the doctrine of eternal torture in a material hell of flaming sulphur under the eye of a personal devil. In rejecting crude mediævalism of this kind, Burns makes fun of hell and friendship with the Deil. In *The Holy Fair* " black Russell " describes the place of torture and " harrows their souls."

> The half-asleep start up wi' fear
> An' think they hear it roarin ;
> When presently it does appear
> 'T was but some neibor snorin.

The *Address to the Deil* runs over the whole ground of kirk teaching and popular superstition, and with mock seriousness preserves the point of view and the emotion proper to each part of the subject ; but at the close the poet and the Deil shake hands.

Combined with this direct teaching of the kirk was a great mass of floating superstition, partly Celtic, partly Norse in its origin, which the kirk likewise consigned to the devil under the elastic name of witchcraft. Burns learnt all of this folk superstition in his childhood from old Betty Davidson,[1] and so vividly was it impressed on his imagination that even in manhood he confessed it "took an effort to shake off these idle terrors." Some of this is worked into the substance of *Halloween*. That is the night when the fairies dance and the natural and supernatural worlds come close together. The spells are all innocent enough, but there is a shadowy background to the scene, in which the powers of Satan darkly shift about and threaten with vague alarms.

> Mony a ane has gotten a fricht
> An' lived an' died deleerit
> On sic a nicht.

But in all the spells tried the dim terrors of the supernatural are softened and made familiar with touches of humor. There is the same familiarizing touch in *Tam o' Shanter*, where the devil and his troop appear in person. The poem takes its departure from a scene of over-jollity; the kirk scene is equally hilarious, though the mirth be the mirth of devils ; the hero's tipsy cry "Weel done, Cutty-sark ! " is a touch of pure humor ; and the fate of mare Meg is not tragic, but comical. In spite of the accumulated horrors that impart such eeriness to Tam's ride, the grewsome paraphernalia that adorn the church walls and the holy table, and the actual presence of Satan and the witches, the poem, though it has much of the tragic circumstance, has nothing of the tragic terror of the witch scenes in *Macbeth*.

Burns's treatment of the Deil in person brings to a head all these qualities of reality, humanism, humor. The devil of kirk theology and popular credence was a mere bugaboo with hardly a remnant of fallen greatness about him. He was the devil of the Miracle plays, to whom Protestant Scotland had fallen heir. In the *Address* Burns takes him as he is.

---

[1] See note on *The Deil*, l. 63.

His Deil is what the Satan who lost paradise has become during eighteen centuries of ecclesiastical bullying and ill usage. He has forgotten the days when he held brusque converse with the Omnipotent in the presence chamber of heaven, and has sunk to bagpiping at a witch's splore. He has lived in Scotland, and been persecuted, maligned, affronted, and nicknamed by the respectabilities of the kirk till he has lost all self-respect and taken to low mischief, — unroofing the churches, making the cows " yeld," frightening the nightly wayfarer by quacking like a wild duck. With a touch of his ancient poetry, he still loves to quit the haunts of men and wander in lonely glens where ruined castles nod to the moon; but hard treatment and lack of sympathy have done their work. Burns gives him sympathy such as he never has got before or since. He calls him away from his ugly business of basting poor wretches with liquid brimstone, talks over old times with him, reminds him of his former glory, — of " Eden's bonie yard," where he gave the infant world a " shog " that nearly ruined all, of the festive time he had with Job, when, with a consummate genius for wickedness, he capped the old man's misery by unloosing his wife's tongue upon him. Probably he is now too far gone for complete restitution, but, believing that even the deil is not so bad as he is painted, the poet bids him a tender good by, with a word of charitable sympathy that is like a message direct from heaven : " O wad ye tak a thocht an' mend."

(e) *God.*

The subject of religion enters to a vital extent into the body of Burns's writings and affects these in three ways, which appear (1) in his objective pictures of the simple faith and practice of the Scottish peasantry, (2) in his satires on the official religion of the kirk, and (3) in personal expressions of religious thought and feeling throughout his poems and letters.

Bred in a religious home like that described in *The Cotter's Saturday Night*, he absorbed its influences with a fervor that made him noted in his boyhood for an enthusiastic and unreasoning piety,[1] and in later years he never forgot the religion he learned at his father's hearth. To this *The Cotter's Saturday Night* is as noble a tribute as any poet ever paid to faith in God. The *English Men of Letters* critic somewhat grudgingly reminds the reader that "the religion there described was his father's faith, not his own"; but a more intimate personal interest is added in the fact that on his father's death the poet took his place as head of the family, and every night conducted the same family worship; long afterwards the hired man remembered those prayers. At Ellisland, too, he regularly held family worship with his servants, and in his letters he always recognizes the necessity of "regular intercourse with the Deity" as a condition of inward peace. He knew the value of this simple faith in the upbuilding of character; and, though *The Cotter's Saturday Night* takes its prime value from its objective as a faithful and loving portrayal of the devout side of Scottish rustic life, it is none the less a subjective revelation of the mind that could thus faithfully see and lovingly express the moral beauty of the scene; the poem derives its color from the light of the poet's soul.

The other side of Scotch religion was that represented in the kirk theology, which had come down inviolate from the days of John Knox and the Westminster Confession, — the ruthless Calvinism of the old Scotch Puritans divested of its old Puritan grandeur. Just as Burns was coming to his maturity and beginning to feel the first pride of intellect, it

---

[1] Letter *To Dr. Moore*, Aug. 2, 1787; cf. *To Mrs. Dunlop*, Dec. 29, 1795.

happened that a broader and milder conception of divine providence, which had for some time been growing among the more enlightened and less ascetic clergy, asserted itself in the church, and Ayrshire in particular was the arena in which the Old Light and the New were arrayed against each other. Burns's intellectual sympathies were all with the New Light clergy; his moral sympathies, too, were aroused against the intolerance, hypocrisy, and uncharitableness bred and fostered by the old orthodoxy; and his sense of humor and power of sarcasm were excited to irrepressible activity by the Herds and Holy Willies and "unco guid" in general who stood for Election and Grace.

His kirk satires, deplored by his *English Men of Letters* biographer, are a class by themselves, and form a chapter in the history of religious liberty. "Not Latimer, not Luther, struck more telling blows against false theology than did this brave singer."[1] But it is more than false theology he arraigns and castigates. He not only exposes cant, hypocrisy, and superstition in general, and holds up to derision dogmas and observances grown worse than obsolete; he drives the theological satire home to the moral life, and for his victims he selects by undisguised name the actual professors and devotees of the ultra-Calvinistic faith, who were known in person to all who read the satires. All of these objects he assails with a vehemence that might be thought vindictive were not the satirist in such splendid good-humor; and he punishes them with a soundness and penetrative force that entitle him to rank as high among religious reformers as mere satire will entitle a man to be placed. As literary works they are marked by keen human sympathy and virile moral strength, a revel of mother wit and humor and blistering sarcasm, daring strokes of imagination that blend the humorous with the sublime, realism to a degree

[1] Emerson on Burns.

that startles, extraordinary facility of versification, and force of language that crushes like a trip-hammer. The outcry about Burns's " want of religion " was largely due to those satires, to the animosity they excited in the church party, and to the scandals encouraged by those who smarted under his lash. In justice to him who thus held up to ridicule and shame what to him was false religion, it should be noted that the essential points for which he contended are now matters of commonplace acceptance even in Scotland, and what he assailed has mostly been allowed to disappear. It should also be remembered that the author of *Holy Willie's Prayer* is likewise author of *The Cotter's Saturday Night.*[1]

Neither the religion of the Cotter, however, nor that of Holy Willie was Burns's own. For one of his intellectual strength, roused as it was to searching activity by the agitations of the modern spirit working within him, the simple faith of his father could not suffice. The remembrance of it, indeed, remained with him always, like an autumnal sunset, but it touched only the emotional side of his nature. It left his intellect unsatisfied. Orthodoxy, again, with its incredible dogmas, its travesty of divine goodness, and its inconsistent practice, affronted alike his intellect and his moral sense. What remained for him in that age ? Only the sterile Deism of the more cultured classes and the " obstinate questionings " and ecstatic aspirations of his

---

[1] For a succinct and sympathetic account of these satires, the student is referred to Professor Nichol's monograph, pp. 21–24. In the present volume the mildest of the series is given, *The Holy Fair*, and the epistle in which he summarizes the fight, *Ep. to McMath*. In the notes to these and to the *Ep. to William Simson* special detail is added. For convenience the complete list is here given: *The Twa Herds, Ep. to Goudie, Ep. to Simson* (postcript), *The Holy Fair, Holy Willie's Prayer* (with the *Epitaph*), *Ep. to McMath, The Ordination,* and *The Kirk's Alarm.* Add *The Calf, Dedication to Gavin Hamilton,* and *To the Unco Guid,* which partake of the same inspiration.

own soul. Beginning in England with Hobbes as a reaction against the dogmatic assumptions of Puritanism, the semi-religious philosophy of Deism passed into the general body of 18th century literature, and was part of Burns's literary inheritance. It appealed to him more directly in the precept and practice of his friends of the New Light. It was poor spiritual diet for a man of his ardent and adoring nature, but it was all the age had to offer him as intellectual support for his adorations, and he accepted it. So far as his faith was positive, it consisted in the Deism of his age, so modified as to accord with the warmer impulses of his heart and his instinctive need of divine sympathy. This is the religion we find in his metrical *Prayers*, and in casual utterances like that in his *Sketch on New Year's Day, 1790*.

But Deism, — the product, as it was the faith, of an age and society that on the moral side were carnal, unfeeling, and insincere, on the spiritual side shallow, skeptical, and materialistic, — while it partially satisfied his intellect, failed to satisfy his emotional needs and the finer part of his spirit. Measured by the standard of both earlier and later times, the 18th century was irreligious ; Burns was formed to be a deeply religious man. His nature seemed to demand the closest relations with Deity, and, finding in the temples no God, but only a formula or else a monster, he broke into importunate beseechings, like a child crying for its absent father. His spiritual disappointment reacted with a violence that overwhelmed him with doubts, and threatened even to shake his foundations. At times, like Hamlet, he almost vainly tried to believe that the soul was "a thing immortal," while he half mistrusted that death might be "a quietus." On other articles of common Christian belief he showed less of creed faith than of the faith that lies in "honest doubt." But through all his darkness and conflict he clung to faith in God, and, as he never spoke otherwise than reverently of things truly sacred, so he ever upheld the value of sincere religion.[1] If by religion we mean an inspiring and sustaining sense of close personal alliance with God, we do not find Burns possessed, to the annihilation of uncertainty, of an absorbing trust of this kind. But this defect of his religion belonged to the age in which he had to work out his own salvation. He came at the close of an era of mundane skepticism, when the new era of spiritual insight was only beginning to dawn. He fretted for what was not. To him, as to Hamlet, the time was out of joint, and the spite was that he was one of those "born to put it right."

The post-revolutionary era has formed a different conception of God, and has given a larger content to the idea of religion, and the influences that produced this renovation were primarily those which found one of their earliest and most substantial embodiments in Burns and Burns's work. It is the function of men of his type to act as regenerative forces ; they sink the plow and bring up the world's subsoil. Even in that materialistic and superstitious age Burns had a strong intuition of the spiritual forces that inform and control the material universe, — that which later became the poetic sense of God in Nature. He had likewise, in spite of personal waywardness, an unfailing realization of allegiance to the forces that make for righteousness and permanence in human life, — that which later became the religion of humanity. A few months before he died he hailed with delight Cowper's *Task*, and recognized its new and kindred spirit, "bating a few scraps of Calvinistic divinity," as "the religion of God and nature, the religion that ennobles man."[2]

---

[1] His letters on this subject form one of the most pathetic chapters in all spiritual autobiography. See especially *To James Candlish*, Mar. 21, 1787 ; *To Mrs. Dunlop*, Feb. 12, 1788, June 21, Sept. 6, and Dec. 13, 1789 ; and *To Cunningham*, Feb. 14, 1790, Aug. 22, 1792, and Feb. 25, 1794. [2] Letter *To Mrs. Dunlop*, Dec. 25, 1795.

And this side of his religion is summed up in his own words:

The heart benevolent and kind
The most resembles God.

(f) *Art and Ethic.*

Since art implies a subjective process as well as an objective result, it is inevitable that the artistic product should take not only its tone and color but its essential meaning and value from the character of the artist's mind. This is what we mean by ἦθος, or ethical quality, and this ethic is the element which gives the artistic product its ultimate worth as a life-giving or life-perverting power, whether the artist wills it or not. Any phase of weakness or disease in the artist's mind will as surely reveal itself in the art he produces, as health, strength, and sympathy with all things good and sound will serve to make his work a human restorative and invigorant. Art absolutely void of this ethical quality does not exist, for this would mean that neither the art product nor the artist nor the life he seeks to portray had any character at all.

The humblest and least artistic way in which this ethic reveals itself is that of direct moral teaching, and for a poet Burns has an unusual amount of this kind of material. Conspicuous among poems with this direct moral bearing are the *Address to the Unco Guid, A Bard's Epitaph*, and *Epistle to a Young Friend.* Closely akin to these are poems of a moralistic turn, like *Friar's Carse Hermitage.* To the same tendency belongs that strain of moralizing in which he loves to indulge in his work in general, as in *Man was Made to Mourn*, some of the *Epistles*, the *Cotter*, the closing stanzas of the *Daisy* and the *Mouse*, the purple patch on *Tam o' Shanter.* In this he merely followed a fashion prevalent in 18th century literature; but, while the 18th century set him the example, the quality of his ethical reflection takes us beyond the moralism of "an understanding age" to the root wisdom of mankind.   No previous moralist taught him,

> But, mousie, thou art no thy lane,

or

> O wad some power the giftie gie us
> To see oursels as ithers see us.

This is the kind of common sense that amounts to an inspired revelation.   It belongs to the seer who is also an artist.   No poet was ever more richly endowed than Burns with this faculty of smelting the common ore of everyday experience.   Even in poems where the theme offers no high material for poetry, like the *Unco Guid* and the *Epistle to a Young Friend*, he brings such a force of sagacity to bear upon them, and so intimately reveals the eternal principles of conduct running through the mixed and drossy ore of human life, that almost every stanza affords some aphorism which has passed into our daily currency as standard coin.

The positive content of his ethic reveals itself, first of all, in the preëminent humaneness of his outlook, shown in his tenderness for the lower animals, his sympathy with the toiling poor, his compassion for the sorrowing and suffering, his beautiful *misericordia*.   Even where the springs of pity are untouched, this loving kindness of nature is equally rich and full in his interpretation of the friendly and domestic affections.   The ethic of friendship has never been more variously or feelingly portrayed than by Burns, from the mere bacchanalian good-fellowship of *Willie Brewed a Peck o' Maut* through the whole gamut of the *Epistles* to the imperishable bonds of *Auld Lang Syne*.   The ethic of the home receives from him its consummate idealization, whether it be in the lyric devotion of *John Anderson my Jo*, or in the domestic picture of the *Cotter* with its proud reflection:

> From scenes like these old Scotia's grandeur springs,

and the noble invocation with which the poem closes; or where he says more personally :

> To mak a happy fireside clime
> For weans an' wife,
> That 's the true pathos an' sublime
> O' human life.

There the ethic is of the richest substance of human nature. More broadly considered, the content of this positive ethic consists in his regard for the simple but eternal qualities that beautify and ennoble character, — truth, sincerity, frankness, magnanimity, loving-kindness. These are simple qualities, but they assume a fresh value in Burns's work from the intensity and force with which he exhibits them. From the reverse side they are especially intensified by his withering hatred for every form of human meanness. Hypocrisy, in particular, whether religious or social, was never so blasted by fire from heaven as it was by the author of *Holy Willie's Prayer* and the *Address to the Unco Guid*. Other perversions of character are not so much held up to obloquy as swept beyond the horizon by the strong breeze of his healthy genius. If at times he exaggerates the negative emphasis, the positive qualities of his ethic will nevertheless be found, taken all in all, to embody an exacting ideal of right, which, in spite of pitiful confessions of failure, dominates both his personal character and his artistic work.

What gives these ethical elements their especial force is the intense individualism of the man's nature. Burns was not imbued with the philosophic individualism into the "dust and powder" of which Burke, at a later time, dreaded lest the French Revolution should reduce the fabric of society. But the revolutionary idea is perceptible in his paramount accentuation of the claims of individual worth, and especially in his aggressive and sometimes defiant asser-

tion of independence. This is not merely the worldly independence of the *Epistle to a Young Friend,* in which he
recommends "gatherin gear by every wile that's justified
by honor."   Rather it is the self-confident, self-respecting
"pride of worth" that is combined with "pith o' sense" in
A Man's a Man; the sentiment which animated him on his
meeting with Lord Daer ; which made him, when he confronted the dazzle of human dignities in Edinburgh, sing in
his heart :

> The man of independent mind,
> He looks an' laughs at a' that;

which enabled him during his dismal years of toil on the
farm and in the excise to "bear himself like a king in exile."
In this regard his organic sentiment, to apply the words of
Emerson, is that of absolute independence resting on a life
of labor.   He does not preach labor as a gospel, he simply
accepts it as a fact.   But he glorifies that fact.   Even round
the most sordid poverty and drudgery in the *Twa Dogs* he
creates an atmosphere of ethical dignity and beauty when
he unfolds the cotter's scenes of joy and homely heroism.
Thus his ethic of independence takes a firmer body from the
reality of labor on which it rests.   It becomes the self-
reliance which is a spiritual resource.   It gives him the
most substantial basis for his "criticism of life," and is at
the same time his keenest inspiration.   All his expressly
ethical work, the matter of which is often scarcely poetical
at all, takes its higher value from his clear recognition of
what constitutes human worth and his allegiance to the
essential nobility of man.   All the more detailed elements
of his ethic become, as it were, focussed in this, and receive
such energy from the glowing mass of the poet's individuality that Burns is one of the strongest ethical forces in
English literature.

In its highest sense, however, this ethic belongs to his art, and is especially that which makes his artistic work a possession for all time.   It is not " unfair " — *pace* Carlyle — to " test him by the rules of art."   It is true he "never once was permitted to grapple with any subject with the full collection of his strength."   True, he never exercised his powers on the large scale of Sophocles or of Shakspere. But even in his most trivial work he showed the same artistic instinct for unity of conception, singleness of impression, beauty and coherence of detail.   Not only had he the fertility of creative resource which made him produce with the ready responsiveness of Nature when seeds are cast into her lap ; but his critical remarks on his songs, many of which are models of perfect art, show that he worked towards this perfection with the sedulous care of Nature when she moulds the frond of the fern or the blossom on the rose tree.   His best poems reveal the same singleness amid variety of conception working out towards beauty of form and finish.   His language always indicates the ease, and commonly the grace, of perfect artistic mastery.   The art criticism which he inherited was merely external and availed him little.   In production he simply obeyed the creative intelligence of his mind.   Art of this kind is the analogue of the work of nature ; the art itself is nature, for the creative instinct of the artist is a mode of the formative force of the universe, which culminates in organic life and operates by intelligent design.   This intelligence and this vitality are sovereign characteristics which give the creative art of Burns its permanent strength.   Amid all the turmoil of his emotions his intellect reigns supreme.   He never works with uncertain or aimless activity.   In him, as in nature, we find imperfections and irregularities, but these cease to be of vital account when the whole makes for healthy vitality.

The art ethic of Burns's work, then, lies in his clear apprehension and strong embodiment of the forces that make for vitality, preservation, permanence. As regards his own life, we know only too well that he often " passed douce Wisdom's door for glaikit Folly's portals," and left a record which has been a favorite pacing ground for theatrical moralists. He has told us all about it in his own words, passed his own verdict on his failings, and characterized both kindly and viciously all his censors, who have done little more than avail themselves of his confessions. *The Bard's Epitaph* is a moral judgment on his own life that in its simple solemnity and pathetic candor outweighs all the homilies ever preached upon it. So far as concerns his occasional coarseness and love of a laugh broader than is permitted in a drawing-room, these are qualities he shares with Chaucer, Shakspere, and others whose wholesomeness is no more called in question than their greatness. These incidental qualities, which can easily be ignored, do not affect the essential value of his poetic work. In the substance of this work we find the ethical vigor and salubrity that come of the sound mental constitution and the healthy outlook on life. Barring a few spiteful but well-provoked epigrams, his view is always magnanimous and humane, his insight always true, his utterance always sincere. His heart is always right. Above all things, he is preëminently sane. He has left somewhat that we can well afford to ignore, but, even if we include the whole, few poets are so conspicuously free from all forms of literary disease as he. In days when art cant is not less prevalent than corrupt art, it is good to go out into the fresh and tonic air of a genius like Burns. It may bring with it a whiff of other odors besides those of the wild flowers and the new-plowed land, but there can be no doubt about its healthfulness and invigorating effect. If we encounter country freshness, we never run across anything sickly, and whatever is amiss or redundant comes of a surplus of health and an exuberant vitality.

As for his fame, Burns is sufficiently well established among civilized peoples as one of the great singers of humanity. This triumph belongs to the artist, not to the moralist; but it is the artist who has so far felt and understood the forces that make for permanence that his interpretation of them embodies a sound and universal ethic. With him, as with the great artists of the race from Homer down, art and ethic are one and indivisible. The art ethic is the world ethic. It is the vital force of nature which builds to resist or to correct decay, whether in physical life or in the social organism. We have seen how Burns caught the organic impulse of the new time that was making for the regeneration of society. First among modern men of great power, he gave this impulse artistic utterance, and, though the doctrine of development was to him unknown, made his art the medium for helping on "the relief of man's estate." In this sense, even more than in point of mere sympathetic interest, he always keeps close to humanity. His interpretation of his art is that which sees in poetry a human restorative and help, and hence he has none of the indifference of spurious "art for art's sake." Nor, for the same reason, has he any of the beauty of decadence. His art, like nature's normal self, derives its strength and beauty from the energy of healthy life. It is this which gives it glow, elasticity, and firmness; this which makes it salutary and good to look upon. Much, therefore, as the moralist may prize the more obvious and positive content of his ethical teaching, his steadfast alliance with justice, truth, kindness, and other forces that bind society together, what gives his art its richest human value is, above all, this unconscious ethic, which rests in the freshness of his health, in the frank and benign sincerity of his outlook, in the life joy and life courage that make his poetry a perpetual fountain of rejuvenation, — the *livsmod* and *livsglæde* that cheered alike in victory and defeat the Vikings, whose blood doubtless ran in his veins.   It was this which sustained him in the misery of his own life, and this he has embodied in his work with a puissance of intellect, a winning grace of wit and humor, and a veracity and firmness of both substance and style that give him just claim to sit among the permanently great and beneficent spirits of the human race.

APPENDICES.

I. PRONUNCIATION.

THE spelling of Scotch words, as they appear in Burns's poems and elsewhere, is only an awkward makeshift for the representation of the living sounds as these are heard from the lips of the people. There is no authoritative spelling, because the language has not received fixity in this respect from written usage. The written usage of the country is English, and in the representation of Scotch sounds the written equivalents are employed with their approximate English values. But most of the vowel sounds, and many of the consonants, do not correspond with those of English ; hence there is a great discrepancy between Burns as he appears in print and Burns as he is read by a native. Add to this that Burns was affected by the process of Anglicizing which had been going on for three hundred years, and largely accommodated his Scotch to English forms. This will easily be seen from a glance at his rhymes ; in many cases the English pronunciation will give no rhyme at all, the Scotch, a perfect rhyme.

This accommodation to English forms is thus misleading. In general, the sounds of Lowland Scotch bear a much closer resemblance to those of Old Norse and modern Norwegian (frequently in its dialectic forms) than they bear to English. High German likewise offers an approximation, but here greater caution is necessary. Care should especially be taken not to mince the consonants nor to thin away the vowel sounds or give them the gliding or vanishing quality they have in English.

VOWEL SOUNDS :

A. This vowel is the shibboleth which distinguishes the two great divisions of dialectic accents in Lowland Scotland, — those north of the river Tay, in which *a* has the broad, open sound of Eng. 'ah,' and those south of the Tay and towards the west, in which the prevailing *a* sound is closer, like Eng. 'awe.'

1. *a* is sounded like Eng. *a* in 'far.' It may be long, as in *warld*, or short, as in *brak*.

(a) This sound is also deepened into that of Eng. *a* in 'fall,' in which case it is usually represented by *au*. It may be long, as *waur*, *awa*, or short, as *maun*, *haud*.

2. It has also a sound similar to Fr. *è*, as in 'père'; e.g., *wale*, *drave*. This sound is frequently represented by *ai*: as *aisle*, *haivers*, *mair*.

(a) This, too, is sharpened into something between Eng. *a* in 'bane' and *e* in 'be': as *hame*, *lanely*. In this value it is frequently represented by other symbols: as *ae* in *sae*, *claes*; *ea* in *mear*, *bear* (barley), *hearse* (hoarse); or light *ai* in *aits*, *claith*.

Sc. *a* has no value corresponding to Eng. *a* in 'man.'

E. This has two main values:

1. Short, almost like Eng. *e* in 'then,' but slightly more open: as *het*, *blether*.

2. Long, like Eng. *e* in 'be.' This is not a characteristically Scotch value; it is oftenest represented by *ee*, as in *weel*, or by *ie* or *ei*, as in *deil*, *niest*, *spier*.

I, Y. These two have nearly the same values; they used to be interchangeable.

1. The prevailing sound is nearly the same as Eng. *e* in 'her' or *i* in 'bird': as *rin*, *hing*. Frequently a *u* quality predominates; e.g., Sc. *will* is pronounced *wull*.

2. In a few words it has a sound nearly like Eng. *i* in 'pin': as *mither*, *thegither*, *brither* (the spelling *brother* is to be so pronounced).

3. Its diphthongal quality is usually much sharper than in English, and corresponds to Norw. *ei* (especially in the Norwegian dialects), i.e., a rapid combination of Eng. *a* in 'fate' and *ee* in 'fee"; e.g., *whyles*, *skyte*, *mind* (pronounced *meynd*; see **EY**).

(a) Occasionally it corresponds to Eng. *i* in 'tire'; e.g., *byre*, *kye*.

Final *y* or *ie* has the same light sound as in English ; e.g., *bonny, bonie.*

O.   This vowel has practically only one value in Scotch, that of Eng. *o* in ' horde '; cf. Fr. ô in 'hôte.'   It may be long, as in *lord, morn,* or short, as in *bonie, gotten* ; but its quality should remain the same.

Most of the open Eng. *o* sounds are to be pronounced in this way.   Sc. *o* has no value like Eng. *o* in ' hot.'

U.   Two main values :

1.   A light, open sound similar to Eng. *u* in ' bun,' with a slight suggestion of an *o* : as *busk, scunner.*

2.   A variety of modifications shifting from Norw. *y* to *ö*, Ger. *ü* to *ö*, or Fr. *u* (in *tu*) to *eu* (in *peur*) : as *fule, blude, sune.* This sound is frequently represented by *ui*, as *guid*, or by *oo*, as *aboon, broo.*

AE, AI have the sound of **A,** 2 : as *gae* (gave), *ain* ; or **A,** 2 (a) : as *gae* (go), *thae, raible.*

EI, IE have the sound of **E,** 2 : as *gie, fient, abeigh.*

EY has the sound of **I,** 3 : as *gley, eydent.*

OO has regularly the sound of **U,** 2 : as *aboon, dool, snool.* English words spelled with *oo* take this pronunciation : as ' moon,' ' fool.'

OU has the regular sound of Fr. *ou* or Eng. *oo* : as *fou, toun, count.*

UI.   Same as **U,** 2 : as *bluid* (also written *blude* ; cf. **OO**).

Consonants :

The only consonants requiring attention are :

1.   **H,** which, except when silent in English words like ' honor,' is always strongly aspirated.

2.   **R,** which always takes the strong Norwegian roll with the tip of the tongue (entirely different from the uvular Ger. and Dan. *r*).   Before other liquids this roll often gives an extra syllable : as

> Till bairns' bairns kindly cuddle.

3. **NG**, which never takes the compound *ng-g* value it has in Eng. 'anger,' but is sounded simply, as in Norw. and Ger. ; e.g., *hung-er, lang-er.*

4. **CH, GH**. Always strongly aspirated as gutturals ; e.g., *laigh, nicht, brought* (pronounced *brocht*), *rough* (pronounced *roch*).

Terminations :

1. **ED** is always pronounced *it* or *et*, and is often so spelled.

2. **ING** always reverts in pronunciation to its ancient form *-and*, of which the *d* is silent as in Norw. *mand.*

3. **URE** is pronounced as if it were *-ur* ; e.g., *picture.*

II. GRAMMAR.

The grammar of Lowland Scotch presents many peculiarities and anomalies. It is not always amenable to rule, and has the freedom and looseness of a speech not yet fixed by literary usage. The following notes merely treat of such variations from English usage occurring in Burns as might puzzle the English student.[1]

Nouns :

1. *Subject.* (*a*) Frequently the subject is mentioned in an absolute construction and then repeated in the form of a pronoun: as

> The lightly-jumpin glowrin *trouts* . . .
> They 're left, etc. (*B. W.*, 9).

2. *Object.* (*a*) It is common to anticipate the object of a statement by placing it first in absolute construction, and then repeating it as a pronoun : as

> The coward *slave*, we pass *him* by. (*A Man's a Man*, 3.)
> A *pint* an' gill, I 'd gie *them* baith. (*Ep. J. L.*, 41.)
> An' her ain *fit*, it brunt *it*. (*H.*, 78.)
> My helpless *lambs*, I trust *them* wi' him. (*P. M.*, 28.)

[1] For an account of historical Scotch grammar, see Dr. J. A. H. Murray's *Dialect of the Southern Counties of Scotland*, pp. 150–230.

The *gentles*, ye wad ne'er envỳ '*em*. (*T. D.*, 190.)
For my last *fou*,
A heapit stimpart, I 'll reserve *ane*. (*M. M.*, 100.)

(*b*) The same often happens when the noun would be the object of a preposition ; i.e., the preposition and pronoun follow : as

Gin ye 'll go there, yon runkled *pair*,
    We 'll get some famous laughin
            At them this day. (*H. F.*, 43.)

(*c*) Frequently a noun is loosely thrown in as an absolute objective where we should expect a preposition or governing verb, but there is none : as

But Mauchline *race* or Mauchline Fair,
I should be proud to meet you there. (*Ep. J. L.*, 97.)
We are na fou, we 're no that fou
But just a drappie in our ee. (*Willie Brewed*, 6.)
Till first ae *caper*, syne anither,
Tam tint his reason a' thegither. (*T. Sh.*, 187.)
My Nanie 's charming, sweet, an' young ;
    Nae artfu' *wiles* to win ye, O. (*My Nanie, O*, 9.)
Ye maist wad think, a wee *touch* langer
And they maun starve o' cauld and hunger. (*T. D.*, 81.)
I . . . would here propone defences —
Their donsie *tricks*, their black *mistakes*. (*U. G.*, 15.)

3. *Possessive.*   (*a*) The sign '*s* is sometimes omitted : as

Wi' arm reposed on the *chair* back. (*H. F.*, 95.)

(*b*) Sometimes, instead of the possessive form, the noun is put down absolutely, and a possessive pronoun follows : as

The harpy, hoodock, purse-proud *race* . . .
    Their tuneless hearts. (*Ep. M. L.*, 38.)

4. The irregularity is sometimes greater than in any of the above cases. A noun or pronoun occurs out of all construction ; i.e., it is merely thrown in and the construction changed according to sense : as

> Its stature seemed lang Scotch ells twa,
> The queerest *shape* that e'er I saw.   (*D. D. H.*, 38.)
> Even *you*, on murderin errands toiled . . .
> The blood-stained roost and sheep-cot spoiled
> My heart forgets.   (*W. N.*, 25.)

PRONOUNS:

1. *Personal.*   (*a*) *Me*, *thee*, and *him*, are sometimes used as subjects.   Scotch usage is greatly affected by French here; cf. the French use of *moi*, *toi*, *lui* : as

> Scotland an' *me* 's in great affliction.   (*E. C. P.*, 14.)
> But gin ye be a brig as auld as *me*.   (*B. A.*, 69.)
> The smith an' *thee* gat roarin fou on.   (*T. Sh.*, 26.)
> There, *him* at Agincourt wha shone
> Few better were or braver.   (*A Dr.*, 95.)

I for *me* in *Ep. D.*, 102, is merely a solecism.

(*b*)   *Ye* as object is very common : as

> Hail, Majesty most Excellent!
> While nobles strive to please *ye*.   (*A Dr.*, 73–81.)

2. *Relative.*   (*a*) Often omitted as subject.   This ellipsis is found also in Middle English (the omission of the relative as object is regular, and in accord with English usage) : as

> To stop those reckless vows
>   ∧ Would soon been broken.   (*V.*, 54.)
> An' gied the infant warld a shog
>   ∧ Maist ruined a'.   (*D.*, 89).
> Or like the snow ∧ falls in the river,
> A moment white — then melts for ever.   (*T. Sh.*, 61.)
> Is there no pity, no relenting ruth,
>   ∧ Points to the parents.   (*C. S. N.*, 87.)
> Forms ∧ might be worshipped on the bended knee.   (*B. A.*, 115.)
> There 's men o' taste ∧ wad tak the Ducat-stream.   (*B. A.*, 79.)

(*b*) *That* for ' to which ' : as

> Fancies that our good Brugh denies protection. (*B. A.*, 124.)

3. *Possessive.*   *His* is often curtailed into '*s* : as

> Whare drucken Charlie brak '*s* neck-bane.   (*T. Sh.*, 92.)
> Labour sair At '*s* weary toil.   (*S. D.*, 34.)

4. *Reflexive.*   *Oursel, themsel,* for 'ourselves,' 'themselves' : as

> That e'er he nearer comes *oursel.* (*D. D. H.*, 11.)
> Till they be fit to fend *themsel.* (*P. M.*, 32.)

5. *Reciprocal.*   *Ither* for ' each other ' : as

> We 've been owre lang unken'd to *ither.* (*Ep. W. S.*, 98.)
> But hear their absent thoughts o' *ither.* (*T. D.*, 221.)

6. *Demonstratives.*   The plural of *this* is *thir*; of *that, thae. Yon* is frequently used for *that, those* : as

> *Thir* breeks o' mine, my only pair. (*T. Sh.*, 155.)
> Quo' I, ' if that *thae* news be true ! ' (*D. D. H.*, 134.)
> *Yon* runkled pair. (*H. F.*, 43.)

ADJECTIVES :

1. Almost any adjective may be used as an adverb : as

> Can *easy* wi' a single wordie
> > Lowse hell upon me. (*Ep. McM.*, 17.)
> My awkward muse *sair* pleads an begs. (*Ep. L.* [II], 11.)
> To right or left *eternal* swervin. (*Ep. J. S.*, 111.)
> When *heavy*-dragged wi' pine an' grievin. (*S. D.*, 27.)

2. *Comparison.*   After comparatives, *nor* is often used for *than* : as

> Waur *nor* their nonsense. (*Ep. McM.*, 24.)

VERBS :

1. *Indicative Present.*   The Anglian *s* forms prevail : as

> An anxious ee I never throw*s.* (*Ep. J. S.*, 145.)

Thou clears the heid o' doitit Lear.   (*S. D.*, 31.)

Unseen thou lurks.   (*D.*, 24.)

Thou lifts thy unassuming head.   (*M. D.*, 27.)

Yarrow an' Tweed to mony a tune

       Owre Scotland rings.   (*Ep. W. S.*, 45.)

2. *Indicative Past.*   No inflection in second singular : as

Thou *sat* as lang as thou *had* siller.   (*T. Sh.*, 24.)

Thou never braing't an' fetch't an' fliskit.   (*M. M.*, 67.)

Thou never *lap*.   (*M. M.*, 81.)

Thou *saw* the fields laid bare an' waste.   (*M.*, 25.)

3. *Indicative Future.*   Besides the usual *shall* and *will* form this takes a peculiar form in *'se* : as

I *'se* no insist.   (*Ep. J. L.*, 88.)

I *'se* ne'er bid better.   (*Ep. M. L.*, 48).

We *'se* hae fine remarkin.   (*H. F.*, 49.)

The *shall* or *will* form takes no inflection in the second singular : as

Ah, Tam! thou *'ll* get thy fairin.   (*T. Sh.*, 201.)

Thou *'ll* break my heart, thou bonie bird.   (*Bonie Doon*, 5.)

4. *Compound tenses with ' have.'*   *Could, would,* and *should have* very frequently omit the *have* (a common Norwegian usage) : as

Kyle-Stewart I could ∧ braggèd wide.   (*M. M.*, 35.)

He should ∧ been tight that . . .   (*M. M.*, 11.)

Till spritty knowes wad ∧ rair't an risket.   (*M. M.*, 71.)

Those reckless vows would soon ∧ been broken.   (*V.*, 54.)

And would to Common Sense for once ∧ betrayed them.
    (*B. A.*, 167.)

Ye wad na ∧ been sae shy.   (*O Tibbie*, 2.)

The wind blew as 't wad ∧ blawn its last.   (*T. Sh.*, 73.)

Ye *'d* better ∧ taen up spades and shools. (*Ep. J. L.* [I], 65.)

The tythe o' what ye waste at cartes

       Wad ∧ stow'd his pantry.   (*Ep. W. S.*, 24.)

5. *Infinitive.* The infinitive often takes ' for to,' as in Middle English: as

> Not *for to* hide it in a hedge.   (*Ep. Y. F.*, 53.)
>
> But *for to* meet the deil her lane.   (*H.*, 183.)

6. *Verbs 'be' and 'have.'* Following the analogy of other verbs (see *Verbs*, 1), these adopt the northern *s* form and take *is, was, has* as a regular inflection for all persons, singular and plural (though in Burns and the modern dialects *hae* is very frequently used for Eng. *have*) : as

> I, here wha sit, *hae* met wi' some
>> An *'s* thankfu' for them yet.   (*Ep. D.*, 90.)
>
> Scotland an' me *'s* in great affliction.   (*E. C. P.*, 8.)
>
> Nor shouts o' war that *'s* heard afar.   (*Go Fetch*, 15.)
>
> There *'s* men o' taste wad tak . . .   (*B. A.*, 79.)
>
> There *'s* mony waur been o' the race.   (*A Dr.*, 25.)
>
> Now thou *'s* turned out for a' thy trouble.   (*M.*, 33.)
>
> Thou ance *was* i' the foremost rank.   (*M. M.*, 13.)
>
> Thou *'s* met me in an evil hour.   (*M. D.*, 2.)
>
> Ye then *was* trottin wi' your minnie.   (*M. M.*, 26.)

PREPOSITIONS :

(*a*) Instead of the construction with *of*, the appositional construction with nouns of quantity and kind is often used, as in Middle English: as

> His wee drap ∧ parritch or his bread
>> Thou kitchens fine.   (*S. D.*, 41.)
>
> They tauld me 't was an odd kin' ∧ chiel.   (*Ep. J. L.*, 23.)
>
> Thy wee bit ∧ housie, too, in ruin.   (*M.*, 19.)
>
> Pickin her pouch as bare as winter
>> O' a' kind ∧ coin.   (*E. C. P.*, 42.)

(*b*) Sometimes the preposition is thrown after its object. This is a poetic license, but Scotch permits greater freedom in this respect: as

> And what poor cot-folk pit their painch *in*.   (*T. D.*, 69.)
>
> But juist the pouchie put the neive *in*.   (*Ep. D.* [II], 33.)

> That dreary hour he mounts his beast *in*.   (*T. Sh.*, 70.)
>
> Every naig ∧ was ca'd a shoe *on*.   (*T. Sh.*, 25.)

(*c*) Sometimes it is used irregularly as an adverb : as

> But ne'er a word o' faith *in*
> > That 's richt that day.   (*H. F.*, 134.)
>
> She pat but little faith *in*.   (*H.*, 184.)
>
> An' just a wee drap sp'ritual burn *in*.   (*S. D.*, 53.)

OTHER IRREGULARITIES:

Burns's language, being drawn largely direct from the speech of the common people, partakes of the structural freedom of such conversational speech.   The uneducated peasantry often make an expressive drive at a thought without strict attention to grammatical form.   Burns avails himself of this liberty, and frequently employs condensed expressions that defy strict analysis.   The same holds of modern Icelandic.   Cf. Vigfusson and Powell's *Icelandic Reader* ; *Grammar*, chap. iv.   Examples :

> An' may a bard no crack his jest
> > What way they 've used him ?   (*Ep. McM.*, 30.)
> > > He 'll still disdain,
> And then cry zeal for gospel laws.   (*Ep. McM.*, 53.)
> Wad gar ye trow ye ne'er do wrang,
> > But aye unerring steady.   (*A Dr.*, 17.)
> Are doomed . . .
> The death o' devils, smoor'd wi' brunstone reek.   (*B. A.*, 8.)
> Or like the snow . . .
> A moment white — then melts for ever.   (*T. Sh.*, 62.)
> The moral man he does define
> > But ne'er a word o' faith in
> > > That 's richt that day.   (*H. F.*, 134.
> But for to meet the deil her lane
> > She pat but little faith in.   (*H.*, 184.)

BIBLIOGRAPHY.

A COMPLETE bibliography of Burns literature would be too extensive to find a place here. Only a few of the most serviceable references are given.

WORKS. — The older editions of Currie, Allan Cunningham, Hogg and Motherwell, and others are now superseded.

1. *Complete Writings*, ed. by W. Scott Douglas : 6 vols., Edinburgh, 1877–79. [Vols. I–III contain the poems and songs in chronological order with valuable notes ; vols. IV–VI, the letters. The able monograph of Professor Nichol (see No. 11 below) is prefixed to vol. I.]

2. *Life and Works*, ed. by R. Chambers, revised by William Wallace : 4 vols., London and New York, 1896. [The writings are incorporated in the *Life* in their chronological order. Mr. Wallace has added much new material and corrected many old errors. This is the best combined *Life* and *Works*.]

3. *Poems, Songs, and Letters*, ed. by Alexander Smith : 1 vol., London and New York, 1893. [The " Globe " edition, a convenient working edition.]

4. *Poetical Works*, ed. by Sir Harris Nicholas, revised by Geo. A. Aitken : 3 vols., London, 1893. [The third " Aldine " edition ; good introduction and notes.]

5. *Poetical Works*, ed. by W. Scott Douglas : 3 vols., 12mo., Edinburgh, 1893. [Complete ; the chronological order is followed and valuable notes are added to each poem ; the binding is poor.]

6. *Poems and Songs*, ed. by A. Lang and W. A. Craigie : 1 vol., 8vo., New York, 1896. [Complete ; chronological order ; good notes and introduction ; excellent typography; bad paper.]

7. *Selections*, ed. by J. Logie Robertson : 1 vol., 8vo., Oxford, 1889. [The notes contain much appreciative criticism, but there are many errors.]

8. "The Centenary Burns." *The Poetry of Robert Burns*, ed. by W. E. Henley and T. F. Henderson : 4 vols., Edinburgh and Boston, 1896–97. [Complete ; chronological order ; valuable notes and discussions ; most complete bibliographical and textual material: printing, paper, etc., very fine.]

("The Cambridge Edition," *Complete Poetical Works*, 1 vol., Boston, 1897, is a reprint of the text of No. 8, with Mr. Henley's biographical and critical essay. This essay is also published separately : Edinburgh, 1898.)

LIFE. — The most trustworthy comment on Burns's life is contained in his poems and letters. Every biography should be checked by a study of these.

The most complete and authoritative *Life* is that by Chambers and Wallace. See No. 2 above.

9. By M. Aug. Angellier, *Robert Burns, Sa Vie, Ses Œuvres*, 2 vols., Paris, 1893. [Up to the appearance of No. 2, the 'most scholarly, most sympathetic and complete *Life* of Burns in any language' ; has a good bibliography.]

10. By J. Gibson Lockhart, revised and enlarged by W. Scott Douglas : 1 vol., 8vo., London, 1882. [Bohn's "Standard Library" series ; long the best work on the subject ; it was Lockhart's *Life* (1828) that produced Carlyle's well-known review. See No. 16 below.]

11. By John Nichol : Edinburgh, 1882. [An excellent summary ; see No. 1 above.]

12. By J. C. Shairp : 1 vol., London, 1879. ["English Men of Letters" series ; the author laments that Burns wrote his satires, and is otherwise "unco guid."]

13. By J. S. Blackie : 1 vol., London, 1888. ["Great Writers" series ; worth little, but contains a good bibliography by J. P. Anderson, of the British Museum.]

14. By Gabriel Setoun : 1 vol., Edinburgh and London, 1896. ["Famous Scots" series.]

[While this book is passing through the press, the first complete edition of the correspondence of Burns and Mrs. Dunlop is announced, edited by William Wallace : London, 1898.]

CRITICISMS. — In addition to the criticisms embodied in many of the foregoing may be mentioned (in alphabetical order) :

15. Brooke, Stopford: *Theology in the English Poets* (London, 1874), pp. 287–339.

16. Carlyle, Thos. : *Miscellaneous Essays*, " Essay on Burns " ; see No. 10, above.

17. Emerson, R. W. : Speech at the Burns Centenary, Boston, 1859 ; *Works* (Boston and New York, 1889), Vol. XI, pp. 303–8.

18. Hazlitt, William : *Lectures on the English Poets* (London, 1819), pp. 245–282.

19. Kingsley, Charles : " Burns and his School," *Works* (London, 1880), Vol. XX ; original printed in *North British Review*, Vol. XVI.

20. Lang, Andrew : *Letters to Dead Authors* (London, 1886), pp. 195–204.

21. Service, John : Ward's *English Poets* (London, 1883), Vol. III, pp. 512–571.

22. Shairp, J. C. : *Poetic Interpretation of Nature* (Edinburgh, 1877), pp. 213–219 ; *Aspects of Poetry* (Oxford, 1881), pp. 192–226.

23. Stevenson, R. L. : *Familiar Studies of Men and Books* (London, 1882), pp. 38–90 ; originally printed in *Cornhill Magazine*, October, 1879.

24. Taine, Henri : *Histoire de la Litt. Anglaise*, translated by Van Laun (London, 1873–4), Vol. III, pp. 389–412.

25. Wilson, John (" Christopher North ") : " Genius and Character of Burns," *Works* (Edinburgh and London, n. d.), Vol. III, pp. 1–211 ; interesting as the criticism of an old-fashioned perfervid Scot.

COLLATERAL MATTER :

26. Walker, Hugh : *Three Centuries of Scottish Literature*, 2 vols., London and New York, 1893.

27. Veitch, John : *The Feeling for Nature in Scottish Poetry*, Edinburgh, 1887.

28. Johnson, James : *Scots Musical Museum*, 5 vols., fol. Edinburgh, 1787–1803 ; reprinted, ed. by W. Stenhouse and D. Laing, 4 vols., Edinburgh, 1853. [A standard work.]

29. Cromek, R. H. : *Reliques of Robert Burns*, 1 vol., London, 1808 ; Philadelphia, 1809. [Contains Burns's critical notes on Scottish Song.]

30. Ritson, Jos. : *Collection of Scottish Songs*, with music, 2 vols., London, 1794; facsimile reprint, Glasgow, 1869. [Good introduction on Scottish Songs and Music.]

31. Herd, David : *Ancient and Modern Scottish Songs*, 2 vols., Edinburgh, 1776 ; reprinted with additions, Glasgow, 1869 ; ed. by S. Gilpin, Edinburgh, 1869. [Scholarly.]

32. Chambers, Robert : *Songs of Scotland Prior to Burns*, with the tunes, Edinburgh, 1862. [Good introduction.]

33. Rogers, Dr. C. : *The Scottish Minstrel*, songs and song writers of Scotland subsequent to Burns, 1 vol., Edinburgh, 1870. [Popular.]

34. *The Songs of Scotland*, chronologically arranged, 1 vol., 8vo., London, 1870 ; Glasgow, 1871. [Valuable introduction.]

35. Hogg, James : *The Jacobite Relics of Scotland*, 2 vols., Edinburgh, 1819–21. [Good enough for lack of a better.]

36. Murray, J. Clarke : *The Ballads and Songs of Scotland*, in view of their influence on the character of the people, 1 vol., Toronto and London, 1874.

37. Robertson, J. Logie ("Hugh Haliburton") : *In Scottish Fields*, 1 vol., Edinburgh, 1890.

38. Hawthorne, Nath. : *Our Old Home* (Haunts of Burns).

39. Hadden, J. Cuthbert : *George Thomson, The Friend of Burns :* His Life and Correspondence : London, 1898.

The student may find interest and edification in the poetical tributes paid to Burns by Wordsworth, Coleridge, Keats, Campbell, Longfellow, and others.

SELECTIONS FROM BURNS.

SONG,—O TIBBIE, I HAE SEEN THE DAY.

CHORUS. — O TIBBIE, I hae seen the day
    Ye wad na been sae shy;
    For laik o' gear ye lightly me,
      But, trowth, I care na by.

    Yestreen I met you on the moor,   5
    Ye spak na, but gaed by like stoure;
    Ye geck at me because I 'm poor,
      But fient a hair care I.

    I doubt na, lass, but ye may think,
    Because ye hae the name o' clink,   10
    That ye can please me at a wink,
      Whene'er ye like to try.

    But sorrow tak him that's sae mean,
    Altho' his pouch o' coin were clean,
    Wha follows ony saucy quean,   15
      That looks sae proud and high.

    Altho' a lad were e'er sae smart,
    If that he want the yellow dirt,
    Ye 'll cast your head anither airt,
      An' answer him fu' dry.   20

But if he hae the name o' gear,
Ye 'll fasten to him like a brier,
Tho' hardly he, for sense or lear,
   Be better than the kye.

But, Tibbie, lass, tak my advice,   25
Your daddie's gear maks you sae nice ;
The deil a ane wad spier your price,
   Were ye as poor as I.

There lives a lass beside yon park,
I 'd rather hae her in her sark,   30
Than you wi' a' your thousand mark,
   That gars you look sae high.

———

SONG,—MARY MORISON.

O MARY, at thy window be,
   It is the wish'd, the trysted hour !
Those smiles and glances let me see,
   That make the miser's treasure poor :
How blythely wad I bide the stoure,   5
   A weary slave frae sun to sun,
Could I the rich reward secure,
   The lovely Mary Morison.

Yestreen when to the trembling string
   The dance gaed thro' the lighted ha',   10
To thee my fancy took its wing,
   I sat, but neither heard nor saw :
Tho' this was fair, and that was braw,
   And yon the toast of a' the town,
I sigh'd, and said amang them a',   15
   " Ye are na Mary Morison."

O Mary, canst thou wreck his peace,
  Wha for thy sake wad gladly die?
Or canst thou break that heart of his,
  Whase only faut is loving thee?   20
If love for love thou wilt na gie
  At least be pity to me shown :
A thought ungentle canna be
  The thought o' Mary Morison.

A PRAYER

IN THE PROSPECT OF DEATH.

OH thou unknown Almighty Cause
  Of all my hope and fear !
In whose dread presence, ere an hour,
  Perhaps I must appear !

If I have wander'd in those paths   5
  Of life I ought to shun —
As something, loudly, in my breast,
  Remonstrates I have done —

Thou know'st that Thou hast formèd me,
  With passions wild and strong ;   10
And list'ning to their witching voice
  Has often led me wrong.

Where human weakness has come short,
  Or frailty stept aside,
Do Thou, All-good ! — for such Thou art —   15
  In shades of darkness hide.

Where with intention I have err'd,
  No other plea I have
But — Thou art good ; and Goodness still
  Delighteth to forgive.   20

THE DEATH AND DYING WORDS OF POOR MAILIE,

THE AUTHOR'S ONLY PET YOWE:

An unco mournfu' Tale.

As Mailie an' her lambs thegither
Was ae day nibblin on the tether,
Upon her cloot she coost a hitch,
An owre she warsl'd in the ditch :
There, groanin, dyin, she did lie,   5
When *Hughoc* he cam doytin by.

  Wi' glowrin een and lifted han's,
Poor *Hughoc* like a statue stan's ;
He saw her days were near-hand ended,
But, wae 's my heart ! he could na mend it.   10
He gapèd wide but naething spak —
At length poor Mailie silence brak.

  " O thou, whase lamentable face
Appears to mourn my woefu' case !
My dying words attentive hear,   15
An' bear them to my Master dear.

  " Tell him, if e'er again he keep
As muckle gear as buy a sheep —
Oh, bid him never tie them mair
Wi' wicked strings o' hemp or hair !   20

But ca' them out to park or hill,
An' let them wander at their will :
So may his flock increase and grow
To· scores o' lambs and packs o' woo' !

"Tell him, he was a Master kin',   25
An' aye was guid to me an' mine ;
An' now my dying charge I gie him —
My helpless lambs, I trust them wi' him.

"Oh, bid him save their harmless lives
Frae dogs, an' tods, an' butchers' knives !   30
But gie them guid cow-milk their fill,
Till they be fit to fend themsel ;
An' tent them duly, e'en an' morn,
Wi' taets o' hay, an' ripps o' corn.

"An' may they never learn the gaets   35
Of ither vile, wanrestfu' pets,
To slink through slaps, an' reave an' steal
At stacks o' peas, or stocks o' kail.
So may they, like their great forbears,
For monie a year come thro' the shears :   40
So wives will gie them bits o' bread, .
An' bairns greet for them when they 're dead.

"My poor toop-lamb, my son an' heir,
Oh, bid him breed him up wi' care ;
An' if he live to be a beast,   45
To pit some havins in his breast !

"An' warn him, what I winna name,
To stay content wi' yowes at hame ;
An' no to rin an' wear his cloots,
Like ither menseless, graceless brutes.   50

" And niest my yowie, silly thing,
Gude keep thee frae a tether string !
Oh, may thou ne'er forgather up
Wi' ony blastit, moorland toop,
But ay keep mind to moop and mell   55
Wi' sheep o' credit like thysel !

" And now, my bairns, wi' my last breath
I lea'e my blessin wi' you baith ;
And when you think upo' your mither,
Mind to be kin' to ane anither.   60

" Now, honest *Hughoc*, dinna fail
To tell my master a' my tale ;
An' bid him burn this cursed tether,
An' for thy pains thou 'se get my blether."

This said, poor Mailie turn'd her head,   65
An' clos'd her een amang the dead !

POOR MAILIE'S ELEGY.

Lament in rhyme, lament in prose,
Wi' saut tears tricklin doun your nose ;
Our Bardie's fate is at a close,
          Past a' remead ;
The last, sad cape-stane o' his woe 's —   5
          . Poor Mailie 's dead !

It 's no the loss o' warl's gear,
That could sae bitter draw the tear,
Or mak our Bardie, dowie, wear

    The mournin weed :   10
He 's lost a friend and neebor dear,
    In Mailie dead.

Thro' a' the toun she trotted by him ;
A lang half-mile she could descry him ;
Wi' kindly bleat, when she did spy him,   15
    She ran wi' speed :
A friend mair faithfu' ne'er cam nigh him,
    Than Mailie dead.

I wat she was a sheep o' sense,
An' could behave hersel wi' mense ;   20
I 'll say 't, she never brak a fence,
    Thro' thievish greed.
Our Bardie, lanely, keeps the spence
    Sin Mailie 's dead.

Or, if he wanders up the howe,   25
Her livin image in her yowe
Comes bleatin till him, owre the knowe,
    For bits o' bread ;
An' down the briny pearls rowe
    For Mailie dead.   30

She was nae get o' moorlan' tips,
Wi' tawted ket, an' hairy hips ;
For her forbears were brought in ships,
    Frae yont the Tweed :
A bonier fleesh ne'er cross'd the clips   35
    Than Mailie 's dead.

Wae worth the man wha first did shape
That vile, wanchancie thing — a rape !
It makes guid fellows girn an' gape,

Wi' chokin dread ;   40
An' Robin's bonnet wave wi' crape,
For Mailie dead.

O a' ye Bards on bonie Doon !
An' wha on Ayr your chanters tune !
Come, join the melancholious croon   45
O' Robin's reed !
His heart will never get aboon —
His Mailie 's dead !

SONG,—MY NANIE, O.

BEHIND yon hills where Lugar flows,
   'Mang moors an' mosses many, O,
The wintry sun the day has clos'd,
   An' I 'll awa to Nanie, O.

The westlin wind blaws loud an' shill :   5
   The night 's baith mirk an' rainy, O ;
But I 'll get my plaid an' out I 'll steal,
   An' owre the hill to Nanie, O.

My Nanie 's charming, sweet, an' young ;
   Nae artfu' wiles to win ye, O :   10
May ill befa' the flattering tongue
   That wad beguile my Nanie, O.

Her face is fair, her heart is true,
   As spotless as she 's bonie, O :
The op'ning gowan, wat wi' dew,   15
   Nae purer is than Nanie, O.

A country lad is my degree,
  An' few there be that ken me, O ;
But what care I how few they be ?
  I 'm welcome aye to Nanie, O.   20

My riches a's my penny-fee,
  An' I maun guide it cannie, O ;
But warl's gear ne'er troubles me,
  My thoughts are a' my Nanie, O.

Our auld guidman delights to view   25
  His sheep an' kye thrive bonie, O ;
But I 'm as blythe that hauds his pleugh,
  And has nae care but Nanie, O.

Come weel, come woe, I care na by,
  I 'll tak what Heav'n will sen' me, O ;   30
Nae ither care in life hae I,
  But live, an' love my Nanie, O.

SONG,—GREEN GROW THE RASHES.

CHORUS.—GREEN grow the rashes, O !
  Green grow the rashes, O !
    The sweetest hours that e'er I spend
  Are spent amang the lasses, O.

There 's nought but care on ev'ry han',   5
  In every hour that passes, O :
What signifies the life o' man,
  An 't were na for the lasses, O ?

The war'ly race may riches chase,
   An' riches still may fly them, O;   10.
An' tho' at last they catch them fast,
   Their hearts can ne'er enjoy them, O.

But gie me a cannie hour at e'en,
   My arms about my dearie, O;
An' war'ly cares, an' war'ly men,   15
   May a' gae tapsalteerie, O.

For you sae douce, ye sneer at this;
   Ye 're nought but senseless asses, O:
The wisest man the warl' e'er saw,
   He dearly lov'd the lasses, O.   20

Auld Nature swears, the lovely dears
   Her noblest work she classes, O:
Her prentice han' she try'd on man,
   An' then she made the lasses, O.

EPISTLE TO DAVIE,

A BROTHER POET.

WHILE winds frae aff Ben-Lomond blaw,
An' bar the doors wi' drivin snaw,
   An' hing us owre the ingle,
I set me down to pass the time,
An' spin a verse or twa o' rhyme,   5
   In hamely westlin jingle.
While frosty winds blaw in the drift,
   Ben to the chimla lug,
I grudge a wee the great-folk's gift,

That live sae bien an' snug :   10
  I tent less, an' want less
    Their roomy fireside ;
  But hanker and canker
    To see their cursed pride.

.It 's hardly in a body's pow'r   15
To keep, at times, frae being sour,
  To see how things are shar'd;
How best o' chiels are whiles in want,
While coofs on countless thousands rant,
  An' ken na how to ware 't ;   20
But Davie, lad, ne'er fash your head,
  Tho' we hae little gear,
We 're fit to win our daily bread,
  As lang 's we 're hale and fier.
    "Mair spier na, nor fear na,"   25
      Auld age ne'er mind a feg ;
    The last o't, the warst o't,
      Is only but to beg.

To lie in kilns an' barns at e'en,
When banes are craz'd, an' bluid is thin,   30
  Is doubtless great distress !
Yet then content could mak us blest;
Ev'n then, sometimes, we 'd snatch a taste
  Of truest happiness.
The honest heart that 's free frae a'   35
  Intended fraud or guile,
However Fortune kick the ba',
  Has ay some cause to smile :
    An' mind still, you 'll find still,
      A comfort this nae sma' ;   40
    Nae mair then, we 'll care then,
      Nae farther can we fa'.

What tho', like commoners of air,
We wander out, we know not where,
   But either house or hal'?   45
Yet nature's charms, the hills and woods,
The sweeping vales, and foaming floods,
   Are free alike to all.
In days when daisies deck the ground,
   And blackbirds whistle clear,   50
With honest joy our hearts will bound
   To see the coming year:
      On braes when we please, then,
        We 'll sit and sowth a tune;
      Syne rhyme till 't, we 'll time till 't,   55
        And sing 't when we hae done.

It 's no in titles nor in rank;
It 's no in wealth like Lon'on bank,
   To purchase peace and rest;
It 's no in making muckle, mair: 60
It 's no in books, it 's no in lear,
   To mak us truly blest:
If happiness hae not her seat
   And centre in the breast,
We may be wise, or rich, or great,   65
   But never can be blest:
      Nae treasures nor pleasures
        Could mak us happy lang;
      The heart ay 's the part ay
        That maks us right or wrang.   70

Think ye, that sic as you and I,
Wha drudge and drive thro' wet an' dry,
   Wi' never ceasing toil, —
Think ye, are we less blest than they,

Wha scarcely tent us in their way,   75
   As hardly.worth their while?
Alas! how aft, in haughty mood,
   God's creatures they oppress!
Or else, neglecting a' that 's guid,
   They riot in excess!   80
      Baith careless, and fearless,
        Of either heav'n or hell!
      Esteeming, and deeming
        It a' an idle tale!

Then let us cheerfu' acquiesce,   85
Nor mak' our scanty pleasures less,
   By pining at our state;
And, even should misfortunes come, —
I, here wha sit, hae met wi' some,
   An 's thankfu' for them yet —   90
They gie the wit of age to youth;
   They let us ken oursel';
They mak us see the naked truth,
   The real guid and ill:
      Though losses an' crosses   95
        Be lessons right severe,
      There 's wit there, ye 'll get there,
        Ye 'll find nae other where.

But tent me, Davie, ace o' hearts!
(To say aught less wad wrang the cartes,   100
   And flatt'ry I detest)
This life has joys for you and I, —
An' joys that riches ne'er could buy, —
   An' joys the very best.
There 's a' the pleasures o' the heart,   105
   The lover and the frien';

Ye hae your Meg, your dearest part,
  And I my darling Jean! ·
    It warms me, it charms me,
      To mention but her name: 110
    It heats me, it beets me,
      An' sets me a' on flame!

O all ye Pow'rs who rule above!
O Thou, whose very self art love!
  Thou know'st my words sincere!   115
The life-blood streaming thro' my heart,
Or my more dear immortal part,
  Is not more fondly dear!
When heart-corroding care and grief
    Deprive my soul of rest,   120
Her dear idea brings relief
  And solace to my breast.
    Thou Being, All-seeing,
      Oh hear my fervent pray'r!
    Still take her, and make her   125
      Thy most peculiar care!

All hail, ye tender feelings dear!
The smile of love, the friendly tear,
  The sympathetic glow!
Long since, this world's thorny ways   130
Had number'd out my weary days,
  Had it not been for you!
Fate still has blest me with a friend,
  In ev'ry care and ill;
And oft a more endearing band,   135
  A tie more tender still.
    It lightens, it brightens
      The tenebrific scene,

   To meet with, an' greet with
     My Davie or my Jean.   140

Oh, how that *Name* inspires my style !
The words come skelpin, rank and file,
   Amaist before I ken !
The ready measure rins as fine,
As Phœbus and the famous Nine   145
   Were glowrin owre my pen.
My spaviet Pegasus will limp,
   Till ance he 's fairly het;
And then he 'll hilch, and stilt, and jimp,
   An' rin an unco fit :   150
     But least then the beast then
      Should rue this hasty ride,
     I 'll light now, and dight now
      His sweaty, wizen'd hide.

SONG,—RANTIN ROVIN ROBIN.

THERE was a lad was born in Kyle,
But whatna day o' whatna style,
I doubt it 's hardly worth the while
   To be sae nice wi' Robin.

CHORUS.— Robin was a rovin boy,   5
       Rantin, rovin, rantin, rovin ;
      Robin was a rovin boy,
       Rantin, rovin Robin.

Our monarch's hindmost year but ane
Was five-and-twenty days begun,   10
'T was then a blast o' Janwar' win'
   Blew hansel in on Robin.

The gossip keekit in his loof,
Quo' scho, "Wha lives will see the proof,
This waly boy will be nae coof;   15
   I think we 'll ca' him Robin.

" He 'll hae misfortunes great and sma',
But aye a heart aboon them a';
He 'll be a credit till us a' —
   We 'll a' be proud o' Robin.   20

" But sure as three times three mak nine,
I see by ilka score and line,
This chap will dearly like our kin',
   So leeze me on thee, Robin."

ADDRESS TO THE DEIL.

O Prince! O Chief of many thronèd pow'rs!
That led th' embattled seraphim to war. — MILTON.

O THOU! whatever title suit thee, —
Auld Hornie, Satan, Nick, or Clootie!
Wha in yon cavern, grim an' sootie,
       Clos'd under hatches,
Spairges about the brunstane cootie   5
       To scaud poor wretches!

Hear me, auld Hangie, for a wee,
An' let poor damnèd bodies be;
I 'm sure sma' pleasure it can gie,
       E'en to a deil,   10
To skelp an' scaud poor dogs like me,
       An' hear us squeel!

Great is thy pow'r, an' great thy fame;
Far ken'd an' noted is thy name;
An' tho' yon lowin heugh's thy hame,   15
       Thou travels far;
An' faith! thou 's neither lag nor lame,
       Nor blate nor scaur.

Whyles, rangin like a roarin lion,
For prey a' holes an' corners tryin;   20
Whyles, on the strong-wing'd tempest flyin,
       Tirlin' the kirks;
Whyles, in the human bosom pryin,
       Unseen thou lurks.

I 've heard my rev'rend grannie say,   25
In lanely glens ye like to stray;
Or whare auld ruin'd castles gray
       Nod to the moon,
Ye fright the nightly wand'rer's way
       Wi' eldritch croon.   30

When twilight did my grannie summon
To say her pray'rs, douce honest woman!
Aft yont the dyke she 's heard you bummin,
       Wi' eerie drone;
Or, rustlin, thro' the boortrees comin,   35
       Wi' heavy groan.

Ae dreary, windy, winter night,
The stars shot down wi' sklentin light,
Wi' you mysel I gat a fright
       Ayont the lough;   40
Ye like a rash-buss stood in sight
       Wi' waving sough.

The cudgel in my nieve did shake,
Each bristl'd hair stood like a stake,
When wi' an eldritch, stoor "Quaick, quaick,"   45
      Amang the springs,
Awa ye squatter'd like a drake,
      On whistlin wings.

Let warlocks grim an' wither'd hags
Tell how wi' you on ragweed nags   50
They skim the muirs an' dizzy crags
      Wi' wicked speed;
And in kirk-yards renew their leagues,
      Owre howket dead.

Thence, countra wives wi' toil an' pain   55
May plunge an' plunge the kirn in vain;
For oh! the yellow treasure 's taen
      By witchin skill;
An' dawtet, twal-pint hawkie 's gaen
      As yell 's the bill.   60

Thence, mystic knots mak great abuse,
On young guidmen, fond, keen, an' crouse;
When the best wark-lume i' the house,
      By cantrip wit,
Is instant made no worth a louse,   65
      Just at the bit.

When thowes dissolve the snawy hoord,
An' float the jinglin icy-boord,
Then water-kelpies haunt the foord
      By your direction,   70
An' nighted trav'lers are allur'd
      To their destruction.

And aft your moss-traversing spunkies
Decoy the wight that late and drunk is:
The bleezin, curst, mischievous monkeys   75
      Delude his eyes,
Till in some miry slough he sunk is,
      Ne'er mair to rise.

When masons' mystic word and grip
In storms an' tempests raise you up,   80
Some cock or cat your rage maun stop,
      Or, strange to tell,
The youngest brither ye wad whip
      Aff straught to hell!

Lang syne, in Eden's bonie yard,   85
When youthfu' lovers first were pair'd,
And all the soul of love they shar'd,
      The raptur'd hour,
Sweet on the fragrant flow'ry swaird,
      In shady bow'r;   90

Then you, ye auld sneck-drawin dog!
Ye cam to Paradise incog,
And play'd on man a cursed brogue,
      (Black be your fa'!)
And gied the infant warld a shog,   95
      Maist ruin'd a'.

D'ye mind that day, when in a bizz,
Wi' reeket duds and reestet gizz,
Ye did present your smoutie phiz
      Mang better folk,   100
An' sklented on the man of Uz
      Your spitefu' joke?

An' how ye gat him i' your thrall,
An' brak him out o' house and hal',
While scabs and blotches did him gall,   .   105
   Wi' bitter claw,
An' lows'd his ill-tongued, wicked scaul,
   Was warst ava?

But a' your doings to rehearse,
Your wily snares an' fechtin fierce,   110
Sin' that day Michael did you pierce,
   Down to this time,
Wad ding a Lallan tongue, or Erse,
   In prose or rhyme.

An' now, auld Cloots, I ken ye 're thinkin,   115
A certain Bardie 's rantin, drinkin,
Some luckless hour will send him linkin,
   To your black pit;
But faith! he 'll turn a corner jinkin,
   An' cheat you yet.   120

But fare you weel, auld Nickie-ben!
O wad ye tak a thought an' men'!
Ye aiblins might — I dinna ken —
   Still hae a stake:
I 'm wae to think upo' yon den,   125
   Ev'n for your sake!

DEATH AND DOCTOR HORNBOOK.

A TRUE STORY.

SOME books are lies frae end to end,
And some great lies were never pen'd:
Ev'n ministers, they hae been ken'd,
    In holy rapture,
A rousin whid at times to vend 5
    An' nail 't wi' Scripture.

But this that I am gaun to tell,
Which lately on a night befell,
Is just as true 's the deil 's in hell
    Or Dublin city : 10
That e'er he nearer comes oursel
    'S a muckle pity.

The clachan yill had made me canty —
I was na' fou, but just had plenty;
I stacher'd whyles, but yet took tent aye 15
    To free the ditches;
An' hillocks, stanes, and bushes ken'd aye
    Frae ghaists and witches.

The rising moon began to glow'r
The distant Cumnock hills out-owre; 20
To count her horns, wi' a' my pow'r,
    . I set mysel;
But whether she had three or four,
    I could na tell.

I was come round about the hill, 25
An' todlin doun on Willie's mill,

Settin my staff wi' a' my skill
    To keep me sicker,
Tho' leeward whiles against my will
    I took a bicker.   30

I there wi' *Something* did forgather,
That pat me in an eerie swither:
An awfu' scythe out-owre ae shouther
    Clear-dangling hang;
A three-taed leister on the ither   35
    Lay large an' lang.

Its stature seem'd lang Scotch ells twa,
The queerest shape that e'er I saw,
For fient a wame it had ava;
    And then its shanks,   40
They were as thin, as sharp and sma'
    As cheeks o' branks.

'Guid-een,' quo' I; 'Friend! hae ye been mawin,
When ither folk are busy sawin?'
It seem'd to mak a kind o' stan',   45
    But naething spak:
At length, says I, 'Friend, whare ye gaun?
    Will ye go back?'

It spak right howe, — 'My name is *Death*,
But be na fley'd.' — Quoth I, 'Guid faith,   50
Ye 're maybe come to stap my breath;
    But tent me, billie:
I red ye weel, tak care o' skaith,
    See, there 's a gully!'

'Gudeman,' quo' he, 'put up your whittle,   55
I 'm no design'd to try its mettle;

But if I did, I wad be kittle
    To be mislear'd ;
I wad na mind it — no that spittle
    Out-owre my beard.' 60

'Weel, weel !' says I, 'a bargain be 't ;
Come, gie 's your hand, an' sae we 're gree 't ;
We 'll ease our shanks an' tak a seat,
    Come, gie 's your news :
'This while ye hae been mony a gait, 65
    At mony a house.'

' Ay, ay !' quo' he, an' shook his head,
' It 's e'en a lang, lang time indeed
Sin' I began to nick the thread
    An' choke the breath : 70
Folk maun do something for their bread,
    An' sae maun *Death*.

'Sax thousand years are near-hand fled
Sin' I was to the butchin bred,
An' mony a scheme in vain 's been laid 75
    To stap or scaur me ;
Till ane *Hornbook's* ta'en up the trade,
    An' faith ! he 'll waur me.

'Ye ken *Jock Hornbook* i' the Clachan —
Deil mak his king's-hood in a spleuchan ! — 80
He 's grown sae well acquaint wi' *Buchan*
    An' ither chaps,
The weans haud out their fingers laughin
    And pouk my hips.

' See, here 's a scythe, and there 's a dart — 85
They hae pierc'd mony a gallant heart ;

But Doctor *Hornbook* wi' his art
      And cursed skill
Has made them baith no worth a [scart],
      Damn'd haet they 'll kill.   90

' 'T was but yestreen, nae farther gaen,
I threw a noble throw at ane ;
Wi' less, I 'm sure, I 've hundreds slain ;
      But deil-ma-care,
It just play'd dirl on the bane,   95
      But did nae mair.

'*Hornbook* was by wi' ready art,
And had sae fortify'd the part,
That when I lookèd to my dart,
      It was sae blunt,   100
Fient haet o 't wad hae pierc'd the heart
      O' a kail-runt.

' I drew my scythe in sic a fury,
I nearhand cowpit wi' my hurry,
But yet the bauld *Apothecary*   105
      Withstood the shock :
I might as weel hae try'd a quarry
      O' hard whin rock.

.   .   .   .

' An' then a' doctor's saws an' whittles,   115
Of a' dimensions, shapes, an' metals,
A' kinds o' boxes, mugs, an' bottles
      He 's sure to hae :
Their Latin names as fast he rattles
      As A B C.   120

'Calces o' fossils, earths, and trees ;
True sal-marinum o' the seas ;
The farina of beans and peas,
      He has 't in plenty ;
Aqua-fontis, — what you please, 125
      He can content ye.

'Forbye some new, uncommon weapons, —
Urinus spiritus of capons ;
Or mite-horn shavins, filins, scrapins,
      Distill'd *per se ;* 130
Sal-alkali o' midge-tail clippins,
      An' mony mae.'

'Wae 's me for *Johnie Ged's Hole* now,'
Quo' I, 'if that thae news be true !
His braw calf-ward, whare gowans grew 135
      Sae white and bonie,
Nae doubt they 'll rive it wi' the plew ;
      They 'll ruin Johnie !'

The creature grain'd an eldritch laugh,
An' says, 'Ye need na yoke the pleugh, 140
Kirkyards will soon be till'd eneugh,
      Tak ye nae fear :
They 'll a' be trench'd wi' mony a sheugh
      In twa-three year.

'Whare I kill'd ane, a fair strae-death 145
By loss o' blood or want of breath,
This night I 'm free to tak my aith,
      That *Hornbook's* skill
Has clad a score i' their last claith,
      By drap and pill. 150

'An honest wabster to his trade,
Whase wife's twa nieves were scarce weel-bred,
Gat tippence-worth to mend her head,
  When it was sair;
The wife slade cannie to her bed,   155
  But ne'er spak mair.

'A countra Laird had taen the batts,
Or some curmurring in his guts,
His only son for *Hornbook* sets
  An' pays him well: 160
The lad for twa guid gimmer-pets
  Was laird himsel.

'A bonie lass, ye ken'd her name,
Some ill-brewn drink had hov'd her wame:
She trusts hersel, to hide the shame,   165
  In *Hornbook's* care;
Horn sent her aff to her lang hame,
  To hide it there.

'That's just a swatch o' *Hornbook's* way;
Thus goes he on from day to day,   170
Thus does he poison, kill, an' slay,
  An's weel pay'd for 't;
Yet stops me o' my lawfu' prey,
  Wi' his damn'd dirt.

'But, hark! I 'll tell you of a plot,   175
Tho' dinna ye be speakin o 't;
I 'll nail the self-conceited sot
  As dead's a herrin.
Niest time we meet, I 'll wad a groat,
  He gets his fairin!'   180

But just as he began to tell,
The auld kirk-hammer strak the bell
Some wee short hour ayont the twal,
    Which rais'd us baith :
I took the way that pleas'd mysel,   185
    And sae did *Death*.

TO JOHN LAPRAIK.

AN OLD SCOTTISH BARD.

WHILE briers and woodbines budding green,
An' paitricks scraichin loud at e'en,
An' morning poussie whiddin seen
    Inspire my muse,
This freedom in an unknown frien'   5
    I pray excuse.

On Fasten-e'en we had a rockin,
To ca' the crack and weave our stockin :
And there was muckle fun and jokin,
    Ye need na doubt;   10
At length we had a hearty yokin
    At sang-about.

There was ae sang amang the rest,
Aboon them a' it pleas'd me best,
That some kind husband had addrest   15
    To some sweet wife :
It thirl'd the heart-strings thro' the breast
    A' to the life.

I 've scarce heard ought describ'd sae weel,
What gen'rous, manly bosoms feel ;   20
Thought I, "Can this be Pope, or Steele,
          Or Beattie's wark ? "
They tauld me 't was an odd kin' chiel
          About Muirkirk.

I pat me fidgin-fain to hear 't,   25
And sae about him there I spier 't ;
Then a' that ken'd him round declar'd
          He had *ingine ;*
That nane excell'd it, few cam near 't,
          It was sae fine ;   30

That, set him to a pint of ale,
An' either douce or merry tale,
Or rhymes an' sangs he 'd made himsel,
          Or witty catches —
'Tween Inverness and Teviotdale   35
          He had few matches.

Then up I gat, an' swoor an aith,
Tho' I should pawn my pleugh and graith,
Or die a cadger pownie's death
          At some dyke-back,   40
A pint an' gill I 'd gie them baith
          To hear your crack.

But, first an' foremost, I should tell,
Amaist as soon as I could spell,
I to the crambo-jingo fell,   45
          Tho' rude an' rough,
Yet crooning to a body's sel
          Does weel eneugh.

I am nae Poet, in a sense,
But just a Rhymer like by chance,   50
An' hae to learning nae pretence ;
      Yet what the matter ?
Whene'er my Muse does on me glance,
      I jingle at her.

Your critic-folk may cock their nose,   55
And say, ' How can you e'er propose,
You wha ken hardly verse frae prose,
      To mak a sang ? '
But, by your leave, my learned foes,
      Ye 're maybe wrang.   60

What 's a' your jargon o' your schools,
Your Latin names for horns an' stools ?
If honest nature made you fools,
      What sairs your grammars ?
Ye 'd better taen up spades and shools,   65
      Or knappin-hammers.

A set o' dull, conceited hashes
Confuse their brains in college classes !
They gang in stirks and come out asses,
      Plain truth to speak ;   70
An' syne they think to climb Parnassus
      By dint o' Greek !

Gie me ae spark o' Nature's fire,
That 's a' the learnin I desire ;
Then, tho' I drudge thro' dub an' mire   75
      At pleugh or cart,
My Muse, though hamely in attire,
      May touch the heart.

O for a spunk o' Allan's glee,
Or Fergusson's, the bauld an' slee,   80
Or bright Lapraik's, my friend to be,
          If I can hit it !
That would be lear eneugh for me,
          If I could get it.

Now, Sir, if ye hae friends enow,   85
Tho' real friends, I b'lieve, are few,
Yet, if your catalogue be fou,
          I 'se no insist ;
But gif ye want ae friend that 's true,
          I 'm on your list.   90

I winna blaw about mysel,
As ill I like my fauts to tell ;
But friends, an' folk that wish me well,
          They sometimes roose me ;
Tho' I maun own, as mony still   95
          As far abuse me.

There 's ae wee faut they whiles lay to me,
I like the lasses — Gude forgie me !
For monie a plack they wheedle frae me,
          At dance or fair ;   100
Maybe some ither thing they gie me
          They weel can spare.

But Mauchline race or Mauchline Fair,
I should be proud to meet you there :
We 'se gie ae night's discharge to care,   105
          If we forgather,
And hae a swap o' rhymin-ware
          Wi' ane anither.

The four-gill chap we 'se gar him clatter,
And kirsen him wi' reekin water ;   110
Syne we 'll sit down and tak our whitter,
          To cheer our heart ;
And faith ! we 'se be acquainted better
          Before we part.

Awa, ye selfish warly race,   115
Wha think that havins, sense and grace,
Ev'n love and friendship should give place
          To catch-the-plack !
I dinna like to see your face
          Nor hear your crack.   120

But ye whom social pleasure charms,
Whose hearts the tide of kindness warms,
Who hold your being on the terms,
          " Each aid the others,"
Come to my bowl, come to my arms,   125
          My friends, my brothers !

But to conclude my lang epistle,
As my auld pen 's worn to the gristle ;
Twa lines frae you wad gar me fissle,
          Who am, most, fervent,   130
While I can either sing or whistle,
          Your friend and servant.

TO WILLIAM SIMSON,

OCHILTREE.

I GAT your letter, winsome Willie ;
Wi' gratefu' heart I thank you brawlie ;
Tho' I maun say 't, I wad be silly,
      An' unco vain,
Should I believe, my coaxin billie,   5
      Your flatterin strain.

But I 'se believe ye kindly meant it,
I sud be lathe to think ye hinted
Ironic satire, sidelins sklented
      On my poor Musie ;   10
Tho' in sic phraisin terms ye 've pen'd it,
      I scarce excuse ye.

My senses wad be in a creel,
Should I but dare a hope to speel
Wi' Allan or wi' Gilbertfield   15
      The braes o' fame ;
Or Fergusson, the writer-chiel,
      A deathless name.

(O Fergusson ! thy glorious parts
Ill suited law's dry, musty arts !   20
My curse upon your whunstane hearts,
      Ye E'nbrugh gentry !
The tythe o' what ye waste at cartes
      Wad stow'd his pantry !)

Yet when a tale comes i' my head,   25
Or lasses gie my heart a screed,
As whiles they 're like to be my dead,
      (Oh sad disease !)

I kittle up my rustic reed :
      It gies me ease.   30

Auld Coila now may fidge fu' fain,
She 's gotten poets o' her ain —
Chiels wha their chanters winna hain,
      But tune their lays,
Till echoes a' resound again   . 35
      Her weel-sung praise.

Nae poet thought her worth his while
To set her name in measur'd style :
She lay like some unken'd-of isle
      Beside New Holland,   40
Or whare wild-meeting oceans boil
      Besouth Magellan.

Ramsay and famous Fergusson
Gied Forth and Tay a lift aboon ;
Yarrow and Tweed to mony a tune   45
      Owre Scotland rings ;
While Irvin, Lugar, Ayr an' Doon
      Naebody sings.

Th' Ilissus, Tiber, Thames, an' Seine
Glide sweet in mony a tunefu' line ;   50
But, Willie, set your fit to mine
      And cock your crest,
We 'll gar our streams and burnies shine
      Up wi' the best !

We 'll sing auld Coila's plains an' fells,   55
Her moors red-brown wi' heather bells,
Her banks an' braes, her dens and dells,
      Where glorious Wallace
Aft bure the gree, as story tells,
      Frae Southron billies.   60

At Wallace' name what Scottish blood
But boils up in a spring-tide flood !
Oft have our fearless fathers strode
      By Wallace' side,
Still pressing onward red-wat-shod,   65
      Or glorious dy'd.

O sweet are Coila's haughs an' woods,
When lintwhites chant amang the buds,
And jinkin hares in amorous whids
      Their loves enjoy,   70
While thro' the braes the cushat croods
      Wi' wailfu' cry !

Ev'n winter bleak has charms to me,
When winds rave thro' the naked tree ;
Or frosts on hills of Ochiltree   75
      Are hoary gray ;
Or blinding drifts wild-furious flee,
      Dark'ning the day !

O Nature ! a' thy shews an' forms
To feeling, pensive hearts hae charms !   80
Whether the summer kindly warms
      Wi' life an' light,
Or winter howls in gusty storms
      The lang, dark night !

The Muse, nae poet ever fand her,   85
Till by himsel he learn'd to wander
Adoun some trottin burn's meander,
      And no think lang ;
O sweet to stray and pensive ponder
      A heart-felt sang !   90

The warly race may drudge and drive,
Hog-shouther, jundie, stretch an' strive :

Let me fair nature's face descrive,
　　　And I wi' pleasure
Shall let the busy, grumbling hive   95
　　　Bum owre their treasure.

Fareweel, my " rhyme-composing brither " !
We 've been owre lang unken'd to ither :
Now let us lay our heads thegither
　　　In love fraternal !   100
May Envy wallop in a tether,
　　　Black fiend infernal !

While Highlandmen hate tolls and taxes,
While moorlan herds like guid fat braxies,
While Terra Firma on her axis   105
　　　Diurnal turns,
Count on a friend in faith an' practice
　　　In Robert Burns.

THE HOLY FAIR.

A robe of seeming truth and trust
　Hid crafty Observation ;
And secret hung, with poison'd crust,
　The dirk of Defamation ;
A mask that like the gorget show'd,
　Dye-varying on the pigeon ;
And for a mantle large and broad,
　He wrapt him in Religion.
　　　　　　Hypocrisy à-la-mode.

Upon a simmer Sunday morn,
　When Nature's face is fair,
I walkèd forth to view the corn
　An' snuff the caller air.

The risin' sun owre Galston muirs   5
 Wi' glorious light was glintin,
The hares were hirplin down the furrs,
 The lav'rocks they were chantin
     Fu' sweet that day.

As lightsomely I glowr'd abroad   10
 To see a scene sae gay,
Three hizzies, early at the road,
 Cam skelpin up the way.
Twa had manteeles o' dolefu' black,
 But ane wi' lyart linin ;   15
The third, that gaed a wee a-back,
 Was in the fashion shinin
     Fu' gay that day.

The twa appear'd like sisters twin
 In feature, form, an' claes ;   20
Their visage wither'd, lang an' thin,
 An' sour as ony slaes :
The third cam up, hap-step-an'-lowp,
 As light as ony lambie,
An' wi' a curchie low did stoop,   25
 As soon as e'er she saw me,
     Fu' kind that day.

Wi' bonnet aff, quoth I, ' Sweet lass,
 I think ye seem to ken me ;
I 'm sure I 've seen that bonie face,   30
 But yet I canna name ye.'
Quo' she, an' laughin as she spak,
 An' taks me by the han's,
' Ye, for my sake, hae gien the feck
 Of a' the ten comman's   35
     A screed some day.

' My name is Fun — your cronie dear,
  'The nearest friend ye hae ;
An' this is Superstition here,
  An' that 's Hypocrisy.   40
I 'm gaun to Mauchline Holy Fair,
  To spend an hour in daffin :
Gin ye 'll go there, yon runkl'd pair,
  We will get famous laughin
                    At them this day.'   45

Quoth I, ' With a' my heart, I 'll do 't :
  I 'll get my Sunday's sark on,
An' meet you on the holy spot ;
  Faith, we 'se hae fine remarkin !'
Then I gaed hame at crowdie-time,   50
  An' soon I made me ready ;
For roads were clad frae side to side
  Wi' mony a wearie body
                    In droves that day.

Here farmers gash in ridin graith   55
  Gaed hoddin by their cotters,
There swankies young in braw braid-claith
  Are springin owre the gutters.
The lasses, skelpin barefit, thrang,
  In silks an' scarlets glitter,   60
Wi' sweet-milk cheese in mony a whang,
  An' farls bak'd wi' butter,
                    Fu' crump that day.

When by the plate we set our nose,
  Weel heapèd up wi' ha'pence,   65
A greedy glowr Black Bonnet throws,
  An' we maun draw our tippence.

Then in we go to see the show:
   On ev'ry side they 're gath'rin,
Some carryin dails, some chairs an' stools,   70
   An' some are busy bleth'rin
             Right loud that day.

Here stands a shed to fend the show'rs
   An' screen our countra gentry;
There Racer Jess an' twa-three whores   75
   Are blinkin at the entry.
Here sits a raw o' tittlin jads,
   Wi' heavin breast and bare neck,
An' there a batch o' wabster lads,
   Blackguardin frae Kilmarnock   80
             For fun this day.

Here some are thinkin on their sins,
   An' some upo' their claes;
Ane curses feet that fyl'd his shins,
   Anither sighs and prays: 85
On this hand sits a chosen swatch,
   Wi' screw'd-up grace-proud faces;
On that a set o' chaps at watch,
   Thrang winkin on the lasses
             To chairs that day.   90

O happy is that man and blest!
   (Nae wonder that it pride him!)
Whase ain dear lass that he likes best,
   Comes clinkin doun beside him!
Wi' arm repos'd on the chair back,   95
   He sweetly does compose him;
Which by degrees slips round her neck,
   An 's loof upon her bosom,
             Unken'd that day.

Now a' the congregation o'er 100
  Is silent expectation ;
For Moodie speels the holy door,
  Wi' tidings o' damnation.
Should Hornie, as in ancient days,
  'Mang sons o' God present him, 105
The vera sight o' Moodie's face
  To's ain het hame had sent him
          Wi' fright that day.

Hear how he clears the points o' faith
  Wi' rattlin an' wi' thumpin! 110
Now meekly calm, now wild in wrath
  He's stampin an' he's jumpin!
His lengthen'd chin, his turn'd-up snout,
  His eldritch squeal and gestures,
Oh, how they fire the heart devout, 115
  Like cantharidian plaisters,
          On sic a day!

But hark! the tent has chang'd its voice :
  There's peace and rest nae langer ;
For a' the real judges rise, 120
  They canna sit for anger.
Smith opens out his cauld harangues,
  On practice and on morals ;
An' aff the godly pour in thrangs,
  To gie the jars an' barrels 125
          A lift that day.

What signifies his barren shine
  Of moral pow'rs and reason ?
His English style an' gesture fine
  Are a' clean out o' season. 130

Like Socrates or Antonine
  Or some auld pagan heathen,
The *moral man* he does define,
  But ne'er a word o' *faith* in
          That 's richt that day.   135

In guid time comes an antidote
  Against sic poison'd nostrum ;
For Peebles, frae the water-fit,
  Ascends the holy rostrum :
See, up he 's got the word o' God   140
  An' meek an mim has view'd it,
While Common Sense has ta'en the road,
  An 's aff, an' up the Cowgate
          Fast, fast that day.

Wee Miller niest the Guard relieves,   145
  An' Orthodoxy raibles,
Tho' in his heart he weel believes
  An' thinks it auld wives' fables :
But faith ! the birkie wants a Manse,
  So cannilie he hums them ;   150
Altho' his carnal wit an' sense
  Like hafflins-wise o'ercomes him
          At times that day.

Now butt an' ben the change-house fills
  Wi' yill-caup commentators :   155
Here 's cryin out for bakes an' gills,
  An' there the pint-stowp clatters ;
While thick an' thrang, an' loud an' lang,
  Wi' logic an' wi' Scripture,
They raise a din, that in the end   160
  Is like to breed a rupture
          O' wrath that day.

Leeze me on Drink ! it gies us mair
   Than either school or college :
It ken'les wit, it waukens lair,   165
   It pangs us fou o' knowledge.
Be't whisky-gill or penny-wheep,
   Or ony stronger potion,
It never fails, on drinkin deep,
   To kittle up our notion   170
              By night or day.

The lads an' lasses, blythely bent
   To mind baith saul an' body,
Sit round the table weel content,
   An' steer about the toddy.   175
On this ane's dress an' that ane's leuk
   They're makin observations;
While some are cozie i' the neuk,
   An' formin assignations
              To meet some day.   180

But now the Lord's ain trumpet touts,
   Till a' the hills are rairin,
An' echoes back return the shouts —
   Black Russell is na sparin.
His piercing words, like highlan' swords,   185
   Divide the joints an' marrow;
His talk o' hell, whare devils dwell,
   Our vera 'sauls does harrow'
              Wi' fright that day.

A vast, unbottom'd, boundless pit,   190
   Fill'd fou o' lowin brunstane,
Whase ragin flame, an' scorchin heat
   Wad melt the hardest whun-stane !

The half-asleep start up wi' fear
   An' think they hear it roarin,   195
When presently it does appear
   'Twas but some neibor snorin,
              Asleep that day.

'Twad be owre lang a tale, to tell
   How mony stories past,   200
An' how they crouded to the yill,
   When they were a' dismist:
How drink gaed round in cogs and caups
   Amang the furms an' benches:
An' cheese and bread frae women's laps   205
   Was dealt about in lunches
              An' dauds that day.

In comes a gaucie, gash guidwife
   An' sits down by the fire,
Syne draws her kebbuck an' her knife;   210
   The lasses they are shyer:
The auld guidmen about the grace
   Frae side to side they bother,
Till some ane by his bonnet lays,
   And gi'es them't like a tether   215
              Fu' lang that day.

Waesucks! for him that gets nae lass,
   Or lasses that hae naething!
Sma' need has he to say a grace,
   Or melvie his braw claithing!   220
O wives, be mindfu' ance yoursel
   How bonie lads ye wanted,
An' dinna for a kebbuck-heel
   Let lasses be affronted
              On sic a day!   225

Now Clinkumbell, wi' rattlin tow,
   Begins to jow an' croon ;
Some swagger hame the best they dow,
   Some wait the afternoon.
At slaps the billies halt a blink,   230
   Till lasses strip their shoon :
Wi' faith an' hope, an' love an' drink,
   They're a' in famous tune
            For crack that day.

How monie hearts this day converts   235
   O' sinners and o' lasses!
Their hearts o' stane, gin night, are gane
   As saft as ony flesh is.
There's some are fou o' love divine,
   There's some are fou o' brandy;   240
An' monie jobs that day begin,
   May end in houghmagandie
            Some ither day.

TO THE REV. JOHN M'MATH.

WHILE at the stook the shearers cow'r
To shun the bitter blaudin show'r,
Or in gulravage rinnin scowr
        To pass the time,
To you I dedicate the hour   5
        In idle rhyme.

My Musie, tir'd wi' monie a sonnet
On gown, an' ban', an' douse black bonnet,
Is grown right eerie now she's done it,
        Lest they shou'd blame her,   10

An' rouse their holy thunder on it,
          And anathem her.

I own 'twas rash, an' rather hardy,
That I, a simple countra bardie,
Shou'd meddle wi' a pack sae sturdy,   15
          Wha, if they ken me,
Can easy wi' a single wordie
          Lowse hell upon me.

But I gae mad at their grimaces,
Their sighin, cantin, grace-proud faces,   20
Their three-mile prayers and hauf-mile graces,
          Their raxin conscience,
Whase greed, revenge, an' pride disgraces
          Waur nor their nonsense.

There's Gau'n, misca't waur than a beast,   25
Wha has mair honour in his breast
Than monie scores as guid's the priest
          Wha sae abus'd him;
An' may a bard no crack his jest
          What way they've used him?   30

See him, the poor man's friend in need,
The gentleman in word an' deed —
An' shall his fame an' honour bleed
          By worthless skellums,
An' no a Muse erect her head   35
          To cowe the blellums?

O Pope, had I thy satire's darts
To gie the rascals their deserts,
I'd rip their rotten, hollow hearts,
          And tell aloud   40
Their jugglin hocus-pocus arts
          To cheat the crowd.

God knows, I 'm no the thing I should be,
Nor am I even the thing I could be,
But twenty times I rather would be   45
          An atheist clean,
Than under gospel colours hid be
          Just for a screen.

An honest man may like a glass,
An honest man may like a lass,   50
But mean revenge and malice fause
          He 'll still disdain,
And then cry zeal for gospel laws,
          Like some we ken.

They tak religion in their mouth;   55
They talk o' mercy, grace, an' truth—
For what? to gie their malice skouth
          On some puir wight,
An' hunt him down, o'er right an' ruth,
          To ruin straight.   60

All hail, Religion ! maid divine !
Pardon a Muse sae mean as mine,
Who in her rough imperfect line
          Thus daurs to name thee
To stigmatize false friends of thine   65
          Can ne'er defame thee.

Tho' blotcht an' foul wi' monie a stain,
An' far unworthy of thy train,
With trembling voice I tune my strain
          To join with those   70
Who boldly daur thy cause maintain
          In spite o' foes,

In spite o' crowds, in spite o' mobs,
In spite of undermining jobs,
In spite o' dark banditti stabs   75
    At worth an' merit,
By scoundrels, even wi' holy robes,
    But hellish spirit.

O Ayr! my dear, my native ground!
Within thy presbyterial bound   80
A candid lib'ral band is found
    Of public teachers,
As men, as Christians too, renown'd,
    An' manly preachers.

Sir, in that circle you are nam'd,   85
Sir, in that circle you are fam'd;
An' some, by whom your doctrine 's blam'd
    (Which gies ye honour),
Even, sir, by them your heart 's esteem'd
    An' winning manner.   90

Pardon this freedom I have ta'en,
An' if impertinent I 've been,
Impute it not, good sir, in ane
    Whase heart ne'er wrang'd ye,
But to his utmost would befrien'   95
    Ought that belang'd ye.

THE BRAES O' BALLOCHMYLE.

THE Catrine woods were yellow seen,
  The flowers decay'd on Catrine lea.
Nae lav'rock sang on hillock green,
  But nature sicken'd on the ee.

Thro' faded groves Maria sang,
  Hersel in beauty's bloom the while,
And aye the wild-wood echoes rang,
  Fareweel the braes o' Ballochmyle! 5

Low in your wintry beds, ye flowers,
  Again ye'll flourish fresh and fair; 10
Ye birdies, dumb in with'rin bowers,
  Again ye'll charm the vocal air.
But here, alas! for me nae mair
  Shall birdie charm, or flow'ret smile,
Fareweel the bonie banks of Ayr, 15
  Fareweel, fareweel! sweet Ballochmyle!

TO A MOUSE,

ON TURNING UP HER NEST WITH THE PLOUGH,
NOVEMBER, 1785.

WEE, sleekit, cowrin, tim'rous beastie,
Oh, what a panic's in thy breastie!
Thou need na start awa sae hasty
        Wi' bickerin brattle!
I wad be laith to rin an' chase thee 5
        Wi' murd'rin pattle!

I'm truly sorry man's dominion
Has broken nature's social union,
An' justifies that ill opinion
        Which makes thee startle 10
At me, thy poor earth-born companion,
        An' fellow-mortal!

I doubt na, whyles, but thou may thieve:
What then? poor beastie, thou maun live!
A daimen icker in a thrave
      'S a sma' request;
I 'll get a blessin wi' the lave,
      An' never miss 't!

Thy wee bit housie, too, in ruin!
Its silly wa's the win's are strewin!
An' naething, now, to big a new ane,
      O' foggage green!
An' bleak December's winds ensuin
      Baith snell an' keen!

Thou saw the fields laid bare and waste,
An' weary winter comin fast,
An' cozie here beneath the blast
      Thou thought to dwell,
Till crash! the cruel coulter past
      Out thro' thy cell.

That wee bit heap o' leaves an' stibble
Has cost thee mony a weary nibble!
Now thou 's turn'd out for a' thy trouble,
      But house or hald,
To thole the winter's sleety dribble
      An' cranreuch cauld!

But, Mousie, thou art no thy lane
In proving foresight may be vain:
The best laid schemes o' mice an' men
      Gang aft a-gley,
An' lea'e us nought but grief an' pain
      For promis'd joy.

Still thou art blest, compar'd wi' me !
The present only toucheth thee :
But, och! I backward cast my ee   45
      On prospects drear !
An' forward, tho' I canna see,
      I guess an' fear !

THE COTTER'S SATURDAY NIGHT.

INSCRIBED TO ROBERT AIKEN, ESQ.

Let not Ambition mock their useful toil,
  Their homely joys and destiny obscure ;
Nor Grandeur hear with a disdainful smile,
  The short and simple annals of the poor. — GRAY.

My lov'd, my honour'd, much respected friend !
  No mercenary bard his homage pays ;
With honest pride, I scorn each selfish end :
  My dearest meed a friend's esteem and praise.
To you I sing, in simple Scottish lays,   5
The lowly train in life's sequester'd scene ;
  The native feelings strong, the guileless ways ;
What Aiken in a cottage would have been ;
Ah ! tho' his worth unknown, far happier there, I ween !

November chill blaws loud wi' angry sugh,   10
  The short'ning winter day is near a close ;
The miry beasts retreating frae the pleugh,
  The black'ning trains o' craws to their repose ;
  The toil-worn Cotter frae his labour goes, —
This night his weekly moil is at an end, —   15
  Collects his spades, his mattocks, and his hoes,
Hoping the morn in ease and rest to spend,
And weary, o'er the moor, his course does hameward bend.

At length his lonely cot appears in view,
   Beneath the shelter of an agèd tree ;	20
Th' expectant wee-things, toddlin, stacher through
   To meet their dad, wi' flichterin noise an' glee.
   His wee bit ingle, blinkin bonilie,
His clean hearth-stane, his thrifty wifie's smile,
   The lisping infant prattling on his knee,	25
Does a' his weary kiaugh and care beguile,
An' makes him quite forget his labour an' his toil.

Belyve, the elder bairns come drappin in,
   At service out amang the farmers roun';
Some ca the pleugh, some herd, some tentie rin	30
   A cannie errand to a neibor toun:
   Their eldest hope, their Jenny, woman-grown,
In youthfu' bloom, love sparkling in her ee,
   Comes hame, perhaps to shew a braw new gown,
Or deposite her sair-won penny-fee,	35
To help her parents dear, if they in hardship be.

With joy unfeign'd brothers and sisters meet,
   An' each for other's weelfare kindly spiers:
The social hours, swift-wing'd, unnotic'd fleet;
   Each tells the uncos that he sees or hears.	40
   The parents, partial, eye their hopeful years ;
Anticipation forward points the view ;
   The mother, wi' her needle an' her sheers,
Gars auld claes look amaist as weel's the new ;
The father mixes a' wi' admonition due.	45

Their master's an' their mistress's command
   The younkers a' are warned to obey ;
An' mind their labours wi' an eydent hand,
   An' ne'er, tho' out o' sight, to jauk or play:

"An' O ! be sure to fear the Lord alway,   50
An' mind your duty, duly, morn an' night !
    Lest in temptation's path ye gang astray,
Implore His counsel and assisting might :
They never sought in vain that sought the Lord aright !"

But hark ! a rap comes gently to the door.   55
    Jenny, wha kens the meaning o' the same,
Tells how a neibor lad cam o'er the moor,
    To do some errands, and convoy her hame.
    The wily mother sees the conscious flame
Sparkle in Jenny's ee, and flush her cheek ;   60
    Wi' heart-struck, anxious care, inquires his name,
While Jenny hafflins is afraid to speak ;
Weel pleas'd the mother hears it's nae wild worthless rake.

Wi' kindly welcome Jenny brings him ben,
    A strappin youth ; he takes the mother's eye ;   65
Blythe Jenny sees the visit's no ill taen ;
    The father cracks of horses, pleughs, and kye.
    The youngster's artless heart o'erflows wi' joy,
But, blate and laithfu', scarce can weel behave ;
    The mother wi' a woman's wiles can spy   70
What maks the youth sae bashfu' an' sae grave,
Weel-pleas'd to think her bairn's respected like the lave.

O happy love ! where love like this is found !
    O heart-felt raptures ! bliss beyond compare !
I've pacèd much this weary, mortal round,   75
    And sage experience bids me this declare —
    "If Heaven a draught of heavenly pleasure spare,
One cordial in this melancholy vale,
    'T is when a youthful, loving, modest pair,
In other's arms breathe out the tender tale,   80
Beneath the milk-white thorn that scents the ev'ning gale."

Is there, in human form, that bears a heart,
　　A wretch! a villain! lost to love and truth!
That can with studied, sly, ensnaring art
　　Betray sweet Jenny's unsuspecting youth?　　85
　　Curse on his perjur'd arts! dissembling smooth!
Are honour, virtue, conscience, all exil'd?
　　Is there no pity, no relenting ruth,
Points to the parents fondling o'er their child,
Then paints the ruin'd maid, and their distraction wild?　　90

But now the supper crowns their simple board,
　　The halesome parritch, chief of Scotia's food;
The sowpe their only hawkie does afford,
　　That yont the hallan snugly chows her cud.
　　The dame brings forth, in complimental mood,　　95
To grace the lad, her weel-hain'd kebbuck fell,
　　An' aft he's prest, an' aft he ca's it guid;
The frugal wifie, garrulous, will tell,
How 'twas a towmond auld, sin' lint was i' the bell.

The cheerfu' supper done, wi' serious face,　　100
　　They round the ingle form a circle wide;
The sire turns o'er with patriarchal grace
　　The big ha'-bible, ance his father's pride;
　　His bonnet rev'rently is laid aside,
His lyart haffets wearing thin and bare;　　105
　　Those strains that once did sweet in Zion glide,
He wales a portion with judicious care;
And, "Let us worship GOD," he says with solemn air.

They chant their artless notes in simple guise;
　　They tune their hearts, by far the noblest aim:　　110
Perhaps *Dundee's* wild-warbling measures rise,
　　Or plaintive *Martyrs*, worthy of the name,
　　Or noble *Elgin* beets the heaven-ward flame,

The sweetest far of Scotia's holy lays.
  Compar'd with these, Italian trills are tame ;   115
The tickl'd ear no heart-felt raptures raise ;
Nae unison hae they with our Creator's praise.

The priest-like father reads the sacred page, —
  How Abram was the friend of GOD on high;
Or Moses bade eternal warfare wage   120
  With Amalek's ungracious progeny;
  Or how the royal bard did groaning lie
Beneath the stroke of heaven's avenging ire ;
  Or Job's pathetic plaint, and wailing cry ;
  Or rapt Isaiah's wild, seraphic fire ;   125
Or other holy seers that tune the sacred lyre.

Perhaps the Christian volume is the theme, —
  How guiltless blood for guilty man was shed;
How HE, who bore in heav'n the second name,
  Had not on earth whereon to lay His head: 130
  How His first followers and servants sped;
The precepts sage they wrote to many a land:
  How he, who lone in Patmos banishèd,
Saw in the sun a mighty angel stand,
And heard great Bab'lon's doom pronounced by Heav'n's
  command.   135

Then kneeling down to HEAVEN'S ETERNAL KING,
  The saint, the father, and the husband prays:
Hope "springs exulting on triumphant wing,"
  That thus they all shall meet in future days:
  There ever bask in uncreated rays,   140
No more to sigh or shed the bitter tear,
  Together hymning their Creator's praise,
  In such society, yet still more dear,
While circling Time moves round in an eternal sphere.

Compar'd with this, how poor Religion's pride   145
   In all the pomp of method and of art,
When men display to congregations wide
   Devotion's ev'ry grace except the heart!
   The Pow'r, incens'd, the pageant will desert,
The pompous strain, the sacerdotal stole;   150
   But haply in some cottage far apart
May hear, well pleased, the language of the soul,
And in His book of life the inmates poor enrol.

Then homeward all take off their sev'ral way;
   The youngling cottagers retire to rest;   155
The parent-pair their secret homage pay,
   And proffer up to Heav'n the warm request,
   That He, who stills the raven's clam'rous nest
And decks the lily fair in flow'ry pride,
   Would, in the way His wisdom sees the best,   160
For them and for their little ones provide;
But chiefly, in their hearts with grace divine preside.

From scenes like these old Scotia's grandeur springs,
   That makes her lov'd at home, rever'd abroad:
Princes and lords are but the breath of kings,   165
   "An honest man 's the noblest work of God":
   And certes, in fair Virtue's heavenly road,
The cottage leaves the palace far behind:
   What is a lordling's pomp? a cumbrous load,
Disguising oft the wretch of human kind,   170
Studied in arts of hell, in wickedness refin'd!

O Scotia! my dear, my native soil!
   For whom my warmest wish to Heaven is sent!
Long may thy hardy sons of rustic toil
   Be blest with health, and peace, and sweet content!   175

And, oh! may Heaven their simple lives prevent
From luxury's contagion, weak and vile!
  Then, howe'er crowns and coronets be rent,
A virtuous populace may rise the while,
And stand a wall of fire around their much-lov'd isle.   180

O Thou! who pour'd the patriotic tide
  That stream'd thro' Wallace's undaunted heart,
Who dar'd to nobly stem tyrannic pride,
  Or nobly die, the second glorious part, —
(The patriot's God peculiarly thou art,   185
His friend, inspirer, guardian, and reward!)
  O never, never Scotia's realm desert,
But still the patriot, and the patriot-bard,
In bright succession raise, her ornament and guard!

HALLOWEEN.

Upon that night, when fairies light
  On Cassilis Downans dance,
Or owre the lays in splendid blaze
  On sprightly coursers prance,
Or for Colean the rout is taen   5
  Beneath the moon's pale beams,
There up the Cove to stray an' rove,
  Amang the rocks and streams
            To sport that night, —

Amang the bonie, winding banks,   10
  Where Doon rins wimplin clear,
Where Bruce ance rul'd the martial ranks
  An' shook his Carrick spear,

Some merry, friendly countra folks
  Together did convene,   15
To burn their nits, an' pou their stocks,
  An' haud their Halloween
          Fu' blythe that night.

The lasses feat an' cleanly neat,
  Mair braw than when they're fine;   20
Their faces blythe fu' sweetly kythe
  Hearts leal an' warm an' kin:
The lads sae trig, wi' wooer-babs
  Weel knotted on their garten,
Some unco blate, an' some wi' gabs,   25
  Gar lasses' hearts gang startin
          Whyles fast at night.

Then first an' foremost, thro' the kail
  Their stocks maun a' be sought ance:
They steek their een, an' grape an' wale   30
  For muckle anes an' straught anes.
Poor hav'rel Will fell aff the drift,
  An' wander'd thro' the bow-kail,
An' pou't, for want o' better shift,
  A runt was like a sow-tail   35
          Sae bow't that night.

Then, straught or crooked, yird or nane,
  They roar and cry a' throu'ther;
The vera wee-things toddlin rin
  Wi' stocks out-owre their shouther: 40
An' gif the custoc's sweet or sour,
  Wi' joctelegs they taste them;
Syne coziely, aboon the door,
  Wi' cannie care, they've placed them
          To lie that night.   45

The lasses staw frae 'mang them a'
  To pou their stalks o' corn;
But Rab slips out, and jinks about,
  Behint the muckle thorn:
He grippet Nelly hard an' fast,   50
  Loud skirl'd a' the lasses;
But her tap-pickle maist was lost
  When kiutlen i' the fause-house
              Wi' him that night.

The auld guidwife's weel-hoordit nits   55
  Are round an' round divided,
An' monie lads' and lasses' fates
  Are there that night decided:
Some kindle couthie side by side,
  An' burn thegither trimly;   60
Some start awa wi' saucy pride,
  An' jump out-owre the chimlie
              Fu' high that night.

Jean slips in twa, wi' tentie ee;
  Wha 't was, she wadna tell;   65
But this is *Jock*, and this is *me*,
  She says in to hersel:
He bleez'd owre her, an' she owre him,
  As they wad never mair part;
Till fuff! he started up the lum,   70
  An' Jean had e'en a sair heart
              To see 't that night.

Poor Willie, wi' his bow-kail runt,
  Was brunt wi' primsie Mallie,
An' Mary nae doubt took the drunt,   75
  To be compar'd to Willie:

Mall's nit lap out wi' pridefu' fling,
   An' her ain fit, it brunt it;
While Willie lap, an' swoor by jing,
   'T was just the way he wanted   80
           To be that night.

Nell had the fause-house in her min';
   She pits hersel and Rab in:
In loving bleeze they sweetly join,
   Till white in ase they're sabbin.   85
Nell's heart was dancin at the view,
   She whisper'd Rab to leuk for 't:
Rab stownlins prie'd her bonie mou
   Fu' cozie in the neuk for 't,
           Unseen that night.   90

But Merran sat behint their backs,
   Her thoughts on Andrew Bell;
She lea'es them gashin at their cracks,
   An' slips out by hersel:
She through the yard the nearest taks   95
   An' to the kiln she goes then,
An' darklins graipet for the bauks,
   An' in the blue-clue throws then,
           Right fear't that night.

And aye she win't and aye she swat,   100
   I wat she made nae jaukin:
Till something held within the pat,
   Guid Lord! but she was quaukin'!
But whether 't was the deil himsel,
   Or whether 't was a bauk-en',   105
Or whether it was Andrew Bell,
   She didna wait on talkin
          To spier that night.

Wee Jenny to her grannie says,
  "Will ye go wi' me, grannie?   110
I 'll eat the apple at the glass,
  I gat frae uncle Johnnie" :
She fuff't her pipe wi' sic a lunt,
  In wrath she was sae vap'rin,
She noticed na an aizle brunt   115
    Her braw new worset apron
        Out thro' that night.

" Ye little skelpie-limmer's face !
  I daur you try sic sportin,
As seek the foul Thief ony place,   120
  For him to spae your fortune :
Nae doubt but ye may get a sight!
  Great cause ye hae to fear it ;
For monie a ane has got a fright,
    An' liv'd an' died deleeret,   125
        On sic a night.

" Ae hairst afore the Sherra-moor,
  I min 't as weel 's yestreen,
I was a gilpey then, I 'm sure
  I was na past fyfteen: 130
The simmer had been cauld an' wat
  An' stuff was unco' green ;
An' ay a rantin kirn we gat,
    An' just on Halloween
        It fell that night.   135

" Our stibble-rig was Rab M'Graen,
  A clever, sturdy fallow ;
His son gat Eppie Sim wi' wean,
  That liv'd in Achmacalla;

He gat hemp-seed, I mind it weel,   140
    An' he made unco light o 't;
But monie a day was by himsel,
    He was sae sairly frighted
            That vera night."

Then up gat fechtin Jamie Fleck,   145
    An' he swoor by his conscience,
That he could saw hemp-seed a peck;
    For it was a' but nonsense:
The auld guidman raught down the pock,
    An' out a handfu' gied him;   150
Syne bad him slip frae 'mang the folk,
    Sometime when nae ane see'd him,
            An' try 't that night.

He marches thro' amang the stacks,
    Tho' he was something sturtin;   155
The graip he for a harrow taks,
    And haurls at his curpin;
And ev'ry now and then he says,
    " Hempseed, I saw thee,
And her that is to be my lass,   160
    Come after me, and draw thee
            As fast this night."

He whistled up Lord Lennox' march
    To keep his courage cheery;
Altho' his hair began to arch,   165
    He was sae fley'd and eerie:
Till presently he hears a squeak,
    And then a grane and gruntle;
He by his shouther gae a keek,
    And tumbl'd wi' a wintle   170
            Out-owre that night.

He roar'd a horrid murder shout
  In dreadfu' desperation!
And young and auld cam' rinnin out
  To hear the sad narration: 175
He swoor 't was hilchin Jean M'Craw,
  Or crouchie Merran Humphie;
Till, stop! she trotted thro' them a',
  And wha was it but grumphie
          Asteer that night?   180

Meg fain wad to the barn gaen
  To winn three wechts o' naething;
But for to meet the deil her lane,
  She pat but little faith in:
She gies the herd a pickle nits   185
  And twa red-cheekit apples
To watch, while for the barn she sets
  In hopes to see Tam Kipples
          That vera night.

She turns the key wi' cannie thraw   190
  An' owre the threshold ventures;
But first on Sawnie gies a ca',
  Syne bauldly in she enters;
A ratton rattl'd up the wa',
  An' she cry'd, Lord preserve her!   195
An' ran thro' midden-hole an' a',
  An' pray'd wi' zeal an' fervour
          Fu' fast that night.

They hoy't out Will wi' sair advice;
  They hecht him some fine braw ane;   200
It chanced the stack he faddom't thrice
  Was timmer-propt for thrawin:

He taks a swirlie, auld moss-oak
  For some black, grousome carlin ;
An' loot a winze, an' drew a stroke,   205
  Till skin in blypes cam haurlin
          Aff 's nieves that night.

A wanton widow Leezie was,
  As cantie as a kittlin :
But och ! that night amang the shaws   210
  She gat a fearfu' settlin !
She thro' the whins an' by the cairn
  An' owre the hill gaed scrievin,
Whare three lairds' lands met at a burn,
  To dip her left sark-sleeve in,   215
          Was bent that night.

Whyles owre a linn the burnie plays,
  As thro' the glen it wimpl't ;
Whyles round a rocky scar it strays ;
  Whyles in a wiel it dimpl't ;   220
Whyles glitter'd to the nightly rays,
  Wi' bickering, dancing dazzle ;
Whyles cookit underneath the braes
  Below the spreading hazel
          Unseen that night.   225

Amang the brachens on the brae,
  Between her an' the moon,
The deil, or else an outler quey,
  Gat up an' gae a croon :
Poor Leezie's heart maist lap the hool ;   230
  Near lav'rock-height she jumpet,
But mist a fit, an' in the pool
  Out-owre the lugs she plumpet
          Wi' a plunge that night.

In order on the clean hearth-stane   235
  The luggies three are ranged ;
And ev'ry time great care is taen,
  To see them duly changed :
Auld uncle John, wha wedlock's joys
  Sin' Mar's-year did desire,   240
Because he gat the toom dish thrice,
  He heav'd them on the fire
      In wrath that night.

Wi' merry sangs, and friendly cracks,
  I wat they did na weary ;   245
And unco tales, an' funnie jokes, —
  Their sports were cheap and cheery :
Till butter'd so'ns wi' fragrant lunt
  Set a' their gabs a-steerin ;
Syne wi' a social glass o' strunt   250
  They parted aff careerin
      Fu' blythe that night.

SCOTCH DRINK.

Gie him strong drink until he wink,
  That 's sinking in despair ;
And liquor guid to fire his bluid,
  That 's prest wi' grief and care :
There let him bouse, and deep carouse,
  Wi' bumpers flowing o'er,
Till he forgets his loves or debts,
  And minds his griefs no more.

SOLOMON'S PROVERBS, xxxi. 6, 7.

LET other poets raise a fracas
'Bout vines, and wines, and drucken Bacchus,
And crabbit names and stories wrack us,

And grate our lug:
I sing the juice Scotch bear can mak us,   5
        In glass or jug.

Oh thou, my Muse! guid auld Scotch drink!
Whether thro' wimplin worms thou jink,
Or, richly brown, ream o'er the brink
        In glorious faem,   10
Inspire me till I lisp and wink,
        To sing thy name!

Let husky wheat the haughs adorn,
An' aits set up their awnie horn,
An' pease and beans at e'en or morn   15
        Perfume the plain:
Leeze me on thee, John Barleycorn,
        Thou king o' grain!

On thee aft Scotland chows her cood,
In souple scones, the wale o' food!   20
Or tumblin in the boiling flood
        Wi' kail an' beef;
But when thou pours thy strong heart's blood,
        There thou shines chief.

Food fills the wame, an' keeps us livin;   25
Tho' life 's a gift no worth receivin,
When heavy-dragg'd wi' pine an' grievin;
        But oil'd by thee,
The wheels o' life gae down-hill scrievin
        Wi' rattlin glee.   30

Thou clears the head o' doited Lear;
Thou cheers the heart o' drooping Care;
Thou strings the nerves o' Labour sair

At 's weary toil :
Thou even brightens dark Despair   35
       Wi' gloomy smile.

Aft, clad in massy siller weed,
Wi' gentles thou erects thy head ;
Yet humbly kind in time o' need,
       The poor man's wine,   40
His wee drap parritch or his bread
       Thou kitchens fine.

Thou art the life o' public haunts ;
But thee, what were our fairs and rants ?
Ev'n godly meetings o' the saunts,   45
       By thee inspir'd,
When gaping they besiege the tents,
       Are doubly fir'd.

That merry night we get the corn in,
O sweetly, then, thou reams the horn in !   50
Or reekin on a New-Year mornin
       In cog or bicker,
An' just a wee drap sp'ritual burn in,
       An' gusty sucker !

When Vulcan gies his bellows breath,   55
And ploughmen gather wi' their graith,
O rare ! to see thee fizz and freath
       I' th' lugget caup !
Then Burnewin comes on like death
       At ev'ry chaup.   60

Nae mercy, then, for airn or steel ;
The brawnie, bainie, ploughman chiel
Brings hard owrehip wi' sturdy wheel

                    The strong forehammer,
        Till block and studdie ring an' reel   65
                    Wi' dinsome clamour.

        When skirlin weanies see the light,
        Thou maks the gossips clatter bright,
        How fumblin cuifs their dearies slight;
                    Wae worth the name !   70
        Nae howdy gets a social night,
                    Or plack frae them.

        When neibors anger at a plea,
        An' just as wud as wud can be,
        How easy can the barley bree   75
                    Cement the quarrel !
        It 's aye the cheapest lawyer's fee
                    To taste the barrel.

        Alake ! that e'er my Muse has reason
        To wyte her countrymen wi' treason !   80
        But mony daily weet their weason
                    Wi' liquors nice,
        An' hardly in a winter's season
                    E'er spier her price.

        Wae worth that brandy, burning trash !   85
        Fell source o' mony a pain an' brash !
        Twins mony a poor, doylt, drucken hash
                    O' half his days ;
        An' sends, beside, auld Scotland's cash
                    To her warst faes.   90

        Ye Scots, wha wish auld Scotland well,
        Ye chief, to you my tale I tell,
        Poor plackless devils like mysel !

It sets you ill,
Wi' bitter, dearthfu' wines to mell,   95
     Or foreign gill.

.   .   .   .

Fortune ! if thou 'll but gie me still
Hale breeks, a scone, an' whisky gill,
An' rowth o' rhyme to rave at will,
     Tak a' the rest,
An' deal 't about as thy blind skill   125
     Directs thee best.

TIIE AULD FARMER'S NEW-YEAR MORNING SALU-
TATION TO HIS AULD MARE, MAGGIE,

ON GIVING IIER TIIE ACCUSTOMED RIPP OF CORN TO IIANSEL
IN THE NEW YEAR.

A GUID New-Year I wish thee, Maggie !
Hae, there 's a ripp to thy auld baggie :
Tho' thou 's howe-backit now, an' knaggie,
     I 've seen the day
Thou could hae gane like ony staggie   5
     Out-owre the lay.

Tho' now thou 's dowie, stiff, an' crazy,
An' thy auld hide 's as white 's a daisie,
I 've seen thee dappl't, sleek an' glaizie,
     A bonie gray: 10
He should been tight that daur't to raize thee,
     Ance in a day.

Thou ance was i' the foremost rank,
A filly buirdly, steeve, an' swank,

An' set weel down a shapely shank   15
    As e'er tread yird ;
An' could hae flown out-owre a stank
    Like ony bird.

It's now some nine-and-twenty year
Sin' thou was my guid-father's meere ;   20
He gied me thee, o' tocher clear,
    An' fifty mark ;
Tho' it was sma', 't was weel won gear,
    An' thou was stark.

When first I gaed to woo my Jenny,   25
Ye then was trottin wi' your minnie :
Tho' ye was trickie, slee and funny,
    Ye ne'er was donsie ;
But hamely, tawie, quiet an' cannie,
    An' unco sonsie.   30

That day ye pranc'd wi' mickle pride,
When ye bure hame my bonie bride :
An' sweet an' gracefu' she did ride,
    Wi' maiden air !
Kyle-Stewart I could braggèd wide   35
    For sic a pair.

Tho' now ye dow but hoyte an' hoble
An' wintle like a saumont-coble,
That day ye was a jinker noble
    For heels an' win' !   40
An' ran them till they a' did wauble
    Far, far behin' !

When thou an' I were young an' skiegh,
An' stable meals at fairs were driegh,

How thou wad prance an' snore an' skriegh   45
    An' tak' the road !
Toun's bodies ran an' stood abiegh
    An' ca't thee mad.

When thou was corn't an' I was mellow,
We took the road ay like a swallow: 50
At brooses thou had ne'er a fellow
    For pith an' speed ;
But ev'ry tail thou pay't them hollow,
    Whare'er thou gaed.

'The sma', droop-rumpl't, hunter cattle   55
Might aiblins waur't thee for a brattle ;
But sax Scotch mile thou try't their mettle
    An' gart them whaizle :
Nae whip nor spur, but just a wattle
    O' saugh or hazel.   60

Thou was a noble fittie-lan'
As e'er in tug or tow was drawn !
Aft thee an' I, in aught hours' gaun
    On guid March-weather,
Hae turn'd sax rood beside our han'   65
    For days thegither.

Thou never braing't an' fetch't an' flisket,
But thy auld tail thou wad hae whisket
An' spread abreed thy weel-fill'd brisket,
    Wi' pith an' pow'r,   70
Till spritty knowes wad rair't and risket
    An' slypet owre.

When frosts lay lang an' snaws were deep
An' threaten'd labour back to keep,

I gied thy cog a wee-bit heap   75
          Aboon the timmer :
I ken'd my Maggie wad na sleep
          For that, or simmer.

In cart or car thou never reestet ;
The steyest brae thou wad hae faced it ;   80
Thou never lap an' sten't an' breastet,
          Then stood to blaw ;
But just thy step a wee thing hastet,
          Thou snoov 't awa.

My pleugh is now thy bairn-time a',   85
Four gallant brutes as e'er did draw ;
Forbye sax mae I 've sell't awa,
          That thou hast nurst :
They drew me thretteen pund an' twa,
          The vera warst.   90

Mony a sair daurg we twa hae wrought,
An' wi' the weary warl' fought !
An' mony an anxious day I thought
          We wad be beat !
Yet here to crazy age we 're brought   95
          Wi' something yet.

And think na, my auld trusty servan',
That now, perhaps, thou 's less deservin,
And thy auld days may end in stervin ;
          For my last fou,   100
A heapit stimpart, I 'll reserve ane,
          Laid by for you.

We 've worn to crazy years thegither ;
We 'll toyte about wi' ane anither ;

Wi' tentie care I 'll flit thy tether   105
    To some hained rig,
Whare ye may noble rax your leather,
    Wi' sma' fatigue.

THE TWA DOGS.

A TALE.

'T was in that place o' Scotland's isle,
That bears the name o' auld King Coil,
Upon a bonie day in June,
When wearin' through the afternoon,
Twa dogs that werena thrang at hame   5
Forgathered ance upon a time.

The first I 'll name, they ca'd him Cæsar,
Was keepit for his Honour's pleasure ;
His hair, his size, his mouth, his lugs,
Showed he was nane o' Scotland's dogs ;   10
But whalpit some place far abroad,
Whare sailors gang to fish for cod.

His lockèd, letter'd, braw brass collar
Show'd him the gentleman and scholar;
But though he was o' high degree,   15
The fient a pride — nae pride had he ;
But wad hae spent an hour caressin,
Even wi' a tinkler-gypsy's messan:
At kirk or market, mill or smiddie,
Nae tawted tyke, though e'er sae duddie,   20
But he wad stan't, as glad to see him,
And stroan't on stanes and hillocks wi' him.

The tither was a ploughman's collie,
A rhymin, rantin, ravin billie,
Wha for his friend and comrade had him,   25
An' in his freaks had Luath ca'd him,
After some dog in Highland sang,
Was made lang syne, — Lord knows how lang.

He was a gash an' faithfu' tyke,
As ever lap a sheugh or dike.   30
His honest, sonsie, baws'nt face
Ay gat him friends in ilka place;
His breast was white, his touzie back
Weel clad wi' coat o' glossy black;
His gawcie tail wi' upward curl   35
Hung owre his hurdies wi' a swirl.

Nae doubt but they were fain o' ither,
An' unco pack an' thick thegither;
Wi' social nose whyles snuff'd and snowket;
Whyles mice and moudieworts they howket;   40
Whyles scour'd awa in lang excursion
An' worry'd ither in diversion;
Until wi' daffin weary grown,
Upon a knowe they sat them down,
An' there began a lang digression   45
About the 'lords o' the creation.'

CÆSAR.

I 've aften wondered, honest Luath,
What sort o' life poor dogs like you have;
And when the gentry's life I saw,
What way poor bodies liv'd ava.   50

Our laird gets in his racket rents,
His coals, his kain, and a' his stents;

He rises when he likes himsel;
His flunkies answer at the bell;
He ca's his coach, he ca's his horse; 55
He draws a bonie silken purse
As lang 's my tail, where through the steeks
The yellow-lettered Geordie keeks.

Frae morn to e'en it 's nought but toilin,
At bakin, roastin, fryin, boilin; 60
And though the gentry first are stechin,
Yet ev'n the ha'-folk fill their pechan
Wi' sauce, ragouts, an' sic like trashtrie,
That 's little short o' downright wastrie.
Our whipper-in, wee blastit wonner, 65
Poor worthless elf, it eats a dinner
Better than ony tenant man
His Honour has in a' the lan';
And what poor cot-folk pit their painch in,
I own it 's past my comprehension. 70

LUATH.

Trowth, Cæsar, whiles they 're fash't eneugh;
A cotter howkin in a sheugh,
Wi' dirty stanes biggin a dyke,
Barin a quarry, and sic like;
Himsel, a wife, he thus sustains, 75
A smytrie o' wee duddie weans,
And nought but his han'-daurg to keep
Them right and tight in thack and rape.

And when they meet wi' sair disasters,
Like loss o' health or want o' masters, 80
Ye maist wad think, a wee touch langer,
And they maun starve o' cauld and hunger;

But how it comes, I never kenn'd yet,
They 're maistly wonderfu' contented :
And buirdly chiels an' clever hizzies   85
Are bred in sic a way as this is.

CÆSAR.

But then to see how you 're neglecket,
How huff'd and cuff'd and disrespecket !
Lord, man, our gentry care as little
For delvers, ditchers and sic cattle ;   90
They gang as saucy by poor folk,
As I wad by a stinkin brock.

I 've noticed, on our Laird's court-day, —
And mony a time my heart 's been wae, —
Poor tenant bodies, scant o' cash,   95
How they maun thole a factor's snash :
He 'll stamp and threaten, curse, and swear
He 'll apprehend them, poind their gear ;
While they maun stan' wi' aspect humble,
And hear it a', and fear and tremble !   100

I see how folk live that hae riches ;
But surely poor folk maun be wretches !

LUATH.

They 're no sae wretched 's ane wad think :
Tho' constantly on poortith's brink,
They 're sae accustom'd wi' the sight,   105
The view o 't gies them little fright.

Then chance and fortune are sae guided,
They 're aye in less or mair provided ;
And tho' fatigu'd wi' close employment,
A blink o' rest 's a sweet enjoyment.   110

The dearest comfort o' their lives,
Their grushie weans and faithfu' wives;
The prattling things are just their pride,
That sweetens a' their fireside.

And whiles twalpennie worth o' nappy   115
Can mak the bodies unco happy:
They lay aside their private cares,
To mind the Kirk and State affairs;
They 'll talk o' patronage an' priests,
Wi' kindling fury i' their breasts,   120
Or tell what new taxation 's comin,
An' ferlie at the folk in Lon'on.

As bleak-fac'd Hallowmas returns,
They get the jovial, ranting kirns,
When rural life o' ev'ry station   125
Unite in common recreation;
Love blinks, Wit slaps, an' social Mirth
Forgets there 's Care upo' the earth.

That merry day the year begins,
They bar the door on frosty winds;   130
The nappy reeks wi' mantlin ream
An' sheds a heart-inspirin steam;
The luntin pipe an' sneeshin mill
Are handed round wi' right guid will;
The cantie auld folks crackin crouse,   135
The young anes rantin thro' the house, —
My heart has been sae fain to see them,
That I for joy hae barket wi' them.

Still it 's owre true that ye hae said,
Sic game is now owre aften play'd.   140

There 's monie a creditable stock
O' decent, honest, fawsont folk
Are riven out baith root an' branch,
Some rascal's pridefu' greed to quench,
Wha thinks to knit himsel the faster   145
In favour wi' some gentle master,
Wha, aiblins thrang a-parliamentin,
For Britain's guid his saul indentin —

CÆSAR.

Haith, lad, ye little ken about it;
For Britain's guid! guid faith! I doubt it.   150
Say rather, gaun as Premiers lead him,
An' saying *ay* or *no*'s they bid him:
At operas an' plays parading,
Mortgaging, gambling, masquerading:
Or maybe, in a frolic daft,   155
To Hague or Calais taks a waft,
To mak a tour an' tak a whirl
To learn *bon ton* an' see the worl'.

There, at Vienna or Versailles,
He rives his father's auld entails;   160
Or by Madrid he taks the rout
To thrum guitars an' fecht wi' nowt;
Or down Italian vista startles,
Whore-hunting amang groves o' myrtles;
Then bouses drumly German-water,   165
To mak himsel look fair and fatter,
And clear the consequential sorrows,
Love-gifts of Carnival signoras.

For Britain's guid! — for her destruction!
Wi' dissipation, feud, and faction.   170

LUATH.

Hech man! dear sirs! is that the gate
They waste sae mony a braw estate?
Are we sae foughten and harass'd
For gear to gang that gate at last?

O would they stay aback frae courts　　175
An' please themsels wi' countra sports,
It wad for ev'ry ane be better,
The Laird, the Tenant, an' the Cotter!
For thae frank, rantin, ramblin billies,
Fient haet o' them 's ill-hearted fellows:　　180
Except for breakin o' their timmer,
Or speakin lightly o' their limmer,
Or shootin o' a hare or moor-cock,
The ne'er-a-bit they 're ill to poor folk.

But will ye tell me, Master Cæsar,　　185
Sure great folk's life 's a life o' pleasure?
Nae cauld nor hunger e'er can steer them,
The vera thought o 't need na fear them.

CÆSAR.

Lord, man, were ye but whyles whare I am,
The gentles ye wad ne'er envy 'em.　　190

It 's true, they need na starve or sweat
Thro' winter's cauld or simmer's heat;
They 've nae sair wark to craze their banes,
An' fill auld age wi' grips an' granes:
But human bodies are sic fools,　　195
For a' their colleges and schools,
That when nae real ills perplex them,
They mak enow themselves to vex them;

An' ay the less they hae to sturt them,
In like proportion less will hurt them.   200

A country fellow at the pleugh,
His acres till'd, he 's right eneugh ;
A country girl at her wheel,
Her dizzens done, she 's unco weel :
But gentlemen, an' ladies warst,   205
Wi' ev'n down want o' wark are curst.
They loiter, loungin, lank, an' lazy ;
Tho' deil-haet ails them, yet uneasy :
Their days insipid, dull, an' tasteless ;
Their nights unquiet, lang, an' restless ;   210

An' ev'n their sports, their balls an' races,
Their galloping thro' public places, —
There 's sic parade, sic pomp, an' art,
The joy can scarcely reach the heart.

The men cast out in party-matches,   215
Then sowther a' in deep debauches.
Ae night, they 're mad wi' drink an' whoring,
Niest day their life is past enduring.

The Ladies arm-in-arm in clusters,
As great an' gracious a' as sisters ;   220
But hear their absent thoughts o' ither,
They 're a' run deils an' jads thegither.
Whiles, o'er the wee bit cup and platie,
They sip the scandal-potion pretty ;
Or lee-lang nights, wi' crabbet leuks,   225
Pore owre the devil's pictur'd beuks ;
Stake on a chance a farmer's stackyard,
And cheat like ony unhang'd blackguard.

There 's some exceptions, man an' woman ;
But this is gentry's life in common.   230

By this, the sun was out o' sight,
And darker gloamin brought the night:
The bum-clock humm'd wi' lazy drone;
The kye stood rowtin i' the loan ;
When up they gat, and shook their lugs,   235
Rejoic'd they were na *men*, but *dogs;*
And each took aff his several way,
Resolv'd to meet some ither day.

EPISTLE TO JAMES SMITH.

Friendship, mysterious cement of the soul!
Sweet'ner of Life, and solder of Society!
I owe thee much.   BLAIR.

DEAR Smith, the slee-ëst pawkie thief
That e'er attempted stealth or rief,
Ye surely hae some warlock brief
            Owre human hearts ;
For n'er a bosom yet was prief   5
            Against your arts.

For me, I swear by sun an' moon
An' ev'ry star that blinks aboon,
Ye 've cost me twenty pair o' shoon
            Just gaun to see you ;   10
An' ev'ry ither pair that 's doon,
            Mair taen I 'm wi' you.

That auld capricious carlin, Nature,
To mak' amends for scrimpet stature,

She 's turn'd you aff, a human creature 15
   On her first plan ;
And, in her freaks, on every feature
   She 's wrote the Man.

Just now I 've taen the fit o' rhyme,
My barmie noddle 's workin prime, 20
My fancy yerket up sublime
   Wi' hasty summon :
Hae ye a leisure moment's time
   To hear what 's comin ?

Some rhyme a neibour's name to lash ; 25
Some rhyme (vain thought !) for needfu' cash ;
Some rhyme to court the country clash,
   And raise a din ;
For me, an aim I never fash —
   I rhyme for fun. 30

The star that rules my luckless lot
Has fated me the russet coat,
And damn'd my fortune to the groat ;
   But, in requit,
Has blest me wi' a random shot 35
   O' countra wit.

This while my notion 's taen a sklent
To try my fate in guid black prent ;
But still the mair I 'm that way bent,
   Something cries " Hoolie ! 40
I red you, honest man, tak tent !
   Ye 'll shaw your folly.

" There 's ither poets much your betters,
Far seen in Greek, deep men o' letters,

Hae thought they had insur'd their debtors   45
  A' future ages;
Now moths deform in shapeless tatters
  Their unknown pages."

Then farewell hopes o' laurel boughs
To garland my poetic brows!   50
Henceforth I 'll rove where busy ploughs
  Are whistlin thrang,
And teach the lanely heights and howes
  My rustic sang.

I 'll wander on, wi' tentless heed   55
How never-halting moments speed,
Till Fate shall snap the brittle thread;
  Then, all unknown,
I 'll lay me with th' inglorious dead,
  Forgot and gone!   60

But why o' death begin a tale?
Just now we 're living, sound and hale!
Then top and maintop crowd the sail,
  Heave Care owre side!
And large before Enjoyment's gale   65
  Let 's tak the tide.

This life, sae far 's I understand,
Is a' enchanted fairy land,
Where Pleasure is the magic wand,
  That, wielded right,   70
Maks hours like minutes, hand in hand,
  Dance by fu' light.

The magic wand then let us wield;
For, ance that five and forty 's speel'd,

See, crazy, weary, joyless Eild,   75
          Wi' wrinkl'd face,
Comes hostin, hirplin owre the field,
          Wi' creepin pace.

When ance life's day draws near the gloamin,
Then fareweel vacant careless roamin,   80
An' fareweel cheerfu' tankards foamin
          An' social noise ;
An' fareweel dear deluding Woman,
          The joy of joys !

O Life ! how pleasant in thy morning   85
Young Fancy's rays the hills adorning !
Cold-pausing Caution's lesson scorning,
          We frisk away,
Like schoolboys, at th' expected warning
          To joy and play.   90

We wander there, we wander here,
We eye the rose upon the brier,
Unmindful that the thorn is near
          Among the leaves :
And tho' the puny wound appear,   95
          Short while it grieves.

Some lucky find a flow'ry spot,
For which they never toil'd nor swat ;
They drink the sweet and eat the fat,
          But care or pain ;   100
And haply eye the barren hut
          With high disdain.

With steady aim some Fortune chase ;
Keen Hope does ev'ry sinew brace ;

Thro' fair, thro' foul, they urge the race,   105
   And seize the prey;
Then cannie in some cozie place
   They close the day.

And others, like your humble servan',
Poor wights! nae rules nor roads observin,   110
To right or left eternal swervin,
   They zig-zag on;
Till curst with age, obscure an' starvin,
   They aften groan.

Alas! what bitter toil an' straining —   115
But truce wi' peevish, poor complaining!
Is Fortune's fickle Luna waning?
   E'en let her gang!
Beneath what light she has remaining
   Let's sing our sang.   120

My pen I here fling to the door,
An' kneel, ye Pow'rs, an' warm implore,
" Tho' I should wander Terra o'er
   In all her climes,
Grant me but this, I ask no more,   125
   Aye rowth o' rhymes.

" Gie dreeping roasts to countra lairds,
Till icicles hing frae their beards;
Gie fine braw claes to fine life-guards
   An' maids of honour!   130
An' yill an' whisky gie to cairds,
   Until they scunner.

" A title, Dempster merits it;
A garter gie to Willie Pitt;

Gie wealth to some be-ledger'd cit, 135
   In cent. per cent.:
But give me real, sterling wit,
   And I 'm content.

" While ye are pleas'd to keep me hale,
I 'll sit down o'er my scanty meal, 140
Be 't water-brose or muslin-kail,
   Wi' cheerfu' face,
As lang 's the Muses dinna fail
   To say the grace."

An anxious ee I never throws 145
Behint my lug or by my nose;
I jouk beneath Misfortune's blows
   As weel 's I may;
Sworn foe to sorrow, care, an' prose,
   I rhyme away. 150

O ye douce folk, that live by rule,
Grave, tideless-blooded, calm an' cool, —
Compar'd wi' you, O fool! fool! fool!
   How much unlike!
Your hearts are just a standing pool, 155
   Your lives a dyke!

Nae harebrained, sentimental traces
In your unlettered, nameless faces!
In *arioso* trills and graces
   Ye never stray, 160
But *gravissimo*, solemn basses
   Ye hum away.

Ye are sae grave, nae doubt ye 're wise;
Nae ferly tho' ye do despise

The hairum-scairum, ram-stam boys, 165
      The rattlin squad:
I see you upward cast your eyes —
      Ye ken the road!

Whilst I — but I shall haud me there:
Wi' you I 'll scarce gang ony where — 170
Then, Jamie, I shall say nae mair,
      But quat my sang,
Content with you to mak a pair,
      Whare'er I gang.

THE VISION.

DUAN FIRST.

THE sun had clos'd the winter day,
The curlers quat their roaring play,
And hunger'd maukin taen her way
      To kail-yards green,
While faithless snaws ilk step betray 5
      Whare she has ben.

The thresher's weary flingin-tree
The lee-lang day had tired me;
And when the day had clos'd his ee
      Far i' the west, 10
Ben i' the spence right pensivelie
      I gaed to rest.

There lanely by the ingle cheek
I sat and ey'd the spewin reek,

That fill'd wi' hoast-provokin smeek   15
      The auld clay biggin,
And heard the restless rattons squeak
      About the riggin.

All in this mottie, misty clime
I backward mus'd on wasted time,   20
How I had spent my youthfu' prime,
      An' done nae thing
But stringin blethers up in rhyme
      For fools to sing.

Had I to guid advice but harket,   25
I might by this hae led a market,
Or strutted in a bank, and clarket
      My cash account:
While here, half-mad, half-fed, half-sarket,
      Is a' th' amount.   30

I started, mutt'ring "Blockhead! coof!"
And heav'd on high my wauket loof,
To swear by a' yon starry roof,
      Or some rash aith,
That I henceforth would be rhyme-proof   35
      Till my last breath, —

When click! the string the sneck did draw:
An' jee! the door gaed to the wa',
And by my ingle-lowe I saw,
      Now bleezin bright,   40
A tight, outlandish hizzie braw
      Come full in sight.

Ye need na doubt, I held my whisht;
The infant aith, half-form'd, was crusht;

I glowr'd as eerie 's I 'd been dusht   45
       In some wild glen ;
When sweet, like modest Worth, she blusht,
       And steppet ben.

Green, slender, leaf-clad holly-boughs
Were twisted gracefu' round her brows ;   50
I took her for some Scottish Muse
       By that same token,
And come to stop those reckless vows,
       Would soon been broken.

A " hair-brain'd sentimental trace "   55
Was strongly market in her face ;
A wildly-witty, rustic grace
       Shone full upon her ;
Her eye, ev'n turn'd on empty space,
       Beam'd keen with honour.   60

Down flow'd her robe, a tartan sheen,
Till half a leg was scrimply seen ;
An' such a leg ! my bonie Jean
       Could only peer it ;
Sae straught, sae taper, light an' clean   65
       Nane else came near it.

Her mantle large, of greenish hue,
My gazing wonder chiefly drew ;
Deep lights and shades, bold-mingling, threw
       A lustre grand,   70
And seem'd to my astonish'd view
       A well known land.

Here, rivers in the sea were lost ;
There, mountains to the skies were toss't ;

Here, tumbling billows mark'd the coast   75
   With surging foam;
There, distant shone Art's lofty boast,
   The lordly dome.

Here, Doon pour'd down his far-fetch'd floods;
There, well-fed Irwine stately thuds;   80
Auld hermit Ayr staw thro' his woods,
   On to the shore;
And many a lesser torrent scuds,
   With seeming roar.

Low in a sandy valley spread,   85
An ancient borough rear'd her head;
Still, as in Scottish story read,
   She boasts a race
To ev'ry nobler virtue bred
   And polish'd grace.   90

By stately tow'r or palace fair,
Or ruins pendent in the air,
Bold stems of heroes, here and there,
   I could discern;
Some seem'd to muse, some seem'd to dare,   95
   With feature stern.

 . . . .

DUAN SECOND.

With musing-deep, astonish'd stare,
I view'd the heav'nly-seeming fair;
A whisp'ring throb did witness bear   135
   Of kindred sweet,
When with an elder sister's air
   She did me greet.

" All hail ! my own inspirèd bard !
In me thy native Muse regard !   140
Nor longer mourn thy fate is hard,
            Thus poorly low !
I come to give thee such reward
            As we bestow.

" Know, the great Genius of this land   145
Has many a light aërial band,
Who, all beneath his high command,
            Harmoniously,
As arts or arms they understand,
            Their labours ply.   150

" They Scotia's race among them share :
Some fire the soldier on to dare ;
Some rouse the patriot up to bare
            Corruption's heart :
Some teach the bard, a darling care,   155
            The tuneful art.

    .   .   .   :   .   .   .   .

" Of these am I — Coila my name ;
And this district as mine I claim,   200
Where once the Campbells, chiefs of fame,
            Held ruling pow'r :
I mark'd thy embryo tuneful flame,
            Thy natal hour.

" With future hope I oft would gaze   205
Fond, on thy little early ways,
Thy rudely caroll'd chiming phrase
            In uncouth rhymes,
Fir'd at the simple, artless lays
            Of other times.   210

"I saw thee seek the sounding shore,
Delighted with the dashing roar;
Or when the North his fleecy store
      Drove through the sky,
I saw grim Nature's visage hoar   215
      Struck thy young eye.

"Or when the deep green-mantled earth
Warm cherish'd ev'ry flow'ret's birth,
And joy and music pouring forth
      In ev'ry grove,   220
I saw thee eye the general mirth
      With boundless love.

"When ripen'd fields and azure skies
Called forth the reaper's rustling noise,
I saw thee leave their evening joys,   225
      And lonely stalk
To vent thy bosom's swelling rise
      In pensive walk.

"When youthful love, warm-blushing, strong,
Keen-shivering, shot thy nerves along,   230
Those accents, grateful to thy tongue,
      Th' adorèd name,
I taught thee how to pour in song
      To soothe thy flame.

"I saw thy pulse's maddening play   235
Wild send thee Pleasure's devious way,
Misled by Fancy's meteor ray,
      By Passion driven;
But yet the light that led astray
      Was light from Heaven.   240

" I taught thy manners-painting strains,
The loves, the ways of simple swains,
Till now, o'er all my wide domains
      Thy fame extends ;
And some, the pride of Coila's plains,   245
      Become thy friends.

" Thou canst not learn, nor can I show,
To paint with Thomson's landscape glow;
Or wake the bosom-melting throe
      With Shenstone's art;   250
Or pour with Gray the moving flow
      Warm on the heart.

" Yet, all beneath the unrivall'd rose,
The lowly daisy sweetly blows ;
Tho' large the forest's monarch throws   255
      His army shade,
Yet green the juicy hawthorn grows
      Adown the glade.

" Then never murmur nor repine ;
Strive in thy humble sphere to shine;   260
And, trust me, not Potosi's mine
      Nor king's regard
Can give a bliss o'ermatching thine,
      A rustic bard.

" To give my counsels all in one —   265
Thy tuneful flame still careful fan :
Preserve the dignity of Man
      With soul erect;
And trust the Universal Plan
      Will all protect.   270

" And wear thou *this*," she solemn said,
And bound the holly round my head :
The polish'd leaves and berries red
      Did rustling play ;
And, like a passing thought, she fled   275
      In light away.

ADDRESS TO THE UNCO GUID, OR THE RIGIDLY RIGHTEOUS.

My son, these maxims make a rule,
  And lump them aye thegither ;
The RIGID RIGHTEOUS is a fool,
  The RIGID WISE anither :
The cleanest corn that e'er was dight,
  May hae some pyles o' caff in ;
So ne'er a fellow-creature slight
  For random fits o' daffin. — SOLOMON, Eccles. vii, 16.

O YE wha are sae guid yoursel,
  Sae pious and sae holy,
Ye 've nought to do but mark and tell
  Your neibour's fauts and folly !
Whase life is like a weel-gaun mill,   5
  Supply'd wi' store o' water,
The heapet happer 's ebbing still,
  And still the clap plays clatter, —

Hear me, ye venerable core,
  As counsel for poor mortals,   10
That frequent pass douce Wisdom's door
  For glaiket Folly's portals ;
I for their thoughtless, careless sakes
  Would here propone defences —

Their donsie tricks, their black mistakes,   15
  Their failings and mischances.

Ye see your state wi' theirs compar'd,
  And shudder at the niffer;
But cast a moment's fair regard,
  What maks the mighty differ?   20
Discount what scant occasion gave,
  That purity ye pride in,
And (what's aft mair than a' the lave)
  Your better art o' hidin.

Think, when your castigated pulse   25
  . Gies now and then a wallop,
'What ragings must his veins convulse
  That still eternal gallop :
Wi' wind and tide fair i' your tail,
  Right on ye scud your sea-way ;   30
But in the teeth o' baith to sail,
  It maks an unco leeway.

See Social Life and Glee sit down,
  All joyous and unthinking,
Till, quite transmugrify'd, they're grown   35
  Debauchery and Drinking :
O would they stay to calculate
  Th' eternal consequences ;
Or — your more dreaded hell to state —
  Damnation of expenses !   40

Ye high, exalted, virtuous Dames,
  Tied up in godly laces,
Before you gie poor Frailty names,
  Suppose a change o' cases :

A dear lov'd lad, convenience snug,   45
  A treacherous inclination —
But, let me whisper i' your lug,
  Ye 're aiblins nae temptation.

Then gently scan your brother man,
  Still gentler sister woman;   50
Tho' they may gang a kennin wrang,
  To step aside is human :
One point must still be greatly dark,
  The moving *Why* they do it;
And just as lamely can ye mark,   55
  How far perhaps they rue it.

Who made the heart, 't is He alone
  Decidedly can try us,
He knows each chord, its various tone,
  Each spring, its various bias :   60
Then at the balance, let 's be mute,
  We never can adjust it ;
What 's *done* we partly can compute,
  But know not what 's *resisted.*

———

SONG COMPOSED IN SPRING.

AGAIN rejoicing Nature sees
  Her robe assume its vernal hues;
Her leafy locks wave in the breeze,
  All freshly steep'd in morning dews.

CHORUS. — An' maun I still on Menie doat,   5
          An' bear the scorn that 's in her ee ?

For it 's jet, jet black, an' it 's like a hawk,
  An' it winna let a body be.

In vain to me the cowslips blaw,
  In vain to me the vi'lets spring ;   10
In vain to me in glen or shaw
  The mavis an' the lintwhite sing.

The merry ploughboy cheers his team,
  Wi' joy the tentie seedsman stalks ;
But life to me 's a weary dream,   15
  A dream of ane that never wauks.

The wanton coot the water skims,
  Amang the reeds the ducklings cry,
The stately swan majestic swims,
  An' every thing is blest but I.   20

The sheep-herd steeks his fauldin-slap,
  An' owre the moorland whistles shill ;
Wi' wild, unequal, wand'ring step
  I meet him on the dewy hill.

An' when the lark 'tween light an' dark   25
  Blythe waukens by the daisy's side,
An' mounts an' sings on flitterin wings,
  A woe-worn ghaist I hameward glide.

Come winter, with thine angry howl,
  An' raging bend the naked tree :   30
Thy gloom will soothe my cheerless soul,
  When nature all is sad like me !

TO A MOUNTAIN DAISY,

ON TURNING ONE DOWN WITH THE PLOUGH, IN APRIL, 1786.

WEE, modest, crimson-tippèd flow'r,
Thou 's met me in an evil hour;
For I maun crush amang the stoure
   Thy slender stem:
To spare thee now is past my pow'r,   5
   Thou bonie gem.

Alas! it 's no thy neibor sweet,
The bonie lark, companion meet,
Bending thee 'mang the dewy weet
   Wi' spreckl'd breast,   10
When upward-springing, blythe, to greet
   The purpling east.

Cauld blew the bitter-biting north
Upon thy early, humble birth;
Yet cheerfully thou glinted forth   15
   Amid the storm,
Scarce rear'd above the parent-earth
   Thy tender form.

The flaunting flowers our gardens yield
High shelt'ring woods an' wa's maun shield: 20
But thou, beneath the random bield
   O' clod or stane,
Adorns the histie stibble-field
   Unseen, alane.

There, in thy scanty mantle clad,   25
Thy snawie bosom sun-ward spread,

Thou lifts thy unassuming head
                    In humble guise ;
But now the share uptears thy bed,
                    And low thou lies!   30

Such is the fate of artless maid,
Sweet flow'ret of the rural shade!
By love's simplicity betray'd
                    And guileless trust ;
Till she, like thee, all soil'd, is laid   35
                    Low i' the dust.

Such is the fate of simple bard,
On life's rough ocean luckless starr'd!
Unskilful he to note the card
                    Of prudent lore,   40
Till billows rage and gales blow hard,
                    And whelm him o'er !

Such fate to suffering Worth is giv'n,
Who long with wants and woes has striv'n,
By human pride or cunning driv'n   45
                    To mis'ry's brink ;
Till, wrench'd of ev'ry stay but Heav'n,
                    He ruin'd sink !

Ev'n thou who mourn'st the Daisy's fate,
That fate is thine — no distant date ;   50
Stern Ruin's ploughshare drives elate,
                    Full on thy bloom,
Till crush'd beneath the furrow's weight
                    Shall be thy doom.

. TO MARY.

Will ye go to the Indies, my Mary,
  And leave auld Scotia's shore?
Will ye go to the Indies, my Mary,
  Across the Atlantic's roar?

O sweet grows the lime and the orange   5
  And the apple on the pine;
But a' the charms o' the Indies
  Can never equal thine.

I hae sworn by the Heavens to my Mary,
  I hae sworn by the Heavens to be true;   10
And sae may the Heavens forget me,
  When I forget my vow!

O plight me your faith, my Mary,
  And plight me your lily-white hand;
O plight me your faith, my Mary,   15
  Before I leave Scotia's strand.

We hae plighted our troth, my Mary,
  In mutual affection to join,
And curst be the cause that shall part us!
  The hour, and the moment o' time!   20

EPISTLE TO A YOUNG FRIEND.

I lang hae thought, my youthfu' friend,
  A something to have sent you,
Tho' it should serve nae ither end
  Than just a kind memento;

But how the subject-theme may gang,   5
   Let time and chance determine;
Perhaps it may turn out a sang,
   Perhaps turn out a sermon.

Ye 'll try the world soon, my lad,
   And, Andrew dear, believe me,   10
Ye 'll find mankind an unco squad,
   And muckle they may grieve ye :
For care and trouble set your thought,
   Ev'n when your end 's attainèd ;
And a' your views may come to nought,   15
   Where ev'ry nerve is strainèd.

I 'll no say, men are villains a' ;
   The real, harden'd wicked,
Wha hae nae check but human law,
   Are to a few restricked :   20
But och ! mankind are unco weak,
   An' little to be trusted ;
If self the wavering balance shake,
   It 's rarely right adjusted !

Yet they wha fa' in fortune's strife,   25
   Their fate we should na censure ;
For still th' important end of life
   They equally may answer :
A man may hae an honest heart,
   Tho' poortith hourly stare him ;   30
A man may tak a neibor's part,
   Yet hae nae cash to spare him.

Ay free, aff han', your story tell,
   When wi' a bosom crony ;
But still keep something to yoursel   35
   Ye scarcely tell to ony.

Conceal yoursel as weel 's ye can
  Frae critical dissection ;
But keek through ev'ry other man
  Wi' sharpen'd, sly inspection.   40

The sacred lowe o' weel-plac'd love,
  Luxuriantly indulge it ;
But never tempt th' illicit rove,
  Tho' naething should divulge it ;
I waive the quantum o' the sin,   45
  The hazard o' concealing ;
But och ! it hardens a' within,
  And petrifies the feeling !

To catch Dame Fortune's golden smile,
  Assiduous wait upon her ;   50
And gather gear by ev'ry wile
  That 's justify'd by honour ;
Not for to hide it in a hedge,
  Nor for a train attendant ;
But for the glorious privilege   55
  Of being independent.

The fear o' hell 's a hangman's whip
  To haud the wretch in order ;
But where ye feel your honour grip,
  Let that aye be your border :   60
Its slightest touches, instant pause —
  . Debar a' side pretences ;
And resolutely keep its laws,
  Uncaring consequences.

The great Creator to revere   65
  Must sure become the creature ;
But still the preaching cant forbear,
  An' ev'n the rigid feature :

Yet ne'er with wits profane to range,
    Be complaisance extended ;   70
An atheist laugh 's a poor exchange
    For Deity offended !

When ranting round in Pleasure's ring,
    Religion may be blinded ;
Or if she gie a random sting,   75
    It may be little minded;
But when on life we 're tempest driv'n,
    A conscience but a canker,
A correspondence fix'd wi' Heav'n
    Is sure a noble anchor !   80

Adieu ! dear, amiable youth,
    Your heart can ne'er be wanting !
May prudence, fortitude, an' truth
    Erect your brow undaunting !
In ploughman phrase, "God send you speed "   85
    Still daily to grow wiser :
An' may you better reck the rede
    Than ever did th' adviser !

A DREAM.

Thoughts, words, and deeds, the statute blames with reason,
But surely *dreams* were ne'er indicted treason.

Guid-Mornin to your Majesty !
    May heaven augment your blisses
On ev'ry new birth-day ye see,
    A humble Bardie wishes.
My Bardship here at your Levee,   5

On sic a day as this is,
Is sure an uncouth sight to see
    Amang thae birth-day dresses
            Sae fine this day.

I see ye 're complimented thrang   10
    By mony a lord an' lady;
"God save the King!" 's a cuckoo sang
    That 's unco easy said aye:
The Poets, too, a venal gang,
    Wi' rhymes weel-turn'd and ready,   15
Wad gar you trow ye ne'er do wrang,
    But aye unerring steady,
            On sic a day.

For me! before a Monarch's face,
    Ev'n there I winna flatter;   20
For neither pension, post, nor place,
    Am I your humble debtor:
So — nae reflection on your Grace,
    Your Kingship to bespatter —
There 's monie waur been o' the race,   25
    And aiblins ane been better
            Than you this day.

'T is very true, my sov'reign King,
    My skill may weel be doubted;
But facts are chiels that winna ding   30
    And downa be disputed:
Your royal nest beneath your wing
    Is e'en right reft an' clouted,
And now the third part of the string,
    And less, will gang about it   35
            Than did ae day.

Far be 't frae me that I aspire
  To blame your legislation,
Or say ye wisdom want, or fire,
  To rule this mighty nation!
But faith! I muckle doubt, my sire,
  Ye 've trusted ministration
To chaps wha in a barn or byre
  Wad better fill'd their station
          Than courts yon day.

And now ye 've gien auld Britain peace
  Her broken shins to plaister,
Your sair taxation does her fleece,
  Till she has scarce a tester:
For me, thank God, my life 's a lease,
  Nae bargain wearin faster,
Or faith! I fear that wi' the geese
  I shortly boost to pasture
          I' the craft some day.

I 'm no mistrusting Willie Pitt,
  When taxes he enlarges,
(An' Will 's a true guid fallow's get,
  A name not envy spairges),
That he intends to pay your debt
  An' lessen a' your charges;
But Gude sake! let nae saving-fit
  Abridge your bonie barges
          An' boats this day.

Adieu, my Liege! may Freedom geck
  Beneath your high protection;
An' may ye rax Corruption's neck,
  And gie her for dissection!

But since I 'm here, I 'll no neglect,
  In loyal true affection,
To pay your Queen with due respect   70
  My fealty an' subjection
      This great birth-day.

Hail, Majesty most Excellent!
  While nobles strive to please ye,
Will ye accept a compliment   75
  A simple poet gies ye?
Thae bonie bairntime Heav'n has lent,
  Still higher may they heeze ye
In bliss, till fate some day is sent,
  For ever to release ye   80
      Frae care that day.

For you, young Potentate o' Wales,
  I tell your Highness fairly,
Down Pleasure's stream wi' swelling sails
  I 'm tauld ye 're driving rarely;   85
But some day ye may gnaw your nails
  An' curse your folly sairly,
That e'er ye brak Diana's pales
  Or rattl'd dice wi' Charlie
      By night or day.   90

Yet aft a ragged cowte's been known
  To mak a noble aiver;
Sae, ye may doucely fill a throne,
  For a' their clish-ma-claver:
There, him at Agincourt wha shone,   95
  Few better were or braver;
And yet wi' funny, queer Sir John
  He was an unco shaver
      For monie a day.

For you, right rev'rend Osnaburg, 100
 Nane sets the lawn-sleeve sweeter,
Altho' a ribban at your lug
 Wad been a dress completer:
As ye disown yon paughty dog
 That bears the Keys of Peter, 105
Then, swith! an' get a wife to hug,
 Or, trowth! ye'll stain the Mitre
   Some luckless day.

Young, royal Tarry Breeks, I learn,
 Ye've lately come athwart her— 110
A glorious galley, stem and stern,
 Weel rigg'd for Venus' barter;
But first hang out, that she'll discern
 Your hymeneal charter,
Then heave aboard your grapple-airn, 115
 An', large upon her quarter,
   Come full that day.

Ye, lastly, bonie blossoms a',
 Ye royal lasses dainty,
Heav'n mak you guid as weel as braw, 120
 An' gie you lads a-plenty!
But sneer na British boys awa,
 For kings are unco scant aye;
An' German gentles are but sma',
 They're better just than want aye 125
   On onie day.

God bless you a'! consider now
 Ye're unco muckle dautet;
But ere the course o' life be through
 It may be bitter sautet: 130

An' I hae seen their coggie fou,
   That yet hae tarrow't at it;
But or the day was done, I trow,
   The laggen they hae clautet
         Fu' clean that day.   135

ON A SCOTCH BARD,

GONE TO THE WEST INDIES.

A' YE wha live by sowps o' drink,
A' ye wha live by crambo-clink,
A' ye wha live and never think,
         Come, mourn wi' me!
Our billie 's gien us a' a jink,   5
         And owre the sea.

Lament him a' ye rantin core,
Wha dearly like a random-splore,
Nae mair he 'll join the merry roar
         In social key;   10
For now he 's taen anither shore,
         And owre the sea!

The bonie lasses weel may wiss him,
And in their dear petitions place him:
The widows, wives, and a' may bless him,   15
         Wi' tearfu' e'e;
For weel I wat they 'll sairly miss him
         That 's owre the sea!

O Fortune, they hae room to grumble!
Hadst thou taen aff some drowsy bummle,   20

Wha can do nought but fyke and fumble,
      'T wad been nae plea;
But he was gleg as ony wumble,
      That 's owre the sea!

Auld cantie Kyle may weepers wear,
And stain them wi' the saut, saut tear;
'T will mak' her poor auld heart, I fear,
      In flinders flee;
He was her laureat mony a year,
      That 's owre the sea!

He saw Misfortune's cauld nor-west
Lang mustering up a bitter blast;
A jillet brak his heart at last,
      Ill may she be!
So, took a berth afore the mast,
      An' owre the sea.

To tremble under Fortune's cummock
On scarce a bellyfu' o' drummock,
Wi' his proud, independent stomach
      Could ill agree;
So, row't his hurdies in a hammock
      An' owre the sea.

He ne'er was gien to great misguidin,
Yet coin his pouches wad na bide in;
Wi' him it ne'er was under hidin,
      He dealt it free:
The Muse was a' that he took pride in
      That 's owre the sea.

Jamaica bodies, use him weel
An' hap him in a cozie biel;

Ye 'll find him ay' a dainty chiel
      And fou o' glee ;
He wad na wrang'd the vera deil,
      That 's owre the sea.

Fareweel, my rhyme-composing billie !   55
Your native soil was right ill-willie ;
But may ye flourish like a lily
      Now bonilie !
I 'll toast ye in my hindmost gillie,
      Tho' owre the sea !   60

A BARD'S EPITAPH.

Is there a whim-inspirèd fool,
Owre fast for thought, owre hot for rule,
Owre blate to seek, owre proud to snool ? —
      Let him draw near ;
And owre this grassy heap sing dool,   5
      And drap a tear.

Is there a bard of rustic song,
Who, noteless, steals the crowds among,
That weekly this area throng ? —
      Oh, pass not by !   10
But with a frater-feeling strong
      Here heave a sigh.

Is there a man whose judgment clear
Can others teach the course to steer,
Yet runs himself life's mad career   15
      Wild as the wave ? —
Here pause — and thro' the starting tear
      Survey this grave.

The poor inhabitant below
Was quick to learn and wise to know,　　　　20
And keenly felt the friendly glow
　　　　And softer flame;
But thoughtless follies laid him low,
　　　　And stain'd his name!

Reader, attend! whether thy soul　　　　25
Soars fancy's flights beyond the pole,
Or darkling grubs this earthly hole
　　　　In low pursuit;
Know, prudent, cautious self-control
　　　　Is wisdom's root.　　　　30

THE BRIGS OF AYR.

'T was when the stacks get on their winter-hap,
And thack and rape secure the toil-won crap;
Potato-bings are snuggèd up frae skaith
Of coming Winter's biting, frosty breath;
The bees, rejoicing o'er their summer toils,　　　　5
Unnumber'd buds' and flow'rs' delicious spoils,
Seal'd up with frugal care in massive waxen piles,
Are doom'd by man, that tyrant o'er the weak,
The death o' devils, smoor'd wi' brimstone reek:
The thundering guns are heard on ev'ry side,　　　　10
The wounded coveys, reeling, scatter wide;
The feather'd field-mates, bound by Nature's tie,
Sires, mothers, children, in one carnage lie:
(What warm, poetic heart but inly bleeds,
And execrates man's savage, ruthless deeds!)　　　　15
Nae mair the flow'r in field or meadow springs;
Nae mair the grove with airy concert rings,

Except, perhaps, the robin's whistlin glee,
Proud o' the height o' some bit half-lang tree:
The hoary morns precede the sunny days, 20
Mild, calm, serene, wide spreads the noon-tide blaze,
While thick the gossamer waves wanton in the rays.

———

'T was in that season, when a simple Bard,
Unknown and poor — simplicity's reward! —
Ae night within the ancient brugh of Ayr, 25
By whim inspired, or haply prest wi' care,
He left his bed, and took his wayward route,
And down by Simpson's wheel'd the left about
(Whether impell'd by all-directing Fate,
To witness what I after shall narrate; 30
Or, whether, rapt in meditation high,
He wandered out he knew not where nor why),
The drowsy Dungeon-clock had number'd two,
And Wallace Tower had sworn the fact was true:
The tide-swoln Firth, with sullen sounding roar, 35
Through the still night dash'd hoarse along the shore:
All else was hush'd as Nature's closèd ee;
The silent moon shone high o'er tow'r and tree;
The chilly frost, beneath the silver beam,
Crept, gently crusting, o'er the glittering stream. 40
When, lo! on either hand the list'ning Bard,
The clanging sugh of whistling wings is heard;
Two dusky forms dart thro' the midnight air,
Swift as the gos drives on the wheeling hare;
Ane on th' Auld Brig his airy shape uprears, 45
The ither flutters o'er the rising piers:
Our warlock Rhymer instantly descry'd
The Sprites that owre the Brigs of Ayr preside.

('That bards are second-sighted is nae joke,
And ken the lingo of the sp'ritual folk ; 50
Fays, Spunkies, Kelpies, a', they can explain them,
And ev'n the vera deils they brawly ken them.)
Auld Brig appear'd of ancient Pictish race,
The very wrinkles Gothic in his face :
He seem'd as he wi' Time had wrastl'd lang, 55
Yet, teughly doure, he bade an unco bang.
New Brig was buskit in a braw new coat,
That he at Lon'on frae ane Adams got ;
In 's hand five taper staves as smooth 's a bead,
Wi' virls and whirlygigums at the head. 60
The Goth was stalking round with anxious search,
Spying the time-worn flaws in ev'ry arch ;
It chanc'd his new-come neibor took his ee.
And e'en a vex'd and angry heart had he !
Wi' thieveless sneer to see his modish mien, 65
He down the water gies him this guid-een : —

AULD BRIG.

I doubt na, frien', ye 'll think ye 're nae sheep-shank,
Ance ye were streekit owre frae bank to bank !
But gin ye be a brig as auld as me —
Tho', faith ! that date, I doubt, ye 'll never see — 70
There 'll be, if that day come, I 'll wad a boddle,
Some fewer whigmeleeries in your noddle.

NEW BRIG.

Auld Vandal ! ye but show your little mense,
Just much about it wi' your scanty sense ;
Will your poor, narrow foot-path of a street, 75
Where twa wheel-barrows tremble when they meet,
Your ruin'd, formless bulk o' stane and lime,
Compare wi' bonie brigs o' modern time ?

There 's men o' taste wou'd tak the Ducat-stream,
Tho' they should cast the vera sark and swim,   80
Ere they would grate their feelings wi' the view
O' sic an ugly, Gothic hulk as you.

AULD BRIG.

Conceited gowk! puff'd up wi' windy pride!
This mony a year I 've stood the flood an' tide;
And tho' wi' crazy eild I 'm sair forfairn,   85
I 'll be a Brig, when ye 're a shapeless cairn!
As yet ye little ken about the matter,
But twa-three winters will inform ye better.
When heavy, dark, continued, a'-day rains,
Wi' deepening deluges o'erflow the plains;   90
When from the hills where springs the brawling Coil,
Or stately Lugar's mossy fountains boil,
Or where the Greenock winds his moorland course,
Or haunted Garpal draws his feeble source,
Arous'd by blust'ring winds an' spotting thowes,   95
In mony a torrent down his snaw-broo rowes;
While crashing ice, borne on the roaring spate,
Sweeps dams, an' mills, an' brigs, a' to the gate;
And from Glenbuck down to the Ratton-Key
Auld Ayr is just one lengthen'd, tumbling sea;   100
Then down ye 'll hurl (deil nor ye never rise!)
And dash the gumlie jaups up to the pouring skies!
A lesson sadly teaching to your cost
That Architecture's noble art is lost!

NEW BRIG.

Fine Architecture, trowth, I needs must say 't o 't;   105
The Lord be thankit that we 've tint the gate o 't!
Gaunt, ghastly, ghaist-alluring edifices,
Hanging with threat'ning jut, like precipices;

O'er-arching, mouldy, gloom-inspiring coves,
Supporting roofs fantastic, stony groves :   110
Windows and doors in nameless sculptures drest,
With order, symmetry, or taste unblest ;
Forms like some bedlam statuary's dream,
The craz'd creations of misguided whim ;
Forms might be worshipp'd on the bended knee,   115
And still the second dread command be free, —
Their likeness is not found on earth, in air, or sea !
Mansions that would disgrace the building taste
Of any mason reptile, bird, or beast ;
Fit only for a doitet monkish race,   120
Or frosty maids forsworn the dear embrace,
Or cuifs of latter times wha held the notion
That sullen gloom was sterling true devotion :
Fancies that our good Brugh denies protection !
And soon may they expire, unblest with resurrection !   125

AULD BRIG.

O ye, my dear-remember'd ancient yealings,
Were ye but here to share my wounded feelings !
Ye worthy Proveses, an' mony a Bailie,
Wha in the paths o' righteousness did toil aye ;
Ye dainty Deacons and ye douce Conveners,   130
To whom our moderns are but causey-cleaners ;
Ye godly Councils wha hae blest this town ;
Ye godly brethren o' the sacred gown,
Wha meekly gae your hurdies to the smiters ;
And — what would now be strange — ye godly Writers ; 135
A' ye douce folk I 've borne aboon the broo,
Were ye but here, what would ye say or do !
How would your spirits groan in deep vexation,
To see each melancholy alteration ;
And agonizing, curse the time and place   140

When ye begat the base, degen'rate race!
Nae langer rev'rend men, their country's glory,
In plain braid Scots hold forth a plain braid story;
Nae langer thrifty citizens and douce,
Meet owre a pint, or in the council-house;   145
But staumrel, corky-headed, graceless gentry,
The herryment and ruin of the country;
Men three-parts made by tailors and by barbers.
Wha waste your weel-hain'd gear on damn'd new brigs
      and harbours.

NEW BRIG.

Now haud you there! for faith ye've said enow,   150
And muckle mair than ye can mak to through.
As for your Priesthood I shall say but little, —
Corbies and *Clergy* are a shot right kittle:
But, under favour o' your langer beard,
Abuse o' Magistrates might weel be spar'd: 155
To liken them to your auld-warld squad,
I must needs say, comparisons are odd.
In Ayr, wag-wits nae mair can hae a handle
To mouth 'a Citizen,' a term o' scandal;
Nae mair the Council waddles down the street,   160
In all the pomp of ignorant conceit;
Men wha grew wise priggin owre hops an' raisins,
Or gather'd lib'ral views in bonds and seisins:
If haply Knowledge, on a random tramp,
Had shor'd them wi' a glimmer of his lamp,   165
And would to Common-sense for once betray'd them,
Plain, dull Stupidity stept kindly in to aid them.

What farther clishmaclaver might been said,
What bloody wars, if Sprites had blood to shed,
No man can tell; but all before their sight   170
A fairy train appear'd in order bright:

Adown the glittering stream they featly danc'd;
Bright to the moon their various dresses glanc'd:
They footed o'er the wat'ry glass so neat,
The infant ice scarce bent beneath their feet: 175
While arts of Minstrelsy among them rung,
And soul-ennobling Bards heroic ditties sung.

  O had M'Lauchlan, thairm-inspiring sage,
Been there to hear this heavenly band engage,
When thro' his dear strathspeys they bore with Highland
      rage ;   180
Or when they struck old Scotia's melting airs,
The lover's raptur'd joys or bleeding cares ;
How would his Highland lug been nobler fir'd,
And ev'n his matchless hand with finer touch inspir'd !
No guess could tell what instrument appear'd,   185
But all the soul of Music's self was heard ;
Harmonious concert rung in every part,
While simple melody pour'd moving on the heart.

  The Genius of the Stream in front appears,
A venerable Chief, advanc'd in years ;   190
His hoary head with water-lilies crown'd,
His manly leg with garter tangle bound.
Next came the loveliest pair in all the ring,
Sweet Female Beauty hand in hand with Spring ;
Then, crown'd with flow'ry hay, came Rural Joy,   195
And Summer, with his fervid-beaming eye ;
All-cheering Plenty, with her flowing horn,
Led yellow Autumn wreath'd with nodding corn ;
Then Winter's time-bleach'd locks did hoary show
By Hospitality with cloudless brow ;   200
Next follow'd Courage with his martial stride,
From where the Feal wild-woody coverts hide ;

Benevolence with mild, benignant air,
A female form, came from the tow'rs of Stair:
Learning and Worth in equal measures trode   205
From simple Catrine, their long-lov'd abode:
Last, white-rob'd Peace, crown'd with a hazel wreath,
To rustic Agriculture did bequeath
The broken, iron instruments of death:
At sight of whom our Sprites forgat their kindling wrath. 210

LINES ON AN INTERVIEW WITH LORD DAER.

THIS wot ye all whom it concerns,
I, Rhymer Robin, alias Burns,
      October twenty-third,
A ne'er-to-be-forgotten day,
Sae far I sprachled up the brae,   5
      I dinner'd wi' a Lord.

I 've been at drucken writers' feasts,
Nay, been bitch-fou 'mang godly priests —
      Wi' rev'rence be it spoken! —
I 've even join'd the honour'd jorum,   10
When mighty Squireships of the Quorum
      Their hydra drouth did sloken.

But wi' a Lord — stand out' my shin !
A Lord — a Peer — an Earl's son !
      Up higher yet, my bonnet!   15
And sic a Lord — lang Scotch ells twa,
Our Peerage he o'erlooks them a',
      As I look owre my sonnet.

But O for Hogarth's magic pow'r
To show Sir Bardie's willyart glow'r,   20

And how he star'd and stammer'd,
When goavan, as if led wi' branks,
An' stumpin on his ploughman shanks,
He in the parlor hammer'd!

I sidling shelter'd in a nook,   25
An' at his Lordship steal't a look,
Like some portentous omen
Except good sense and social glee,
An' (what surprised me) modesty,
I markèd nought uncommon.   30

I watch'd the symptoms o' the great,
The gentle pride, the lordly state,
The arrogant assuming:
The fient a pride, nae pride had he,
Nor sauce nor state that I could see,   35
Mair than an honest ploughman.

Then from his lordship I shall learn,
Henceforth to meet with unconcern
One rank as weel 's another:
Nae honest worthy man need care   40
To meet with noble youthful Daer,
For he but meets a brother.

A WINTER NIGHT.

Poor naked wretches, wheresoe'er you are,
That bide the pelting of this pitiless storm!
How shall your houseless heads and unfed sides,
Your loop'd and window'd raggedness, defend you
From seasons such as these?   SHAKESPEARE.

WHEN biting Boreas, fell and doure,
Sharp shivers thro' the leafless bow'r;

When Phœbus gies a short lived glow'r
    Far south the lift,
Dim-darkening thro' the flaky show'r   5
    Or whirling drift ;

Ae night the storm the steeples rocked,
Poor Labour sweet in sleep was locked,
While burns, wi' snawy wreaths up-choked,
    Wild-eddying swirl,   10
Or, thro' the mining outlet bocked,
    Down headlong hurl :

Listening the doors and winnocks rattle,
I thought me on the ourie cattle,
Or silly sheep, wha bide this brattle   15
    O' winter war,
An' through the drift, deep-lairing, sprattle
    Beneath a scaur.

Ilk happin bird — wee, helpless thing !—
That in the merry months o' spring   20
Delighted me to hear thee sing,
    What comes o' thee?
Whare wilt thou cow'r thy chittering wing
    An' close thy ee?

Ev'n you on murd'ring errands toil'd,   25
Lone from your savage homes exil'd, —
The blood-stain'd roost an' sheep-cot spoil'd
    My heart forgets,
While pitiless the tempest wild
    Sore on you beats.   30

Now Phœbe, in her midnight reign,
Dark muffled, viewed the dreary plain ;

Still crowding thoughts, a pensive train,
  Rose in my soul,
When on my ear this plaintive strain,   35
  Slow-solemn, stole : —

"Blow, blow ye winds with heavier gust!
And freeze, thou bitter-biting frost!
Descend, ye chilly, smothering snows!
Not all your rage, as now united, shows   40
 More hard unkindness, unrelenting,
 Vengeful malice, unrepenting,
Than heaven-illumined man on brother man bestows!

"See stern Oppression's iron grip,
 Or mad Ambition's gory hand,   45
Sending, like blood-hounds from the slip,
 Woe, Want, and Murder o'er a land!
Ev'n in the peaceful rural vale,
Truth, weeping, tells the mournful tale:
How pamper'd Luxury, Flatt'ry by her side,   50
 The parasite empoisoning her ear,
 With all the servile wretches in the rear,
Looks o'er proud Property, extended wide;
 And eyes the simple, rustic hind,
 Whose toil upholds the glitt'ring show—   55
 A creature of another kind,
 Some coarser substance, unrefin'd —
Plac'd for her lordly use, thus far, thus vile, below!

"Where, where is Love's fond, tender throe,
With lordly Honour's lofty brow,   60
 The pow'rs you proudly own?
Is there, beneath Love's noble name,
Can harbour, dark, the selfish aim,
 To bless himself alone?

Mark Maiden-Innocence a prey
  To love-pretending snares :
This boasted Honour turns away,
Shunning soft Pity's rising sway,
Regardless of the tears and unavailing pray'rs!
  Perhaps this hour, in Misery's squalid nest,   70
  She strains your infant to her joyless breast,
And with a mother's fears shrinks at the rocking blast!

"O ye! who, sunk in beds of down,
  Feel not a want but what yourselves create,
  Think, for a moment, on his wretched fate,   75
Whom friends and fortune quite disown !
  Ill-satisfy'd keen nature's clam'rous call,
Stretched on his straw, he lays himself to sleep ;
While through the ragged roof and chinky wall,
  Chill, o'er his slumbers piles the drifty heap!   80
  Think on the dungeon's grim confine,
  Where Guilt and poor Misfortune pine !
  Guilt, erring man, relenting view !
  But shall thy legal rage pursue
  The wretch, already crushèd low   85
  By cruel Fortune's undeservèd blow?
Affliction's sons are brothers in distress ;
A brother to relieve, how exquisite the bliss!"

I heard nae mair, for chanticleer
  Shook off the pouthery snaw,   90
And hailed the morning with a cheer —
  A cottage-rousing craw.

But deep this truth impress'd my mind —
  Through all His works abroad,
The heart benevolent and kind   95
  The most resembles GOD.

TO A HAGGIS.

Fair fa' your honest, sonsie face,
Great chieftain o' the puddin-race!
Aboon them a' ye tak your place,
       Painch, tripe, or thairm:
Weel are ye wordy o' a grace   5
       As lang 's my arm.

The groaning trencher there ye fill,
Your hurdies like a distant hill,
Your pin wad help to mend a mill
       In time o' need,   10
While thro' your pores the dews distil
       Like amber bead.

His knife see rustic Labour dight,
And cut you up wi' ready slight,
Trenching your gushing entrails bright   15
       Like ony ditch;
And then, O what a glorious sight,
       Warm-reekin, rich!

Then horn for horn they stretch an' strive:
Deil tak' the hindmost! on they drive,   20
Till a' their weel-swall'd kytes belyve
       Are bent like drums;
Then auld guidman, maist like to rive,
       " Bethanket! " hums.

Is there that owre his French ragout,   25
Or *olio* that wad staw a sow,
Or *fricassee* wad mak her spew
       Wi' perfect scunner,
Looks down wi' sneering, scornfu' view
       On sic a dinner?   30

Poor devil ! see him owre his trash,
As feckless as a wither'd rash,
His spindle shank a guid whip-lash,
      His nieve a nit ;
Thro' bloody flood or field to dash   35
      Oh how unfit !

But mark the rustic, haggis-fed,
The trembling earth resounds his tread,
Clap in his walie nieve a blade,
      He 'll mak it whissle ;   40
And legs an' arms an' heads will sned
      Like taps o' thrissle.

Ye pow'rs wha mak mankind your care,
And dish them out their bill o' fare,
Auld Scotland wants nae skinking ware   45
      That jaups in luggies ;
But, if ye wish her gratefu' pray'r,
      Gie her a haggis !

ANSWER TO VERSES ADDRESSED TO THE POET

BY THE GUIDWIFE OF WAUCHOPE-HOUSE.

GUIDWIFE,

I mind it weel in early date,
When I was beardless, young, and blate,
   An' first could thresh the barn,
Or haud a yokin at the pleugh,
An' tho' forfoughten sair eneugh,   5
   Yet unco proud to learn :
When first amang the yellow corn

A man I reckon'd was,
And wi' the lave ilk merry morn
  Could rank my rig and lass,   10
    Still shearing, and clearing
      The tither stookèd raw,
  Wi' claivers an' haivers
      Wearing the day awa:

Ev'n then a wish (I mind its power),   15
A wish that to my latest hour
  Shall strongly heave my breast;
That I for poor auld Scotland's sake
Some usefu' plan or beuk could make,
  Or sing a sang at least.   20
The rough burr-thistle, spreading wide
  Amang the bearded bear,
I turn'd the weeder-clips aside
  An' spar'd the symbol dear:
    No nation, no station   25
      My envy e'er could raise;
  A Scot still, but blot still,
      I knew nae higher praise.

But still the elements o' sang
In formless jumble, right an' wrang,   30
  Wild floated in my brain;
Till on that hairst I said before,
My partner in the merry core
  She rous'd the forming strain:
I see her yet, the sonsie quean,   35
  That lighted up my jingle,
Her witching smile, her pauky een,
  That gart my heart-strings tingle;
    I firèd, inspirèd,

At ev'ry kindling keek,   40
But bashing, and dashing,
I fearèd aye to speak.

Health to the sex! ilk guid chiel says,
Wi' merry dance on winter days,
  An' we to share in common: 45
The gust o' joy, the balm of woe,
The saul o' life, the heav'n below,
  Is rapture-giving Woman.
Ye surly sumphs, who hate the name,
  Be mindfu' o' your mither: 50
She, honest woman, may think shame
  That ye 're connected with her.
    Ye 're wae men, ye 're nae men,
      That slight the lovely dears;
    To shame ye, disclaim ye,   55
      Ilk honest birkie swears.

For you, no bred to barn and byre,
Wha sweetly tune the Scottish lyre,
  Thanks to you for your line:
The marl'd plaid ye kindly spare   60
By me should gratefully be ware;
  'T wad please me to the nine.
I 'd be more vauntie o' my hap,
  Douce hingin owre my curple,
Than ony ermine ever lap,   65
  Or proud imperial purple.
    Farewell then, lang hale then
      An' plenty be your fa':
    May losses and crosses
      Ne'er at your hallan ca'!   70

THE BIRKS OF ABERFELDY.

Now simmer blinks on flowery braes,
And o'er the crystal streamlet plays;
Come, let us spend the lightsome days
  In the birks of Aberfeldy.

CHORUS. — Bonie lassie, will ye go,   5
    Will ye go, will ye go,
    Bonie lassie, will ye go
      To the birks of Aberfeldy?

The little birdies blythely sing,
While o'er their heads the hazels hing,   10
Or lightly flit on wanton wing
  In the birks of Aberfeldy.

The braes ascend, like lofty wa's,
The foaming stream deep-roaring fa's,
O'erhung wi' fragrant spreading shaws,   15
  The birks of Aberfeldy.

The hoary cliffs are crown'd wi' flowers,
White o'er the linns the burnie pours,
An', rising, weets wi' misty showers
  The birks of Aberfeldy.   20

Let Fortune's gifts at random flee,
They ne'er shall draw a wish frae me,
Supremely blest wi' love and thee
  In the birks of Aberfeldy.

THE HUMBLE PETITION OF BRUAR WATER

TO THE NOBLE DUKE OF ATHOLE.

My lord, I know your noble ear
  Woe ne'er assails in vain ;
Embolden'd thus, I beg you 'll hear
  Your humble slave complain,
How saucy Phœbus' scorching beams,   5
  In flaming summer-pride,
Dry-withering, waste my foamy streams
  And drink my crystal tide.

The lightly-jumpin glowrin trouts,
  That thro' my waters play,   10
If, in their random, wanton spouts,
  They near the margin stray ;
If, hapless chance ! they linger lang,
  I 'm scorching up so shallow,
They 're left the whitening stanes amang,   15
  In gasping death to wallow.

Last day I grat wi' spite and teen,
  As poet Burns came by,
That to a bard I should be seen
  Wi' half my channel dry :   20
A panegyric rhyme, I ween,
  Even as I was he shor'd me ;
But had I in my glory been,
  He, kneeling, wad ador'd me.

Here, foaming down the skelvy rocks,   25
  In twisting strength I rin ;
There, high my boiling torrent smokes,
  Wild-roaring o'er a linn :

Enjoying large each spring and well
    As Nature gave them me,   30
I am, altho' I say 't mysel,
    Worth gaun a mile to see.

Would then my noble master please
    To grant my highest wishes,
He 'll shade my banks wi tow'ring trees   35
    And bonie spreading bushes.
Delighted doubly then, my lord,
    You 'll wander on my banks,
And listen monie a grateful bird
    Return you tuneful thanks.   40

The sober laverock, warbling wild,
    Shall to the skies aspire ;
The gowdspink, Music's gayest child,
    Shall sweetly join the choir ;
The blackbird strong, the lintwhite clear,   45
    The mavis mild and mellow,
The robin, pensive Autumn cheer
    In all her locks of yellow.

This, too, a covert shall ensure
    To shield them from the storm ;   50
And coward maukin sleep secure,
    Low in her grassy form :
Here shall the shepherd make his seat
    To weave his crown of flow'rs,
Or find a sheltering safe retreat   55
    From prone-descending show'rs.

And here, by sweet endearing stealth,
    Shall meet the loving pair,

Despising worlds with all their wealth
  As empty, idle care :   60
The flow'rs shall vie in all their charms
  The hour of heav'n to grace,
And birks extend their fragrant arms
  To screen the dear embrace.

Here haply too at vernal dawn   65
  Some musing bard may stray,
And eye the smoking, dewy lawn
  And misty mountain gray ;
Or by the reaper's nightly beam,
  Mild-chequering thro' the trees,   70
Rave to my darkly dashing stream,
  Hoarse-swelling on the breeze.

Let lofty firs and ashes cool
  My lowly banks o'erspread,
And view, deep-bending in the pool,   75
  Their shadows' wat'ry bed :
Let fragrant birks in woodbines drest
  My craggy cliffs adorn ;
And, for the little songster's nest,
  The close embow'ring thorn.   80

So may old Scotia's darling hope,
  Your little angel band,
Spring, like their fathers, up to prop
  Their honour'd native land !
So may thro' Albion's farthest ken   85
  To social-flowing glasses
The grace be — " Athole's honest men
  And Athole's bonie lasses ! "

THE BANKS OF THE DEVON.

How pleasànt the banks of the clear winding Devon,
  With green spreading bushes, and flowers blooming fair!
But the boniest flower on the banks of the Devon
  Was once a sweet bud on the braes of the Ayr.
Mild be the sun on this sweet blushing flower,   5
  In the gay rosy morn as it bathes in the dew ;
And gentle the fall of the soft vernal shower,
  That steals on the evening each leaf to renew.

O spare the dear blossom, ye orient breezes,
  With chill hoary wing as ye usher the dawn!   10
And far be thou distant, thou reptile that seizes
  The verdure and pride of the garden and lawn !
Let Bourbon exult in his gay gilded lilies,
  And England, triumphant, display her proud rose ;
A fairer than either adorns the green valleys,   15
  Where Devon, sweet Devon, meandering flows.

BLYTHE, BLYTHE AND MERRY WAS SHE.

  By Ochtertyre grows the aik,
    On Yarrow banks the birken shaw;
  But Phemie was a bonier lass
    Than braes o' Yarrow ever saw.

CHORUS. — Blythe, blythe and merry was she,   5
    Blythe was she but and ben :
    Blythe by the banks of Earn,
    An' blythe in Glenturit glen.

Her looks were like a flow'r in May,
   Her smile was like a simmer morn :   10
She trippèd by the banks o' Earn,
   As light 's a bird upon a thorn.

Her bonie face it was as meek
   As ony lamb upon a lea ;
The evening sun was ne'er sae sweet   15
   As was the blink o' Phemie's ee.

The Highland hills I 've wander'd wide,
   An' o'er the Lawlands I hae been ;
But Phemie was the blythest lass
   That ever trod the dewy green.   20

M'PHERSON'S FAREWELL.

FAREWELL, ye dungeons dark and strong,
   The wretch's destinie !
M'Pherson's time will not be long
   On yonder gallows tree.

CHORUS. — Sae rantinly, sae wantonly,   5
     Sae dauntinly gaed he ;
     He play'd a spring and danc'd it round,
     Below the gallows tree.

O what is death but parting breath ? —
   On monie a bloody plain   10
I 've dar'd his face, and in this place
   I scorn him yet again !

Untie these bands from off my hands
   And bring to me my sword,

And there 's no man in all Scotland,   15
   But I 'll brave him at a word.

I 've liv'd a·life of sturt and strife;
   I die by treacherie :
It burns my heart I must depart
   And not avengèd be.   20

Now farewell light, thou sunshine bright,
   And all beneath the sky!
May coward shame distain his name,
   The wretch that dare not die!

MY HOGGIE.

WHAT will I do gin my Hoggie die?
   My joy, my pride, my Hoggie?
My only beast, I had nae mae,
   And vow but I was vogie !

The lee-lang night we watch'd the fauld,   5
   Me and my faithfu' doggie;
We heard nocht but the roaring linn
   Amang the braes sae scroggie;

But the howlet cry'd frae the castle wa',
   The blitter frae the boggie,   10
The tod reply'd upon the hill,
   I trembled for my Hoggie.

When day did daw and cocks did craw,
   The morning it was foggie;
An unco tyke lap o'er the dyke,   15
   And maist has kill'd my Hoggie !

EPISTLE TO HUGH PARKER.

In this strange land, this uncouth clime,
A land unknown to prose or rhyme;
Where words ne'er crost the Muse's heckles
Nor limpit in poetic shackles;
A land that Prose did never view it,   5
Except when drunk he stacher't through it;
Here, ambush'd by the chimla cheek,
Hid in an atmosphere of reek,
I hear a wheel thrum i' the neuk, —
I hear it, for in vain I leuk.   10
The red peat gleams, a fiery kernel,
Enhuskèd by a fog infernal:
Here, for my wonted rhyming raptures,
I sit and count my sins by chapters;
For life and spunk like ither Christians,   15
I 'm dwindled down to mere existence,
Wi' nae converse but Gallowa' bodies,
Wi' nae ken'd face but Jenny Geddes.
Jenny, my Pegasean pride!
Dowie she saunters down Nithside,   20
And ay a westlin leuk she throws,
While tears hap o'er her auld brown nose!
Was it for this wi' canny care
Thou bure the Bard through many a shire?
At howes or hillocks never stumbled,   25
And late or early never grumbled? —
O had I power like inclination,
I 'd heeze thee up a constellation,
To canter with the Sagitarre,
Or loup the ecliptic like a bar;   30
Or turn the pole like any arrow;
Or, when auld Phœbus bids good-morrow,

Down the zodiac urge the race,
And cast dirt on his godship's face ;
For I could lay my bread and kail   35
He 'd ne'er cast saut upo' thy tail. —
Wi' a' this care and a' this grief,
And sma', sma' prospect of relief,
And nought but peat reek i' my head,
How can I write what ye can read ? —   40
Tarbolton, twenty-fourth o' June,
Ye 'll find me in a better tune ;
But till we meet and weet our whistle,
Tak this excuse for nae epistle.

OF A' THE AIRTS THE WIND CAN BLAW.

Of a' the airts the wind can blaw
  I dearly like the west,
For there the bonie lassie lives,
  The lassie I lo'e best :
There 's wild woods grow an' rivers row,   5
  An' mony a hill between ;
But day and night my fancy's flight
  Is ever wi' my Jean.

I see her in the dewy flow'rs,
  I see her sweet an' fair :   10
I hear her in the tunefu' birds,
  I hear her charm the air :
There 's not a bonie flow'r that springs
  By fountain, shaw, or green ;
There 's not a bonie bird that sings,   15
  But minds me o' my Jean.

AULD LANG SYNE.

SHOULD auld acquaintance be forgot,
　　And never brought to min'?
Should auld acquaintance be forgot,
　　And auld lang syne?

CHORUS. — For auld lang syne, my dear,　　　　5
　　　　For auld lang syne,
　　　　We 'll tak a cup o' kindness yet
　　　　For auld lang syne.

And surely ye 'll be your pint-stowp,
　　And surely I 'll be mine !　　　　10
And we 'll tak a cup o' kindness yet
　　For auld lang syne.

We twa hae run about the braes,
　　And pu'd the gowans fine ;
But we 've wander'd mony a weary fit　　　　15
　　Sin' auld lang syne.

We twa hae paidl't i' the burn,
　　From mornin' sun till dine ;
But seas between us braid hae roar'd
　　Sin' auld lang syne.　　　　20

And there 's a hand, my trusty fier,
　　And gie 's a hand o' thine ;
And we 'll tak a right guid-willie waught
　　For auld lang syne.

GO FETCH TO ME A PINT O' WINE.

Go fetch to me a pint o' wine,
   And fill it in a silver tassie ;
That I may drink, before I go,
   A service to my bonie lassie :
The boat rocks at the pier o' Leith,   5
   Fu' loud the wind blaws frae the Ferry;
The ship rides by the Berwick-law,
   And I maun leave my bonie Mary.

The trumpets sound, the banners fly,
   The glittering spears are rankèd ready,   10
The shouts o' war are heard afar,
   The battle closes deep and bloody ;
It 's not the roar o' sea or shore
   Would mak me langer wish to tarry;
Nor shouts o' war that 's heard afar —   15
   It 's leaving thee, my bonie Mary !

JOHN ANDERSON MY JO.

John Anderson my jo, John,
   When we were first acquent,
Your locks were like the raven,
   Your bonie brow was brent;
But now your brow is beld, John,   5
   Your locks are like the snaw ;
But blessings on your frosty pow,
   John Anderson my jo.

John Anderson my jo, John,
   We clamb the hill thegither;   10

And monie a canty day, John,
   We 've had wi' ane anither:
Now we maun totter down, John,
   And hand in hand we 'll go,
And sleep thegither at the foot,   15
   John Anderson my jo.

TAM GLEN.

My heart is a-breaking, dear tittie,
   Some counsel unto me come len';
To anger them a' is a pity,
   But what will I do wi' Tam Glen?

I 'm thinking, wi' sic a braw fellow,   5
   In poortith I might mak a fen':
What care I in riches to wallow,
   If I maunna marry Tam Glen?

There 's Lowrie, the laird o' Dumeller,
   "Guid-day to you,"—brute! he comes ben: 10
He brags and he blaws o' his siller,
   But when will he dance like Tam Glen?

My minnie does constantly deave me,
   And bids me beware o' young men;
They flatter, she says, to deceive me;   15
   But wha can think sae o' Tam Glen?

My daddie says, gin I 'll forsake him,
   He 'll gie me guid hunder marks ten:
But, if it 's ordain'd I maun take him,
   O wha will I get but Tam Glen?   20

Yestreen at the valentines' dealing,
    My heart to my mou gied a sten:
For thrice I drew ane without failing,
    And thrice it was written, " Tam Glen " !

The last Halloween I was waukin   25
    My droukit sark-sleeve, as ye ken:
His likeness cam up the house staukin,
    And the very gray breeks o' Tam Glen!

Come counsel, dear tittie, don't tarry;
    I 'll gie ye my bonie black hen,   30
Gif ye will advise me to marry
    The lad I lo'e dearly, Tam Glen.

WILLIE BREWED A PECK O' MAUT.

O, WILLIE brew'd a peck o' maut,
    An' Rob an' Allan cam to see:
Three blyther hearts that lee-lang night
    Ye wad na found in Christendie.

CHORUS. — We are na fou, we 're nae that fou,   5
        But just a drappie in our ee;
      The cock may craw, the day may daw,
        And aye we 'll taste the barley bree.

Here are we met, three merry boys,
    Three merry boys, I trow, are we;   10
An' mony a night we 've merry been,
    And mony mae we hope to be !

It is the moon, I ken her horn,
    That 's blinkin in the lift sae hie;

She shines sae bright to wile us hame,　　　15
　　But, by my sooth, she 'll wait a wee !

Wha first shall rise to gang awa',
　　A cuckold, coward loon is he !
Wha first beside his chair shall fa',
　　He is the king amang us three !　　　20

TO MARY IN HEAVEN.

Thou ling'ring star, with less'ning ray,
　　That lov'st to greet the early morn,
Again thou usher'st in the day
　　My Mary from my soul was torn.
O Mary! dear departed shade !　　　5
　　Where is thy place of blissful rest?
See'st thou thy lover lowly laid?
　　Hear'st thou the groans that rend his breast?

That sacred hour can I forget,
　　Can I forget the hallowed grove,　　　10
Where by the winding Ayr we met
　　To live one day of parting love?
Eternity will not efface
　　Those records dear of transports past,
Thy image at our last embrace —　　　15
　　Ah ! little thought we 't was our last !

Ayr, gurgling, kiss'd his pebbl'd shore,
　　O'erhung with wild woods, thick'ning green ;
The fragrant birch and hawthorn hoar
　　Twin'd amorous round the raptur'd scene :　　　20

The flow'rs sprang wanton to be prest,
  The birds sang love on every spray,
Till too, too soon the glowing west
  Proclaim'd the speed of winged day.

Still o'er these scenes my mem'ry wakes,   25
  And fondly broods with miser care !
Time but th' impression stronger makes,
  As streams their channels deeper wear.
My Mary, dear departed shade !
  Where is thy place of blissful rest?   30
See'st thou thy lover lowly laid?
  Hear'st thou the groans that rend his breast?

TO DR. BLACKLOCK.

Wow, but your letter made me vauntie !
And are ye hale, and weel, and cantie ?
I ken'd it still, your wee bit jauntie
      Wad bring you to :
Lord send ye aye as weel 's I want ye,   5
      And then ye 'll do.

The Ill-Thief blaw the Heron south !
And never drink be near his drouth !
He tauld mysel' by word o' mouth,
      He 'd tak' my letter ;   10
I lippen'd to the chield in trouth,
      And bade nae better.

But aiblins honest Master Heron,
Had at the time some dainty fair one,

To ware his theologic care on,   15
   And holy study;
And, tir'd o' sauls to waste his lear on,
   E'en tried the body.

But what d' ye think, my trusty fier?
I 'm turn'd a gauger — Peace be here!   20
Parnassian queens, I fear, I fear
   Ye 'll now disdain me!
And then my fifty pounds a year
   Will little gain me.

Ye glaiket, gleesome, dainty damies, '   25
Wha, by Castalia's wimplin streamies,
Lowp, sing, and lave your pretty limbies,
   Ye ken, ye ken,
That strang necessity supreme is
   'Mang sons o' men.   30

I hae a wife and twa wee laddies, —
They maun hae brose and brats o' duddies;
Ye ken yoursels my heart right proud is,
   I need na vaunt,
But I 'll sned besoms, thraw saugh woodies,   35
   Before they want.

Lord help me thro' this warld o' care!
I 'm weary — sick o 't late and air!
Not but I hae a richer share
   Than monie ithers;   40
But why should ae man better fare,
   And a' men brithers?

Come, firm Resolve, take thou the van,
Thou stalk o' carl-hemp in man!

And let us mind, faint heart ne'er wan 45
    A lady fair:
Wha does the utmost that he can,
    Will whyles do mair.

But to conclude my silly rhyme,
(I 'm scant o' verse, and scant o' time,) 50
To make a happy fire-side clime
    To weans and wife,
That 's the true pathos and sublime
    Of human life.

My compliments to sister Beckie 55
And eke the same to honest Lucky:
I wat she is a daintie chuckie
    As e'er tread clay:
And gratefully, my guid auld cockie,
    I 'm yours for aye. 60

ON CAPTAIN MATTHEW HENDERSON,

A GENTLEMAN WHO HELD THE PATENT FOR HIS HONOURS IMMEDIATELY FROM ALMIGHTY GOD.

But now his radiant course is run,
    For Matthew's course was bright:
His soul was like the glorious sun,
    A matchless, Heavenly light.

O DEATH! thou tyrant fell an' bloody!
The meikle devil wi' a woodie
Haurl thee hame to his black smiddie
    O'er hurcheon hides,
An' like stock-fish come o'er his studdie 5
    Wi' thy auld sides!

He 's gane ! he 's gane ! he 's frae us torn,
The ae best fellow e'er was born !
Thee, Matthew, Nature's sel shall mourn
      By wood an' wild,   10
Where, haply, Pity strays forlorn,
      Frae man exil'd !

Ye hills ! near neibors o' the starns,
That proudly cock your cresting cairns !
Ye cliffs, the haunts of sailing yearns,   15
      Where Echo slumbers!
Come join ye, Nature's sturdiest bairns,
      My wailing numbers!

Mourn, ilka grove the cushat kens !
Ye haz'ly shaws an' briery dens !   20
Ye burnies, wimplin down your glens,
      Wi' toddlin din,
Or foaming strang wi' hasty stens
      Frae linn to linn !

Mourn, little harebells o'er the lea ;   25
Ye stately foxgloves fair to see ;
Ye woodbines, hanging bonilie
      In scented bow'rs ;
Ye roses on your thorny tree,
      The first o' flow'rs.   30

At dawn, when ev'ry grassy blade
Droops with a diamond at his head ;
At ev'n, when beans their fragrance shed
      I' th' rustling gale, —
Ye maukins whiddin thro' the glade,   35
      Come join my wail.

Mourn, ye wee songsters o' the wood;
Ye grouse that crap the heather bud;
Ye curlews calling thro' a clud;
      Ye whistling plover;   40
And mourn, ye whirring paitrick brood;
      He's gane for ever!

Mourn, sooty coots and speckled teals;
Ye fisher herons, watching eels;
Ye duck and drake, wi' airy wheels   45
      'Circling the lake;
Ye bitterns, till the quagmire reels,
      Rair for his sake.

Mourn, clam'ring craiks at close o' day,
'Mang fields o' flow'ring clover gay;   50
And when ye wing your annual way
      Frae our cauld shore,
Tell thae far warlds wha lies in clay,
      Wham we deplore.

Ye houlets, frae your ivy bow'r   55
In some auld tree or eldritch tow'r,
What time the moon, wi' silent glow'r,
      Sets up her horn,
Wail thro' the dreary midnight hour
      Till waukrife morn!   60

O rivers, forests, hills, and plains!
Oft have ye heard my canty strains:
But now, what else for me remains
      But tales of woe?
And frae my een the drappin rains   65
      Maun ever flow.

Mourn, Spring, thou darling of the year !
Ilk cowslip cup shall kep a tear :
Thou, Simmer, while each corny spear
　　　　Shoots up its head,　　　　　　　　　70
Thy gay, green, flow'ry tresses shear,
　　　　For him that 's dead !

Thou, Autumn, wi' thy yellow hair,
In grief thy sallow mantle tear !
Thou, Winter, hurling thro' the air　　　　75
　　　　The roaring blast,
Wide o'er the naked world declare
　　　　The worth we 've lost !

Mourn him, thou Sun, great source of light !
Mourn, Empress of the silent night !　　　　80
And you, ye twinkling starnies bright,
　　　　My Matthew mourn !
For through your orbs he 's taen his flight,
　　　　Ne'er to return.

O Henderson ! the man ! the brother !　　　　85
And art thou gone, and gone for ever ?
And hast thou crost that unknown river,
　　　　Life's dreary bound ?
Like thee, where shall I find another,
　　　　The world around ?　　　　　　　　　90

Go to your sculptur'd tombs, ye Great,
In a' the tinsel trash o' state !
But by thy honest turf I 'll wait,
　　　　Thou man of worth !
And weep the ae best fellow's fate　　　　95
　　　　E'er lay in earth.

TAM O' SHANTER.

A TALE.

Of Brownyis and of Bogillis full is this Buke. — GAWIN DOUGLAS.

WHEN chapman billies leave the street,
And drouthy neibors neibors meet,
As market-days are wearing late,
And folk begin to tak the gate;
While we sit bousin at the nappy,   5
And gettin fou and unco happy,
We think na on the lang Scots miles,
The mosses, waters, slaps, and stiles,
That lie between us and our hame,
Whare sits our sulky, sullen dame,   10
Gathering her brows like gathering storm,
Nursing her wrath to keep it warm.

This truth fand honest Tam o' Shanter,
As he frae Ayr ae night did canter :
(Auld Ayr, wham ne'er a town surpasses,   15
For honest men and bonie lasses.)

O Tam ! had'st thou but been sae wise
As taen thy ain wife Kate's advice !
She tauld thee weel thou was a skellum,
A bletherin, blusterin, drunken blellum ;   20
That frae November till October,
Ae market-day thou was na sober;
That ilka melder wi' the miller,
Thou sat as lang as thou had siller ;
That ev'ry naig was ca'd a shoe on,   25
The smith and thee gat roarin fou on ;
That at the Lord's house, ev'n on Sunday,
Thou drank wi' Kirkton Jean till Monday.

She prophesied, that, late or soon,
Thou would be found deep drown'd in Doon ;   30
Or catch't wi' warlocks in the mirk,
By Alloway's auld haunted kirk.

Ah, gentle dames ! it gars me greet,
To think how mony counsels sweet,
How mony lengthened sage advices,   35
The husband frae the wife despises !

But to our tale : — Ae market night,
Tam had got planted unco right,
Fast by an ingle, bleezin finely,
Wi' reamin swats that drank divinely ;   40
And at his elbow, Souter Johnie,
His ancient, trusty, drouthy crony :
Tam lo'ed him like a vera brither ;
They had been fou for weeks thegither.
The night drave on wi' sangs and clatter ;   45
And ay the ale was growing better :
The landlady and Tam grew gracious
Wi' secret favours, sweet, and precious :
The souter tauld his queerest stories ;
The landlord's laugh was ready chorus :   50
The storm without might rair and rustle,
Tam did na mind the storm a whistle.

Care, mad to see a man sae happy,
E'en drown'd himsel amang the nappy :
As bees flee hame wi' lades o' treasure,   55
The minutes wing'd their way wi' pleasure ;
Kings may be blest, but Tam was glorious,
O'er a' the ills o' life victorious !

But pleasures are like poppies spread,
You seize the flow'r, its bloom is shed ;   60

Or like the snow falls in the river,
A moment white — then melts for ever;
Or like the borealis race,
That flit ere you can point their place;
Or like the rainbow's lovely form   65
Evanishing amid the storm.
Nae man can tether time or tide:
The hour approaches Tam maun ride, —
That hour, o' night's black arch the key-stane,
That dreary hour he mounts his beast in;   70
And sic a night he taks the road in,
As ne'er poor sinner was abroad in.

The wind blew as 't wad blawn its last;
The rattling show'rs rose on the blast;
The speedy gleams the darkness swallow'd;   75
Loud, deep, and lang the thunder bellow'd:
That night, a child might understand,
The Deil had business on his hand.

Weel mounted on his gray mear, Meg,
A better never lifted leg,   80
Tam skelpit on thro' dub and mire,
Despising wind and rain and fire;
Whiles holding fast his guid blue bonnet,
Whiles crooning o'er some auld Scots sonnet,
Whiles glowrin round wi' prudent cares,   85
Lest bogles catch him unawares.
Kirk-Alloway was drawing nigh,
Whare ghaists and houlets nightly cry.

By this time he was cross the ford,
Whare in the snaw the chapman smoor'd;   90
And past the birks and meikle stane,
Whare drucken Charlie brak 's neck-bane;

And thro' the whins, and by the cairn,
Whare hunters fand the murder'd bairn;
And near the thorn, aboon the well,   95
Whare Mungo's mither hang'd hersel.
Before him Doon pours all his floods;
The doubling storm roars thro' the woods;
The lightnings flash from pole to pole,
Near and more near the thunders roll;   100
When, glimmering thro' the groaning trees,
Kirk-Alloway seemed in a bleeze;
Thro' ilka bore the beams were glancing,
And loud resounded mirth and dancing.

Inspiring bold John Barleycorn!   105
What dangers thou can'st make us scorn!
Wi' tippenny we fear nae evil;
Wi' usquebae we'll face the devil!
The swats sae ream'd in Tammie's noddle,
Fair play, he car'd na deils a boddle.   110
But Maggie stood right sair astonish'd,
Till, by the heel and hand admonish'd,
She ventur'd forward on the light;
And, wow! Tam saw an unco sight!

Warlocks and witches in a dance;   115
Nae cotillon brent new frae France,
But hornpipes, jigs, strathspeys, and reels
Put life and mettle in their heels:
A winnock bunker in the east,
There sat Auld Nick in shape o' beast;   120
A towzie tyke, black, grim, and large,
To gie them music was his charge;
He screw'd the pipes and gart them skirl,
Till roof and rafters a' did dirl. —

Coffins stood round like open presses, 125
That shaw'd the dead in their last dresses ;
And by some devilish cantraip sleight
Each in its cauld hand held a light,
By which heroic Tam was able
To note upon the haly table 130
A murderer's banes in gibbet airns ;
Twa span-lang, wee, unchristen'd bairns ;
A thief, new-cutted frae the rape —
Wi' his last gasp his gab did gape ;
Five tomahawks, wi' blude red-rusted ; 135
Five scymitars, wi' murder crusted ;
A garter, which a babe had strangled ;
A knife, a father's throat had mangled,
Whom his ain son o' life bereft —
The gray hairs yet stack to the heft ; 140
Wi' mair o' horrible and awfu',
Which ev'n to name wad be unlawfu'.

As Tammie glowr'd, amaz'd and curious,
The mirth and fun grew fast and furious :
The piper loud and louder blew, 145
The dancers quick and quicker flew ;
They reel'd, they set, they cross'd, they cleekit,
Till ilka carlin swat and reekit
And coost her duddies to the wark
And linket at it in her sark ! 150

Now Tam, O Tam ! had thae been queans,
A' plump and strapping in their teens !
Their sarks, instead o' creeshie flannen,
Been snaw-white seventeen hunder linen ! —
Thir breeks o' mine, my only pair, 155
That ance were plush, o' gude blue hair,

I wad hae gien them aff my hurdies,
For ae blink o' the bonie burdies !

But wither'd beldams, auld and droll,
Rigwoodie hags wad spean a foal,   160
Lowping and flinging on a crummock,
I wonder didna turn thy stomach.

But Tam ken'd what was what fu' brawlie ;
There was ae winsome wench and walie,
That night enlisted in the core   165
(Lang after ken'd on Carrick shore :
For mony a beast to dead she shot,
And perish'd mony a bonie boat,
And shook baith meikle corn and bear,
And kept the country-side in fear);   170
Her cutty sark o' Paisley harn,
That while a lassie she had worn,
In longitude tho' sorely scanty,
It was her best, and she was vauntie.
Ah ! little kent thy reverend grannie,   175
That sark she coft for her wee Nannie,
Wi' twa pund Scots ('t was a' her riches),
Wad ever graced a dance o' witches !

But here my Muse her wing maun cow'r,
Sic flights are far beyond her pow'r ;   180
To sing how Nannie lap and flang,
(A souple jad she was and strang,)
And how Tam stood like ane bewitch'd,
And thought his very een enrich'd ;
Even Satan glowr'd and fidg'd fu' fain,   185
And hotch'd and blew wi' might and main :
Till first ae caper, syne anither,
Tam tint his reason a' thegither,

And roars out, "Weel done, Cutty-sark!"
And in an instant all was dark :   190
And scarcely had he Maggie rallied,
When out the hellish legion sallied.

As bees bizz out wi' angry fyke,
When plundering herds assail their byke ;
As open pussie's mortal foes,   195
When, pop ! she starts before their nose ;
As eager runs the market-crowd,
When " Catch the thief ! " resounds aloud ;
So Maggie runs, the witches follow,
Wi' mony an eldritch skriech and hollo.   200

Ah, Tam ! ah, Tam ! thou 'll get thy fairin !
In hell they 'll roast thee like a herrin !
In vain thy Kate awaits thy comin !
Kate soon will be a woefu' woman !
Now, do thy speedy utmost, Meg,   205
And win the key-stane of the brig :
There at them thou thy tail may toss,
A running stream they dare na cross.
But ere the key-stane she could make,
The fient a tail she had to shake !   210
For Nannie, far before the rest,
Hard upon noble Maggie prest,
And flew at Tam wi' furious ettle ;
But little wist she Maggie's mettle —
Ae spring brought aff her master hale,   215
But left behind her ain gray tail :
The carlin claught her by the rump,
And left poor Maggie scarce a stump.

Now, wha this tale o' truth shall read,
Ilk man and mother's son, take heed,   220

Whene'er to drink you are inclin'd,
Or cutty-sarks run in your mind,
Think, ye may buy the joys owre dear,
Remember Tam o' Shanter's mear.

BONIE DOON.

YE flowery banks o' bonie Doon,
   How can ye blume sae fair?
How can ye chant, ye little birds,
   And I sae fu' o' care?

Thou'll break my heart, thou bonie bird,   5
   That sings upon the bough;
Thou minds me o' the happy days,
   When my fause luve was true.

Thou'll break my heart, thou bonie bird,
   That sings beside thy mate;   10
For sae I sat, and sae I sang,
   And wist na o' my fate.

Aft hae I rov'd by bonie Doon
   To see the wood-bine twine,
And ilka bird sang o' its luve,   15
   And sae did I o' mine.

Wi' lightsome heart I pu'd a rose
   Frae aff its thorny tree;
And my fause luver staw my rose
   But left the thorn wi' me.   20

O FOR ANE–AND–TWENTY, TAM.

CHORUS. — An' O for ane-and-twenty, Tam !
    And hey, sweet ane-and-twenty, Tam !
I 'll learn my kin a rattlin sang,
    An I saw ane-and-twenty, Tam.

THEY snool me sair an' haud me down,   5
    An' gar me look like bluntie, Tam !
But three short years will soon wheel roun',
    An' then comes ane-and-twenty, Tam.

A gleib o' lan', a claut o' gear,
    Was left me by my auntie, Tam :   10
At kith or kin I need na spier,
    An I saw ane-and-twenty, Tam.

They 'll hae me wed a wealthy coof,
    Tho' I mysel hae plenty, Tam ;
But hear'st thou, laddie ! there 's my loof,   15
    I 'm thine at ane-and-twenty, Tam.

FLOW GENTLY, SWEET AFTON.

FLOW gently, sweet Afton, among thy green braes,
Flow gently, I 'll sing thee a song in thy praise ;
My Mary 's asleep by thy murmuring stream,
Flow gently, sweet Afton, disturb not her dream.

Thou stock-dove whose echo resounds thro' the glen,   5
Ye wild whistling blackbirds in yon thorny den,
Thou green-crested lapwing, thy screaming forbear,
I charge you disturb not my slumbering fair.

How lofty, sweet Afton, thy neighbouring hills,
Far mark'd with the courses of clear winding rills; 10
There daily I wander as noon rises high,
My flocks and my Mary's sweet cot in my eye.

How pleasant thy banks and green valleys below,
Where wild in the woodlands the primroses blow;
There oft, as mild Evening weeps over the lea, 15
The sweet-scented birk shades my Mary and me.

Thy crystal stream, Afton, how lovely it glides,
And winds by the cot where my Mary resides;
How wanton thy waters her snowy feet lave,
As gathering sweet flow'rets she stems thy clear wave. 20

Flow gently, sweet Afton, among thy green braes,
Flow gently, sweet river, the theme of my lays;
My Mary 's asleep by thy murmuring stream,
Flow gently, sweet Afton, disturb not her dream.

AE FOND KISS.

Ae fond kiss, and then we sever;
Ae fareweel, and then for ever!
Deep in heart-wrung tears I 'll pledge thee,
Warring sighs and groans I 'll wage thee.
Who shall say that Fortune grieves him, 5
While the star of hope she leaves him?
Me, nae cheerfu' twinkle lights me;
Dark despair around benights me.

I 'll ne'er blame my partial fancy,
Naething could resist my Nancy; 10
But to see her was to love her;
Love but her, and love for ever.

Had we never lov'd sae kindly,
Had we never lov'd sae blindly,
Never met — or never parted —   15
We had ne'er been broken-hearted.

Fare thee weel, thou first and fairest!
Fare thee weel, thou best and dearest!
Thine be ilka joy and treasure,
Peace, enjoyment, love, and pleasure!   20
Ae one fond kiss, and then we sever;
Ae fareweel, alas, for ever!
Deep in heart-wrung tears I 'll pledge thee,
Warring sighs and groans I 'll wage thee !

THE DEUK'S DANG O'ER MY DADDIE.

THE bairns gat out wi' an unco shout:
  "The deuk 's dang o'er my daddie, O !"
"The fient-ma-care," quo' the feirie auld wife,
  "He was but a paidlin body, O !
He paidles out, and he paidles in,   5
  An' he paidles late and early, O;
This seven lang years I hae lien by his side,
  An' he is but a fusionless carlie, O."

"O haud your tongue, my feirie auld wife,
  O haud your tongue now, Nansie, O!   10
I 've seen the day, and sae hae ye,
  Ye wadna been sae donsie, O ;
I 've seen the day ye butter'd my brose
  And cuddl'd me late and early, O ;
But downa-do 's come o'er me now,   15
  And, och, I find it sairly, O !"

THE DEIL'S AWA WI' THE EXCISEMAN.

THE deil cam fiddling through the town,
  An' danced awa wi' the Exciseman,
And ilka wife cries, "Auld Mahoun,
  I wish you luck o' the prize, man!"

CHORUS. — The deil's awa, the deil's awa,   5
    The deil's awa wi' the Exciseman;
  He's danc'd awa, he's danc'd awa,
    He's danc'd awa wi' the Exciseman!

We'll mak our maut, and we'll brew our drink,
  We'll laugh, sing, an' rejoice, man;   10
And mony braw thanks to the meikle black deil
  That danc'd awa wi' the Exciseman.

There's threesome reels, there's foursome reels,
  There's hornpipes and strathspeys, man;
But the ae best dance e'er cam to the land
  Was — The deil's awa wi' the Exciseman.   15

BESSY AND HER SPINNIN WHEEL.

O LEEZE me on my spinnin wheel,
O leeze me on my rock and reel;
Frae tap to tae that cleeds me bien,
And haps me fiel and warm at e'en!
I'll set me down and sing and spin,   5
While laigh descends the simmer sun,
Blest wi' content, and milk and meal —
O leeze me on my spinnin wheel.

On ilka hand the burnies trot,
And meet below my theekit cot;
The scented birk and hawthorn white
Across the pool their arms unite,
Alike to screen the birdie's nest,
And little fishes' caller rest:
The sun blinks kindly in the biel',
Where blythe I turn my spinnin wheel.

On lofty aiks the cushats wail,
And echo cons the doolfu' tale;
The lintwhites in the hazel braes,
Delighted, rival ither's lays;
The craik amang the claver hay,
The paitrick whirrin o'er the ley,
The swallow jinkin round my shiel,
Amuse me at my spinnin wheel.

Wi' sma' to sell, and less to buy,
Aboon distress, below envy,
O wha wad leave this humble state,
For a' the pride of a' the great?
Amid their flarin, idle toys,
Amid their cumbrous, dinsome joys,
Can they the peace and pleasure feel
Of Bessy at her spinnin wheel?

BONIE LESLEY.

O SAW ye bonie Lesley
  As she gaed o'er the border?
She 's gane, like Alexander,
  To spread her conquests farther.

To see her is to love her,   5
   And love but her for ever ;
For Nature made her what she is,
   And never made anither !

Thou art a queen, fair Lesley,
   Thy subjects, we before thee :   10
Thou art divine, fair Lesley,
   The hearts o' men adore thee.

The Deil he could na scaith thee,
   Or aught that wad belang thee ;
He 'd look into thy bonie face,   15
   And say, " I canna wrang thee."

The Powers aboon will tent thee ;
   Misfortune sha' na steer thee ;
Thou 'rt like themselves sae lovely,
   That ill they 'll ne'er let near thee.   20

Return again, fair Lesley,
   Return to Caledonie !
That we may brag, we hae a lass
   There 's nane again sae bonie.

————

MY AIN KIND DEARIE.

When o'er the hill the eastern star
   Tells bughtin time is near, my jo,
An' owsen frae the furrow'd field
   Return sae dowf an' weary, O ;

Down by the burn, where scented birks 5
  Wi' dew are hangin clear, my jo,
I 'll meet thee on the lea rig,
  My ain kind dearie, O.

In mirkest glen, at midnight hour,
  I 'd rove, an' ne'er be eerie, O, 10
If thro' that glen I gaed to thee,
  My ain kind dearie, O.
Altho' the night were ne'er sae wild,
  An' I were ne'er sae weary, O.
I 'd meet thee on the lea rig, 15
  My ain kind dearie, O.

The hunter lo'es the morning sun,
  To rouse the mountain deer, my jo;
At noon the fisher seeks the glen,
  Along the burn to steer, my jo; 20
Gie me the hour o' gloamin gray,
  It maks my heart sae cheery, O,
To meet thee on the lea rig,
  My ain kind dearie, O.

HIGHLAND MARY.

YE banks, and braes, and streams around
  The castle o' Montgomery,
Green be your woods and fair your flowers,
  Your waters never drumlie!
There simmer first unfauld her robes, 5
  And there the langest tarry;
For there I took the last fareweel
  O' my sweet Highland Mary.

How sweetly bloom'd the gay green birk,
  How rich the hawthorn's blossom, 10
As underneath their fragrant shade
  I clasp'd her to my bosom!
The golden hours, on angel wings,
  Flew o'er me and my dearie;
For dear to me as light and life, 15
  Was my sweet Highland Mary.

Wi' monie a vow and lock'd embrace
  Our parting was fu' tender;
And, pledging aft to meet again,
  We tore oursels asunder; 20
But O! fell death's untimely frost,
  That nipt my flower sae early!
Now green 's the sod, and cauld 's the clay,
  That wraps my Highland Mary!

O pale, pale now, those rosy lips, 25
  I aft hae kiss'd sae fondly!
And closed for aye the sparkling glance,
  That dwelt on me sae kindly!
And mould'ring now in silent dust,
  That heart that lo'ed me dearly! 30
But still within my bosom's core
  Shall live my Highland Mary.

DUNCAN GRAY.

Duncan Gray came here to woo,
  Ha, ha, the wooin o' t!
On blythe Yule night when we were fou,
  Ha, ha, the wooin o' t!

Maggie coost her head fu hiegh,   5
Look'd asklent and unco skiegh,
Gart poor Duncan stand abiegh;
    Ha, ha, the wooin o't!

Duncan fleech'd, and Duncan pray'd;
    Ha, ha, the wooin o't!   10
Meg was deaf as Ailsa Craig,
    Ha, ha, the wooin o't!
Duncan sigh'd baith out and in,
Grat his een baith bleer't and blin',
Spak o' lowpin owre a linn;   15
    Ha, ha, the wooin o't!

Time and chance are but a tide,
    Ha, ha, the wooin o't!
Slighted love is sair to bide,
    Ha, ha, the wooin o't!   20
" Shall I, like a fool," quoth he,
" For a haughty hizzie die?
She may gae to—France for me!"
    Ha, ha, the wooin o't!

How it comes let doctors tell,   25
    Ha, ha, the wooin o't!
Meg grew sick as he grew hale,
    Ha, ha, the wooin o't!
Something in her bosom wrings,
For relief a sigh she brings;   30
And O! her een, they spak sic things!
    Ha, ha, the wooin o't!

Duncan was a lad o' grace,
    Ha, ha, the wooin o't!
Maggie's was a piteous case,   35
    Ha, ha, the wooin o't!

Duncan could na be her death,
Swelling pity smoor'd his wrath;
Now they 're crouse and cantie baith;
    Ha, ha, the wooin o 't!   40

GALA WATER.

Braw braw lads on Yarrow braes,
    Ye wander thro' the blooming heather;
But Yarrow braes nor Ettrick shaws
    Can match the lads o' Gala Water.

But there is ane, a secret ane,   5
    Aboon them a' I lo'e him better;
And I 'll be his, and he 'll be mine,
    The bonie lad o' Gala Water.

Altho' his daddie was nae laird,
    And tho' I hae nae meikle tocher;   10
Yet rich in kindest, truest love,
    We 'll tent our flocks by Gala Water.

It ne'er was wealth, it ne'er was wealth
    That coft contentment, peace, or pleasure;
The bands and bliss o' mutual love,   15
    O that 's the chiefest warld's treasure!

WANDERING WILLIE.

Here awa, there awa, wandering Willie,
    Here awa, there awa, haud awa hame;
Come to my bosom, my ae only dearie,
    And tell me thou bring'st me my Willie the same.

Loud tho' the winter blew cauld at our parting, 5
 'Twas na the blast brought the tear in my ee;
Welcome now simmer and welcome my Willie,
 The simmer to nature, my Willie to me.

Rest, ye wild storms, in the cave of your slumbers,
 How your dread howling a lover alarms! 10
Wauken, ye breezes, row gently, ye billows,
 And waft my dear laddie ance mair to my arms.
But O, if he's faithless, and minds na his Nannie,
 Flow still between us, thou wide-roaring main!
May I never see it, may I never trow it, 15
 But, dying, believe that my Willie's my ain!

WHISTLE, AND I'LL COME TO YOU, MY LAD.

CHORUS. — O whistle, an' I'll come to you, my lad!
    O whistle, an' I'll come to you, my lad!
    Tho' father an' mither an' a' should gae mad,
    O whistle, an' I'll come to you, my lad!

 BUT warily tent, when ye come to court me, 5
 And come na unless the back-yett be a-jee;
 Syne up the back-style, and let naebody see,
 And come as ye were na comin to me.

 At kirk, or at market, whene'er ye meet me,
 Gang by me as tho' that ye car'd na a flie: 10
 But steal me a blink o' your bonie black ee,
 Yet look as ye were na lookin at me.

 Ay vow and protest that ye care na for me,
 And whiles ye may lightly my beauty a wee;
 But court na anither, tho' jokin ye be, 15
 For fear that she wyle your fancy frae me.

SCOTS WHA HAE.

Scots, wha hae wi' Wallace bled,
Scots, wham Bruce has aften led ;
Welcome to your gory bed,
   Or to victory !
Now 's the day, and now 's the hour ;   5
See the front o' battle lour ;
See approach proud Edward's power —
   Chains and slavery !

Wha will be a traitor knave ?
Wha can fill a coward's grave ?   10
Wha sac base as be a slave ?
   Let him turn and flee !
Wha for Scotland's king and law
Freedom's sword will strongly draw,
Freeman stand, or Freeman fa',   15
   Let him follow me !

By oppression's woes and pains !
By your sons in servile chains !
We will drain our dearest veins,
   But they shall be free !   20
Lay the proud usurpers low !
Tyrants fall in every foe !
Liberty 's in every blow ! —
   Let us do, or die !

THE LOVELY LASS OF INVERNESS.

The lovely lass o' Inverness,
   Nae joy nor pleasure can she see ;
For e'en and morn she cries, "alas !"

And aye the saut tear blin's her ee:
"Drumossie moor, Drumossie day,   5
    A waefu' day it was to me;
For there I lost my father dear,
    My father dear, and brethren three.

"Their winding-sheet the bluidy clay,
    Their graves are growing green to see;   10
And by them lies the dearest lad
    That ever blest a woman's ee!
Now wae to thee, thou cruel lord,
    A bluidy man I trow thou be;
For monie a heart thou hast made sair,   15
    That ne'er did wrang to thine or thee."

CA' THE YOWES TO THE KNOWES.

CHORUS. — Ca' the yowes to the knowes,
        Ca' them where the heather grows,
        Ca' them where the burnie rows,
            My bonie dearie.

HARK! the mavis' evening sang   5
Sounding Cluden's woods amang,
Then a-fauldin let us gang,
    My bonie dearie.

We 'll gae down by Cluden side,
Thro' the hazels spreading wide,   10
O'er the waves that sweetly glide
    To the moon sae clearly.

Yonder Cluden's silent towers,
Where at moonshine midnight hours,

O'er the dewy-bending flowers,   15
  Fairies dance sae cheery.

Ghaist nor bogle shalt thou fear;
Thou 'rt to love and Heaven sae dear,
Nocht of ill may come thee near,
  My bonie dearie.   20

Fair and lovely as thou art,
Thou hast stown my very heart;
I can die — but canna part,
  My bonie dearie.

THE WINTER OF LIFE.

But lately seen in gladsome green,
  The woods rejoiced the day;
Thro' gentle showers the laughing flowers,
  In double pride were gay;
But now our joys are fled   5
  On winter blasts awa;
Yet maiden May, in rich array,
  Again shall bring them a'.

But my white pow — nae kindly thowe
  Shall melt the snaws of age;   10
My trunk of eild, but buss or beild,
  Sinks in Time's wintry rage.
Oh, age has weary days,
  An' nights o' sleepless pain !
Thou golden time o' youthfu' prime,   15
  Why comes thou not again?

CONTENTED WI' LITTLE.

CONTENTED wi' little, and cantie wi' mair,
Whene'er I forgather wi' Sorrow and Care,
I gie them a skelp as they 're creepin alang,
Wi' a cog o' gude swats and an auld Scottish sang.

I whyles claw the elbow o' troublesome Thought;   5
But man is a soger, and life is a faught:
My mirth and gude humour are coin in my pouch,
And my freedom's my lairdship nae monarch dare touch.

A towmond o' trouble, should that be my fa', —
A night o' gude fellowship sowthers it a';   10
When at the blythe end of our journey at last,
Wha the deil ever thinks o' the road he has past?

Blind Chance, let her snapper and stoyte on her way,
Be't to me, be't frae me, e'en let the jad gae:
Come ease or come travail, come pleasure or pain,   15
My warst word is — "Welcome, and welcome again!"

MY NANIE'S AWA.

Now in her green mantle blythe Nature arrays,
And listens the lambkins that bleat o'er the braes,
While birds warble welcomes in ilka green shaw;
But to me it's delightless — my Nanie's awa.

The snaw-drop and primrose our woodlands adorn,   5
And violets bathe in the weet o' the morn:
They pain my sad bosom, sae sweetly they blaw,
They mind me o' Nanie — and Nanie's awa.

Thou laverock that springs frae the dews o' the lawn,
The shepherd to warn o' the gray-breaking dawn,   10
And thou, mellow mavis, that hails the night-fa',
Give over for pity — my Nanie's awa.

Come autumn sae pensive, in yellow and gray,
And soothe me wi' tidings o' nature's decay ;
The dark, dreary winter, and wild-driving snaw   15
Alane can delight me — now Nanie's awa.

A MAN'S A MAN FOR A' THAT.

Is there, for honest poverty,
   That hings his head, an' a' that?
The coward slave, we pass him by,
   We dare be poor for a' that !
     For a' that, an' a' that,   5
      Our toils obscure, an' a' that ;
     The rank is but the guinea's stamp ;
      The man's the gowd for a' that.

What tho' on hamely fare we dine,
   Wear hodden-gray, an' a' that ;   10
Gie fools their silks, and knaves their wine,
   A man's a man for a' that.
     For a' that, an' a' that,
      Their tinsel show, an' a' that ;
     The honest man, tho' e'er sae poor,   15
      Is king o' men for a' that.

Ye see yon birkie, ca'd a lord,
   Wha struts, an' stares, an' a' that ;
Tho' hundreds worship at his word,
   He's but a coof for a' that :   20

For a' that, an' a' that,
   His riband, star, an' a' that,
The man o' independent mind,
   He looks and laughs at a' that.

A prince can mak a belted knight,   25
   A marquis, duke, an' a' that;
But an honest man 's aboon his might,
   Guid faith he mauna fa' that!
     For a' that, an' a' that,
       Their dignities, an' a' that,   30
    The pith o' sense, an' pride o' worth,
     Are higher rank than a' that.

Then let us pray that come it may,
   As come it will for a' that,
That sense and worth, o'er a' the earth,   · 35
   May bear the gree, an' a' that.
     For a' that, an' a' that,
       It's coming yet, for a' that,
    That man to man, the warld o'er,
     Shall brothers be for a' that.   40

THE LASS OF ECCLEFECHAN.

"Gat ye me, O gat ye me,
   O gat ye me wi' naething?
Rock and reel, and spinnin' wheel,
   A mickle quarter basin.
Bye attour, my gutcher has   5
   A heigh house and a laigh ane,
A' forbye my bonie sel,
   The toss of Ecclefechan."

"O haud your tongue now, luckie Laing,
   O haud your tongue and jauner;   10
I held the gate till you I met,
   Syne I began to wander:
I tint my whistle and my sang,
   I tint my peace and pleasure;
But your green graff, now, luckie Laing,   15
   Wad airt me to my treasure."

LAST MAY A BRAW WOOER.

LAST May a braw wooer cam down the lang glen,
   And sair wi' his love he did deave me;
I said there was naething I hated like men:
   The deuce gae wi 'm to believe me, believe me,
   The deuce gae wi 'm to believe me.   5

He spak o' the darts in my bonie black een,
   And vow'd for my love he was diein;
I said he might die when he liked for Jean:
   The Lord forgie me for liein, for liein,
   The Lord forgie me for liein!   10

A weel-stocked mailen, himsel for the laird,
   And marriage aff-hand, were his proffers:
I never loot on that I ken'd it, or cared,
   But thought I might hae waur offers, waur offers,
   But thought I might hae waur offers.   15

But what wad ye think? in a fortnight or less,
   (The deil tak his taste to gae near her!)
He up the lang loan to my black cousin Bess,
   Guess ye how, the jad! I could bear her, could bear her,
   Guess ye how, the jad! I could bear her.   20

But a' the niest week as I fretted wi' care,
　I gaed to the tryste o' Dalgarnock,
And wha but my fine fickle lover was there.
　I glowr'd as I 'd seen a warlock, a warlock,
　I glowr'd as I 'd seen a warlock.　　　　25

But owre my left shouther I gae him a blink,
　Lest neibors might say I was saucy;
My wooer he caper'd as he 'd been in drink,
　And vow'd I was his dear lassie, dear lassie,
　And vow'd I was his dear lassie.　　　　30

I spier'd for my cousin fu' couthy and sweet,
　Gin she had recover'd her hearin,
And how her new shoon fit her auld shachl't feet —
　But, heavens! how he fell a swearin, a swearin,
　But, heavens! how he fell a swearin.　　　35

He begged, for gudesake, I wad be his wife,
　Or else I wad kill him wi' sorrow:
So e'en to preserve the poor body in life,
　I think I maun wed him to-morrow, to-morrow,
　I think I maun wed him to-morrow.　　　40

EPISTLE TO COLONEL DE PEYSTER.

My honour'd Colonel, deep I feel
Your interest in the Poet's weal;
Ah! now sma' heart hae I to speel
　　　　The steep Parnassus,
Surrounded thus by bolus pill,　　　　5
　　　　And potion glasses.

O what a canty warld were it,
Would pain and care and sickness spare it;
And fortune favour worth and merit,
        As they deserve: 10
And ay a rowth, roast beef and claret;
        Syne wha wad starve?

Dame Life, tho' fiction out may trick her,
And in paste gems and fripp'ry deck her,
O! flick'ring, feeble, and unsicker   15
        I 've found her still,
Aye wav'ring like the willow-wicker,
        'Tween good and ill.

Then that curst carmagnole, auld Satan,
Watches, like baudrons by a ratton,   20
Our sinfu' saul to get a claut on
        Wi' felon ire;
Syne, whip! his tail ye 'll ne'er cast saut on,
        He 's aff like fire.

Ah Nick! ah Nick! it isna fair,   25
First shewing us the tempting ware,
Bright wine and bonie lasses rare,
        To put us daft;
Syne weave, unseen, thy spider snare
        O' hell's damn'd waft.   30

Poor man, the flie, aft bizzes by,
An' aft, as chance he comes thee nigh,
Thy damn'd auld elbow yeuks wi' joy,
        And hellish pleasure, —
Already in thy fancy's eye,   35
        Thy sicker treasure.

Soon, heels-o'er-gowdie! in he gangs,
And like a sheep-head on a tangs,
Thy girnin laugh enjoys his pangs
         And murd'ring wrestle,   40
As, dangling in the wind, he hangs
         A gibbet's tassel.

But lest you think I am uncivil,
To plague you with this draunting drivel,
Abjuring a' intentions evil,   45
         I quat my pen:
The Lord preserve us frae the Devil!
         Amen! amen!

O, WERT THOU IN THE CAULD BLAST.

O, WERT thou in the cauld blast,
  On yonder lea, on yonder lea,
My plaidie to the angry airt,
  I 'd shelter thee, I 'd shelter thee.
Or did misfortune's bitter storms   5
  Around thee blaw, around thee blaw,
Thy beild should be my bosom,
  To share it a', to share it a'.

Or were I in the wildest waste,
  Sae black and bare, sae black and bare,   10
The desert were a paradise,
  If thou wert there, if thou wert there.
Or were I monarch o' the globe,
  Wi' thee to reign, wi' thee to reign,
The brightest jewel in my crown   15
  Wad be my queen, wad be my queen.

FAIREST MAID ON DEVON BANKS.

CHORUS.— Fairest maid on Devon banks,
      Crystal Devon, winding Devon,
    Wilt thou lay that frown aside,
      And smile as thou wert wont to do?

    FULL well thou know'st I love thee dear,   5
    Couldst thou to malice lend an ear?
    O, did not Love exclaim, " Forbear,
      Nor use a faithful lover so "?

    Then come, thou fairest of the fair,
    Those wonted smiles, O, let me share ;   10
    And by thy beauteous self I swear,
      No love but thine my heart shall know.

NOTES.

Burns's earliest poetical efforts were love songs. They represent actual passages of his life, and they were generally composed to the humming of a melody. Hence, from the first his work has that air of reality and truth which is its most distinctive characteristic, and his songs, in particular, possess that 'singing' quality which marks them above those of every other song writer.

O TIBBIE, I HAE SEEN THE DAY (1776).

Air, 'Invercauld's Reel.'

'This song I composed about the age of seventeen.'—*B.* The record of Burns's loves is more diversified than even Goethe's. 'Sometimes,' he says, 'I was received with favor, and sometimes mortified with a repulse.' Tibbie was one of those who mortified him, and the touch of temper is just enough to add sprightliness. Combined with this there is a note of jealousy against riches and social superiority which later becomes a familiar strain. The lively measure of the reel is well marked.

1 1. **Tibbie**: Scotch for Isabella.

1 2. **wad na been**: for the idiom, see Gram. Introd.

1 4. **care na by**: 'care not for that'; cf. obs. Eng. use of 'let by,' e.g., 'Clothed as a loller, and lytel y-lete by,' i.e., 'thought of' (*Piers Plowman*).

1 6. **like stoure**: 'like the wind'; *stoure* = dry dust.

2 22. **brier**: pron. 'breer.'

2 25. **tak my advice**: 'take my word for it'; cf. obs. Eng. use of *advice* = opinion.

2 27. **spier your price**: 'make a bid for you,' 'ask your hand.' The phrase, idiomatic for 'signify a desire to have,' is commonly used with a negative, = 'have no use for.'

MARY MORISON (1781).

This is the fifteenth number in Mr. Scott Douglas's edition, and all before it are love songs. The subject was a servant girl whom Burns seriously desired to marry, to whom he wrote the earliest of his preserved letters, and whose charms he had already sung, — Ellison Begbie, Bonie Peggie Alison, the Lass on Cessnock Banks. Handsome Nell (see *Ep. Mrs. S.*), Montgomerie's Peggie, Annie of the Barley Riggs, and others successively touched the tinder of his heart; but to Ellison Begbie he proposed marriage. She refused his offer — Burns himself says 'jilted' him — but did not break his heart. The elasticity of his temper was no less remarkable than the variety of his moods and the violence of their revulsions.

In sending the song to Thomson (March 20, 1793) he apologized for its juvenility and said he 'did not think it remarkable for either its merits or demerits.' The poet was an erratic judge of his own work. This lyric (not strictly to be called juvenile, as he had reached the capable age of twenty-two) contains one of the finest pieces of suggestive idealization in literature, and it shows also that the poet had reached his full, rich note of pure song.

2 1.   As originally printed the song began at ' Yestreen.'

2 2.   **stoure**: see Vocab.; it is not 'dust' here.

2 9.   See introd. note to this song. The 'lighted ha'' was a barn with a clay floor, rough stone walls, and exposed rafters covered with dirt and cobwebs, lighted with a few guttering tallow dips stuck in bits of wood; planks raised on logs against the walls offered seats; and the 'trembling string' — worthy of a royal minstrel in a palace — was that of the rustic amateur fiddler in the corner.

2 13.   **braw**: here = 'finely dressed.'

3 23.   The same sentiment occurs in the first of his letters to Ellison Begbie.

A PRAYER (1781).

The date is Mr. Scott Douglas's. The poem appears in his *Comm. Pl. Bk.* under August, 1784, with an entry that points back two or three years.

THE DEATH AND DYING WORDS OF POOR MAILIE
(1782, Spring).

The incident was genuine.   One day, as Burns and his brother were going out with their teams at noon, Hugh Wilson, a neighbor herdboy, ' an odd, glowrin, gapin callan, about three-fourths wise,' came running to tell them what had happened to Mailie.   The ewe was soon released, but the ludicrous side of Hughoc's alarm and appearance touched the poet's fancy, and at the plow during the afternoon he composed this tragical-comical-historical-pastoral.   The humor, though slighter, has already something of the rich ethical flavor of *The Twa Dogs*, and here the sympathetic self-identification with the brute in her point of view is equally tender and more playful.   Burns had in mind Hamilton of Gilbertfield's *Dying Words of Bonny Heck, a Famous Greyhound*.

4 2.   **Was:** Burns originally wrote *were*.   Only Mailie was on the tether, but the form 'was' would be legitimate Scots grammar in either case; cf. the ballad *There* Was *Three Kings into the East*.

4 6.   **Hughoc:** the dimin. *-oc* (cf. Eng. *-ock* in *hillock*) is an alternative for *-ie*; e.g., *lassoc, lassie; Davoc, Davie.*   Sometimes the two are united, as in Dr. Geddes's song, —

> ' There was a wee bit wifikie was comin frae the fair
> Had gotten a bit drappikie that bred her muckle care.'

4 7–11.   Gilbert Burns tells us his brother 'was much tickled with Hughoc's appearance and postures '; Mailie sustains the humor in l. 13.

4 17.   **keep:** Burns already had a poet's contempt for 'geargathering,' which Mailie quite understands.

5 28, 32.   **them, themsel:** see Gram. Introd.

5 38.   **stocks o' kail:** heads of cabbage, or 'cabbage-stocks.'

5 45.   **beast:** i.e., full-grown.

5 49–56.   The advice is that of a 'douce' Scottish mother to her children as to the company they should keep.

6 51.   **silly:** the epithet is Homeric applied to sheep.

6 64.   **thou 'se:** see Gram. Introd.

6 64.   **blether:** the gift was one highly prized by the country urchin; hence the droll dignity of the bequest.

POOR MAILIE'S ELEGY.

As this poem does not occur in the *Comm. Pl. Bk.* immediately after the preceding, the date is probably somewhat later.   The verse form is that introduced by Robert Sempill in his *Life and Death of Habbie Simpson, the Piper of Kilbarchan*, about the middle of the 17th century. It was adopted by Ramsay and Fergusson, and by them passed on to Burns.

The poet *may* have drawn suggestions from *The Piper of Kilbarchan*, but he certainly had in mind *The Ewie wi' the Crookit Horn*, by the Rev. John Skinner.   In this year, 1782, Skinner was alive and sixty-one years of age; Burns afterwards made his acquaintance by letter, but they never met.

6 6. **Mailie's dead**: Burns uses the same stanza for elegiac purposes, both serious and comic, in the *Elegy on Captain Henderson* and *Tam Samson's Dead*; in the latter the refrain is employed as here.

7 21. **I'll say 't**: formula of solemn affirmation.   Cf. Mailie's dying words, ll. 35–38.

7 29. **pearls**: the roll of the *r* makes a dissyllable.

7 34. **Frae yont the Tweed**: English wool had an historic renown from Plantagenet times, when the exportation of sheep was by law prohibited.

7 37. **Wae worth**: sorrow befall.   **Wae** is a noun; **man** is a dative; for **worth**, see Vocab.   Cf. Scott's

> ' Woe worth the chase, woe worth the day.'
>
> *Lady of the Lake*, I. 9.

8 43. **O a' ye Bards**: there are several echoes of Skinner's poem throughout, but the resemblance is clear in the last stanza of both,—

> ' But thus, poor thing, to lose her life
> Aneath a bleedy villain's knife!
> I 'm really fley 't that our guidwife
>   Will never win aboon 't ava:
> O a' ye bards benorth Kinghorn,
> Call your muses up an' mourn
> Our ewie wi' the crookit horn
>   Stown frae 's an' fell 't an' a'.'

It may be noted that 'bonie Doon' and Ayr had as yet no bards.   As late as 1785 Burns had still to lament the fact.   See *Ep. W. S.*, 47.

MY NANIE, O (1782).

This, too, Burns ingenuously writes in his *Comm. Pl. Bk.*, was at the time *real*.   The virginal sweetness of the emotion is likewise to be observed.

8 1. **Lugar**: only as late as 1792, Oct. 26, Burns suggested this name, or *Girvan*, as a substitute for the cacophonous actual name of the stream, Stinchar.

8 4. **Nanie**: Scotch for Agnes. She has been identified as Agnes Fleming, but she need not have been called Nanie at all; cf. Peggie Alison.

8 7. **plaid**: the highland substitute for overcoat. It is wound about the chest and shoulders, and its length, about four yards, makes it a convenient wrap for two. Cf. Hector Macneill's song, *Come under my Plaidie*.

8 8. **hill**: the Carrick hills, west of Lochlea.

9 21. These circumstances are imaginary: Burns never worked under any master except his father.

GREEN GROW THE RASHES (1783, Summer).

This song is created out of an old snatch of the same name. It is the earliest of those *rifacimenti* whose importance is twofold: they show how keen and true was the singer's instinct in Burns, and they reveal the extent of the debt under which he has laid the literature of song. (See Gen. Introd.)

For all its lightness and *brusquerie*, the song embodies the poet's serious conviction, as his letters repeatedly show. In his *Comm. Pl. Bk.* (August, 1784) the verses are given as 'the genuine language of my heart'; and, writing of this period to Dr. Moore (Aug. 2, 1787), he says: '*Vive l'amour et vive la bagatelle* were my sole principles of action.'

This was after his sojourn in Irvine, where he got that copy of Fergusson's poems which made him 'string his lyre with emulating vigor.'

10 19, 20. Burns, though not bred a Puritan, was remarkably well read in the Bible, and took delight in making scriptural allusions; see notes to *C. S. N.*, *To the D.*, *H. F.*, etc.

10 21-24. This stanza was added later. The conceit is old. Steele uses it in his *Christian Hero* (1701): 'He (Adam) saw a creature who had, as it were, heaven's second thought in her formation.' It occurs earlier, in *Cupid's Whirligig*, a comedy published in 1607: 'Since we were made before you [women], should we not admire you as the last and therefore perfect work of nature? Man was made when Nature was but an apprentice, but woman when she was a skilful mistress of her art.' This passage was copied into a book not scarce in Burns's

day, — *The British Muse, a Collection of Thoughts, by Thomas Heywood, Gent.*, 4 vols., London, 1738.

During 1783 came the collapse of his father's affairs and another distressing circumstance in the poet's life. His father died in February, 1784, 'just saved from a jail by phthisical consumption.' Soon after, Burns wrote *Man was Made to Mourn*, in which he records the indignant protest of poverty against wealth and social injustice, for with him these two are nearly synonymous. At the same time he took up the subject from a humorous point of view in his letter to Davie, a 'Brother-poet, Lover, Ploughman, and Fiddler.'

EPISTLE TO DAVIE (1784; Completed January, 1785).

Gilbert Burns states that in the summer of 1784, while he and his brother were weeding in the 'kailyard,' Robert recited the greater part of this epistle; and he believes that the idea of Robert's becoming an author was started on that occasion. He was already inspired by Fergusson, and was looking to poetry as a serious vocation, but he had not yet thought of publishing.

Man was Made to Mourn and this poem are to each other as obverse and reverse; the former serious and English, the latter humorous and Scotch; in the former 'man's inhumanity to man makes countless thousands mourn,' and the spirit of independence frets against social fetters; in the latter the poet, though at times he cannot help being sour, finds consolation at every turn, even in the prospect of a release offered in beggardom.

Davie Sillar, to whom the epistle is addressed, has no claim on posterity beyond this recognition of him, though he, too, published a volume of poems at Kilmarnock.

The stanza, which, in spite of its awkward form, Burns appears to have mastered at the first effort, is supposed to have been invented by Alexander Montgomerie in *The Banks of Helicon*, and is that employed by Allan Ramsay in *The Vision*.

10 1.   **winds**, etc.: so *M. M. M.* begins, —

> ' When chill November's surly blast.'

10 6.   **westlin jingle** : the Ayrshire dialect has peculiarities, but more of accent than vocabulary.   Some are noted in the Vocab.

10 9.   gift : what is given *to* them. For the sentiment, cf. *M. M. M.,*—

> ' Where hundreds labour to support
> A haughty lordling's pride.'

11 15.   **a body's** : this is the regular Scotch indefinite, = ' one '; e.g.,

> ' Gin a body meet a body.'

11 25.   Burns notes this line as borrowed from Ramsay. It is from the *Response of the Oracle to the Poet's Wish,* —

> ' Mair speir na and flir na,
> But set thy mind at rest.'

11 28.   **to beg** : see Scott's introd. to *The Antiquary,* and the character of Edie Ochiltree; Scott believed that Burns may have looked forward to the possibility of becoming a ' bluegown,' and Burns, in a letter to Charles Sharpe (April 22, 1791), assumes that character over the signature ' Johnny Faa.'

11 29.   **kilns** : for making malt, in days when people brewed their own ale.

11 29 ff.   Vagabondage and Bohemianism had a charm for Burns, as they had for Shakspere; the genius that conjured up the scenes in Eastcheap had his compeer in the creator of the revelry that ' sheuk the kebars ' at Poosie Nansie's.

11 39–42.   Cf. the poet's second song in *The Jolly Beggars,* —

> ' Life is all a variorum,
> We regard not how it goes ;
> Let them cant about decorum
> Who have characters to lose.'

12 43–56.   The spirit of this beautiful stanza is strikingly reproduced by Jean Richepin in the idyllic portion of his *Chanson des Gueux.* The process described in ll. 54–56 is that followed by Burns in the composition of his songs. See his letter to Thomson, September, 1793; and cf. Gen. Introd., p. xlvi. ff.

12 57–59.   Cf. *Gala Water,* 13, 14, p. 162.

12 60.   **making muckle, mair** : ' making much grow to be more.'

12 71.   With this stanza cf. *The T. D.,* 71–100, p. 73.

13 90.   **An's** : ' and am.' See Gram. Introd.

13 92.   ' No one has moralised better on the " uses of adversity " than Burns; few so finely as when he says misfortunes " let us ken oursel." ' — Professor Nichol, Introd. to Mr. Scott Douglas's ed., vol. i.

13 109.   **I** ; a mere sacrifice to rhyme; not a Scotch idiom.

14 108. Jean: Jean Armour, afterwards his wife. She was the daughter of a builder in the neighboring town of Mauchline, and socially rather above the poet. He first met her in April or May of this year, and passion sprang full-grown between them. The impetuosity of the poet's emotions renders it unnecessary to adopt any theory involving a later date for these ardent references to Jean. The fact stands that when Burns saw Jean he had seen his fate.

14 130. world's: dissyll. on account of rolled *r*.

14 138. tenebrific: one of his few bombastic words; cf. *terraefilial*, *frater-feeling*, and a few more.

15 145. As: ' as if.'

15 147. Pegasus has for Burns all the reality of Jenny Geddes; cf. *Ep. to Willie Chalmers*, 1–8, —

> ' Wi braw new branks an' muckle pride,
> An' eke a braw new brechan,
> My Pegasus I 'm got astride
> An' up Parnassus pechin,' etc.

RANTIN ROVIN ROBIN (probably early in 1785).

Burns was now fired with the ambition to become a poet, and henceforth poetry was his only successful undertaking.

This song was composed to the air '*Dainty Davie*,' and there is extant in Burns's handwriting the following opening:

> ' There was a birkie born in Kyle,
> But whatna day o' whatna style,
> I doubt it 's hardly worth my while
> To be sae nice wi' Davie.
> Leeze me on thy curly pow,
> Bonie Davie, dainty Davie;
> Leeze me on thy curly pow,
> Thou 's aye my dainty Davie.'

15 1. Kyle: the districts of Ayrshire were Cunningham, north of the Irvine; Kyle, between the Irvine and the Doon; Carrick, south of the Doon. From Kyle he names his muse *Coila*.

15 2. style: for some time after the change in the calendar (1751) dates were reckoned according to both ' old style ' and ' new style.'

15 6. rantin, rovin: almost the same combination occurs in *The Twa Dogs*, 24, p. 72; the third *Ep. to Lapraik* is signed *Rab the Ranter;* the words imply a jovial and Bohemian disposition.

15 9. **Our monarch's . . . begun**: George II; Jan. 25, 1759.

16 13. **gossip**: sponsor in baptism. Tradition has it that an itinerant 'spaewife' uttered prophecies on the child's future, and there may have been palmistry, such practice being common.

16 20. The words were prophetic, but Burns was by no means blown up with anticipated fame. His self-judgment was remarkably keen, and at all times he rather underestimated than overestimated his powers.

16 26. The following stanza is found with variations in some editions. This version is taken from the second *Comm. Pl. Bk.*

> 'Guid faith,' quo' scho, 'I doubt you, Stir,
> Ye gar the lasses lie aspar ;
> But twenty fauts ye may hae waur —
> So blessins on thee, Robin !'

TO THE DEIL.

Gilbert Burns states that Robert recited this poem to him during the winter after the *Ep. to Davie*. He heard the latter during the summer of 1784, and therefore the present poem is consigned to the winter of 1784–5. He may have altered and improved it later.

Originating in a humorous freak as he ran over 'the many ludicrous accounts we have of this august personage,' this poem, so realistic as to make us believe in this devil, and so familiarly tender as to make us love him, with its variety of contrasts, its daring combination of banter and awe, familiarity and respect, indignation and compassion, with its rich play of fancy and observation woven into a warp of humanity and supernaturalism, is one of the most remarkable compositions in literature. The theological element belongs to Scotch Calvinism; the legendary to northern folklore and to medieval superstition.

16 1. **O thou**: Burns, like Byron, curiously had a great regard for the chief of the school whose overthrow his own work proclaimed. Here he adapts Pope's apostrophe to Swift, —

> 'O thou, whatever title please thine ear,
> Dean, Drapier, Bickerstaff, or Gulliver.'
>
> *Dunciad*, I.

16 2. **Hornie . . . cavern . . . brunstane**: the conception of a horned devil in a fiery cavern torturing the damned is a product of medieval Christianity, and was a prominent feature of the Miracle

Plays.   It still lingers in Scotland in a modified form.   For the picture, cf. *Holy Fair*, 190, p. 41 :

> ‘ A vast unbottom’d boundless pit,
>   Filled fou o’ lowin brunstane,’ etc.

16 5.   cootie: Satan has a foot pail for the purpose of basting his victims with liquid brimstone.   The humor of **Spairges** cannot be expressed in English.

17 19.   roarin lion: I Peter, v, 8.

17 21.   tempest: Ephesians, ii, 2.   The storm is congenial to the Prince of the Powers of the Air;   see also below, ll. 49–52, and cf. *Tam O' Shanter*, 73–78, p. 147.

17 22.   kirks: it was part of the devil’s business to unroof these; ruined churches were favorite haunts of his; cf. Kirk Alloway.

17 25–30.   This touch of pathos in the deil’s romantic love of solitude finds its full expression at the close of the poem.

17 33–42.   bummin . . . rash-buss . . . drake: the humorist reverses the situation.   It might have been a droning beetle, etc., but it was the deil.

18 55–60.   There are two pieces of witchcraft here, — the bewitching of the churn and that of the cow.   Both superstitions still linger in Scotland and in Scandinavia, and various charms are employed to remove the spell. — **twal-pint** :   giving twelve pints (Scotch) of milk, or three gallons at a ‘ milking.’

18 69.   water-kelpies : see Gen. Introd., §§ I and VI (d).   The kelpie usually took the form of a black horse, and, inducing travellers to mount him, plunged with them into a pool.   See *Folk-lore of the Northeast of Scotland*, pp. 66, 67 (Rev. W. Gregor, F.L.S., 1881).

19 73.   spunkies : see Vocab.   Cf. *B. A.*, 51, p. 111.

19 79.   masons’ : Burns was an ardent freemason.   He wrote poems to the brethren, signed his name with a masonic mark, spoke of himself as a ‘ mason-maker,’ and was at all times ready for masonic conviviality.

19 85.   This stanza originally ran :

> ‘ Lang syne in Eden’s happy scene,
>   When strappin Adam’s days were green
>   And Eve was like my bonie Jean,
>   My dearest part,
>   A dancin, sweet, young handsome quean,
>   O’guileless heart.’

This is quite in the strain of *Ep. D.*, 108, etc., p. 14. But before the Kilmarnock edition appeared the Armour parents had loosed upon him the 'dogs of the law'; hence the alteration. Cf. the similar alteration in *The V.*, 63, p. 87. 'Eden's bonie yard' is a reminiscence of Fergusson's *Caller Water*, —

> 'When Father Adie first put spade in
> The bonie yard o' ancient Eden.'

19 92. **Paradise**: Genesis, iii, 1. The identity of the serpent with Satan is an essential part of Scotch theology.

19 97. **that day**: Job, i.

20 111. **Michael**: Burns gives the reference to Milton (*Par. Lost*, vi, 325) where the sword of Michael

> 'deep-entering, shared
> All his right side ; then Satan first knew pain.'

20 113. **Lallan . . . Erse**: 'Lowland . . . Highland.' Erse is properly Irish as distinct from Scotch Gaelic.

20 115. **auld Cloots**: 'old Cloven-feet': cf. l. 2. He preserves the familiarity, but softens it almost to fondness in the next stanza.

20 122. **tak a thought**: regular Scotch idiom for 'reflect.'

20 125. **den**: cf. 'Crookie-den,' a name for hell ; as in the song, —

> 'I hae been to Crookie-den,
> Bonie laddie, Highland laddie.'

DEATH AND DR. HORNBOOK (1785, ' Seedtime ').

The subject was John Wilson, schoolmaster and grocer in Tarbolton, who, having become 'hobby-horsically attached to the study of medicine,' added drugs to his store and offered advice *gratis*. At a masonic meeting, when Burns was present, he made such a parade of medical knowledge that Burns determined to 'nail the self-conceited sot as dead's a herrin.' The poem, like *Tam O' Shanter*, was written at a heat, and, when it circulated, Wilson had to shut shop and school and quit the district. But its breadth of elaboration, richness of descriptive detail, and grotesque supernaturalism lift it far beyond the character of an occasional satire.

Dr. Hornbook: the title is meant to suggest the puerile character of the 'doctor's' knowledge. Children's reading primers used to be called 'hornbooks' from the covering of 'translucent horn' that protected the letters. See Cowper, *Tirocinium*, 119, 120.

21 5. Var. 'Great lies and nonsense baith to vend.'

21 13. The rôle of inebriate, which is purely dramatic, is so successful that even Wordsworth enjoyed it. For the general subject in Burns's life, see Introd. to *Sc. Dr.*

21 20. **Cumnock hills**: southeast of Tarbolton. Burns gives local particulars without invention; so 'Willie's mill,' below.

22 33. **scythe**: Burns had in mind the allegorical figure of Time. Death is commonly represented as a skeleton, but this figure, though little more than skin and bone, has a beard, and flesh on his hips ll. 41, 60, 84.

22 37. **Scotch ells twa**: 6 ft. 2 in. See *T. S.*, 84, note.

22 44. **sawin**: 'This rencontre happened in seedtime.' — *B.*

22 47. **whare ye gaun**: the rapid colloquial utterance causes the blending of *whare* and *are.* Frequently, too, the *r* drops out of the pronunciation of *are* before *we* and *ye*, — 'a'e we,' 'a'e ye.'

23 57 f. **kittle to be mislear'd**: the meaning of this passage is doubtful. 'Misleared' means ill-taught,' hence, 'unmannerly, mischievous'; 'kittle' = 'ticklish.' Thus the whole phrase probably means, 'I should be a ticklish person to deal with if I became mischievous.'

23 62. **gie's**: give us.

23 65. **This while**: for some time past. There is reference to an epidemic then raging in the district.

23 73. **sax thousand**: from the Creation, B.C. 4004.

23 80. **in**: into; 'may the devil make a tobacco-pouch of his second stomach.'

23 81. **Buchan**: 'Buchan's *Domestic Medicine.*' — *B.*

24 95. **play'd dirl**: struck sharp and quivered without penetrating. This is a common, graphic use of 'play.' Cf. *To the U. G.*, 8, p. 92 : 'An' still the clap plays clatter.' Note that the pronunciation of *r* gives *dirl* two syllables.

25 133. **Johnie Ged's Hole**: the grave. Cf. 'Davie Jones' Locker'; Johnie Ged is here humorously taken for the parish gravedigger.

25 135. **calf-ward**: the churchyard had been used by Johnie as a calf pasture; now that every one was getting cured it would be plowed up. Johnie would thus find both his pasture and his occupation gone.

25 140. **pleugh**: note the spelling and pronunciation. In l. 131 it was *plew* (ploo); here it is guttural, rhyming with *eneugh, sheugh.*

25 144. **twa-three**: the same law holds here as in *whare ye gaun* (l. 47). A further attrition makes it *tworree.*

25 145. **strae-death** : i.e., natural death in bed, referring to the olden-time beds of straw.

26 151. **honest wabster to his trade** : honest (cf. *honestus*) = respectable. The line is condensed, = ' A respectable man, a weaver,' etc.

26 152. She used her fists too freely on her husband, who profited by her headache to get Hornbook to cure her. In the same way the young laird gets rid of his father.

26 169–174. Where Hornbook kills, the killing is murder; and where he cures, the cure is cheating Death.

27 183. **wee short hour ayont the twal** has now become a current phrase for the stroke of one o'clock.

EPISTLE TO JOHN LAPRAIK (1785, April 1).

John Lapraik was a neighbor farmer, 'a very worthy, facetious old fellow.' He, too, published poems, but, like Davie's, his only fame is that given him by Burns. The song which was the occasion of this epistle was one which Lapraik had 'borrowed' from the *Weekly Magazine, or Edinburgh Amusement* (Oct. 14, 1773), and slightly altered into Scotch. Burns never knew of the plagiarism.

27 1. This is ' Aprille with his shoures sote.' Cf. Chaucer, *Prol.* 1.

27 7. **Fasten-e'en** : Shrovetide. — **rockin** : before the days of the spinning wheel, women used to carry their rocks or distaffs with them when they went visiting. By and by the original signification disappeared, and the phrase was used indiscriminately by men and women ; a *rockin* became a social gathering, with singing and other amusements, to which the women brought their knitting (l. 8).

27 8. **ca' the crack** : keep the conversation going.

27 11 f. **yokin at sang-about** : set-to at singing songs in turn.

27 13. **ae sang** : see note above. Burns liked it so well that he had it printed in Johnson's *Museum*.

28 21. **Pope**, etc. : notice the men whom he cites. The original had been in English, and it seems as if Burns almost looked through the fraud of Lapraik's Scotch. James Beattie (1735–1803) was a leading name in the fashionable Scotch-English school of Burns's day, professor of ethics and logic in Aberdeen, and author of an *Essay on Truth* (1770), and *The Minstrel ; or, The Progress of Genius*, a poem in the Spenserian stanza (1771–4). His collected works were published in Philadelphia in ten volumes, 1809.

28 23. **odd kin' chiel**: odd kind of a fellow.   See Gram. Introd.

28 31.   **That, set him**: imperat. used as condit.   'That, if you put him,' etc.

28 35.   **Inverness**: then the northern limit of Scotch civilization.

28 39.   **cadger pownie's death**: a picturesquely exaggerated way of saying he would think no exertion too great to go to see him.   Fish-cadgers' ponies are notoriously overdriven.

28 41.   **pint an' gill**: pint of ale and gill of whisky, an old-fashioned Scotch treat for two.   For **them**, see Gram. Introd.

29 50.   **like**: 'as it were,' interjectional.

29 60.   **maybe**: in Scotch, an adv. = perhaps; 'are' is not redundant.

29 65.   **ye 'd better taen**: you had better have taken; see Gram. Introd.

29 66.   **knappin-hammers**: or taken to breaking road metal.

29 67–72.   With occasional misgivings, as in his Kilmarnock preface, this contempt for academic learning was his confirmed opinion.

30 79, 80.   Allan Ramsay and Robert Fergusson; see Gen. Introd., pp. xxv–xxix.

30 103.   **Mauchline . . . Fair**: celebrated on the road near Mossgiel.

31 109.   **four-gill chap**: the mutchkin measure; it is of pewter, and has a lid; hence the clatter.   Whisky is meant, and 'toddy' is to be brewed.

EPISTLE TO WILLIAM SIMSON (1785, May).

Burns's first theological satire, *The Twa Herds; or, The Holy Tulzie*, had already circulated in MS., and met with roars of applause.   A copy reached William Simson, schoolmaster and poet, who addressed an epistle to Burns.   The latter replied in this poem, which is not only intensely patriotic, but intensely local in its patriotism.

32 2.   **brawlie**: heartily; for this rare use, cf. *The Deil's Awa*, 11, p. 156, —

> 'An' mony braw thanks to the muckle black deil.'

A popular Norwegian use of *bra* corresponds.

32 13.   Proverbial, = I would show I had completely lost my head.

32 15.   **Gilbertfield**: William Hamilton of Gilbertfield.   See Gen. Introd., p. xxiv.

32 17. **writer-chiel**: 'writer' is Scotch for attorney or lawyer. Fergusson worked in a law office in Edinburgh (l. 21). See Gen. Introd., p. xxviii.

32 27. **dead**: a noun, = 'death.'

33 30. **ease**: see *The V.*, 150, note.

33 31. **Coila**: see *Rantin Rovin Robin*, 1, and *The V.*, 109, notes.

33 32. **poets**: Davie Sillar, Lapraik, Simson, and himself.

33 43 ff. Cf. with this the entry in his *Comm. Pl. Bk.* for August, 1784 (?) (*Works*, vol. iii, p. 91): 'However I am pleased with the works of our Scotch poets, particularly the excellent Ramsay and the still more excellent Fergusson, yet I am hurt to see other places of Scotland ... immortalized in such celebrated performances, whilst my dear native country, the ancient ..., famous ..., a country where ..., the birth-place of ..., the scene of ..., particularly the actions of the GLORIOUS WALLACE, the SAVIOUR of his country; yet we have never had one Scotch poet of any eminence to make the fertile banks of Irvine, the romantic woodlands and sequestered scenes on Aire, and the healthy mountainous source and winding sweep of Doon emulate Tay, Forth, Ettrick, Tweed, etc.' Mr. Scott Douglas arbitrarily places the above passage under the year 1785; Burns gives the month August. More probably it was written in August, 1784, and used, according to his practice (cf. *To the U. G.*, introd. and note, and *C. S. N.*, l. 64, note), in the composition of the poem instead of conversely.

33 58. **Wallace**: type of the Scottish patriot and liberator before Bruce. By treachery he fell into the hands of the English, was taken to London and hanged, drawn, and quartered. In his boyhood Burns made a pilgrimage to the Leglen Wood, a haunt of Wallace, and 'explored every den and dell.' Blind Harry, the minstrel, wrote an exaggerated account of his adventures in rude rhyme, entitled ' *Ye Actis and Deidis of ye Illuster and Vailzeand Champioun, Schir William Wallace*' (ed. by Dr. Jamieson, 4°, Edin., 1820). Cf. Gen. Introd., p. xxxix, and see Scott's *Tales of a Grandfather*, ch. vii.

34 65. **red-wat-shod**: 'wat-shod' is an old compound, 'with wet feet'; the 'red' added by Burns is all the more terrible from being merely suggestive.

34 73. **ev'n winter**: see his poems *A. W. N.*, p. 117, and *Winter, a Dirge*. He loved to describe winter, not more for graphic effect than for the suggestions of humanity it stirred.

34 75. **Ochiltree**: on the Lugar; Simson was schoolmaster there.

34 85. **The Muse**: cf. *The V.*, 211–228, p. 90.

34 88. **think lang**: 'feel the time heavy'; usually with a negative.

35 95. **grumbling hive**: Burns may have read Bernard Mandeville's *Fable of the Bees; or, The Grumbling Hive of Knaves turned Honest.*

35 103. **tolls and taxes**: these were pet aversions of the highlanders. The former were satirized in a comic ballad just before Burns's day, the *Turningpike* (turnpike). Tolls were universal on the highways of Scotland until recent years.

There is a long postscript to this epistle in which the quarrel of the Auld and New Lichts is humorously disposed of as a squabble about the old and the new moon, a 'moonshine matter.' It was not so, and the quarrel was soon to draw from Burns some of his heaviest shot. The Auld Lichts were those who held firmly to the Westminster Confession of Faith and the theology of Calvin; the New Lichts were the 'moderates,' who admitted humane culture and a kindlier creed.

THE HOLY FAIR (1785; probably August).

There is no longer any doubt that this poem belongs to 1785; the discovery of the poet's later *Comm. Pl. Bk.* has settled the point.[1]

In several places this poem touches *Ep. McM.*, which more probably echoes this poem than conversely (see *Ep. McM.*, p. 43, and notes). The poem, moreover, is manifestly the result of fresh inspiration, and the Holy Fair of Mauchline was then held in August. The stanza beginning 'Leeze me on Drink!' is evidently the germ of *Sc. Dr.*, and not a reminiscence of that poem.

A Holy Fair was a kind of cross between an old Catholic festival and a Methodist camp meeting. It was held for the celebration of the Lord's Supper and the conversion of souls. Burns had no particle of reverence for this kind of religion, but his descriptive details are not distorted ; they are true to fact, and therein lies the sting of the satire. When plowmen engaged themselves to a master they used to stipulate that they should be allowed to attend so many fairs or so many sacraments during the year ; a fair and a sacrament being thus to them practically identical, they used to behave at the one as they did at the other. To find anything like this poem, we must go back to Dunbar and Lindsay.

'Holy Fair' being a common phrase for a sacramental occasion, there is no need to suppose the title borrowed from Fergusson's *Hallow*

---

[1] Mr. Scott Douglas gives this *Comm. Pl. Bk.* in an appendix to vol. vi, but in vol. iii he strangely places *The Holy Fair* under 1786, and feels 'bound to regard it as later than February.'

Fair. Both plan and metre of the poem, however, are taken from that poet's *Leith Races.* Burns had been studying Fergusson since 1782, so that his request of February, 1786, that his friend Richmond should send him a copy of Fergusson's poems is of no account in fixing the date. He may, however, have improved the poem later.

36 1. Cf. Fergusson's opening, —

> ' In July month, ae bonie morn,
>   When Nature's rokelay green
> Was spread owre ilka rig o' corn
>   To charm our rovin een.'

36 5. **Galston**: next parish north of Mauchline. Burns never seeks to disguise localities. Cf. *D. and Dr. H.*, 20, p. 21.

36 10. Fergusson has

> ' Glowrin about I saw a quean
>   The fairest neath the lift.'

36 15. **lyart linin**: the garb of Hypocrisy.

36 23. **The third**: Burns appears to follow Fergusson here quite closely ; compare the two for a study in true 'originality.'

37 37. **my name is Fun**: 'They ca' me Mirth.'—*Fergusson.*

37 50. **crowdie-time**: here = 'breakfast-time' ; see l. 229.

37 57. **braw braid-claith**: it is still a point of etiquette among the country people in Scotland to have a 'stand o' Sabbath claes.'

37 59. **barefit**: a country custom, practiced as much to ease the feet as to save the fine shoes.

37 61. **cheese . . . farls**: the lasses took lunch with them and treated the lads during intervals. Cf. ll. 217–225.

37 64 **by the plate**: observe the local details. The fair was held in the churchyard, which in country parishes always surrounds the church, and is itself enclosed by a stone wall ; the ' plate,' a large pewter vessel usually set at the church door to receive the 'collection,' is here placed by the churchyard gate. They were about to pass ('gae by ') the plate.

37 66. **Black Bonnet**: the ' elder ' who stood beside the plate commonly wore a John Knox bonnet.

37 67. **tippence**: i.e., a penny each ; the satirist treats the whole affair as a penny 'show' (l. 68).

38 75. **Racer Jess**: the long-limbed, half-witted daughter of Poosie Nansie of *Jolly Beggars.*

38 81. **fun**: the ' fun ' is heightened by the fact that the 'black guards ' must have come ten miles to enjoy it. Kilmarnock is a weaving town about ten miles from Mauchline.

38 86. **chosen swatch**: the Unco Guid, who were soon to receive their own special castigation.

38 91. **O happy**, etc. : Psalm cxlvi, 5. This stanza was extravagantly praised by Hogg, the ' Ettrick Shepherd.'

39 102. **Moodie** : one of the Twa Herds of the *H. T.* He and all the others mentioned later were clergymen of the district ; Burns did with men as he did with places (see l. 5, note).

39 103. **damnation**: ' salvation ' in the Kilmarnock edition. The change was suggested by Dr. Hugh Blair, of ' Rhetoric ' fame.

39 105. **'Mang sons o' God** : Job, i, 6. Cf. *To the D.*, 97, p. 19.

39 107. **Var.**:

> ' Aff straucht to hell had sent him
> Fast, fast that day.'

39 120. **real judges**: the ' Auld Licht ' evangelicals ; disgusted with mere moral preaching, they go off to have a different kind of spiritual refreshment.

40 131. **Antonine** : Marcus Aurelius, of the *Meditations.*

40 134. **faith in** : the grammar is forced to suit the rhyme.

40 138. **water-fit** : ' foot of the water,' mouth of the river. Newton-on-Ayr is meant.

40 142. **Common Sense** : merely a personification here, though Dr. Mackenzie, of Mauchline, one of the ' New Lichts,' wrote under this *nom de plume.* The reference is to common sense in matters of dogma, or to the ' New Licht ' party.

40 143. **Cowgate** : the street facing the exit from the churchyard.

40 152. **Like hafflins-wise** : ' like,' ' -lins,' and ' wise ' all have the same force, — ' as it were,' ' in a manner,' ' after a fashion.'

40 154. **change-house** : the tavern, formerly an almost universal annex to the kirk in rural Scotland.

41 163. **Leeze me**, etc.: see introd. note. It is very improbable that Burns would have inserted such a digression *after* he had written *Sc. Dr.*

41 181. **touts** : see Vocab. Russel's preaching voice was audible a mile off.

41 187. **hell** : cf. *To the D.* and notes.

41 188. **sauls does harrow** : ' Shakespeare's *Hamlet.*' — B.

> ' I could a tale unfold whose lightest word
> Would harrow up thy soul.'
>
> i, v, 14.

42 200. **stories** : ' incidents,' the recital of which would be ' stories.'

42 205. **cheese and bread** : cf. l. 62, note.

42 215. **like a tether**: cf. ‘half-mile graces’ (*Ep. McM.*, 21, p. 44); ‘as lang ’s my airm’ (*To a H.*, 5, p. 121). He himself composed some famous graces, notably the Selkirk Grace, for which see *To a Haggis*, l. 24, note.

42 217–225. Explained by the custom above, l. 62.

43 226. **Clinkumbell**: the beadle.   Cf. ‘Burnewin’ (blacksmith, ‘burn-the-wind’), ‘Clout the caudron’ (tinker).—**Rattlin** refers to the chain usually forming the bell-pull.

43 231. **strip their shoon**: see l. 59, note; they had put on their shoes on approaching the meeting; now they doffed them to return ‘barefit’ as they had come.

EPISTLE TO REV. JOHN McMATH (1785, Sept. 17).

In July, Gawin Hamilton, a generous, upright man, but not conspicuously devout, was brought up before the presbytery of Ayr for irregularity in church attendance, whistling on a Fast Day, and saying ‘Dammit.’ His chief persecutor was a sanctimonious hypocrite who afterwards robbed the poor-box, and died drunk in a ditch, William Auld. Burns followed up the trial by a merciless satire on Holy Willie’s devotions, which was also a burlesque of the extreme ‘Auld Licht’ doctrines. McMath, one of the ‘New Lichts,’ asked Burns for a copy of *H. W. Pr.*, and it was sent along with this Epistle.

43 1. **shearers**: because they used sickles. The bad weather of this season destroyed half of the Mossgiel crop.

43 7. **monie a sonnet**: e.g., *H. T.*, *H. W. Pr.*, *Ep. to G.*, *H. F.* He would hardly have said ‘monie a’ if the last were not included. See introd. note on *H. F.* **Sonnet** has its larger meaning.

43 8. **gown, ban’**: these are the canonicals of the Scotch clergy,— the Geneva gown and the ‘bands,’ or brôad-tailed white necktie worn in the pulpit. **Bonnet** is the flat John Knox cap, mentioned *H. F.*, 66, p. 37.

44 17, 18. Ref. to the weak joint in his armor. They did attack him, and he had to sit on the ‘cutty-stool.’

44 20. **grace-proud faces**: another echo of *H. F.*, 87, p. 38.

44 25. **Gau’n**: Gavin Hamilton; see introd. note.

44 30. **What way**: condensed for ‘at the way in which.’

45 53. **And then**: the construction is broken,—‘he ’ll still disdain revenge,’ etc., ‘and [disdain] then to cry,’ etc. **Still** = always.

45 60.　**straight**: rimes with 'wight'; both are guttural.

45 61.　**All hail, Religion!**　True religion remains unsullied by all of Burns's satires.　Presently he was to express his reverence for such in *C. S. N.*　When Carlyle said Burns had 'no religion,' his judgment was partially warped by the very Puritanism which Burns so ruthlessly exposed.

46 91.　**freedom**: referring to the preceding complimentary stanza.

46 96.　**belang'd ye**: i.e., 'to you.'　Cf. *Bonie Lesley*, 14, p. 158.

THE BRAES O' BALLOCHMYLE (1785, October (?)).

In the midst of ecclesiastical and theological bickerings Burns still preserved a note of pure song.　This is only one of several detached songs of this period, and it was about this time that he composed his cantata, *The Jolly Beggars*, his work of greatest artistic promise.

The Ballochmyle estate was noted for its scenery, and was a favorite resort of Burns.　The Whiteford family had to part with the property for financial reasons, and Maria, who sings this *Farewell*, is Miss Whiteford.　Here, again, we have real scenery, real places, and actual names.

TO A MOUSE (1785, November).

Here we have the promise of *Mailie* fulfilled; the tenderness is deepened, the same playfulness is combined with a richer pathos, and the ethic is made to broaden out into life itself.

47 5, 6.　Burns was plowing with four horses.　When the mouse ran, the boy who was 'gaudsman' to the leading pair rushed to kill it with the 'pattle.'　Burns saved the mouse's life, and, as he went on plowing, composed this poem.　*To a M. D.* was composed under similar circumstances, and much of his best verse was composed at the plow.　It was a favorite place of his for composition, and never more so than when farming began to fail him.

48 33.　**For**: in spite of; cf. 'For a' that.'—**Trouble** rhymes with 'nibble,' a local pronunciation.

48 37.　**thy lane**: 'alone by thyself'; cf. the old Eng. usage 'my lone.'

THE COTTER'S SATURDAY NIGHT (1785, November).

There is no need to question the November of l. i.   He was doubt-less composing *Halloween* at the same time.

Fergusson's *Farmer's Ingle*, though it suggested the title and fur-nished the model on which Burns improved, explains as little of the origin as it does of the workmanship of this poem.   Having in previous satires exposed the ugly side of Scotch religion, it is not strange that he should desire to do justice to the beauty of Scotch family devotion.   It was the religious aspect of the picture which first drew him to portray it.   He had frequently remarked to his brother Gilbert that to him there was something peculiarly venerable in the phrase 'Let us worship God,' used by the head of a family introducing family worship.   So closely allied to this sincere religion as to form part of it is the ethical element that gives the picture its human beauty.

The easy and quiet swing of the verse is suggestive.   It no doubt points to a careful study of Shenstone, but it also means that Hypocrisy and Superstition and Cant, with their 'holy robes and hellish spirit,' their 'mean revenge' and 'malice false,' and all the sickening and irri-tating thoughts of the Herds and Holy Willies have been dismissed. He had summed them up in *Ep. McM.* and put them away, and now he turns with a calm spirit to the simple dignity of the cotter's home and bids 'All hail' to the religion of his father's fireside.   This serious picture is as true to fact as the contemptuous humors of *H. F.*

49 12.   **pleugh**: pron. here 'plooch' to rime with **sugh** (sooch).   See *D. and Dr. H.*, 134, note.

49 14.   **Cotter**: the life selected is socially a degree below that of his father's home.   Burns's father, like himself, was a yeoman rather than a peasant.   For another description of the cotter's life, see *T. D.*, p. 71.

49 17.   **the morn**: regular Scotch for 'to-morrow'; so we have *the day, the nicht, the streen.*

50 21.   Burns was a student and admirer of Gray; this is a remi-niscence of the *Elegy*, —

> 'For them no more the blazing hearth shall burn,
>   Nor busy housewife ply her evening care,
>   No children run to lisp their sire's return
>   Or climb his knees the envied kiss to share.'

Burns headed the poem by a quotation from the same source.

50 26.   **Does**: see Gram. Introd. — **Kiaugh and care**: var. 'carking cares.'

50 29. **At service:** even the small farmers sent their sons and daughters out into 'service.'

50 31. **toun:** 'farm-toun.' See Vocab.

50 35. **deposite:** old Sc. pron. due to Fr. influence; cf. *envý*.

50 42. **Anticipation:** the contrast between this strikingly eighteenth-century line and the couplet that follows is so violent that only a false admiration for his English predecessors can explain it. There are other feeblenesses due to the same cause.

50 47. **warned:** not *warnèd*. The roll of the *r* gives the extra syllable.

51 50-54. These lines embody the groundwork of the old Scotch training, always liable to perversion, and now disappearing.

51 58. **hame:** i.e., back to her 'place.' When a farm-servant is 'fee'd,' his or her new place of abode is 'hame.' To 'gae hame' in this connection is to go to begin work in the new place.

51 70. **wiles:** 'penetration'; cf. wily, above, l. 50.

51 77. **If Heaven,** etc.; versified from *Comm. Pl. Bk.*, April, 1873.

52 93. **sowpe:** applied to any kind of liquid; see Vocab.

52 103. **ha'-bible:** a possession in almost every Scottish home. The scene is described from his father's household; Burns, too, in his own home was punctilious in the observance of family worship.

52 111. **Dundee . . . Martyrs . . . Elgin:** names of favorite old church melodies: note that the *g* of Elgin is hard.

53 116. **ear . . . raise:** grammar according to sense, — 'trills that tickle the ear raise no,' etc.; 'they' (l. 108) = the trills.

53 118-135. Burns was very familiar with the Bible, and here he rapidly traverses both Old and New Testaments. In the latter stanza he speaks of the Gospels (128-130), Acts (131), Epistles (132), and Apocalypse (133-5).

53 129. **second name:** i.e., second person of the Trinity.

53 138. 'Pope's *Windsor Forest.'* — *B.*

> ' See! from the brake the whirring pheasant springs
>   And mounts exulting on triumphant wings.' — ll. 111, 112.

54 145-153. This stanza is a direct and deliberate offset to the religion of the Holy Fair and the pulpit.

54 158, 159. **raven . . . lily:** Psalm cxlvii, 9; Matthew, vi, 28.

54 163. The late Professor John Nichol, in the Introductory Essay to Mr. Scott Douglas's edition, finds the secret of Scotland's greatness to 'rely on the influence of a few men of such character as the father of Burns.' When Carlyle with filial adoration compares his father with

Burns, to the latter's disadvantage, he should have made the comparison between his own and the poet's father.

54 166. Pope, *Essay on Man*, iv, 248. The cast of the preceding line is taken from Goldsmith, —

> ' Princes and lords may flourish and may fade, —
> A breath can make them, as a breath has made.'
>
> *Deserted Village*, 53.

54 171. Cf. *The T. D.*, pp. 71 ff. This inveterate jealousy and suspicion of rank grew on Burns in his later life.

55 176. **prevent from luxury**: the old dread alike of Roman Stoic and Scotch Puritan. **Prevent** is simply 'shut off.' The peculiarity is in the noun 'contagion,' where we should expect 'from being contaminated,' or infected. ·

55 182. **Wallace**: see *Ep. W. S.*, 58, note.

HALLOWEEN (1785; about the same time as the foregoing).

The eve of All Saints (Oct. 31) is a Catholic festival, but, like those celebrations elsewhere, it had in Scotland drawn to itself much of the Pagan tradition and folk superstition of the country. Burns omits several practices that still survive in rural districts, — e.g., masquerading and singing Halloween songs, ducking for apples, eating mashed potatoes out of a common pot which contains a ring, a piece of silver, etc., that bring special destinies on the finder. Those preserved by Burns have now almost entirely disappeared, and may have begun to fall into desuetude in the poet's day. Naturally, therefore, Burns in localizing the poem goes back to the scenery and associations of his childhood, when credulity and imagination were equally brisk.

John Mayne (1759-1836), author of *The Siller Gun, Helen of Kirkconnell, Logan Braes*, etc., wrote a poem on Halloween, which appeared in the *Weekly Magazine*, November, 1780 (cf. *Ep. J. L.*, introd. note). Burns probably made use of it. It is quoted after *Halloween* in the 3 vol. edition of Burns's works, published by Jas. R. Osgood & Co., Boston, 1877. Mayne introduces the 'guidwife's nits,' the reference to people 'trying their nits,' the charms of the 'blue-clue,' and the 'hemp-seed,' the incident of falling into a 'peatpot.' The composition of Burns's *Halloween* evinces great care, and while, like the *Holy Fair*, the poem points to the inspiration of recent occurrences, it was by no means hurriedly written. The poet's descriptive power is here at its best. As a picture of a different phase of Scottish country life, it is a striking comparison to *C. S. N.*, and another offset to *H. F.* Burns fully annotated the poem himself, as if conscious that he was preserving traditions that were soon to be obsolete.

55 1. **that night**: 'when witches, devils, and other mischief-making beings are all abroad, . . . particularly the fairies.' — *B.* The fairies were supernatural beings about the height of quart bottles; they dressed in green, and loved to dance on sequestered spots of fine sward and grassy knolls. The superstitious Scot sought to propitiate them in various ways, e.g., by calling them 'the gude bodies' (cf. the Gr. *Eumenides*).

55 2. **Cassilis Downans**: 'certain little, romantic, rocky, green hills in the neighborhood of the ancient seat of the Earls of Cassilis.' — *B.* They are on the lower Doon, near Burns's birthplace.

55 5. **Colean**: Culzean, or Colean, House is another seat of the Cassilis family, situated on the cliffy Carrick coast; the cove, another haunt of the fairies, is right under the castle.

55 13. **Carrick**: see *R. R. R.*, 1, note. King Robert Bruce was originally Earl of Carrick.

56 20. 'Better looking than when they have fine clothes on.'

56 23. **wooer-babs**: rosettes to set off the knee-breeches then worn.

56 29. **stocks**: 'The first ceremony of Halloween is pulling each a stock, or plant, of kail. They must go out, hand in hand, with eyes shut and pull the first they meet with: its being big or little, straight or crooked, is prophetic of the size and shape of the grand object of all their spells, — the husband or wife. If any "yird," or earth, stick to the root, that is "tocher," or fortune; and the taste of the "custoc," that is, the heart of the stem, is indicative of the natural temper or disposition. Lastly the stems, or to give them their proper appellation, the "runts," are placed above the head of the door: and the Christian names of people whom chance brings into the house are, according to the priority of placing the runts, the names in question.' — *B.*

56 32. **fell aff the drift**: 'dropped away from the others.'

57 47-52. 'They go to the barnyard and pull each, at three several times, a stalk of oats. If the third stock wants the "top-pickle," that is, the grain at the top of the stalk, the party in question will come to the marriage-bed anything but a maid.' — *B.*

57 53. **fause-house**: 'When the corn is in a doubtful state, by being too green or wet, the stack-builder, by means of old timber, etc., makes a large apartment in his stack, with an opening in the side which is fairest exposed to the wind: this he calls a "fause-house." ' — *B.*

57 55. **weel-hoordit nits** : ' Burning the nuts is a favorite charm : they name the lad or lass to each particular nut as they lay them in the fire ; and according as they burn quietly together or start from beside one another the course and issue of the courtship will be.' — *B.*

57 62. **chimlie**: ' mantel-piece ' (not ' chimney,' which is ' lum,' l. 70).

57 67. **says in** : ' inwardly ' : opposed to ' say oot,' i.e., aloud.

57 74. **Mallie** : i.e., Mary.

58 98. **blue-clue**: ' Steal out, all alone, to the kiln, and darkling throw into the " pot " a clue of blue yarn : wind it in a new clue off the old one ; and toward the latter end something will hold the thread : demand " Wha hauds ? " and answer will be returned from the kiln-pot by naming the Christian and surname of your future spouse.' — *B.*

58 100. **win't** : i.e., ' winded ' (wound).   See Gram. Introd.

58 102. **pat** : the kiln-pot, or bottom of the kiln.

58 107. **wait on talkin** : wait for words.

59 111. **apple at the glass** : ' Take a candle and go alone to a looking-glass : eat an apple before it (and some traditions say you should comb your hair all the time) : the face of your conjugal companion to be will be seen in the glass as if peeping over your shoulder.' — *B.* It might be the deil.

59 118. **skelpie-limmer's face** : ' a technical term in female scolding.' — *B.*   Something like ' bold-faced gadabout.'

59 127. **Sherra moor** : battle of Sheriffmuir, which quelled the Jacobite rising of 1715 : the clans were raised by the Earl of Mar, whence ' Mar's year,' below, l. 240.

59 128. **min 't** : ' mind it ': cf. **win't,** l. 100. Grannie is dramatically longwinded in her reminiscences, like Juliet's nurse.

59 132. **stuff** : regular term for the grain crops.

59 133. **kirn** : ' harvest-home ' : cf. *Sc. Dr.,* 49, p. 65; *The T. D.,* 124, p. 75.

60 140. **hemp-seed** : ' Steal out unperceived and sow a handful of hemp-seed, harrowing it with anything you can conveniently draw after you.   Repeat now and then, " Hemp-seed, I saw thee : and him (her) that is to be my true love, come after me an' pou thee."   Look over your left shoulder and you will see the appearance of the person invoked in the attitude of pulling hemp.' — *B.*

60 163. **Lord Lennox' march** : cf. *Tam o' Shanter,* 84, —

' Whiles croonin owre some auld Scots sonnet.'

61 181. **barn gaen** : ' barn ' has two syll. ; for ' wad gaen,' see Gram. Introd.

61 182. **three wechts o' naething**: see Vocab. 'wecht.' 'This charm must likewise be performed unperceived and alone. You go to the barn and open both doors, taking them off their hinges if possible. . . . Then take a "wecht," and go through all the attitudes of letting down corn against the wind. Repeat it three times, and the third time an apparition will pass through the barn, in at the windy door and out at the other, having the figure in question.' — *B*.

61 192. **on Sawnie gies a ca'**: Sandy is the herd of l. 185. Note the stroke of truth : Meg is about to trust herself to supernatural powers, and the call to Sandy is a kind of link with the natural world.

61 201. **faddom't thrice**: 'Take an opportunity of going unnoticed to a "bear-stack," and fathom it thrice round. The last fathom of the last time you will catch in your arms the appearance of your future conjugal yoke-fellow.' — *B*. Fathoming is measuring round with the arms at full stretch. The others had promised Will a 'braw ane,' i.e., a fine-looking lass.

61 202. **timmer-propt for thrawin** : the stack had timbers set against it in case of its twisting as it settled.

62 211. **settlin** : quieting ; the friskiness was taken out of her.

62 214. **three lairds' lands met**: 'You go out, one or more (for this is a social spell), to a south running spring or rivulet where three lairds' lands meet, and dip your left shirt-sleeve. Go to bed in sight of a fire, and hang your wet sleeve before it to dry. Lie awake, and some time near midnight an apparition having the exact figure of the grand object in question will come and turn the sleeve as if to dry the other side.' — *B*.

62 217-225. Often quoted as an unequalled piece of condensed description.

62 228. **The deil**: as in *To the D.*, 41, 47, p. 18 ; the deil has the preference.

63 236. **luggies three** : 'Take three dishes, put clean water in one, foul water in another, and leave the third empty : blindfold a person and lead him to the hearth where the dishes are ranged : he dips his hand, — if in the first, he will marry a maid ; if in the second, a widow ; the third foretells no marriage at all. It is repeated three times, and each time the arrangement of the dishes is altered.' — *B*.

63 240. **Mar's-year** : see l. 127, note.

63 248. **butter'd so'ns** : 'Sowens with butter instead of milk to them is always the Halloween supper.' — *B*.

SCOTCH DRINK (composed probably about the festive time of
Yule and the New Year, 1785–86).

The poem is a development of the stanza of the *Holy Fair*, beginning 'Leeze me on Drink!' (ll. 163–171) and contains other echoes
from the same source. For the earlier date of *H. F.*, see that poem,
notes.

This poem is an offset to Fergusson's *Caller Water*, and the two run
on parallel lines. Burns reverts to this subject so frequently, and with
such gusto, that a word in general may here be set down. In Scotland,
as in other European countries during the last century, ale, whisky,
wine, etc., were not only universal accessories to social enjoyment, but
recognized essentials of ordinary hospitality. To get drunk in company was a venial offence, and among the higher and even professional
classes was a fashionable peccadillo. Scotch butlers took it as a sign
of coming degeneracy when 'gentlemen' were able to go to bed without assistance. This explains the poet's light and humorous handling
of the subject. He himself was no ascetic, and before he died he had
drunk many a glass more than was good for him; but only ignorance
can find the inspiration of his genius in liberal Scotch drink. Of
poems written before this date he has drawn pleasantry from the subject in *D. Dr. H.*, *To the D.*, *Ep. to L.* (1), *H. F.*, *J. B.*, *H. W. Pr.*, and
others. But Gilbert Burns testifies that during the whole Lochlea
period (1777–84) he never saw his brother intoxicated, 'nor was he
at all given to drinking.' Burns himself speaks of scenes of 'riot and
debauchery'; but the fact that up to the publication of his book his
expenses never exceeded his annual income of £7, or $35, puts any
degree of revelry in liquor out of the question. Burns was not a hard
drinker until he went to Dumfries; even then he was not what one
would term a drunkard; and before that his drinking was probably less
than that of the average Scotsman of his day.

63 1. The fourth stanza of Fergusson's *Caller Water* begins .

    'The fuddlin bardies now-a-days
    Rin maukin-mad in Bacchus praise.'

64 6. **glass or jug**: i.e., whisky or ale. So in ll. 8–10.
64 17. **John Barleycorn**: barley is almost the only grain used in
Scotland for brewing and distilling.
64 20. **souple scones**: barley-meal scones, baked without yeast, and
therefore thin and pliant.
64 22. **kail an' beef**: i.e., Scotch broth.

64 23.   **strong heart's blood**: 'barley-bree,' esp. whisky.

64 31.   **doited Lear**: cf. 'It waukens Lear' (*H. F.*, 165, p. 41).
'Lear,' 'Care,' etc., are eighteenth-century personifications: see Gen.
Introd., p. xli and note 1.

65 37.   **siller weed**: arrayed in silver; i.e., served in silver tankards at
the tables of the gentry.

65 41.   **drap parritch**: porridge and small ale, the 'penny-wheep'
of *H. F.*, was a regular poor man's dish.   Carlyle well notices this
poetic interpretation of 'the poor man's wine.'   **Drap**, because porridge
is 'poured' into the dishes in Scotland.

65 45.   **meetings o' the saunts**: assemblages like the Holy Fair.

65 47, 48.   **besiege the tents**: 'crowd open-mouthed round the out-
door pulpits.'   Cf. *H. F.*, 102, 107, p. 39.   **Doubly**: i.e., both by the
'Cantharidian plaisters' and by the 'jars an' barrels' (*H. F.*, 116, 126).

65 49.   **corn in**: see Vocab., *Kirn* 2; *H.*, 133, p. 59; and *T. D.*, 124,
p. 75.

65 51.   **New-Year mornin**: the same custom is described in *T. D.*,
129–138, p. 75.   It used to be customary, and is still common, in Scotland to 'handsel' the new year with potations of whisky.   The custom of 'first-footing' is not yet extinct.   The luck for the year is supposed to depend on the first who enters across the threshold.   Friends,
accordingly, start soon after midnight to first-foot each other with a full
hand and a good wish.   Large quantities of cheese and whisky are
consumed.

65 53.   **sp'ritual burn in**: 'ardent spirits therein.'

65 55.   **Vulcan**: the blacksmith, 'Burnewin' (l. 60).   The smithy is
also the place where Tam o' Shanter gets 'roarin fou' every time he
gets the mare shod.

65 62.   **ploughman**: it is still the custom of the plowmen, when they
go to the smithy with their plow-irons, to give the blacksmith a 'chaup'
(i.e., swing the sledge for him).

66 90.   **warst faes**: Burns here assumes the English attitude towards
the French: all the traditions of Scotland from Malcolm Canmore
down had been those of friendship with France.

67 96.   Four stanzas are omitted here.

MARE MAGGIE (1786, January).

This is the *John Anderson, my jo*, of Burns's poems.   It portrays a
long and tried friendship and those relations of human intimacy that
are common between the country people of Scotland and their domes-

tic animals, and is lightened up by a glow of autobiographic reminiscence. Burns had a favorite mare which he named Jenny Geddes, his companion in many adventures, and his description of her, besides illustrating this poem, furnishes a good example of his Scotch prose: —

' My auld ga'd gleyde o' a meere has huchyall'd up hill and down brae, in Scotland and England, as teugh and birnie as a vera devil wi' me. It 's true she 's as poor as a sangmaker and as hard 's a kirk, and tippertaipers when she taks the gate like a hen on a het girdle, but she 's a yauld poutherie girran for a' that. . . . When ance her ring-banes and spavies, her cruicks and cramps, are fairly soupled, she beets to, beets to, and aye the hindmost hour the tightest. I could wager her price to a thretty pennies that for twa or three wooks ridin at fifty mile a day the deil-sticket a five gallopers acqueesh Clyde & Whithorn could cast saut upon her tail.' — *Letter to W. Nichol, June 1, 1787.*

67 11. **should been tight:** ' had need to be girt for action.' For ' should been,' see Gram. Introd. **Tread** (l. 16) is past tense.

68 21. **o' tocher clear:** his wife brought Maggie and fifty marks as dowry. Fifty marks (Eng. money) would be about $165.

68 23. **weel won:** ' earned by honest toil.'

68 35. **Kyle-Stewart:** the northern division of Central Ayrshire, between the Irvine and the Ayr, in which Mossgiel lay; in the southern division, King Kyle, Burns was born.

68 44. **stable meals:** horse feed was poor at the fair.

69 47. **Toun's bodies:** said with a countryman's commiseration.

69 53. **ev'ry tail:** humorously for ' every head.'

69 57. **Scotch mile:** long miles, commonly called ' hielant miles.'

69 63. **aught hours' gaun:** eight hours' going. **Say rood** = $1\frac{1}{2}$ acre.

69 67–72. ' Thou didst never fret, or plunge and kick, but thou wouldst have whisked thy old tail, and spread abroad thy large chest with pith and power, till hillocks, where the earth was full of tough-rooted plants, would have given forth a crackling sound and the clods fallen gently over.' — *Shairp.*

70 75. **a wee-bit heap aboon:** ' filled her wooden measure of oats rather above the brim.' He knew she would be hard put to it with the spring work ere summer came with rest. **For that:** ' on account of the late season.'

70 85. **pleugh:** plowing team of four horses.

70 89. **thretteen pund an' twa:** fifteen pounds sterling. Not Scots money, which would only be six dollars. Cf. l. 21, note.

70 100. **For my last fou:** for is a conjunction, and **fou** a substantive in apposition to ane. See Gram. Introd.

This stanza ought to be enough to explode the derivation of *stimpart* from *huitième part;* no farmer would feed an old mare with a 'heaped half-peck' of oats at a time.　See Vocab., *stimpart.*

THE TWA DOGS (1786, some time before February 17).

In a letter of this date he refers to it as 'finished.'　He had 'nearly taken' his resolution to go into print, and this poem was composed partly with that resolution in mind.　He indicated his estimation of its importance by placing it first in the Kilmarnock edition.

The poem originated in a desire to perpetuate the memory of a favorite dog, Luath, that had been wantonly killed.　But this idea grew into the tale of the two dogs, in which with an inimitable blending of canine humor and human seriousness the social circumstances of the peasant-farmer are shown forth in clear relief against the upper landed proprietary, — a tale in which homily rises to poetry.　In its account of the Cotter's life the poem is a companion picture to *C. S. N.*, but it is not a sermon on rustic contentment. Cæsar is an invention introduced as a foil to Luath, and it is to be observed that the peasant dog has a fairly favorable estimate of the laird class; it is Cæsar who is better informed and brings disillusion.

71 2.　**King Coil**: see *A. M. M.*, 35, note.　This poem, like *Halloween,* takes us back to the Mount Oliphant days.　The district is said to have taken its name from Coilus, a Pictish king.

71 12.　**cod**: Cæsar was a Newfoundland dog.　His freedom from pride is at once the result of his being a good dog and the cause of his being a severe critic of the class to which he belongs.　In his letter to Dr. Moore (Aug. 2, 1787), Burns speaks of his boyish friendship with social superiors and their kindness to him, adding, 'It takes a few dashes into the world to give the young Great man that proper, decent, unnoticing disregard for the poor, insignificant, stupid peasantry.'

71 21.　**stan't**: 'have stood.'

72 24.　**rantin, ravin**: an echo of the song *Rantin, Rovin Robin.*

72 26.　**Luath**: named after 'Cuchullin's dog in Ossian's *Fingal.*' — *B.*

72 37.　**Nae doubt**: observe the implied sarcasm on the 'lords of creation' and their relations.　For the study of animal life, cf. *A. M. M.*

72 51. **racket rents**: a recollection of the 'ruinous bargain' of Mount Oliphant.

73 58. **Geordie**: golden guineas bearing King George's head.

73 65. **whipper-in**: Burns's hatred of fox-hunting here shows itself as contempt for the huntsman, — ' worthless elf,' 'it.'

73 71 ff. In this bitterly realistic picture of the cotter's life, Luath can scarcely be regarded as preaching the contentment he closes with; and Burns was no cynic.

73 78. **thack and rape**: metaphor here for 'the necessaries of life'; for a literal use of the term, see *B. A.*, 2, p. 109, and note.

74 93. **court-day**: the day on which the tenants have to go to the factor's office with their rents; if they fail, the sequel. is apt to be as described in the lines that follow.

74 96. **factor**: landlord's agent. ' We fell into the hands of a factor who sat for the picture I have drawn of one in my Tale of the *Twa Dogs* ... My indignation yet boils at the scoundrel factor's insolent, threatening letters which used to set us all in tears.'—*B.* (Letter to Dr. Moore.)

74 102. **wretches**: 'wretched beings.'

74 105–6. This confession is so grim that it makes Luath appear almost as a foil to Cæsar rather than conversely.

75 111 ff. Few have spoken so feelingly of domestic joys as Burns; cf. *Ep. D. B.*, 52–54, p. 141, and elsewhere.

75 115. **twalpennie worth**: = a Scots pint; but Scots pints were four times as large as English pints, and a Scots penny was only a twelfth of an English one.

75 118. **Kirk and State**: until the year 1874 the clergy of the Church of Scotland were appointed by ' patrons ' of the various livings. Patronage was much discussed in Burns's time, and ultimately caused the Disruption of 1843, when a section of the church decided to 'gie the brutes themsel the power to choose their herds ' (*T. H.*, 89, 90), a privilege which since 1874 has been universal.

75 123. **Hallowmas . . . kirns**: cf. *Sc. Dr.*, 49, note.

75 129. **the year begins**: cf. *Sc. Dr.*, 51, note.

76 144. **rascal**: this is the factor once more; the 'gentle (i.e., of gentle birth) master ' is the laird, who does not rack the tenants except through the factor. Luath's guilelessness is a trifle overdone here to give Cæsar a good cue.

76 157. **tour**: those were still the days of the 'grand tour.'

76 160. **entails**: entail is the law by which property, especially real estate, passes to the next male heir, and is thus preserved intact. It

cannot be sold except by breaking the entail, and for this an act of Parliament is required. Nearly all landed property in Britain is en tailed.

76 162. **nowt**: again the contempt for sports that mean suffering to dumb animals; cf. l. 65. The word 'nowt' takes all the romance from bull-fighting.

76 165. **drumly German-water**: the German spas were coming into vogue.

77 175. **frae courts**: for similar ingenuousness, cf. the reference to 'kings' palaces' in Luke, vii. 25; cf. also Ramsay, *The Vision*, 317, —

> ' Syne wallopt to tar courts and bleizt
> Till riggs and shaws were spent.'

77 180. **Fient haet**: for this defence, cf. l. 144, note.

77 183. **hare or moor-cock**: referring to violation of the game laws, a crime more severely punished in Scotland than wife-beating.

77 195. **bodies**: 'folk,' 'people.'

77 196. **their colleges**: cf. *Ep. J. L.*, 61–72, p. 29, and note.

78 203. **girl**: two syllables on account of rolled *r*.

78 204. **dizzens**: 'dozens' of hanks of thread to be wound for weaving.

78 215. **cast out**: 'quarrel,' ' mak a pley.'

78 216. **sowther a'**: 'cement the whole,' 'make it all up.'

78 222. **run**: 'out-and-out,' 'thorough-paced.'

78 226. **devil's pictur'd beuks**: Puritanic name for cards.

78 227. **stackyard**: i.e., the value of a whole year's crop.

78 230. **this is, etc.**: Burns had small means of knowing the life he so confidently portrayed; but his account represents the current belief of the rural population.

EPISTLE TO JAMES SMITH (1786, early in the year).

Just before this Burns had returned to two subjects which he had simultaneously treated before, — Scotch Drink and Scotch Religion, — and written *The Author's Earnest Cry and Prayer*, and *The Ordination.* Both are poems of extraordinary vivacity and vigor, but have a dash of hardness, the one political, the other theological. Here the poet mellows to the touch of friendship.

James Smith, a shop-keeper of Mauchline, was 'a person of ready wit and lively manners, and much respected by the poet.' When trouble with the Armour family was gathering round him, Burns wrote (February 17): 'I am extremely happy with Smith; he is the only friend I now have in Mauchline.' This is the mood in which the poet has written one of the finest of all familiar epistles, whether prose or verse. He has a happy impulse, his 'barmie noddle 's workin prime,' and the bright movements of his fancy as he plays with wisdom are reflected in the easy ripple of the verse. The poem is especially rich in interest of more than the merely biographical kind.

80 30. **for fun**: this is no mere affectation; it represents one of his moods in which riming seemed merely an idle pastime. Cf. *Ep. J. L.*, 49-54, p. 28; but see below, and also next poem.

80 36. **countra wit**: cf. l. 137, and *Ep. J. L.*, 73, p. 29.

80 37. **This while**: the confidence in his own abilities which this step indicates is frankly stated in the preface to the Kilmarnock edition, qualified by the same diffidence we find here.

80 40. **cries Hoolie**: cf. 'Now that he appears in the public character of an author, he does it with fear and trembling.'—*Pref. Kilm. Ed.*

80 44. **Greek**: represented to Burns the acme of college learning and culture; cf. *Ep. J. L.*, 71-72, p. 29, —

> 'climb Parnassus by dint o' Greek.'

81 52. **whistlin**: may refer to the plowman's habit of whistling at his work; or it may be used figuratively = 'bustling.'

82 75. **joyless Eild**: in one of his characters Burns was prematurely old, just as in another he was always a boy. Here he seems to dread old age. Cf. *The Winter of Age*, notes.

82 89. **expected warning**: the call 'Minutes,' signal for the fore-noon recess of a few minutes for play about 11 o'clock.

83 117. **Luna**: cf. **Terra** (l. 123). Burns's Latin used to be a standing joke in the family, but he took pride in it next to his French. He knew, however, 'small [French] and less [Latin].'

83 126. **rowth o' rhymes**: in *Sc. Dr.* he had stipulated

> 'Hale breeks, a scone an' whisky gill,
> An' rowth o' rhymes to rave at will.'

Here he leaves whisky to the 'cairds' (l. 131).

83 133. **Dempster**: a patriotic Scotsman and member of Parliament.

83 134. **Pitt**: Pitt the younger, then Prime Minister, who is frequently complimented by Burns; cf. *A Dream*, 55-58, p. 103. At a late hour he recognized the similarity of the genius of Burns to that of Shakspere.

84 137. **wit**: last century use of the word, more akin to 'good sense.' A person of 'little wit' in Scotch is a foolish person, not a dull one; add polish, and you have the 'wit' of Pope.

84 145. **throws**: see Gram. Introd.

84 163–8. This stanza is an anticipation of the *Address to the Unco Guid*. The poems touch at other points.

THE VISION (1786, about the same time as the preceding).

The opening lines need not be questioned. This poem bears a very close relation to *Ep. J. S.* Its subject is that which gives its personal interest to the earlier epistle, — his plans, prospects, poetry, capabilities. There he plays over the subject with humorous and familiar fancy; here he settles down to a serious estimate of himself as a poet. The humor disappears, and the fancy warms to a glow of passion. The diffidence, too, which still pursues him, melts away as he accepts the consecration of his life and genius.

Here, again, Burns drew from Ramsay, in whose poem *The Vision* a specter similarly appears to the poet, clad in a 'rainbow-colourt plaid,' and utters words of ardent patriotism. But, as in every case, what he borrows is the merest trifle to what he brings.

Duan: 'a term of Ossian's for the different divisions of a digressive poem; see his *Cath-loda.*' — *B.*

85 2. **roaring**: the 'roaring game' is named both from the noise made by the stones on the ice, and from the boisterousness of the players.

85 7. **flingin-tree**: there were no threshing-mills in those days; all grain was threshed with the flail. Cf. *G. W. H.*, 3.

86 20. **I backward mus'd**: cf. *To a Mouse*, 45, —

> 'I backward cast an ee
> On prospects drear.'

86 23. **stringin blethers**: cf. *Ep. J. S.*, 30, and note, —

> 'I rhyme for fun.'

86 25. **harket**: for the worldly wisdom to which he did not harken, see *Ep. Y. Fr.*, 49–56, p. 100.

87 55. **hair-brain'd sentimental trace**: this and the 'wildly-witty air' would, according to Arnold, be of Celtic origin; the *Duans* and the tartan robe (l. 61) give the same indication.

87 63. **Jean.** So it was originally written, but when the poems were already in press he changed it to 'my Bess, I ween,' on account of his trouble with the Armours. In 1787 'my bonie Jean' was restored.

87 72. **well known land** : Ayrshire, or, more strictly, Kyle.

88 86. **an ancient borough** : the charter of Ayr is probably the oldest known; it was granted about 1200 by William the Lion, who made the town a royal burgh and royal residence.

88 96. Here follow seven stanzas celebrating the Wallaces, first introduced into the Edinburgh edition. Thirteen more stanzas of the first *Duan*, chiefly panegyrical of patrons, Burns was impulsive enough to write, but had the good sense to keep in MS.

88 133. **musing-deep** : i.e., deep-musing.

89 139. **inspirèd bard** : his confident self-possession here is in striking contrast with the hesitancy of *Ep. J. S.*, 37 ff., p. 80.

89 146. **aërial band** : similarly, the spirit of Caledon, in Ramsay's *Vision*, has aërial attendants.

89 157. Seven stanzas describing the offices of the several orders of spirits are here omitted.

89 199. **Coila : from Coil.** See *T. D.*, 2, p. 71, and *K. R. R.*, 1, p. 15. Burns tells us he took the idea from Scota, the muse of Alexander Ross. (See Gen. Introd, p. xxix, n. 2.)

89 209. **Fir'd** : agrees with *thee* contained in *thy*. The 'artless lays' are those of the Song Collection, his *vade mecum* at Mount Oliphant, and the version of Blind Harry's *Wallace* by Hamilton (*Ep. W. S.*, 15 and 58, notes).

90 211. **shore** : if Burns did this, it is strange that the sea should occupy so insignificant a place in his poetry. (See Gen. Introd., pp. liii–liv.)

90 215. **grim Nature** : see *Ep. W. S.*, 73, p. 34, and Gen. Introd., p. liii ff.

90 234. **soothe thy flame** : 'My passions raged like so many devils till they got vent in rhyme; and then conning over my verses, like a spell, soothed all into quiet' (Letter to Dr. Moore). Cf. *Ep. W. S.*, 30, —

'It gies me ease.'

Tennyson speaks of similar relief in the 'mechanic exercise' of verse, — *In Memoriam*, v.

90 233–246. **I taught . . . friends** : ref. esp. to *C. S. N.* Burns's fame was as yet only local, but it was well established. MS. copies of his poems had freely circulated and won him friends among the country gentry, notably Mrs. Dunlop and Mrs. Stewart of Stair.

91 247–252. Of pure description, like that of Thomson, Burns has very little. Shenstone was an early favorite, whose 'bosom-melting' powers he much exaggerated. Gray's 'moving flow' is that of the *Elegy.* The last two influences affected the *C. S. N.*, which see.

91 256. **army** : branching, many-armed.

92 276. Ramsay is more specific, —

> ' He mountit upwards frae my sicht
> Straicht to the Milky Way.'

TO THE UNCO GUID (1786, soon after the preceding).

At the close of *Ep. J. S.* there is a hint that this subject was occupying his mind. He was now approaching a crisis of those misfortunes which, as he says, 'let us ken oursel'; and this poem is to some extent a personal plea. But the same reflections had passed through his mind and been noted long before, when he was in similar distress :

'Let any of the strictest character for regularity of conduct among us examine impartially how many of his virtues are owing to constitution and education; how many vices he has never been guilty of, not from any care or vigilance, but from want of opportunity or some accidental circumstance intervening; how many of the weaknesses of mankind he has escaped because he was out of the line of such temptation; and what often, if not always, weighs more than all the rest, how much he is indebted to the world's good opinion because the world does not know all: I say any man who can thus think, will scan the failings, nay, the faults and crimes of mankind around him with a brother's eye.' — *Comm. Pl. Bk.,* March, 1784.

The poem, no less remarkable for its penetration than for its kindliness, is at once a plea for the ethical right and a condemnation of the Pharisaism which turns goodness into the 'righteousness over much' of the Unco Guid.

The fact that it had such a distinct personal application to his case at this time may have induced Burns to omit the poem from the Kilmarnock edition. It first appeared in the Edinburgh edition.

92 8. **plays clatter** : cf. 'played dirl,' *D. and Dr. H.,* 95, note.

92 10. **counsel** : advocate, a law term. So 'propone defences,' l. 14.

93 21. **Discount** : see introd. note. They are asked to discount, not all their purity, as a comma after 'gave' would imply, but as much of it as is due to scanty opportunity : 'what scant occasion, and your better art of hiding, gave to that purity,' etc.

93 30. **your . . . hell**: these people are as narrow in pocket as in mind, and dread of expense is often a more powerful deterrent than dread of 'the eternal consequences.'

94 48. **nae temptation**: possessed of few attractions, hence unlikely either to tempt or be tempted.

94 49. **Then gently scan**, etc.: from this point on the poem has become a sheaf of familiar quotations.

Early in this year Burns had contracted a Scotch marriage, valid in point of law, with Jean Armour. About April 13, her parents, furious at her connection with Burns, made her surrender the writing, and destroyed it. Burns felt himself deserted as well as shamed. He thought, too, that he foresaw Jean 'on the road to eternal ruin.' His distraction broke out in that passionate *Lament*, which, but for the circumstances, would be ranked beside his lines to the memory of Highland Mary. The same anguish of recollection and disappointment appears in this song.

SONG COMPOSED IN SPRING (1786).

From its chorus it has also been named *Menie's Ee*. Burns threw disguises over it. He adopted a chorus entirely out of keeping; he appended a note stating that the chorus was 'part of a song composed by a gentleman in Edinburgh'; and he reminded us that *Menie* is for *Marianne*. But he himself was the 'gentleman in Edinburgh,' and 'Menie' was simply Jeanie. The explanation of the apparently bizarre chorus may be found in his note of June 12 to David Brice: 'What she thinks of her conduct now I don't know: one thing I do know, *she has made me completely miserable*. Never man loved, or rather adored, a woman more than I did her; and to confess the truth . . . *I do still love her to distraction*.' (The italics are mine.)

95 14. **tentie seedsman**: 'careful sower'; 'stalks' aptly describes the measured gait of the plowman sowing by hand.

95 23-24. A reminiscence of Gray's *Elegy*, —

> 'Brushing with hasty step the dews away.'

See letter quoted *To a M. D.*, 31, note.

95 25. **'tween light an' dark**: a nice touch of nature; the lark raises his first song before daybreak. Cf. also *To a M. D.*, 7-12, p. 96.

TO A MOUNTAIN DAISY (1786, April).

This poem was originally entitled *The Gowan* ; for the circumstances, cf. *To a Mouse.* In estimating the originality and value of such poems we must bear in mind that Burns preceded Wordsworth.

96 2. **Thou 's**: 'thou has.' See Gram. Introd.

96 8. **The bonie lark**: see above, *Song Composed in Spring*, 25, p. 95.

97 31–54. In a letter to John Kennedy (April 20), in which he encloses this poem, Burns refers to these sentiments as the 'querulous feelings of a heart which, as the elegantly melting Gray says, "Melancholy has marked for her own." ' But these 'sentiments' are far more than reflections on the tragedy of human life; they are cries of anguish wrung from him by dire fate. See preceding song, introd. note.

97 38. **luckless starr'd**: Burns moralized magnificently, but when the pinch came, he often, like a creature of emotion, cursed his evil star, and then his excitable temperament charged the air with blackness, e.g., below, l. 50. It was now, too, that he wrote his *Stanzas to Ruin* and *Ode to Despondency.*

TO MARY (1786, May).

His farming on Mossgiel being a failure, Burns resolved to try his fortune in Jamaica. At the same time, his apparent desertion by Jean Armour and the fancied annulment of his marriage 'cut his veins.' Both ruin and disgrace confronted him, and he felt himself 'nine parts and nine-tenths out of ten stark staring mad.' Now with all the abandon of his passionate nature he threw himself into that love of his about which there hung so much secrecy and out of whose secrecy there developed so much romance. This was Highland Mary, whom Burns's song has raised to a consecrated niche beside Dante's Beatrice.

Mary Campbell was at this time probably a nurserymaid in the family of Gavin Hamilton. She had not been there long, and when Burns speaks of a 'pretty long reciprocal attachment,' his words must be taken as we take his other statement, that this is a song of his 'very early years.' An earlier date for the Highland Mary episode is now known to be wrong, and, strange and disappointing as it may seem, there is no longer doubt that the episode must be fitted into this crucial period of the poet's life. It is further probable that it was as brief as it was rash.

The story of their romantic parting is a familiar legend. Prior to Mary's return to her West Highland home for a season, the lovers met by appointment on the second Sunday of May and spent a farewell day together on the banks of the Ayr. Burns gave Mary a Bible in two volumes (now kept in the Ayr monument) with writing and masonic marks in each, and they parted, never to meet again. Five months later, October 20, Mary died in Greenock, and was buried there in the West Kirkyard, a spot neglected for all but her.

See also notes on *To Mary in Heaven* and *Highland Mary ;* and, for a full discussion, see *Works,* I. 294–299 and IV. 121–130.

EPISTLE TO A YOUNG FRIEND (1786, May).

This unique composition is addressed to a son of Robert Aiken, the lawyer, to whom Burns dedicated his *Cotter's Saturday Night.* More 'sermon' than 'sang,' it marks a revulsion into a mood of dispassionate worldly wisdom. In his trouble he had given way to grief and despair, to hot self-reproach and bitter scorn. Now he arrays his experience of the world and his knowledge of human nature to point the way to that respectability and mundane success which he himself had failed to attain. Still, the epistle, with all its cold prudence, is only a mood. The same mood often occurs incidentally ; here it is unique by being sustained. It reads, too, as if the writer were advising himself rather than some one else, and it has in it *inter alia* more of the ordinary 'canny Scot' than anything else he has written.

99 25. **they** : repeated in 'their' (next line) ; see Gram. Introd.

99 27–28. **end . . . answer** : 'answer an end' is Scotch for 'serve a purpose.'

100 37–40. These lines may be simply a bit of the common worldly prudence of the 'pawky' Scot, but they find a striking parallel in Chesterfield's *Letters,* which Burns may have read. 'Sly' has no mean sense here ; it is simply 'shrewd' ; cf. *Ep. J. S.,* 1, —

'Dear Smith, the slee-ëst pawkie thief.'

100 48. Here followed a stanza which Burns tried to suppress. It is weak, but it throws interesting light on the state of his mind :

> ' If ye hae made a step aside,
>   Some hap mistak o'ertaen ye,
> Yet still keep up a decent pride
>   An ne'er o'er far demean ye :
> Time comes wi' kind oblivious shade
>   An' daily darker sets it ;
> And if nae mair mistaks are made,
>   The warld soon forgets it.'

-100 51.   **wile** : cf. the use of ' sly ' above, l. 40.

100 56.   **independent** : see Gen. Introd. pp. lxxvii–lxxviii.

100 57–58.   This couplet has become proverbial in Scotland.

100 61.   **touches** : see Gram. Introd.

100 65–68.   With these lines cf. *C. S. N.* and *H. F.*

101 80.   cf. the closing lines of his *Comm. Pl. Bk.*, — ' Let my pupil, as he tenders his own peace, keep up a regular warm intercourse with the Deity.'

A DREAM (1786, June).

' On reading in the public papers the Laureate's *Ode*, with other parade of June 4, the author was no sooner dropt asleep than he imagined himself transported to the Birthday Levee, and in his dreaming fancy made the following Address.' — *B.* The poet laureate in 1786 was the well-known author of the *History of English Poetry*, Thomas Warton, the opening lines of whose *Ode* may be quoted to illustrate by contrast Burns's frank touch of reality, —

> ' When Freedom nursed her native fire
>   In ancient Greece and ruled the lyre,
> Her hands disdainful from the tyrant's brow
>   The tinsel gifts of flattery tore,
> But paid to guiltless power the willing vow
>   And to the throne of virtuous kings,' etc.

The *Dream* is not a sublime production, but it is full of character. Even the easy gallop of the verse contributes to the *brusquerie* of the poem. Mrs. Dunlop and others advised him to omit this piece from the Edinburgh edition, as it contained ' perilous stuff.' His reply was characteristic : — ' Poets, much my superiors, have so flattered those who possessed the adventitious qualities of wealth and power, that I am determined to flatter no created being. I set as little store by princes,

lords, clergy, critics, etc., as all these respective gentry by my bardship.'
(*Letter to Mrs. D.*, April 30, 1787.)   Yet the *Dream* was neither written
nor printed out of defiance, and its perfect good nature disarms all
offence.   Its familiarity is disillusioning, but this is merely the frank
raillery and plain speech of one to whom princes, being only human
beings, are not above a word of honest sense.

The peculiar verse, which is a sort of double four-in-hand after the
pattern of Ramsay's *Edinburgh's Salutation to the Earl of Carnarvon*,
helps to give rapidity to the movement.   Burns did not publish this
poem.   It first appeared in the *Edinburgh Magazine* for February, 1818.

101 4.   **wishes :** usually pronounced as here, 'wisses.'

102 14.   **a venal gang :** those were still the days of 'patrons,' and
flattering addresses and dedications.

102 26.   **aiblins ane :** a 'canny' way of saying 'not a few.'

102 33.   **reft an' clouted :** 'the British Empire is much torn and
patched ; since the loss of the American Colonies a piece of twine one-
third as long will go round the parcel.'

103 43.   **chaps :** like Lord North and the Duke of Grafton.   **Yon
day** refers to the origin of the trouble with America.

103 46.   **peace :** Treaty of Paris, September, 1783.

103 50.   **For me :** a grim allusion to his hopeless circumstances.
'Thank God, death will soon come to save me from beggary.'   Cf. his
humorous anticipation of beggary, *Ep. D.*, 29–56, p. 11.

103 55.   **Willie Pitt :** see *Ep. J. S.*, 134, p. 83.

103 62.   **barges :** ref. to a recent discussion in Parliament over sup-
plies for the navy, in which reductions were proposed to curtail expenses.
England was even then 'Mistress of the Seas.'

104 82.   **Potentate o' Wales :** Prince of Wales, afterwards George
IV, for whom see Thackeray's *Four Georges*.

104 89.   **rattl'd dice wi' Charlie :** Charles James Fox, the statesman,
whom Burns had already stigmatized in his *Earnest Cry and Prayer :*

> 'Yon ill-tongued tinkler, Charlie Fox,
>   May taunt you wi' his jeers an' knocks ;
>   But gie him 't het, my hearty cocks !
>   E'en cowe the cadie !
>   An' send him to his dicin box
>   An' sportin lady.'

104 95.   **him at Agincourt :** 1415 ;   Henry V, formerly the wild
'prince Hal' who held revels in Eastcheap with Falstaff ('funny queer
Sir John '); see Shakspere's *Henry IV.*

105 100. **Osnaburg:** Frederick, first a Bishop and afterwards Duke of York.

105 109. **Tarry Breeks:** Prince-William Henry, afterwards King William IV, who was in the navy. In his youth he married Mrs. Jordan, an actress.

105 124. **sma':** either 'of small account,' or 'petty princelings.'

105 130. **bitter sautet:** Allan Cunningham discovered prophecy in this, referring to the malady of the King's last years.

106 131–135. I have seen petted children sulk over a full dish, who were by and by glad to scrape it out clean.

ON A SCOTCH BARD (1786, June).

Burns's early departure for the Indies was now decided upon, and he had begun to bid his farewells. This one is conspicuous for its playfulness, though it can hardly be said to 'shine out cheerfully.' He laughs, but there is a dash of bitterness in the laughter. The gaiety is rendered all the more effective by an undertone of seriousness, and by a sadness that he only makes believe to laugh away.

106 2. **crambo-clink:** cf. 'crambo-jingle,' *Ep. J. L.*, 45, p. 28.

106 3. **and never think:** poets are with Burns 'the thoughtless clan.' In an *Epistle to Major Logan*, 31–36, he says, —

> 'A blessing on the cheery gang
> Wha dearly like a jig or sang,
> And never think o' right or wrang
> > By square or rule,
> But as the clegs o' feeling stang
> > Are wise or fool.'

107 34. **Ill may she be:** Burns mixed some very hard feelings with his vexation at Jean ; see his letters of this time.

107 43–48. Cf. what he says of himself in *Ep. D., Ep. J. L., Ep. W. S.*, etc.

108 53. **He wad na :** see *Address to the Deil*, last stanza, p. 20.

A BARD'S EPITAPH (1786, June).

This poem closes the Kilmarnock volume. It represents one of those times of keen introspection that are frequent in both Burns's poems and his letters. His self-examinations are seldom morbid, and of this one Wordsworth said, — 'Here is a sincere and solemn avowal — a confession at once devout, poetical, and human — a history in the shape of a prophecy.' In *The Vision* he measured himself with pride as a man of genius; in the *Unco Guid* he held before the poor sinner a shield of scorn for his accusers. Here pride and scorn are laid aside, and he reads his own weaknesses with a manly humility and pathetic truth which turn the sting of every assault upon his character.

108 1. **Is there**: cf. the closing entry in his *Comm. Pl. Bk.*, Oct. 5, 1785.

108 9. **area**: var. *arena*. The country churchyard is meant, lying round the church ; 'weekly,' therefore, means 'every Sunday,' when the people come to church.

108 13–16. So in his second *Epistle to Davie*, he says, —

> 'An' whiles, but aye owre late, I think
> Braw sober lessons.'

THE BRIGS OF AYR (1786, September).

The old bridge of Ayr is one of the most ancient historic structures in Scotland, and the date cut on the parapet, 1232, is generally accepted as authentic. To relieve this, a new bridge was planned and was in process of erection when Burns wrote this poem (see ll. 46, 59–60, 68). Mr. John Ballantyne, then Provost, a friend of Burns, was chiefly instrumental in having the new bridge built, and to him the poem is dedicated in lines similar to the dedication to Mr. Robert Aiken that prefaces *The Cotter's Saturday Night.* The old bridge is still in use, and only in the summer of 1894 its foundations were successfully repaired and strengthened. The line,

> 'I'll be a Brig when ye're a shapeless cairn !'

seems likely to be prophetic, for in 1877 a spate almost proved fatal to the New Brig.

Like *The Vision*, this poem is unequal. There is the same introduction of incongruous matter, and the same blending of Scotch and English, with a similar uncertainty of stroke in the use of the latter.

The influence of Fergusson is marked. There is no mere borrowing, but the poem takes something of its plan, character, and finish from the

Dialogue between Brandy and Whisky, from *The Ghaists*, and from the better known *Mutual Complaint of Plainstanes and Causey*.

109 2.   **thack and rape**: the stacks of grain are thatched with straw and the thatch is then roped down.   See also *T. D.*, 78, note.

109 3.   **Potato-bings**: long heaps, covered with straw and then with earth against winter; the covered heaps are called ' tatie-pits.'

109 9.   **death . . . smoor'd**: Gram. acc. to sense; see Gram. Introd.

109 10.   For Burns's detestation of field-sports and sympathy with the lower animals, see Gen. Introd., § VI (b).

110 19.   **half-lang**: half-grown, a corruption of *halflin*.

110 25.   **ancient brugh**: see *The V.*, 86, note.

110 26.   **By whim inspired**: cf. ' whim-inspired fool,' *Bard's Ep.*, 1, p. 108.

110 28.   **Simpson's**: 'a noted tavern at the Auld Brig-end.' — *B.*

110 33.   **Dungeon-clock**: orig. written ' Steeple-clock,' the steeple being over the old jail.   It exists no longer.

110 34.   **Wallace Tower**: the other steeple, a piece of antique masonry surmounted by a spire in the High Street.   It was removed in 1835, but a new Wallace tower occupies its place.

110 35-36.   Noteworthy as one of Burns's few references to the sea; cf. *The V.*, 211-2, p. 90, where the language is curiously like this.

110 40.   **gently crusting**: the ' infant ice ' serves another purpose later on, l. 175.

111 53.   **Pictish**: popularly applied in Scotland to very ancient structures.   ' Gothic ' is similarly loose here; cf. *Vandal*, l. 73.

111 58.   **Adams**: the architect.   The next couplet refers to the ' rising piers ' above, l. 46.

111 66.   **down the water**: the new bridge is about 100 yards below.

111 69.   **as me**: quite good Scotch ; cf. the French use of *moi*.

111 74.   **much about it**: idiomatic for ' much the same.'

111 75-76.   This couplet is not in the MS.; if it was inserted in proof-correction, it was a remarkably happy second thought.

112 79.   **Ducat-stream**: 'a noted ford just above the Auld Brig.'—*B.*

112 86.   **I 'll be a Brig**: see Introd. note.

112 94.   **haunted Garpal**: 'ghaists still inhabit there.' — *B.*

112 99.   **Glenbuck . . . Ratton-Key**: i.e., 'from source to mouth.' ' Key ' = quay.

112 102.   The whole ' Poussin-like ' picture is a striking one of a Scotch stream in a ' spate.'   See Carlyle's *Essay on Burns*.

113 110.   **groves**: a description of Gothic architecture in general, the idea of whose columns and arched recesses is taken from the woods.

113 115. **Forms** [that] **might**: the Second Commandment forbids worshipping any likeness of anything 'in heaven above, or the earth beneath, or the waters under the earth.'

113 119. **mason**: used as an adj., 'that builds.'

113 122. **cuifs**: ref. to the Auld Licht Puritans.

113 133. **godly brethren**: in the pre-Reformation times Ayr had two monasteries. Cf. l. 120, above.

113 135. A dig at the easy-going lawyers of his own day.

113 136. **aboon the broo**: over the water.

114 151. **mak to through**: 'succeed in making through with, or good.'

114 157. **odd**: the rhyme originally stood, 'bodies . . . odious.'

114 159. **Citizen**: the 'city gent' of *Ep. Lapraik*, II, 61 ; contemptuously shortened into 'cit.' in *Ep. J. S.*, 135, p. 84:

> 'Gie wealth to some be-ledger'd cit.'

114 171. **A fairy train**: this is like a flash from *A Midsummer Night's Dream ;* the incongruity lies in the later application, ll. 201–6.

115 178. **M'Lauchlan**: 'a well-known performer of Scottish music on the violin.' — *B.*

115 180. **strathspeys**: commonly called 'Scotch reels'; but the strathspey is the slow movement; the reel, the quick time that follows. The name is taken from the *Strath* (or valley) of the river *Spey* (Invernesshire).

115 181. **melting airs**: those to which Burns wrote his songs.

115 201. **Courage**: the Montgomeries, famous in battle story, are here complimented, esp. " Soger Hugh "; the Teal passes their country seat, Coilsfield House.

116 203. **Benevolence**: Mrs. Stewart of Stair, one of his earliest patrons.

116 205. **Learning and Worth**: Dugald Stewart of Catrine House, professor of Mental Philosophy in the University of Edinburgh. Dining with him, Burns met his first 'lord' ; see next selection.

The poem breaks off abruptly, but the subject is not one suited for expanded treatment. It offers little evidence for or against Burns's ability to handle elaborate work. As a matter of fact, Burns never did produce an extended work, but it would be rash criticism to affirm that the author of the *Jolly Beggars* had no genius that way.

LORD DAER (1786, October).

Being introduced to Professor Stewart by Dr. Mackenzie of Mauch-line, Burns was invited to dine at Catrine House (see *B. A.*, 205, note), and there met Lord Daer, son and heir-apparent of the Earl of Selkirk, who incidentally called.　This was the poet's first interview with a member of the British aristocracy, and he was agreeably disappointed in his impressions.　Two days later he sent the verses to Dr. Mackenzie, with a note saying that they were 'really *extempore*, but a little corrected since.'

116 13.　**stand out, my shin**: as in a pompous stage-strut.

117 29.　**what surprised me**: for his preconceived notions of such rank, see *T. D.*, p. 71.

117 31.　**watch'd**: i.e., looked for.

117 34.　Repeated from his description of *Cæsar* (*T. D.*, 16, p. 71).

117 37.　Upon this he acted when he entered the world of rank and fashion in Edinburgh.

The immediate success of his volume did not at once affect the poet's plans for emigration.　He bought a passage to Jamaica, sent his baggage to Greenock, wrote a last farewell song, — *The Gloomy Night is Gathering Fast*, and otherwise prepared to go.　His departure was staved off mainly by receipt of a letter written by Dr. Blacklock, the blind poet of Edinburgh, who expressed the demand for a second edition, and recommended a visit to the capital, then a strong literary centre.　Burns tried his Kilmarnock printer, but the latter declined the risk.　He continued to harp on the Jamaica string for a whole year to come, but the prospect of Edinburgh and the flattering recognition of Dr. Blacklock allured him and unsettled his plans.　Finally he rather drifted to the capital, in the uncertain hope that something, probably a place on the Excise, might come of it.

A WINTER NIGHT (1786, November).

He sent a copy of this poem to Provost Ballantyne of Ayr on November 20, exactly one week before the author set out for Edinburgh.

Like the *Brigs of Ayr*, this poem opens with vigorous Scotch, pity for the suffering animals being another point of identity, and passes into ambitious English.　That Burns could write effective English is abundantly proved, but here he drops into a bombastic imitation of the eighteenth-century ode. The motive is genuine, but both sentiment and language are yeasty. The Scotch portion is as strong, beautiful, and true descriptive writing as he ever produced. The opening description is modeled on Fergusson's *Daft Days.*

118 25. **you**: anticipated from 'you' in l. 30. Forces are meant.

118 37. **Blow, blow**: paraphrased from the song in *As You Like It:*

> 'Blow, blow, thou winter wind,
>   Thou art not so unkind
>   As man's ingratitude,' etc.

119 44. The three stilted strophes in irregular metre which follow are in the mood of *Man was Made to Mourn.* The return to common sense in 'I heard,' etc., is as happy as it is natural.

120 93–96. This furnished Coleridge with the closing thought of the *Ancient Mariner,—*

> 'He prayeth best who loveth best,' etc.

On the 28th of November Burns entered Edinburgh and took up his abode in a poor lodging. His fame had preceded him. His acquaintance with Professor Stewart almost immediately gave him *entrée* to the world of letters. Another of the Ayrshire gentry introduced him to the Earl of Glencairn, who immediately led him into the world of fashion. In a few weeks his wonderful personality had brought the whole capital to his feet. Presently Henry Mackenzie (author of the *Man of Feeling*) announced in the *Lounger* the rise of a new poetic genius; Lord Glencairn introduced him to the favor of Creech, the publisher; the gentlemen of the Caledonian Hunt took up the subscription list, and the financial success of a new edition was assured. Meanwhile the poet collected material hitherto unpublished and produced some new work.

TO A HAGGIS (1786, December).

On December 20 it appeared in the *Caledonian Mercury*, a long-established Scottish newspaper, though not the first by a century.

A Haggis is a peculiarly Scottish dish, consisting of a mixture of oatmeal, chopped meat, suet, and seasoning, boiled in the stomach of a sheep; the chopped meat is usually the vitals of the same animal. Allan Cunningham comments: 'The vehement nationality of this poem is but a small part of its merit. The haggis of the north is the mince-pie of the south.   Both are characteristic of the people; the ingredients which compose the former are all of Scottish growth, including the bag which contains them; the ingredients of the latter are gathered from the four quarters of the globe.   The haggis is the triumph of poverty; the mince-pie the triumph of wealth.'

121 1.   **Fair fa'** : 'fair befal,' a form of good greeting.

121 6.   **as lang 's my arm** : cf. 'like a tether,' *H. F.*, 215 (note).

121 9.   **pin** : the wooden pin used for fixing the opening of the haggis.

121 13.   **dight** : pron. 'dicht,' = 'wipe.'

121 19.   **horn for horn** : 'spoonful for spoonful'; the horns are horn-spoons, and they helped themselves out of a common dish in the middle of the table.

121 24.   **Bethanket** : 'grace after meat'; cf. the 'Selkirk' grace, —

> 'Some hae meat that canna eat,
>   And some wad eat that want it;
> But we hae meat, and we can eat,
>   An' sae the Lord *be thanket.*'

121 25.   Cf. the contempt he pours with similar good nature on French brandy, *Sc. Dr.*, 79, p. 66.

122 33.   'His spindle leg no thicker than a good whip lash.'

122 43.   **Ye pow'rs** : in the *Mercury* this verse ran, —

> 'Ye powers wha gie us a that 's gude,
>   Still bless auld Caledonia's brood
> Wi' great John Barley-corn's heart's blude
>   In stoups an' luggies;
>   And on our board that king o' food,
>   A glorious haggice.'

Chambers asserted that this was an impromptu grace, out of which the 'Address' grew.

TO THE GUIDWIFE OF WAUCHOPE-HOUSE (1787, March).

This lady, Mrs. Scott, struck with the power displayed in the Kilmarnock volume, addressed to Burns a clever epistle in rhyme, in which she affected to doubt that he was 'wi' plowmen schooled, wi' plowmen fed.'

> ' Gude troth, your saul and body baith
>   Were better fed, I 'll gie my aith,
>   Than theirs wha sup sour milk an' parritch,
>   And bummle through the single carritch,'

(i.e., single or shorter catechism). Burns in reply tells how he came to be a poet. In his autobiographical letter to Dr. Moore (Aug. 2, 1787), he repeated the substance of this poem, and gave at length the episode of ' Handsome Nell.'

122 3. thresh the barn: thresh the grain crop with the flail; cf. *V.*, 6, note.

122 4. yokin: from 6 to 11 A.M. is the forenoon, and from 1 to 6 P.M. the afternoon ' yoking.'

122 5. forfoughten: in his autob. letter he calls it the ' unceasing moil of a galley slave.'

123 10. rig and lass: it was the country custom to pair off men and women on the harvest field; a pair took a ' rig ' between them.

123 15–20. For this early patriotic ambition, cf. *Ep. W. S.* and notes, and see also *The Vision*, Duan Second.

123 29. the elements o' sang: cf. *V.*, 117, —

> ' Thy rudely carolled chiming phrase
>   In uncouth rhymes.'

123 32. that hairst ... my partner: see above. He was then fifteen, and the girl was Nelly Kilpatrick, — ' Handsome Nell ' of his first song. ' Among her other love-inspiring qualities she sang sweetly, and it was her favorite reel to which I attempted giving an embodied vehicle in rhyme.' — (*Letter to D. M.*)

124 53. Ye 're wae men: cf. *Green Grow the Rashes*, —

> ' For you sae douce, ye sneer at this;
>   Ye 're nought but senseless asses, O.'

124 57. For you: ref. to Mrs. Scott's epistle; she was the wife of a country laird, and therefore not bred to feeding and milking cows.

124 60. marl'd plaid: note the rolled *r*. She had said in her epistle, —

> ' O gif I ken'd but where ye baide,
>   I 'd send to you a marled plaid.'

Burns called at Wauchope-House on his border tour, but was not charmed with the ' guidwife,' nor do we hear more of the plaid.

124 61. **ware**: worn. This is Burns, but it is neither Scots nor English; Douglas has a preterite 'ware.'

124 65. 'Than any one whom ermine ever covered.'

Early in the year the Earl of Buchan advised Burns to 'fire his muse at Scottish story.' The poet answered that he 'wished for nothing more than to make a leisurely pilgrimage through his native country, ... and, catching the inspiration, to pour the deathless names in song.' But Prudence, he says, counsels differently. 'I must return to my humble station and woo my rustic muse in my wonted way at the plow-tail.' — (*Letter to the Earl of Buchan*, Feb. 3, 1787).

Still the proceeds of his Edinburgh edition enabled him partially to satisfy his longing. May and part of June he spent in a tour over the Border country, and on August 25 he started with William Nichol (who afterwards brewed the peck o' maut) on a tour through part of the Northern Highlands. With Burns the Border tour was poetically unproductive; it remained for Scott to reawaken the Border minstrelsy. But the Highlands, besides touching the romantic chord of Burns's Jacobite fancy, brought his mind more finely into tune with the old Scottish melodies. He was now returning to pure song, and for the rest of his life songs were to form, with only one exception of first importance, the entire bulk of his poetical production. On May 4 he had begun his connection with Johnson's *Musical Museum*, to which he contributed in all 184 songs.

THE BIRKS OF ABERFELDY (1787, Aug. 30).

'I composed these stanzas standing under the Falls of Moness, near Aberfeldy.'—*B.* They are partly an echo of an old Aberdeenshire ditty, *The Birks of Abergeldy*. The melody is old Scottish, and bears the impression of the ancient scale.

HUMBLE PETITION OF BRUAR WATER (1787, Sept. 5).

Passing through the north of Perthshire, Burns spent two days at Blair-Athole with the Duke and his family. Athole entertained him with Highland hospitality, and on his departure recommended a visit to the falls of Bruar. Burns went, and found that they were 'exceedingly picturesque and beautiful, but their effect was much impaired by the want of trees and shrubs.' Three days later he sent this poem to Mr. Walker, the Duke's family tutor, afterwards professor of Latin in the University of Edinburgh.

126 11. **spouts**: spoutings or leapings.

126 26. **twisting strength**: 'A happy picture of the upper part of the fall.' — *Walker*.

127 34. **wishes**: the petition was, of course, granted.

127 47. **robin**: the Scotch robin, the redbreast, is a different bird from the American, and is about the size of a sparrow. It is Scotland's only song-bird in late autumn, and its soft, clear trill is in fine accord with the 'pensive' season.

128 62. **hour of heav'n**: hour of heavenly bliss.

128 69. **reaper's nightly beam**: light of the harvest moon.

128 71. **darkly dashing**: an Ossianic epithet. Under the circumstances, it shows how closely Burns observed.

128 81-88. 'The Duke's fine family attracted much of his admiration; he drank their health as "honest men and bonie lasses," an idea which was much applauded by the company.' —*Walker*.

THE BANKS OF THE DEVON (1787, October.)

This was composed to one of the melodies he picked up on his northern tour, — 'True old Highland,' a Gaelic air he heard sung at Inverness, *Bannerach dhon a chri*. The heroine was Charlotte Hamilton, sister of his friend Gavin (the 'Gau'n' of *Ep. M'M.*, 25, p. 44). The song is 'singular as a compliment to a handsome woman, in which he did not assume the character of a lover.' —*Lockhart*. See also *Fairest Maid on Devon Banks*, note.

129 3-4. 'Miss Charlotte Hamilton . . . was born on the banks of the Ayr, but was, at the time I wrote these lines, residing at Harvieston, on the romantic banks of the little river Devon.' — *B*.

BLYTHE, BLYTHE AND MERRY WAS SHE (1787, October).

'I composed these verses while I stayed at Ochtertyre with Sir William Murray. The lady . . . was the well-known toast, Miss Euphemia Murray of Lintrose, the Flower of Strathmore.' —*B*.

The air is that of the old song *Andro an' his Cutty Gun*, which gave
Burns the first two lines and the strain of the last stanza.

129 2. **Yarrow banks**: taken for poetic associations. See *Gala
Water*.

129 6. **but and ben**: 'all over the house she made gladness.'

129 8. **Glenturit**: pron. *turret*. In this wild glen was Loch Turit,
the scene of his lines *On Scaring Wildfowl*.

130 17. Cf. the last four lines of the old song, —

> ' I hae been east, I hae been west,
>   I hae been far ayont the sun,
> But the blythest lad that e'er I saw
>   Was Andro wi' his cutty gun.'

M'PHERSON'S FAREWELL (1787, October).

Another of the themes he brought with him from the north. James
Macpherson was a famous Highland reaver, who, after terrorizing several
counties, was taken and hanged on the Gallow Hill of Banff in 1700.
There is a tradition that he was skilled in music and poetry, and that
while lying in prison he composed the air and song, *Macpherson's Rant;*
at the place of execution he played the *Rant*, and then broke the violin
over his knee. His sword is preserved at Duff House, Banff.

The tame ballad given in Herd's Collection (I, 99), bears, beyond the
subject, no relation to this ' wild, stormful song.' Burns drew the chorus
and the idea from another *Rant*.

> ' I 've spent my time in rioting,
>   Debauched my health and strength ;
>   I squandered fast as pillage came,
>   And fell to shame at length.
>   But dantonly and wantonly
>   And rantonly I 'll gae,
>   I 'll play a tune and dance it roun'
>   Beneath the gallows' tree.'

MY HOGGIE (1787).

This was written for Johnson (see note preceding *The Birks of Aberfeldy*) to a melody which he picked up from the 'diddling' of an old

woman in Liddesdale. She said its name was, '*What'll I do gin my hoggie die?*' It was a favorite of Sir Walter Scott's.

Cromek (*Select Scottish Songs*) remarks that it is 'a silly subject treated sublimely.' Without conceding either the silliness or the sublimity, the reader may recognize the tenderness of *Poor Mailie* invested in humorously tragic array of dark and vague circumstance.

131 1.   **Hoggie**: a 'hogg' is a sheep before it has lost its first fleece.

TO HUGH PARKER (1788, June).

Having realized about £500 from his Edinburgh edition, Burns gave his brother Gilbert £180 to help him at Mossgiel, and himself took a lease of the poetically fine but agriculturally wretched farm of Ellisland, March 13. He arrived at Ellisland June 12. In April he had been regularly married to Jean Armour, and now he was preparing a home for her. He was getting a new house built, and meanwhile had only the accommodation described in the text.

132 2.   **unknown to rhyme**: 'As for the Muses, they [the people hereabout] have as much idea of a rhinocerós as of a poet.' — *Letter to Mr. Bengo*, Sept. 9, 1788.

132 11.   **peat**: used in the hill districts of Scotland as a substitute for coal; it is dug from the mosses, cut into blocks, and then dried and stacked.

132 17.   **Gallowa'**: Galloway is the older name for the extreme southwest counties of Scotland, in one of which Ellisland lies.

132 18.   **Jenny Geddes**: name of the mare he rode on his border tour and after; for a description of her, see *A. M. M.*, note.

132 21.   **westlin**: towards Ayrshire, where Jean was.

133 36.   **cast saut upo' thy tail**: i.e., get near enough to catch or overtake. He uses the same phrase in his Scotch letter to W. Nichol, already quoted (see *A. M. M.*, p. 67).

OF A' THE AIRTS THE WIND CAN BLAW (1788, June).

Burns had hoped for some kind of an honest living to come out of all the huge admiration he received in Edinburgh, something that might enable him to realize his genius. Nothing came, and he was now more than ever unfit for farming. It was in this bitterness of disappointment (see his *Letters*) that he began farming on Ellisland, and no better illustration of his elastic temper can be found than the perfect happiness of this love-lyric in which he greets his coming wife. Mrs. Burns was then with the poet's mother and sisters at Mossgiel, learning dairy matters.

133 5–8. The first draft of these four lines may be found in an earlier fragment, beginning ' Though Cruel Fate.'

> ' Though mountains rise and deserts howl,
>   And oceans roar between,
> Yet, dearer than my deathless soul,
>   I still would love my Jean.'

133 16. The sixteen lines usually sung in addition to those of the text were written by Mr. John Hamilton of Edinburgh, who later contributed to Scott's *Border Minstrelsy*.

> ' O blaw, ye wastlin winds, blaw saft,
>   Amang the leafy trees.
> Wi balmy gale, frae muir and dale
>   Bring hame the laden bees:
> And bring the lassie back to me
>   That 's aye sae neat an' clean ;
> Ae blink o' her wad banish care,
>   Sae lovely is my Jean.

> ' What sighs an' vows amang the knowes
>   Hae passed atween us twa !
> How fond to meet, how wae to part
>   That night she gaed awa !
> The powers aboon alane can ken
>   To whom the heart is seen,
> That nane can be sae dear to me
>   As my sweet, lovely Jean.'

AULD LANG SYNE (1788, December).

Sent to Mrs. Dunlop in a letter of December 17. When sending a copy of it to Thomson (September, 1793), Burns affected that he had taken down ' this olden song of the olden time from an old man's singing.' The phrase, ' Auld lang syne,' is traditional; so likewise is the melody, and from time unknown there have been words to it. To Mrs. Dunlop, Burns spoke of it as a fragment, — ' Light be the turf on the breast of the heaven-inspired poet who composed this glorious fragment.' But Burns knew Allan Ramsay's version of the song, and perhaps also Sempill's — perhaps one even earlier than Sempill's. The earliest known begins, —

> ' Should old acquaintance be forgot
> And never thought upon ?
> The flames of love extinguished
> And freely past and gone ? '

This is attributed to Francis, son of Robert, Sempill (see notes to *P. M.*), and occurs in *A Choice Selection of Comic and Serious Scots Poems*, edited by James Watson (Edin., 1713). Ramsay's version, distinguished by eighteenth-century classicism, begins, —

> ' Should auld acquaintance be forgot,
> Though they return with scars ?
> These are the noble hero's lot,
> Obtained in glorious wars.'

134 9. **And surely**: in Thomson's *Collection* this stanza is placed last; the order of the text is that of Johnson's *Museum.*

134 23. **guid-willie waught**: this is sometimes erroneously written ' guid willie-waught': there is no such word.

GO FETCH TO ME A PINT O' WINE (1788, December).

Sent to Mrs. Dunlop, along with the preceding, as ' two old stanzas,' which, he said, pleased him mightily. The first four lines are old; for the rest, he is said to have been inspired by seeing a young soldier, ordered abroad, taking leave of his sweetheart on the ' pier o' Leith.'

135 5. **Leith**: the ' Piræus ' of the ' Modern Athens.'

135 6. **frae the Ferry**: i.e., seaward, from Queensferry up the Firth.

135 7. **Berwick-law**: a conspicuous hill near the shore by North Berwick, and a landmark for sailors. For ' law,' see Vocab.

135 12. **deep**: var. ' thick,' but ' deep ' sings better.

JOHN ANDERSON MY JO (1789, some time before July).

This was a very old song, reworked by Burns. The melody was originally a solemn chant. In Reformation times in Scotland it was quickened and fitted with a set of ribald words. This ribald version prevailed until Burns rescued the lovely melody and clothed it anew in words that idealize and glorify their subject for all time. This is, more-over, the very best example of the purification Burns gave to Scottish song.

The minor mode of the air suggests pathos, but the sentiment of the song is one of supreme happiness. In Allan's drawing, which illus-trated the song in Thomson's work, 'the old couple are seated by the fireside, the gude-wife in great good humor is clapping John's shoulder, while he smiles and looks at her with such glee as to show that he fully recollects the pleasant days when they were "first acquent." '— *Letter of Thomson to Burns*, August, 1793.

135 1. **my jo**: 'my sweetheart.' The punctuation, 'my jo John,' makes no sense. For 'jo,' see Vocab.

135 4, 5. The discrepancy between the two brows, the ' brent ' and the ' beld,' need not cause difficulty.

TAM GLEN (1789).

Mrs. Begg, Burns's sister, declared that this was an old song retouched. But of the old song nothing is known except the burden, and in the *Museum* the song appears with Burns's name. Its *naïveté* is unique, though not unlike that of *Last May a Braw Wooer*.

136 6. **In poortith**: this was the gospel Burns preached in the Bachelor's Club at Tarbolton.

136 10. **"Guid-day to you,"** — **brute!** This is sometimes punctu-ated "*Guid-day to you, brute!*" and defended on the ground that 'brute' was a familiar salutation of Lord K——, the subject of John Rankine's curious dream: ' Gae 'wa wi' ye,' quoth Satan, ' ye canna be here; ye 're ane o' Lord K——'s d—d brutes; hell 's fou o' them already.'

136 19. **ordain'd**: the word has a theological flavor, fore-ordination being a leading idea in the Scotch religious economy.

137 21. **valentines' dealing**: alluding to the custom of writing names of lads and lasses on separate slips and drawing partners.

137 25. **Halloween**: see *H.*, 215, p. 62, and Burns's note. ' Waukin ' is, of course, ' waking,' to watch the sark-sleeve.

WILLIE BREWED A PECK O' MAUT (1789, September).

In the summer of 1789 Burns and Allan Masterton, the musician, went to visit William Nichol (the hot-headed schoolmaster who ruled Burns on his northern tour), who was then spending his vacation at Moffat. They held a symposium, in celebration of which Burns wrote this song and Masterton composed the air. The Burns punch-bowl in the British Museum has nothing to do with this 'browst.'

137 2. **see**: the commoner, but less authentic, reading is 'pree.'

138 19. **first**: some versions read 'last,' and Burns once quotes it, with 'last' in italics, but there is reason to believe that he changed for the occasion.

Baroness Nairne succeeded in having this song debarred from Smith's *Scottish Minstrel*. She might have better turned the point of its imagined tendencies by getting Smith to quote below it a verse written some years later by John Struthers as a sequel:

'Nae mair in learnin Willie toils, nor Allan wakes the meltin lay,
  Nor Rob, wi fancy-witchin wiles, beguiles the hour o' dawnin day;
  For tho' they were na very fou, that wicked 'wee drap in the ee'
  Has done its turn: untimely now the green grass waves o'er a' the three.'

TO MARY IN HEAVEN (1789, October).

For Mary Campbell, see notes to *To Mary*. Burns did not know of Mary's illness until some days after her death. They had parted in May; Mary died in October. In the interval Mary had drifted from Burns's life, and in the excitements that then surrounded him he had forgotten her. But the shock of her sudden death, and perhaps a sting of remorse, so affected his emotional mind that her memory became to him ever after a sacred idealization.

The melodramatic account of the composition of this lyric accords well with the rest of the romance that surrounds Mary's name. On the anniversary of Mary's death he was observed by his wife to 'grow sad about something, and to wander solitary on the banks of the Nith and about his farmyard in the extremest agitation of mind nearly the whole night. He screened himself on the lee side of a corn-stack from the cutting edge of the night wind, and lingered till approaching dawn wiped out the stars one by one from the firmament.' Finally, after repeated entreaties of his wife, he entered, and wrote the lines as they now stand.

138 1. **ling'ring star:** this is the 'one planet that shone like another moon' of the legend.

138 17. **Ayr:** the spot is still pointed out, — 'a grove more pathetically hallowed than the fountain of Vaucluse or Julie's bosque. There is no spot in Scotland so created for a modern idyl, none leaves us with such an impression of perfect peace as this, where the river, babbling over a shelf of pebbles to the left, then hushed through "birch and hawthorn" and Narcissus willows, murmuring on heedless of the near and noisy world, keeps the memory green of our minstrel and his Mary.' — Nichol's Monograph on Burns.

TO DR. BLACKLOCK (1789, October 21).

It was he who practically turned the drift of the poet's life (see note preceding *W. N.*), and he remained true to Burns till his death in 1791. This epistle was written in answer to a friendly letter, also in rhyme, from the blind poet, August 24. We trace in it something of the bitter humor of that *Extemporaneous Effusion*, —

> ' Searchin auld wives' barrels,
>> Ochone the day !
> That clarty barm should stain my laurels !'

But the Excise had been Burns's early choice. His thoughts first went that way during the dark days of 1786. The subject comes up repeatedly during his Edinburgh season and later. With a return to farming in view, he partially gave up the Excise idea, but a single season's experience of Ellisland convinced him that on farming and poetry alone he and his family would come to grief, and on September 10, 1788, he begged Mr. Graham of Fintry to get him placed. In a letter to Miss Peggy Chalmers, September 16, he says, — 'If I could set *all* before your view, whatever disrespect you, in common with the world, have for this business, I know you would approve my idea.' After waiting another year, he acknowledges receipt of his appointment in a 'sonnet' dated August 10, 1789, and then in his *Extemporaneous Effusion* gives his reason for accepting it, —

> ' Thae movin things ca'd wives an' weans
> Would move the very hearts o' stanes.'

He entered on his duties probably in the beginning of November.

139 5.   **as weel 's I want ye**: a formula of health-drinking; 'want' = 'wish.'

139 7.   **Heron**: Robert Heron, author of a History of Scotland and of a Life of Burns.

140 21.   **Parnassian queens**: to Mr. Graham he writes on November 9, — 'I do not find my hurried life greatly inimical to my correspondence with the Muses. Their visits . . . are short and far between; but I meet them now and then as I jog through the hills of Nithsdale, just as I used to do on the banks of Ayr.' The muses did not desert him to his dying hour, but that gaugership was as detrimental to Burns as it was discreditable to his country. For **queens** some editors read 'queires' = 'books.'

140 25.   **damies**: 'dames,' the 'Parnassian queens' above.

140 35.   **sned besoms**: in the country, brooms are made of furze or 'broom.' The plant is cut ('sned'), the twigs bound together and trimmed, and this head fastened to a handle. The heather plant is similarly utilized. These articles are made by travelling tinkers, and sold as 'besoms,' the distinction being 'broom-besoms' and 'heather-besoms.' The name 'broom' always refers to the plant — never, by itself, in Scotch, to the article. — **thraw saugh woodies**: 'twist willow ropes,' 'make wicker-baskets,' another occupation of the travelling tinker, whom Burns had in mind.

140 39.   **Not but**: the full idiomatic expression is 'no but what.'

140 41–42.   Cf. his *Epistle to Davie*, p. 10.

ELEGY ON CAPTAIN MATTHEW HENDERSON (1790, July).

Of this gentleman little is known except that he was an honored citizen of Edinburgh, and devoted to 'a friend and a bottle.' Burns's very high regard for him is shown in the sub-title to the poem. On Henderson's death, Nov. 21, 1788, Burns composed 'an elegiac stanza or two,' and now he returned to the subject and completed this *Elegy*. The incongruous opening no doubt belongs to the earlier effort. The descriptive detail of the poem is wonderfully close, true, and graphic, and in spite of the invocation, 'Mourn,' the character of the composition is descriptive rather than elegiac; as an elegy it lacks object. Contrast, in this respect, Shelley's *Adonais*.

One MS. has, instead of the motto given in the text, —

'Should the poor be flattered ?'

Shakspere.

TAM O' SHANTER (1790, October).

When Captain Grose was at Carse House, working up his *Antiquities of Scotland*, Burns suggested to him that he should include Alloway Kirk, and roused his interest by relating witch stories connected with it. Grose agreed to do so if Burns would write him letterpress to accompany the picture. Burns sent him three legends in prose and the tale of *Tam o' Shanter*, in which he gives the second legend and part of the third in verse.

This was his first and only tale, just as the *Jolly Beggars* was his only effort towards drama, and between these two, critics have been divided in determining his masterpiece. Carlyle, Arnold, and others have given the preference to the *Jolly Beggars;* Scott and Burns himself decided in favor of *Tam o' Shanter.* There is no need to choose. The kind of art is different; and if the one connects his genius with him who created the comedy of Eastcheap, the other as surely allies him with the author of the *Canterbury Tales.*

The composition is said to have been finished in one day, — 'the best day's work done in Scotland since Bannockburn,' Carlyle says. Through the colored haze of tradition we can see Burns gesticulating with excitement, and believe that his wife saw the tears 'happin owre his cheeks.'

145 1. **chapman billies**: the fairs in Scotland are a harvesting time for all sorts of travelling hucksters; they carry their wares and a stall with them, and follow the market-days from town to town; the stalls are ranged along the side of the street.

145 5. **we sit**: Burns had been there, and he sympathetically includes the reader in 'we.'

145 22. **market-day**: ref. to the weekly market. What with market-days, meal-makings, horse-shoeings, and occasional Sundays, Tam had not much time to get sober.

145 25–26. The construction is, — 'that the smith and you got roaring full on [the occasion of] every naig on [which] a shoe was ca'd.'

145 28. **Kirkton**: a common name for the village or farm near the kirk; here, however, it may mean Kirkoswald, a place which even now lays proud claim to the originals of all the characters, even 'Cutty-Sark.' For proximity of kirk and tavern, cf. *H. F.*, 1 54, p. 40.

146 32. **haunted kirk**: this is the first link between the human and the supernatural in the poem; the second occurs ll. 77–78. Carlyle strangely says that this chasm is 'nowhere bridged over.'

146 40. **drank divinely**: one thinks of the old Teutonic blood, and the gods of old who loved their ale.

146 41. **Souter Johnie**: as the Souter lived in Ayr, Tam must have absented himself from home during the ' weeks ' he and the souter had been ' fou thegither.' No wonder Kate scolded.

146 59–66. This curious streak of sentimental English in a poem otherwise Scotch and humorous is intelligible in Burns, who never hesitated to combine the most conflicting emotions. But here the success of the experiment is open to question.

147 71–78. Taken from the first legend sent to Grose, — 'a stormy night amid whistling squalls of wind and bitter blasts of hail, — in short, on such a night as the devil would choose to take the air in.'

147 84. **crooning . . . Scots sonnet**: 'Scots ' is the more correct form of the adj., still preserved in ' Scots law,' ' Scots guards,' etc. The form ' Scottish ' is also legitimate, but ' Scotch ' is a later corruption to suit the parallel forms ' French,' ' Welsh,' etc. **Sonnet** is used in its freer sense. It is a question whether it was the swats or fear that made Tam sing.

147 85. **glowrin round**: Burns himself had a vein of superstition, as he confesses in his *Letter to Dr. Moore* (Aug. 2, 1787), — 'To this hour in my nocturnal rambles I sometimes keep a sharp look-out in suspicious places'; cf. *D. and Dr. H.*, 17, p. 21, —

> 'An' hillocks, stanes, an' bushes ken'd aye
> Frae ghaists and witches.'

147 87. **Kirk-Alloway**: it is now a ruin, and in Burns's day, though it had a roof, it was a deserted centre of superstitious fears and rumors. Round it lies the churchyard, and the so-called Burns cottage is near by.

147 89. **By this time**: the ground referred to is now all private and enclosed property, and is so changed that it is impossible to trace Tam's steps. This cumulation of subsidiary effects is after the manner of Shakspere, and the device is repeated later, ll. 131–140.

148 105. **Inspiring, etc.**: so in the first legend of his letter to Grose, the plowman had got 'courageously drunk at the smithy.'

148 110. **Fair play**: ' so long as things went fair and square '; or it may be a mere exclamation. The s of **deils** is a phonetic accretion.

148 116. **Nae cotillon**: cf. what he says in a letter from a place unknown during his mysterious rush to the West Highlands (June 30, 1787): 'Our dancing was none of the French and English insipid, formal movements; we flew at Bab at the Bowster, Tullochgorum, etc., etc.'

149 120. **Auld Nick** is Scandinavian, but the pipes are Celtic.

149 127.　**cantraip sleight**: cf. 'magic sleights,' *Macbeth*, Act iii, v. 26.

149 130.　**holy table**: the communion table.

149 131–8.　A reminiscence of the witches' hell broth in *Macbeth*, Act iv, sc. 1.

149 140.　Here Burns originally had two more couplets upon 'three lawyers' tongues seamed with lies,' and 'three priests' hearts rotten.'

149 143.　**As Tammie glowr'd**: to illustrate the creative growth of the tale in Burns's mind, cf. this with the bare statement in the prose version: 'The farmer, stopping his horse to observe them a little, could plainly descry the faces of many old women of his acquaintance and neighborhood.　How the gentleman was dressed tradition does not say, but the ladies were all in their smocks.'　This, it is said, was the point in the composition where Burns found relief in gesticulation, and finally in frantic tears as he came to 'Now, Tam! O, Tam!' etc.

149 154.　**seventeen hunder linen**: linen woven in a reed of 1700 divisions, consequently very fine; cf. 'twal hunder linen.'

150 158.　**burdies**: see Vocab., and cf. Campbell's *Lord Ullin's Daughter*, —

> 'And by my word the bonny burd
> In danger shall not tarry.'

150 164.　**ae winsome wench and walie**: contrary to his custom, Burns does not acknowledge that this line is Ramsay's.

150 177.　**twa pund Scots**: 3*s*. 4*d*. English money; eighty cents.

150 219–220.　The prose version closes more naturally: 'The unsightly tailless condition of the vigorous steed was an awful warning to the Carrick farmers not to stay too late at Ayr markets.'

BONIE DOON (1791, March).

There are three versions of this song,— (1) a rough copy sent to Alex. Cunningham, March 11, which he improved into (2) the version of the text, and (3) the altered and less perfect version generally known. No. 1 is here quoted to show this winged creature in its unawakened chrysalis.　It consists of two twelve-line stanzas:

> ' Sweet are the banks — the banks o' Doon,
> The spreading flowers are fair,
> And everything is blithe and glad
> But I am fou o' care.

Thou 'll break my heart, thou bonie bird
    That sings upon the bough ;
Thou minds me o' the happy days
    When my fause love was true.
Thou 'll break my heart, thou bonie bird
    That sings beside thy mate,
For sae I sat an' sae I sang
    An' wist na o' my fate.

'Aft hae I roved by bonie Doon
    To see the woodbine twine,
And ilka bird sang o' its love,
    And sae did I o' mine.
Wi' lightsome heart I pu'd a rose
    Upon its thorny tree,
But my fause lover staw my rose
    And left the thorn wi' me :
Wi' lightsome heart I pu'd a rose
    Upon a morn in June,
And sae I flourished in the morn,
    And sae was pu'd or noon.'

Until Mr. Scott Douglas's edition appeared, this lyric was chronologically misplaced by four years, and had a touching association with the bitterly real romance of Miss Margaret Kennedy, the 'bonie young Peggy' of an earlier song of Burns. That association is now shown to be fanciful, and we are indebted to its editor for the history and transformations of the poem. Unfortunately, Mr. Douglas, not content to let well alone, must not only furnish a new and 'original' melody, but, in order to accommodate this poor music, and at the same time obviate his objection that the closing couplet of Burns's rough copy is 'a very palpable instance of the "art of sinking" from pathos to bathos,' must 'restore' Burns's perfect lyric with an original variation that makes even bathos pathetic.

152 5. **Thou 'll break**: the grammar here should be noted.

152 6. **bough**: a Scotsman would ordinarily say 'brainch,' but if he used this word he would pronounce it 'boo.' It therefore rimes with 'true' without the canine howl given it by Mr. Scott Douglas, — 'bow-oo.'

O FOR ANE-AND-TWENTY, TAM (1791).

This is a humorous specimen of the dramatic [1] kind of which the foregoing is the best pathetic example.   But it is difficult to draw the line
between the personal and the dramatic songs.   Not all those songs are
personal in which he gives utterance to passion in the language of
absolute sincerity; and again there is a wealth of purely personal emotion in songs that are dramatic in form.   *Bonie Doon* is as genuine as
Ae Fond Kiss, and *O for Ane-and-Twenty* is not less so than *O Tibbie,
I Hae Seen the Day*.   Burns had the dramatic faculty of making others'
experience real, as well as the lyric faculty of making it tuneful.

153 3.   **learn**: good Scotch.   **A rattlin sang** is one with 'go' in it.
She means to 'make them skip.'
153 11.   **spier**: ask leave; she will be her own mistress.
153 13.   **a wealthy coof**: this is the converse of *Tibbie*, where he
says with the same lightness, —

> ' Ye geck at me because I 'm poor,
> But fient a hair care I.'

FLOW GENTLY, SWEET AFTON (1791 [?]).

This song is generally known among Scots people by the name *Afton
Water*.   'A kind of holy calm pervades the soul of the reader who pe-
ruses, or the auditor who listens to the music of this unique strain.
The " pastoral melancholy " which Wordsworth felt at St. Mary's Loch
steals over his heart and laps him in a dreamy elysium of sympathetic
repose' (Scott Douglas's note).   It is a fine example of Burns's lyric
power in English, and a good offset to his statement to Thomson
(Oct. 19, 1794), — ' These English songs gravel me to death: I have
not that command of the language that I have of my native tongue.'
Gilbert Burns said that the song referred to Highland Mary; Currie,
followed by Lockhart, gave it to Mrs. Stewart of Stair (see *B. A.*, 204,
p. 116); but the circumstantials of the song do not harmonize with
either of these claims, both of which rest on the assumption that the
name Afton is taken from Afton Lodge, near Coilsfield, and not, as the
text clearly bears, to Glen Afton, at the head of Nithsdale.   The

----

[1] The word is used in the sense adopted by Browning in his *Dramatic Lyrics*.

heroine was probably some casual fancy of the poet's New Cumnock acquaintance in the Vale of Afton (see *Works*, II, 241).

AE FOND KISS (1791, December 27).

This is one of the poet's earliest productions after his removal to Dumfries. Its subject, Mrs. Maclehose, was a young 'grass widow' whom Burns first met at a friend's house in Edinburgh, Dec. 4, 1784. They were mutually smitten, the lady more deeply, but the poet with greater gush. Then began a correspondence in some respects beautiful and touching as the romantic epistolary of Heloïse, in others among the most nauseating in literature. Burns, under the name of *Sylvander*, wrote to Mrs. Maclehose as *Clarinda* almost every day, and sometimes twice a day, for a period of three months. They were both in Edinburgh, but they behaved like boy and girl lovers who are not allowed to meet too often. Clarinda wrote verses to Sylvander and grew eloquent upon ' Friendship's pure and lasting joys '; Sylvander replied with the excited ardors of a youth of eighteen. She also worked upon his religious sentiment, and, while she subdued his passion, fed it into an infatuation that blinded his common sense. Burns told Mrs. Maclehose all about Jean Armour, and when he decided to go back to the woman who had sacrificed all for him, and give her honorable marriage, Mrs. Maclehose wrote to him that he was a villain. Their Arcadian love thus ended, but their friendship was renewed in the autumn of 1791, when Burns revisited Edinburgh on other business. Mrs. Maclehose was then about to sail for the West Indies to join her husband, and Burns took farewell of her. On his return to Dumfries he sent her this song. Clarinda sailed in February. Six months later she returned to Edinburgh, and lived there to the age of eighty-three, but she and Burns never met again. But see *My Nanie's Awa*, note.

154 9. **I 'll ne'er blame:** he uses the same expression in his letter of March 9, 1789, in which he replies to the lady's charge of villainy.

155 13–16. These four lines were prefixed by Byron to his *Bride of Abydos*. Scott said that they contained ' the essence of a thousand love-tales.' Mrs. Jameson's language was even stronger, — ' the essence of an existence of pain and pleasure distilled into one burning drop.'

THE DEUK'S DANG O'ER MY DADDIE (1792).

This song, which first appeared in Johnson's *Museum*, is founded on an old ballad, set to a melody which is found in Playford's *Dancing Master* (1657), entitled 'The Buff Coat.' The second four lines of that ballad run, —

> ' The bairns they a' set up the cry,
>   " The deuk's dang o'er my daddie, O."
> " There 's no meikle matter," quo' the gudewife,
>   " He's aye been a daidlin body, O." '

For a companion study, read *John Anderson my jo.*

155 2. **dang** : the more correct participle would be *dung.*

THE DEIL'S AWA WI' THE EXCISEMAN (1792, Feb. 27).

Lockhart gives a circumstantial account of the composition of this song, furnished him by Supervisor Train, who succeeded Lewars, Burns's associate. A smuggling brig was stranded in the Firth of Solway, and as she promised fight, Lewars went to Dumfries for a squad of Dragoons. Burns grew impatient at his delay, and composed the song while pacing up and down the shingly beach. This was the brig, four of whose cannon Burns bought and sent to the French Assembly with his compliments.

The idea of the devil dancing away with an Exciseman, however, occurs in a song current before Burns's day, written by one Thomas Whittell, a Northumberland poet, who died in 1736. The first stanza runs, —

> ' Did you not hear of a new found dance
>   That lately was devised on,
> And how the Devil was tired out
>   By dancing with an Exciseman ? '

156 1. **fiddling** : Scotch Puritanism made the fiddle *par excellence* the devil's instrument, chiefly on account of its association with dancing ; but in *Tam o' Shanter* the fiend plays the bagpipe.

156 13. **reels** : cf. *Tam o' Shanter*, 117, note :

> ' But hornpipes, jigs, strathspeys, and reels
>   Put life and mettle in their heels.'

BESSY AND HER SPINNIN WHEEL (1792, Summer).

Into this song of perfect rural peace neither love nor any other disturbing element enters (see notes to *For a' That*).

156 2. **rock and reel:** 'distaff and spindle'; see *Ep. L.*, 1, note.
157 25-26. **sma':** 'little.' Cf. Ben Jonson's saying of Shakspere, '*Small* Latin and less Greek.' Note the French accent of *envý*.

BONIE LESLEY (1792, August).

On the 22d he wrote to Mrs. Dunlop, enclosing this song, which he had composed a few days before on the occasion of a visit from Mr. Baillie and his two daughters on their way to England. Burns had been smitten with spasms of admiration for Miss Lesley Baillie, — 'So delighting and so pure were the emotions of my soul,' he says. He 'convoyed' the party fifteen miles on their way, and as he rode home the old ballad of *Lizzie Baillie* floated through his mind and crooned itself into this song. The ballad begins, —

> 'O bonie Lizzie Baillie,
> I 'll rowe thee in my plaidie.'

158 5-6. Adapted from *Ae Fond Kiss*, 11, 12, p. 154.
158 8. Thomson would have altered this to, ' And ne'er made sic anither'; but Burns defended his own line as ' more poetical.'
158 13-16. For this quaintly original conceit, cf. *Ca' the Yowes*, 17–20, p. 166.
158 22. **Caledonie:** here again Thomson objected, but Burns again defended the word on the sanction given it by Ramsay.

In September of this year began his connection with Mr. George Thomson, who was editing a collection of Scottish music, a work of the same kind as Johnson's *Museum*, but meant to be of a higher tone. For this work Burns wrote in all 65 songs. When soliciting Burns's aid in the work Thomson had stipulated, — ' One thing only I beg, that however gay and sportive the muse may be, she may always be decent. Let her not write what beauty would blush to speak, nor wound that charming delicacy which forms the most precious dowry of our daughters' (*Letter of Thomson to Burns*, Oct. 13, 1792). The same gentleman also recommended English songs (which Burns found so troublesome to compose), probably because the Scottish muse was too little of a prude. Burns objected to his fastidiousness, but he himself had already for years past, and that without making the least concession to pod-snappery, been giving Scottish song a κάθαρσις, or clarification, both poetical and ethical, which finds its best parallel in what Shakspere did for English drama.

MY AIN KIND DEARIE (1792, October).

This is the first song he wrote specially for Thomson, though he had sent others composed earlier. A light pastoral song to the same tune, *The Lea-rig*, had appeared in the first volume of Johnson's *Museum*. This was by Fergusson, and may have been the one Burns had been 'reading over.' There is, however, an older ballad, more beautiful than Fergusson's, but rather broad, beginning, —

> ' I 'll rowe thee owre the lea-rig.'

159 5. **scented birks:** var. 'birken buds,' which is not consistent with the dewy time of year.

159 6. **clear:** ' shining,' ' bright,' as commonly.

159 17. **The hunter:** this stanza was added December 1. Burns was no sportsman, and habitually inveighed against field sports, but he sometimes handled a fishing rod. The story of the Englishmen, however, who claimed to have found him fishing up a tree with a claymore is too silly.

HIGHLAND MARY (1792, October).

Sent to Thomson November 14. For the story, see notes to *To Mary* and *To Mary in Heaven*. This song, too, was written about the time of year of Mary's death, and though his surroundings were entirely different, the same recollections, scenery, and sentiment recur. Inspired by the same idealized memory, this song is a far higher flight than *To Mary in Heaven*. It was composed to a melody, *Catherine Ogie*, one of the oldest preserved Scottish melodies, and so beautifully plaintive that it draws tears to the cheeks of old men. Burns thought it was 'in his happiest manner.' It is interesting to observe how the artist's passionate music of language here rises superior to the shackles of rhyme.

DUNCAN GRAY (1792, December).

There was an old ribald ditty of the same name and air printed in Johnson's *Museum*. Burns adopted the first quatrain. His version is one of the best illustrations of the κάθαρσις referred to in the note before *My Ain Kind Dearie*. In his note of December 4, Burns says : 'Duncan Gray is a light-horse gallop of an air which precludes senti-ment'; but he has succeeded in giving it a humor both rich and tender.

160 2. **o 't**: 'of it'; an idiomatic phrase, really redundant, but giving a certain dramatic round-off to an expression.

161 5. **hiegh**: the rime is gutteral; pron. 'heech.'

161 11. **Ailsa Craig**: a rocky islet in the Firth of Clyde, off Ayr-shire.

161 15. **spak o'** . . . : i.e., 'drowning himself.' Hon. Andrew Ers-kine said this was 'a line which itself should make him immortal.'

161 17. **tide**: i.e., it ebbs and flows and brings reversals.

162 39. **baith**: here a conjunction; idiomatic Scotch order for 'baith crouse and canty.'

GALA WATER (1793, January).

There were several versions of an old song, one of which is given by Herd as the oldest ; another is quoted by Mr. Scott Douglas ; and there was at least one more, *The Braw, Braw Lass o' Gala Water*. Burns first modified the old song and then rewrote it. The subject is a remi-niscençe of his Border tour of May, 1787. The song is a remarkable adaptation of words and sentiment to the melody, which is old and was a favorite of Haydn's.

162 1-2. Var. 'There 's braw . . . They wander.'

162 3. **Yarrow** . . . **Ettrick**: some of the finest of the Border min-strelsy is associated with the 'dowie dens o' Yarrow.' Ettrick is another district on Tweedside, renowned in Border song and the mother country of James Hogg, 'the Ettrick Shepherd.'

162 4. **Gala Water**: a tributary of the Tweed. 'Water' is the general name, = 'river,' e.g., *Water Tay ;* cf. the philologically famous *Wansbeckwater* in the north of England ; but there the usage varies, e.g., *Ullswater* is a lake.

WANDERING WILLIE (1793, March).

An old song of the same name (published in Herd's collection) gave Burns the suggestion and the first two lines.

162 2. **haud awa**: idiomatic Sc. for 'take the road,' 'make tracks.'

163 8. **The simmer**: Thomson's correction, 'As simmer . . . so,' destroys the fine beauty of the implied comparison, by rendering it explicit.

WHISTLE, AND I'LL COME TO YOU, MY LAD (1793, August).

This song was inspired by Jean Lorimer, for some time his reigning beauty, and the subject of about a dozen of his songs. The title and melody are old.

162 1. Var.:

> 'O whistle and I'll come to you, my jo,
> O whistle and I'll come to you, my jo;
> Though father an' mither an' a' should say no,
> Thy Jeanie will venture wi' ye, my jo.'

163 6-7. **yett . . . style**: the meaning is plain enough, but the local particulars are not quite clear.

163 9. **kirk . . . market**: the two great *rendezvous* of Scotch country people.

In singing, the last line of each quatrain is repeated.

SCOTS WHA HAE (1793, Aug. 31).

The original title is *Robert Bruce's March to Bannockburn*. The germ of the ode may be found in the entry of his journal for the first day of his Highland tour, Aug. 25, 1787, when he visited the field of Bannockburn. 'Here no Scot can pass uninterested. I fancy to myself that I can see my gallant, heroic countrymen coming down upon the plunderers of their country, the murderers of their fathers, noble revenge and just hate glowing in every vein, striding more eagerly as they approach the oppressive, insulting, bloodthirsty foe.' In writing to Thomson, Sept. 1, 1793, he mentions a tradition that the air, 'Hey tuttie, taitie,' was Bruce's March at Bannockburn.[1] 'This thought in

------

[1] Cromek points out the absurdity of this; the only martial music the Scots had in Bruce's days was what could be produced from bullocks' horns.

my yesternight's evening walk warmed me to a pitch of enthusiasm . . .
which I threw into a kind of Scotch ode that one might suppose to be
the royal Scot's Address on that eventful morning.'   The sensational
story of its composition, which Carlyle is mainly responsible for propa-
gating, — 'dithyrambic on horseback,' 'wildest Galloway moor,' 'throat
of the whirlwind,' etc., etc., — finds no support from Burns's own account,
and it is contradicted by what he repeatedly says about his methods
of composition.

William Wordsworth objected to this song as 'little more than school-
boy rodomontade.'   But the only *essential* of a song is that it 'sing,' i.e.,
have not merely lyrical but musical emotion ; and about the singing
quality of *Scots Wha Hae* there is no shadow of doubt.   It is remarkable, however, that the melody, which Burns said had often filled his eyes
with tears, should, with all its suggestion of the defiant blare of trumpets,
be the identical melody of the *Land o' the Leal*, one of the most plaintive of all songs.   Urbani noticed the delicacy of the melody and begged
Burns to compose soft verses to it ; but Burns took fire differently.

164 **7.**   **Edward's power** : in 1314 Edward II marched into Scotland
with 100,000 men to relieve an English garrison in Stirling Castle and
reduce the country.   Bruce met him with 30,000 on the field of Bannockburn, and gained a victory which decided the independence of
Scotland, acknowledged by England fourteen years later.

164 **16.**   Var. 'Let him on wi' me !'   Most of the other variations
are due to the persistent obtuseness of Thomson.

164 **21–24.**   'I have borrowed the last stanza from the common stall
edition of *Wallace*' [see *Ep. W. S.*, 15, note] :

> 'A false usurper sinks in every foe,
> And liberty returns with every blow.' — *B.*

THE LOVELY LASS OF INVERNESS (1794, Spring).

This is another reminiscence of his Highland tour.   The entry in
his Journal (Sept. 6, 1787) states that he 'came over Culloden Moor,'
and had 'reflections on the field of battle.'   There was an old song of
the same name, but only four lines of it were left.

165 **5.**   **Drumossie Moor** : another name for Culloden, where the
Jacobite rebellion of 1745–6 was crushed.

CA' THE YOWES TO THE KNOWES (1794, September).

In 1787 Burns made a note of this lovely melody and of words sometimes attributed to wild Tibbie Pagan ; in 1790 he made some alterations
and additions and sent it to Johnson ; now 'in a solitary stroll' he added
the walk at fauldin-time and the mavis' evening sang, the glimpses of the
moon on water and Abbey ruin, where the fairies dance on dewsprent
flowers, the prayer for protection from unholy influences and then the
cry of utter love ; we can see the song tremble, breathe, and start
blushing into warm life in his hands.

165 13.　**Cluden's . . . towers** : the ruins of Lincluden Abbey at the
confluence of the Cluden and the Nith.

166 17.　**ghaist nor bogle** : for similar guardianship from malevolent
spirits, cf. Shakspere's song in *Cymbeline*, —

> ' No exorciser harm thee
> Nor no witchcraft charm thee.'

THE WINTER OF LIFE (1794, Oct. 19).

Burns wrote this to an air which he called 'a musical curiosity, — an
East Indian air which you would swear was a Scottish one.'

The verses are 'dramatic,' but there is a strong undercurrent of personal feeling (cf. note on *O For Ane-and-Twenty, Tam*).　Very early
Burns could moralize with effect on youthful folly and the evanescence
of its joys.　Now he knew that he was about to suffer for those follies,
and already he felt the chills of premature old age stiffening his frame.
On June 25 of this year he had written to Mrs. Dunlop, — 'To tell you
that I have been in poor health will not be excuse enough for neglecting
your correspondence, though it is true.　I am afraid that I am about to
suffer for the follies of my youth.'　In this connection the student
should read his noble letter to Mr. Cunningham, Feb. 25, 1794.

166 15–16.　Cf. *Man was Made to Mourn*, 27, 28 :

> ' Miss-spending all thy precious hours,
> Thy glorious youthful prime.'

CONTENTED WI' LITTLE (1794, November).

In a letter of May, 1795, Burns refers to this song as 'a picture of his mind.' Cunningham says it was written when 'the frozen finger of the Excise pointed to a supervisorship.' But the mood is a characteristic one. Cf. *Rantin Rovin Robin*, 17, 18, p. 16:

> 'He'll hae misfortunes great and sma',
> But aye a heart aboon them a'.

MY NANIE'S AWA (1794).

Sent to Thomson in December, but the song may have been composed earlier, and he doubtless had Mrs. Maclehose in mind. In one of Clarinda's letters (January, 1788) a passage occurs which evidently furnished the motive of this composition, — 'Oh, let the scenes of nature remind you of Clarinda: in winter remember the dark shades of her fate ; in summer, the warmth of her friendship ; in autumn, her glowing wishes to bestow plenty on all; and let spring animate you with the hopes that your friend may yet surmount the wintry blasts of life.' Burns replied, — 'I shall certainly steal it and set it in some future production, and get immortal fame by it.'

167 1–2. **arrays . . . listens**: the first is intrans., the second trans., 'listens to.' The freedom of construction permitted in Scotch made Burns occasionally twist English to suit his convenience.

A MAN'S A MAN FOR A' THAT (1795, Jan. 1).

'This piece is no song, but will be allowed, I think, to be two or three pretty good prose thoughts put into rhyme. I do not give you the song for your book, but merely by way of *vive la bagatelle*, for the piece is not really poetry' (*Letter to Thomson*, January 15). If not a song, and it is more suitable for declamation than for singing, this lyric contains the double-distilled essence of the spirit that produced American independence. The sentiment was not uncommon in the eighteenth century, but it was only a fashion. It served to give a turn to rhetorical couplets, but it meant nothing to Europe until the Parisian *faubourgs* took up the cry in deadly earnest. In this year the French revolutionary spirit was finding its chief apostle in Napoleon Bonaparte, and here the blaze of *Liberté, Égalité, Fraternité,* is concentrated into a burning focus.

168 17. **Ye see:** Burns knew that a 'lord' need not be a 'coof,' but not even the friendship of men like Glencairn subdued his inveterate jealousy of rank and social superiority.

169 25-28. Cf. *C. S. N.,* 165-6, and note, —

> ' Princes and lords are but the breath of kings,
>   "An honest man 's the noblest work of God." '

THE LASS OF ECCLEFECHAN (1795, February).

In a note to Thomson of this date, the poet described himself as snowed up and driven to distraction in this 'unfortunate, wicked little village,' and he elsewhere gives the village a bad name for drunkenness. The place is now better known as the birthplace of Thomas Carlyle, whose parents were resident there, and who was himself born in December of this year. Carlyle's father saw Burns and noted the fact with indifference.

For this lively matrimonial skirmish, cf. *The Deuk 's Dang O'er My Daddie,* p. 155. The proud little beauty in a fit of temper twits her husband with the 'tocher' she brought him besides her 'bonie sel.' In the second stanza the 'worser half' retaliates with another treasure he has in his eye if he only saw the 'green graff' growing over her.

169 8. **toss:** 'toast.' Cf. 'An' yon the toast of a' the town,' — *Mary Morison.*

LAST MAY A BRAW WOOER (1795).

An imitation of the old ballad song like *Tak Your Auld Cloak About Ye, Muirland Willie,* etc. Cf. *Tam Glen.* Its humor and *naïveté* are well suited in the melody.

170 18. **lang loan:** Burns's original reading was 'Gateslack,' the name of a picturesque pass in the Lowther hills. Thomson prevailed upon Burns to alter the word, which he did, under protest, into 'lang loan.' But a touch of locality is thereby lost.

171 **22.** **Dalgarnock**: the name of a romantic spot near the Nith, with the ruins of a church and an old burial ground still to be seen. The *tryste*, or market, was held near by.

171 **33.** Popular usage has made this line, —

> ' And how my auld shoon fitted her schachl' feet.'

The point of this change is that 'auld shoon' is a familiar expression for a rejected lover who pays his addresses to another. No wonder, then, he ' fell a-swearin.'

EPISTLE TO COLONEL DE PEYSTER (1796, early in the year).

The circumstances are those of the first stanza: Burns was now suffering from his mortal sickness.

Colonel de Peyster was commandant of the Gentlemen Volunteers of Dumfries, a company raised in the previous year on the scare of invasion from France. Burns was a private in that corps, and in its honor had written a stirring battle-cry, *Does Haughty Gaul Invasion Threat?* This was the company Burns referred to when he said on his death-bed, ' Don't let the awkward squad fire over me.'

173 **38.** **on a tangs :** i.e., being singed previous to cooking.

GLOSSARY.

A.S. = Anglo-Saxon; M.E. = Middle English; O.N. = Old Norse; Norw. = Norwegian; Dan. = Danish; Sw. = Swedish; Du. = Dutch; C. = Celtic; Fr. = French; M.L.G. = Middle Low German; unk. = unknown; wh. = whence.

a-, prefix used often where Eng. uses *be-,* as in *afore, ahint, ayont, aside.*

abeigh, *adv.* off, aloof. [Etym. dub. Perh. *a,* on, and O.N. *beig,* fear.]

aboon, *adv.* and *prep.* above. [M.E. *abowen, aboven ;* A.S. *abufan.*]

abreed, *adv.* abroad. [*a-* and *braid: ee* is local.]

acquent, *adj.* acquainted. [For *-ted,* see Gram. Introd.]

ae, *adj.* one : also used to intensify superlatives, as in 'The ae best dance ' (*Deil's awa*).

a-fauldin, *ptc.* 'a-folding,' bringing the sheep to fold.

aff, *adv.* and *prep.* off.

afore, *adv.* and *prep.* before.

aft, aften, *adv.* often.

agley, agly, *adv.* amiss, crookedly [*gley* to squint; M.E. *glien ;* O.N. *gljá,* to glitter].

ahint, *adv.* and *prep.* behind.

aiblins, *adv.* perhaps, possibly. [*able* and *-lins,* wh. see.]

aik, *n.* oak. [A.S. *āc ;* cf. O.N. *eik.*]

ain, *adj.* own. [A.S. *āgen ;* cf. O.N. *eigin.*]

aince, see *ance.*

air, see *ear.*

airn, *n.* iron. [Cf. O.N. *járn,* older form *earn.*]

airt, *n.* direction, quarter of the compass : *v.* guide, direct. [C. *aird.*]

aisle, aizle, *n.* burning ash, 'cinder.' [Also *eisle ;* A.S. *ysle.*]

aith, *n.* oath. [A.S. *āð;* cf. O.N. *eið-r.*]

aits, *n.* oats, 'corn.' [A.S. *āte, æte.*]

aiver, *n.* full-grown horse. [Also *aver ;* O.Fr. *aver, aveir,* havings, stock, cattle.]

ajee, *adv.* ajar. [*jee* or *gee,* to stir.]

amaist, *adv.* almost. [See *maist.*]

amang, *prep.* among. [A.S. *onmang.*]

an', *conj.* and: if, 'gin.' [Cf. early use of Eng. *and, an.*]

anathém, *v.* anathematize, curse.

ance, aince, *adv.* once. [Early form *anys ;* adv. gen. of *ane.*]

ane, *adj.* one.

anent, *prep.* relative to, about; beside. [*aneven;* A.S. *on. efen, on emn,* on even (ground), with excrescent *t.*]

anither, *adj.* another. [See *ither.*]

an's, 'and is.' [See Gram. Introd.]

ase, *n.* ash, ashes. [A.S. *æsce.*]

aside, *prep.* beside.

asklent, *adv.* aslant, sideways. [See *sklent.*]

asteerin, *ptc.* stirring, moving. [A.S. *styrian.*]

attour, *prep.* or *adv.* out-over, besides. [*at-our, at-owre;* see *owre.*]

aught (pron. **acht**), *adj.* eight. [M.E. *aht;* A.S. *eahta.*]

auld, *adj.* old. [M.E. *ald;* A.S. *eald, ald.*]

ava, *adv.* at all. [*af a'* = of all.]

awa, *adv.* away.

awnie, *adj.* bearded (of grain). [*awn,* beard of grain, usu. barley; O.N. *ögn,* pl. *agnar;* Gothic *ahana.*]

ayont. *adv.* beyond. [For the *t,* cf. *ahint.*]

Bab, *n.* knot of ribbons. [Same as *bob;* M.E. *bobbe,* a cluster; cf. C. *babag.*]

backlins, *adv.* back. [See *-lins.*]

bade, *v.* past of *bide,* wh. see.

baggie, *n.* dim. of *bag,* stomach.

baillie, *n.* magistrate next to the provost in a royal borough: alderman. [O.Fr. *bailli.*]

bairn, *n.* child. [A.S. *bearn;* O.N. *barn.*]

bairn-teme, } offspring, brood.
bairn-time, } [A.S. *bearn-team.*]

baith, *adj.* and *conj.* both. [M.E. *bāðe;* O.N. *bāðar* (not A.S. *bātwā*).]

bake, *n.* biscuit.

bands, *n.* Genevan clerical necktie worn officially.

bane, *n.* bone. [A.S. *bān;* cf. O.N. *bein.*]

bang, *n.* knock. [Cf. O.N. *bang,* hammering.]

bardie, *n.* dim. of *bard.*

barefit (pron. **berfit**), *adj.* barefooted.

barley-bree, *n.* malt-liquor. [See *bree.*]

barm, *n.* yeast, barm. [M.E. *berme;* A.S. *beorma.*]

barmie, *adj.* fermented, excited, active.

bashin, *ptc.* of *bash,* knocking down (grain), reaping. [?Dan. *baske,* to beat.]

batch, *n.* group, gang. [M.E. *bacche,* a quantity baked at once; fr. A.S. *bacen,* baked.]

batts, *n.* botts, colic.

baudrons (also **bauthrons**), *n.* cat. [Prob. C.]

bauk, *n.* crossbeam. [Same as Eng. *balk;* A.S. *balca.*]

bauk-en', *n.* end of the beam.

bauld, *adj.* bold. [A.S. *beald, bald.*]

bawsnt, *adj.* having a white spot or streak on the face (of a cow, etc.), brindled, blazed. [O.Fr. *bausant.*]

bear, bere, *n.* barley. [A.S. *bere.*]

beast, *n.* a full-grown head of stock.

beet, beit, *v.* to help by adding, add fuel to, incite. [A.S. *bētan;* O.N. *bæta,* to mend.]

bein, *adj.* snug, comfortable, well-to-do. [M.E. *bene,* pleasant. Origin unknown.]

belang, *v.* belong to.

beld, *adj.* bald.

belyve, *adv.* presently. [M.E. *bi life,* 'with life.']

ben, *adv.* and *prep.* into the interior, into the parlor. [A.S. *be-innan, binnan.*] See *but.*

bere, see *bear.*

besom, *n.* broom; see *Ep. D. B.,* 23, note. [A.S. *besema, besma.*]

bethankit, *n.* 'be thanked': grace after meat.

beuk, see *buik.*

1. **bicker,** *n.* a wooden cup. [O.N. *bikarr;* M.E. *biker;* Eng. *beaker.*]

2. **bicker,** *n.* a hurried run. [M.E. *biker,* to skirmish.]

bid, *v.* ask, pray for. [A.S. *biddan.*]

bide, *v.* wait for, endure, 'thole.' [A.S. *bīdan.*]

bield, *n.* shelter, refuge. [Perh. same as A.S. *bieldo,* M.E. *belde,* boldness, resource, help.]

bien, see *bein.* [In no way conn. w. Fr. *bien,* well.]

big, *v.* build; orig. to settle, inhabit. [M.E. *bigge;* O.N. *byggja,* to inhabit, build (*búa,* to dwell).]

biggin, *n.* building, edifice. [From above.]

bill, *n.* bull. [The *i* is local.]

billie, *n.* fellow, 'chield.' [Perh. same word as *bully.*]

bing, *n.* heap (of grain, etc.). [O.N. *bing-r.*]

birk, *n.* birch. [A.S. *beorc, berc;* cf. O.N. *björk;* Dan. *birk.*]

birkie, *n.* smart young fellow (in both good and bad sense). [Etym. unknown.]

birr, *v.* 'whirr.' [Imit. word.]

bit, used idiom. as an adj. = little.

bizz, *n.* bustle, flurry. [Imit. word.]

blae, *adj.* dark blue, livid. [O.N. *blá-r.*]

blastit, *adj.* withered; used as an epithet of condemnation. Burns has also the *n. blastie.*

blate, *adj.* shy, bashful. [Etym. dub. Murray rejects A.S. *blēat,* soft, and prefers *blāt,* pale.]

blaud, *n.* large piece, fragment broken off by a stroke. 'Screed' (of writing): *v.* to strike, abuse, beat down (as windy showers on grain).

blaw, *v.* blow; boast. [A.S. *blāwan.*]

bleer't, *ptc.* bleared. [M.E. *bleren.*]

bleeze, *n.* blaze. [A.S. *blæse,* a torch.]

blellum, *n.* idle talker, 'blatherskite.'

1. **blether,** *v.* talk nonsense.

2. **blether,** *n.* bladder. [O.N. *blaðra;* A.S. *blǣdre.*]

blethers, *n.* nonsense. [O.N. *blaðra.* For vowel, cf. gather, gether.]

blink, *n.* gleam, twinkle; brief moment.

blitter, *n.* snipe : prop. bittern.

bluid, blude, *n.* blood.

bluntie, *adj.* dull, stupid. [M.E. *blunt.*]

blype, *n.* strip, peeling (of skin).

bock, *v.* vomit, belch, pour out. [M.E. *bolken.*]

bodle, *n.* a copper coin = 2 pennies Scots, said to have been named after mint-master *Bothwell.*

body, bodies, *n.* person, folk; often contemptuous.

bog-hole, *n.* quagmire, 'wall-ee.' [C. *bog*, soft ; *bogach*, a morass.] Dim. *boggie.*

bogle, *n.* goblin, 'doolie.' [Prob. C. *bwg, bwgwl*, hobgoblin ; cf. obs. Eng. *bug* as in *bug-bear*, and Eng. *boggle*, to start aside for fear.]

bonie, bonnie, *adj.* good-looking, beautiful, winsome. [Fr. *bon.*]

boord, buird, *n.* board.

boortree, bourtree, *n.* elder. [Also *bountree ;* der. *boretree*, from its soft pith, questionable.]

boost, *v.* must, ought. [M.E. *boes, bus ;* past *bude, bood ;* orig. impers., contr. fr. (it) *behoves.*]

bore, *n.* hole, burrow, crevice. [A.S. *borian ;* O.N. *bora.*]

bouse, *v.* drink deeply: *n.* drinking-bout. [M.E. *bousen ;* M.Du. *busen.*]

bow-kail, *n.* cabbage.

bow't, (pron. **boo'd**), *ptc.* crooked, bent.

bracken, *n.* fern. [M.E. *braken ;* cf. Sw. *bräken ;* Eng. *brake*, fern.]

brae, *n.* slope, rising ground. [O.N. *brā*, eyebrow, brow of a hill.]

braid, *adj.* broad. [A.S. *brād;* cf. O.N. *breiðr.*]

braik, *n.* a heavy harrow for pulverizing. [Same word as Eng. *break.*]

braindge, *v.* plunge (of a horse): also *breendge.*

brak, *v.* broke.

branks, *n.* a wooden bridle for cows. [C. *brang*, part of a horse's halter.]

brash, *n.* a sudden sickness. [Used generally of a sudden attack ; prob. imit.]

brat, *n.* any article of clothing, esp. an apron ; rag, 'dudd.' [A.S. *bratt*, fr. C. *brat*, a cloth.]

brattle, *n.* clatter ; scamper, 'spurt.' [Imit. word.]

braw, *adj.* fine, excellent, hearty, fine-looking, handsome ; finely dressed. [Fr. *brave.*]

brawlie, *adv.* very well; heartily.

braxie, *n.* a disease among sheep ; wh. the flesh of sheep that die on the hills. [Cf. A.S. *bræc-sēocnes*, falling sickness, fr. *bræc-rheum.*]

breastit, *v.* put the breast to, sprung up a forward.

bree, *n.* juice, liquor, water. [Perh. A.S. *brīw.*]

breef, brief, *n.* spell. [O.Fr. *brief* (*bref, brevet*), talisman.]

breeks, *n.* breeches, trousers. [A.S. *brēc.*]

1. **brent,** *adj.* high, straight: of the forehead, used as opposed to

bald, perh. because well covered with hair and thus having a steep appearance. [A.S. *brant*, steep.]

2. **brent**, *adv.* in comp., *brent-new*, brandnew.

brier (pron. **breer**), *n.* wild-rose. [A.S. *brĕr.*]

brig, *n.* bridge. [A.S. *brycg;* M.E. *brigge.*]

brisket, *n.* breast, stomach. [O.Fr. *brischet* or *bruschet.*]

brither, *n.* brother. [Cf. *ither.*]

brock, *n.* badger. [A.S. *broc*, fr. C. *broch.*]

brogue, *n.* trick. [Etym. unk.]

broo (pron. **brö**), *n.* juice, liquor, water. [Perh. O.Fr. *bro, breu*, whence dim. *broez.* See *brose.*]

broose, *n.* a race at a country wedding. [Perh. same word as brose, as a dish of brose sometimes formed the prize.]

brose, *n.* on dry uncooked oatmeal, with salt, boiling water is poured sufficient to soak the meal; it is then allowed to stand until the meal swells, whereupon it is eaten with milk. This is water-brose. *Kail-brose* is made with broth instead of water. A generation ago this was the staple food of the Scottish plowman. [Older forms are *browis, browes;* M.E. *broys;* O.Fr. *broez.*]

brugh (pron. **bruch**), *n.* burgh. [Cf. *brunt* and *burnt*, and, conversely, *girn, grin*, etc.]

brunstane, *n.* brimstone, sulphur. [M.E. *brynstan.*]

brunt, *ptc.* burnt.

bught (pron. **bucht**), *n.* sheep-fold, pen: *v.* to pen (sheep). [Prob. conn. w. *bight;* A.S. *byht*, a bend.]

bughtin-time, *n.* time for the ewes to be penned and milked.

buik, beuk, buk, *n.* book.

buird, *n.* see *boord.*

buirdly, *adj.* large and strong-looking, of robust appearance.

bum, *v.* and *n.* buzz, hum. [Imit. word.]

bum-clock, *n.* drone-beetle. [*bum*, from its droning flight; *clock*, a beetle.]

bunker, *n.* large box or bin sometimes used as a seat. [Cf. Eng. *bunk.*]

burdie, dim. of **burd**, *n.* bride, damsel. [Perh. A.S. *brȳd*, Dan. *brud*, w. transp. *r.*]

bure, past of bear: bore.

burn, *n.* brook. [A.S. *burna, burne.*]

burr-thistle, *n.* Scotch thistle. [M.E. *burre;* Dan. Sw. *borre.*]

busk, *v.* dress, adorn. [M.E. *busken;* O.N. *būask*, to get oneself ready.]

buss, *n.* bush, covert. [Cf. *wiss* for *wish.*]

bussle, *n.* bustle, 'bizz.'

büt, *prep.* without: *n.* the kitchen end of the house: *adv.* in the kitchen. The cotter's house consists of 'a but and a ben.' [A.S. *be-ūtan, būtan.*]

butchin, *n.* butcher's trade. [*Ptc.* of *butch*, to butcher.]

by, *prep.* past, beyond; *by himsel*, crazy; *by this*, by this time: *adv. I care na by*, I care not for that. (See *Tibbie, I hae seen the day*, 4, note.)

byke, *n.* nest of wild bees or wasps. [Etym. unk.]

byre, *n.* cowhouse. [A.S. *b̄yre.*]

1. **Ca',** *v.* call, name. [O.N. *kalla.*]

2. **ca',** *v.* drive (e.g., a cart, nail, flock of sheep). [Same word as *ca'* 1.]

cadger, *n.* itinerant fishmonger. [From *cadge*, to carry about, hawk; of doubtful etym.]

caird, *n.* tinker. [C. *ceard.*]

cairn, *n.* pile of stones. [C. *carn.*]

caller, cauler, *adj.* fresh; wh. cool. [Older form *caloure, callour*, applied to flesh recently killed; perh. fr. *calver*, an epithet used of newly caught fish. Cf. *silver, siller.*]

canker, *n.* irritation: *v.* be irritated; wh. *cankrie*, irritating, peevish.

canna, *v.* cannot.

cannie, *adj.* sagacious, cunning; careful, quiet, harmless. [*can*, to know how.]

cantie, *adj.* happy, cheerful. [Prob. *cant*, brisk and bold; a Low German word.]

cantrip, *n.* a mischievous trick usually connected with charms or magic. [Etym. dub.]

capestane, *n.* copestone.

carl, carle, *n.* man, boor, old man. [M.E. *carl*; O.N. *karl*; cf. A.S. *ceorl.*]

carl-hemp, *n.* the strongest stalk of hemp, form. supposed to be the male-plant, but really the female.

carlin, *n.* fem. of carl: old woman.

carmagnole, fiend, wild revolutionist. [Fr. *carmagnole*, a wild dance popular among the French revolutionaries.]

cartes, *n.* playing cards. [The *t* is Fr.]

cattle, *n.* all beasts constituting property.

cauld, *adj.* cold. [M.E. *cald*; A.S. *ceald*; O.N. *kald-r.*]

caup, *n.* wooden bowl. [Also *cap* (the *au* being local; cf. *chaup, chap*; *cauler, caller*); A.S. *copp*; O.N. *kopp-r.*]

causey, *n.* causeway. [O.Fr. *caucie, caucile*, a beaten track, *via calciata.*]

certes, *adv.* forsooth, 'fegs.' [Fr.]

changehouse, *n.* tavern; wayside inn where horses were changed.

chanter, *n.* the pipe of a bagpipe, recorder. [Older form *chantour*; O.Fr. *chanteor.*]

1. **chap,** *n.* fellow. [Short for *chapman*; cf. *callant*, fr. Du. *kalant*, a customer.]

2. **chap, chaup,** *n.* stroke (of a hammer), knock. [M.E. *chappen*; conn. w. *chop, chip.*]

chiel, chield, *n.* young man, fellow. [A.S. *cild.*]

chimla, *n.* fireplace, mantelpiece; not 'chimney' in the sense of 'flue,' wh. in Scotch is 'lum.' [O.Fr. *cheminée.*]

chittering, *ptc.* shivering, fluttering, usu. w. cold. [M.E. *chiteren;* cf. chatter.]

chow, chaw, *v.* chew. [A.S. *cēowan.*]

cit, *n.* 'citizen,' contemptuously.

clachan, *n.* village. [C.]

claes, *n.* clothes. [Cf. *mou'*, mouth, *wi'*, with.]

claith, *n.* cloth. [A.S. *clāð;* O.N. *klæði.*]

claivers, clavers, *n.* gossip, idle talk. [Prob. C. *clabaire*, a gabbler; but cf. obs. Du. *kalaberen*, and Ger. *klaffern*, to chatter.]

clamb, *v.* past of climb.

1. **clap,** *v.* put quickly. [O.N. *klappa*, to pat; M.E. *clappen.*]

2. **clap,** *n.* clapper (of a mill). [Same.]

clarkit, *ptc.* clerked, figured accounts.

clash, clashes, *n.* idle gossip, scandal. [Imit. word.]

claught, *ptc.* clutched. [Past of *cleek* wh. corr. to M.E. *clecchen*, pp. *claht.*]

claut, *v.* scrape: *n.* something scraped together, hoard. [Prob. same root as *claw.*]

claw, *v.* scratch. [A.S. *clāwan.*]

clean, *adv.* altogether.

cleed, *v.* clothe. [O.N. *klæða*, Dan. *klæde*, Du. *kleeden;* and cf. Eng. *clad* for *clothed.*]

cleek, *n.* hook: *v.* link together. [North. form of M.E. *clechen*, to catch.]

1. **clink,** *n.* money, wealth, 'chink.'

2. **clink,** *v.* accord, come in aptly.

clips, *n.* shears.

clish-ma-claver, *n.* idle gossip, 'clashes.' [*clish* is a doublet of *clash;* see *claiver.*]

clock, *n.* a beetle. [Etym. unk.]

cloot (pron. **cluit**), *n.* one of the divisions of a cloven hoof. [Perh. O.N. *klō*, claw.]

Clootie, Cloots, *n.* Satan. [*cloot.*]

clud, *n.* cloud. [A.S. *clūd*, a hill, 'cumulus.']

coble, *n.* small, broad-beamed rowboat, usu. for salmon-fishing. [? C.]

coft, *v.* bought. [Past tense and p. p. from *cope;* cf. M.Du. *cōpen.* The pres. *coff* was formed from *coft.*]

cog, *n.* wooden bowl, bigger than a *caup.* [Prob. C. *cawg*, a basin.] Dim. *coggie.*

convoy, *v.* accompany on the way. [O.Fr. *convoie.*]

cood (pron. **cuid**), *n.* cud.

coof, cuif, *n.* fool, blockhead. [Perh. cf. Eng. *cove* (slang).]

cookit, *v.* past of *cook*, to appear and disappear by turns. [Etym. dub.]

coost, cuist, past of *cast.*

cootie (pron. **cuitie**), *n.* tub.

corbie, *n.* raven, crow. [O.Fr. *corb, corbin.*]

core, *n.* company, gang. [Fr. *corps.*]

corn, *n.* grain, oats.

corn't, *ptc.* fed with oats.

cosie, cozie, *adj.* snug, warm. [Etym. unk.]

cot-folk, *n.* cotters.

cotter, *n.* one who inhabits a cottage dependent on a farm.

couthy, *adj.* kindly, loving. [A. S. *cūð*, known ; cf. M. E. *cuði.*]

cove, *n.* cave ; recess, nook. [A.S. *cofa.*]

cowe, *v.* intimidate, surpass. [Perh. O.N. *kūga ;* Dan. *kue.* Dist. fr. *cowe*, to cut short (M.E. *colle*).]

cowpit, past of *cowp*, upset. [Prob. same word as *cope*, fr. Fr. *couper*, orig. to strike.]

cowte, *n.* colt.

cozie, *adj.* see *cosie.*

crack, *v.* talk : *n.* conversation. [Orig. to talk loud or boastfully ; same as Eng. *crack.*]

craft, *n.* croft, field. [A.S. *croft.*]

craik, *n.* corn-craik, land-rail. [Imit. word.]

crambo-clink, crambo-jingle, *n.* versification. [*crambo*, a game of verses, and *clink*, jingle.]

cranreuch, *n.* hoarfrost. [C. *crann*, a tree ; *reodhadh*, freezing (from the forms of vegetation it takes).]

1. **crap**, *n.* and *v.* crop.

2. **crap**, *v.* past of creep.

1. **craw**, *n.* crow (of chanticleer).

2. **craw**, *n.* rook.

creel, *n.* large, round, open wicker basket ; *senses in a creel* = 'having lost one's head.' [? C.]

creeshie, creishie, *adj.* greasy. [*creish*, grease ; O.Fr. *craisse*, *cresse ;* cf. C. *créis* (pron. *krēsh*).]

crony, *n.* intimate companion. [No conn. w. *crone* has been traced.]

1. **crood**, *n.* crowd.

2. **crood**, *v.* coo (as a dove). [Imit. word.]

1. **croon**, *n.* crown, top of the head, 'pow.'

2. **croon**, *v.* make a low mournful sound : *n.* hum. [M.Du. *crōnen*, to lament.]

crouchie, *adj.* hump-backed. [M.E. *cruchen*, to cower ; cf. O.Fr. *crochir*, cower.]

crouse, *adj.* brisk and bold, spirited. [M.E. *crus ;* M.L.G. *krūs.*]

crowdie, *n.* porridge, brose. [Cf. O.N. *graut-r.*]

crummock, *n.* staff with a crooked head. [A.S. *crumb*, crooked ; *-ock*, dim. termin. ; C. *cromag.*]

crump, *adj.* crisp, short (of cakes). [Cf. *crimp, crumple.*]

cuddle, *v.* caress. [Prob. a corruption of 'couth-le,' a frequentative from M.E. *couth*, and so same root as *couthie.*]

cuif, see *coof.*

cummock, *n.* stick with a crooked head. [Also *cammock, cambock ;* M.E. *kambok ;* L.Lat. *cambuca*, of C. origin.]

curchie, *n.* curtsy.

curmurrin, *n.* rumbling sound, grumbling. [Imit. word ; cf. Du. *koeren-morren.*]

curpin, curple, *n.* crupper, back. [Var. form of *croupon ;* O.Fr. *croupon*, rump.]

cushat, *n.* wood-pigeon. [A.S. *cūscote.*]

custoc, castock, *n.* pith of the stem of a cabbage. [*cal*, kail, and *stock.*]

cutty, *adj.* short. [C. *cutach*, short, docked.]

Daddie, *n.* father. [C.]

daffin, *n.* making fun, romping. [M.E. *daffe*, to be foolish.]

daft, *adj.* foolish, crazy. [P. p. of M.E. *daffe.*]

dail, deal, *n.* deal board.

daimen, *adj.* occasional, 'antrin.' [Etym. dub.]

dainty (pron. denty), *adj.* good, lovable. [O.Fr. *daintié*, agreeableness, fr. Lat. *dignitatem.*]

damies, *n.* dames. [Dim.]

darg, daurg, *n.* lit. a day's work; wh. a spell of work in general. [*daurk*, syncop. form of *day-werk*, day-work.]

darklins, *adv.* secretly. [See *-lins.*]

daud, *n.* large piece. [Also *dad;* a piece broken off by a *dad* or blow; fr. *v. dad*, strike firmly. Imit. word.]

daur, *v.* dare.

daurk, see *darg.*

daut, dawt, *v.* pet, caress. [Etym. unk.]

daw, *v.* dawn. [M.E. *dawen;* A.S. *dagian.*]

dead, *n.* death. [M.E. (North.) *ded;* A.S. *dēað;* cf. O.N. *dauð-r* (Dan. Sw. *död*).]

dearthfu, *adj.* costly, dear.

deave, *v.* stupefy with noise;
annoy by repetition, pester. [A.S. *dēafian* in *ādēafian* (f = v), to wax deaf.]

dee, *v.* die. [M.E. *deyen;* O.N. *deyja.*]

deevil, deil, *n.* devil.

deil-ma-care, *interj.* 'no matter.'

deleerit, *adj.* delirious, raving.

1. den, *n.* dell. [M.E. *dere;* A.S. *denu*, valley.]

2. den, *n.* cavern. [M.E. *den;* A.S. *denn.*]

descrive, *v.* describe. [M.E. *descriven;* O.Fr. *descrivre.*]

deuk, *n.* duck. [Same as Eng. *duck;* see *jouk.*]

dicht, dight, *v.* wipe. [A.S. *dihtan*, to prepare.]

dike, see *dyke.*

din, *n.* noise; discord.

dine, *n.* dinnertime, noon.

ding, *v.* knock; beat, baffle. [M.E. *dingen;* cf. O.N. *dengja*, to hammer.]

dinsome, *adj.* noisy.

dirl, *n.* a stroke that produces vibration but does not penetrate : *v.* throb, tingle. [Cf. *thirl, thrill,* etc.]

dizzen, *n.* dozen.

doited, *adj.* stupid. [*doit* may be *dote*, M.E. *doten;* O.N. *dotta*, to nod sleepily.]

doitin, doytin, *ptc.* walking in a stupid manner. [*doit, doiter;* see above.]

donsie, *adj.* wicked, morally bad (*U. G.*); vicious, ill tempered (*A. M. M.*); wh. ill to please, over-nice.

dool, dule, *n.* sorrow. [O.Fr. *doel = deuil.*]

douce, *adj.* solemn, grave. [O. Fr. *douse, douce.*]

dour, doure, *adj.* stubborn, unyielding, stern. [Cf. Fr. *dur ;* L. *durus.*]

dow, *v.* can; past *dought.* [M. E. *dowen ;* A.S. *dugan.*]

dowff, *adj.* dull, spiritless; pointless. [O.N. *dauf-r,* deaf.]

dowie, *adj.* dull, low-spirited. [Earlier form, *dollie,* prob. same as A.S. *dol.*]

downa, *v.* cannot. [*dow.*]

downans, *n.* green hillocks. [C. *dūn.*]

doylt, *adj.* stupid. [Perh. orig. p. p. of *dullen,* to dull ; cf. M.E. *dult.*]

drag, *n.* and *v.* break (of a vehicle) : *dragged, ptc.* having the break applied.

drappie, *n.* dim. of *drap,* drop.

drave, *v.* past of *drive.*

dree, *v.* endure, suffer. [M.E. *dreien, dreghen ;* A.S. *drēogan.*]

dreep, *v.* drip.

dreigh, *adj.* tedious. [M.E. *dregh;* see *dree,* and cf. O.N. *drjūg-r.*]

droop-rumpl't, *adj.* drooping at the crupper. [O.N. *drūpa ;* and *rumple* = rump.]

droukit, *ptc.* drenched. [O.N. *drukna,* to be drowned.]

drouthy, *adj.* thirsty. [*drouth ;* M.E. *drougð(e) ;* A.S. *drūgað,* fr. *drūgian,* to dry.]

drucken, *adj.* drunken. [Norw. and Dan. *drukken ;* O.N. *drukkinn.*]

drumly, *adj.* muddy. [Also *drumbly.*]

drummock, *n.* raw oatmeal stirred in cold water; thin 'crowdie.' [Prob. C.]

drunt, *n.* pique, huff.

duan, *n.* division of a poem, canto. [C.]

dub, *n.* pool, puddle. [C. *dob,* gutter.]

duddie, *adj.* ragged. [*duds.*]

duds, duddies, *n.* rags, clothes. [M.E. *dudde,* a cloak.]

dung, *v.* past of *ding.*

dusht, *ptc.* astounded (as with a heavy blow). [M.E. *duschen,* to strike, doublet of *dash.*]

dyke, dike, *n.* stone or turf fence ; orig. a mound thrown up by digging a trench. [A.S. *dīc,* a ditch.]

Earn, ern, *n.* eagle. [A.S. *earn ;* M.E. *ern.*]

Earse, Erse, *n.* Highland, Gaelic. [= Irish.]

ee, *n.* eye. Pl. **een.** [A.S. *ēage, ēagan ;* M.E. *eye, eyen.*]

e'en, *n.* evening.

eerie, *adj.* frightened, weird ; prop. it suggests ghostliness and the apprehension of something unknown. [M.E. *eri,* prob. fr. A.S. *earh,* timid.]

eild, *n.* old age ; Eng. *eld.* [A.S. *eldo, yldu.*]

elbock, *n.* elbow. [Cf. A.S. *elboga.*]

eldritch, *adj.* unearthly. [A form *elphrish* favors a connection with *elf.*]

eneuch, *n.* enough. [M.E. *inoh;* A.S. *genoh.*]

ettle, *v.* and *n.* aim, endeavor. [O.N. *ætla*, to intend.]

eydent, *adj.* diligent. [Also written *ithand*; O.N. *iðinn*, assiduous; *ið*, restless motion.]

Fa, *v.* get, secure; 'he maunna fa that.' Cf. old song, 'For fient a crum o' thee she faus.' [A.S. *fōn*; O.N. *fā*; Dan. *faae*.]

fa', *n.* lot, destiny: *v.* to befall.

faddom, *n.* and *v.* fathom; the outstretched arms. [A.S. *faðm*; M.E. *fadme*.]

fae, *n.* foe.

faem, *n.* foam.

fain, *adj.* desirous, fond. [A.S. *fægen*.]

fair fa', = 'fair befall,' 'good luck to.'

fairin, *n.* present given at a fair; reward.

fallow, *n.* fellow.

fa'n, *ptc.* fallen.

fancy, *n.* love, amour (as in Shakspere).

fand, *v.* past of find.

farl, *n.* coarse meal cake. [Also *fardel*, lit. a fourth part of anything; wh. a cake cut in four; A.S. *feorða dæl*.]

fash, *v.* and *n.* trouble. [O.Fr. *fascher*.]

Fasten-een, *n.* Shrove Tuesday. [Fast.]

faught, *n.* fight.

fauld, *n.* fold: *v.* to bring the sheep home.

fause, *adj.* false. [Cf. Fr. *fausse*.]

faut, *n.* fault. [Cf. Fr. *faute*.]

fawsont, *adj.* seemly, respectable. [M.E. *fasoun*, fashion; Fr. *façon*; *t* is p. p. ending.]

fear't (pron. **fear'd**), *adj.* afraid. [Cf. Eng. *afeard*.]

feat, *adj.* trim, smart. [M.E. *feit, fait*; Fr. *fait*.]

fecht, *n.* and *v.* fight.

feck, *n.* greater part, substance. [Corrup. of *effect*.]

feckless, *adj.* insubstantial, pithless. [*feck*.]

feg, *n.* fig. [Dist. fr. interj. *fegs!*]

feil, *adj.* comfortable, cosy. [Perh. A.S. *fæle*; M.E. *fele*, proper, good.]

feir, fier, *adj.* strong, lusty. [M.E. *fere*; O.N. *færr*, capable.]

feirie, *adj.* vigorous, active. [*feir*.]

1. **fell,** *adj.* strong (of taste). [M.E. *fel*.]

2. **fell,** *n.* hill. [O.N. *-fell, fjall*.]

fen', *n.* shift, provision: *v.* to make provision. [M.E. *fenden*; Fr. *défendre*.]

ferly, *n.* and *v.* wonder. [M.E. *ferli*; A.S. *færlic*, sudden.]

fetch, *v.* pull intermittently.

fidge, *v.* move uneasily, fidget. [See *fyke*.]

fidgin-fain, *adj.* fidgeting with eagerness.

fient, *n.* fiend. Used in emphatic negatives; 'fient a' = 'devil a'; 'fient haet' = 'devil a whit.'

fier, see *feir*.

fiere, *n.* comrade. [M.E. *fere*; A.S. *gefera*.]

filabeg, *n.* kilt.　[C. *filleadh beag.*]

fine, *adv.* nicely, 'brawly.'

fissle, *v.* hustle, get excited. [Freq. of *fuss.*]

fit, *n.* foot.

fittie-lan', *n.* 'foot-the-land'; the horse of the hinder pair in plowing which does not step in the furrow.

fizz, *v.* effervesce.

flang, *v.* past of *fling.*

flannen, *n.* flannel.

fleech, *v.* cajole, flatter.　[Perh. M.Du. *fletsen,* to fawn.]

fleesh, *n.* fleece.　[Cf. *creesh, grease.*]

fleg, fley, *v.* and *n.* scare.　[M.E. *fleyen;* A.S. * *flēgan, āfȳgan.*]

flichter, *v.* flutter.　[Same root as *flight.*]

flie (pron. **flee**), *n.* and *v.* fly.

flinders, *n.* splinters.　[Cf. Norw. *flindra,* dial. *flinter.*]

fling, *v.* kick out; dance a 'fling.'　[Cf. O.N. *flengja,* to flog; Dan. *flänge,* to move impetuously, to romp.]

flingin-tree, *n.* flail.

flisk, *v.* caper, 'balk' (of a horse).　[Imit. word; cf. *whisk.*]

flit, *v.* remove one's household. [M.E. *flitten;* cf. O.N. *flytja.*]

foggage, *n.* rank grass.　[Sc. Law Lat. *fogagium,* prob. fr. M.E. *fogge,* grass, esp. aftermath.]

for, *prep.* in spite of.

forbears, *n.* ancestors, progenitors. [Prob. *fore; bear,* produce.]

forby, *adv.* in addition, besides. [M.E. *forbi.*]

forfairn, *ptc.* jaded, worn out. [A.S. *forfaran,* to destroy, perish.]

forfoughten (pron. **forfoch'n**), *ptc.* over-exerted, 'trachl't.'　[*for-,* intensive ; A.S. *fohten, p. p.* of *feohtan,* to fight.]

forgather, *v.* meet, associate with.

1. **fou** (pron. **foo**), *adj.* full, drunk.

2. **fou, fow,** *n.* measure of grain, 'fill' of the measure.

foughten (pron. **foch'n**), *ptc.* harassed; cf. *forfoughten.*

fouth, *n.* plenty.　[M.E. *fulthe; ful,* '*fou.*']

fracas, *n.* ado, fuss.　[Fr.]

frae, *prep.* from.　[O.N. *frā.*]

freath, *n.* froth, 'ream.'　[M.E. *frodĕ;* O.N. *frodĕa;* the *ea* is local.]

fu', *adv.* quite, very.　Same word as *fou* 1, but the pronunc. is much lighter.

fur, furr, *n.* furrow.　[A.S. *furh.*]

furm, *n.* form, bench.　[L. *forma.*]

fushionless, *adj.* foisonless, weak, 'thowless.'　[O.Fr. *foison,* abundance.]

fyke, fike, *n.* agitation, fuss, anxiety about petty things.　[M.E. *fiken;* O.N. *fīkja,* to move nimbly.]

fyle, *v.* soil, dirty.　[M.E. *fylen;* A.S. (*a*) *fȳlan,* fr. *fūl,* dirty.]

1. **Gab,** *n.* mouth.　[See *gab* 2.]

2. **gab,** *v.* chatter, prate.　[M.E. *gabben,* to talk idly; O.Fr. *gaber.*]

gae, gang, *v.* go. *P. gaed, p.p. gane.*

gaet, gate, *n.* road, way; manner. [M.E. *gate*, way; O.N. *gata;* cf. A.S. *geat*, an opening.]

gane, gang, see *gae.*

gar, *v.* compel. [M.E. *garren;* O.N. *göra*, vulg. *gera*, to cause; cf. A.S. *gearwian*, to prepare.]

gart, *p.p.* of *gar.*

garten, *n.* garter. [C. *gartan.*]

gash, *adj.* sagacious, shrewd; talkative: *v.* talk much.

gat, *v.* past of *get.*

gate, *n.* see *gaet.*

gaucie, gawsie, *adj.* big and lusty, plump; jolly.

gauger, *n.* exciseman, one who 'gauges' (ale-barrels, etc.).

gaun, *ptc.* and *n.* going. (The *n* repres. *ptc.* *-in.*)

gear, *n.* goods, wealth. [M.E. *gere;* A.S. *gearwe*, furnishings.]

geck (*g* hard), *v.* toss the head; mock. [Dan. *gekken.*]

Ged, in 'Johnny Ged's hole,' the grave. [Perh. fr. *ged*, a greedy person; metaph. fr. *ged*, a pike.]

gentles, *n.* gentle-folks, gentry.

get, gett, *n.* breed, offspring. [Cf. *beget.*]

ghaist, *n.* ghost. [A.S. *gāst.*]

gie (*g* hard), *v.* give.

gif (*g* hard), *conj.* if. [A.S. *gif.*]

gillie (*g* soft), *n.* dim. of *gill*, fourth part of a mutchkin or pint.

gilpey (*g* hard), *n.* frolicsome girl. [Used also of boys.]

gimmer (*g* hard), *n.* young ewe. [O.N. *gymb-r.*]

gin (*g* hard), *prep.* by the time of: *conj.* by the time that; if. [Also *gen;* A.S. *gēan-*, against.]

girn, *v.* gnash the teeth with chagrin, rage or ill temper. [Same as *grin.*]

gizz, *n.* face. [Perh. Fr. *guise.*]

glaikit, *adj.* light, giddy, thoughtless. [*glaik*, obs. Eng. *gleek.*]

glaizie, *adj.* shining, glossy. [*glaze.*]

gleib, *n.* small farm (usu. attached to the church), glebe. [Fr. *glèbe.*]

glen, *n.* small valley. [C. *gleann.*]

glint, *n.* and *v.* glance. [M.E. *glenten.*]

gloamin, *n.* gloaming, twilight. [A.S. *glōmung.*]

glower, *v.* stare, glare. [M.E. *gloren.*]

glunch, *n.* frown, surly look. [Also *glumch*, fr. *glum.*]

goavan, *ptc.* staring in a dazed way. [Also *gove, goif.*]

gos, *n.* goshawk, falcon.

gowan, *n.* daisy; -y, *adj.* daisied. [C. *gugan.*]

gowd, *n.* gold; -en, *adj.* golden.

gowdspink, *n.* goldfinch. [*spink* is same word as *finch*, A.S. *finc;* cf. Gr. σπίγγος.]

gowk, *n.* fool. [M.E. *gowke;* cf. O.N. *gauk-r*, cuckoo (which in Scotl. is still *gowk*); cf. also Eng. *gawk.*]

grain, grane, *n.* groan.

1. **graip,** *n.* short pitchfork. [Cf. Dan. *greb;* Sw. *grepe.*]

2. **graip,** *v.* grope. [A.S. *grā-pian;* conn. w. above.]

graith, *n.* implements ; harness, attire. [M.E. *greithe ;* O.N. *greiði,* preparation.]

grane, see grain.

granny, *n.* grandmother. [*grannam,* grandam, Fr.]

grat, past of *greet.*

gree, *n.* prize, superiority. [O. Fr. *gré.*]

greet, *v.* weep. [A.S. *grǣtan,* to bewail ; cf. O.N. *grāta.*]

grissle, *n.* gristle, stump.

groat, *n.* an old silver coin = 8 cents. [M.E. *grote ;* O.L.G. *grote.*]

grousome, *adj.* horrible. [*grew,* to shiver ; cf. Dan. *grue.*]

grumph, *n.* grunt ; wh. **grumphie,** *n.* pig. [Imit. word.]

gruntle, *n.* snout, visage ; grunt.

grushie, *adj.* thick, of thriving growth.

gude, guid, *adj.* good : *n.* goodness ; God.

gudefather, *n.* goodfather, father-in-law.

gudeman, *n.* master of the household, husband.

gude-willie, *adj.* good-willed, friendly.

gully, *n.* large pocketknife, bowieknife.

gulravage, *n.* disorder, tumult.

gumlie, *adj.* muddy. [*gummle,* to stir up ; same as *jumble ;* Dan. *gumpe,* to jolt.]

gusty, *adj.* tasty, toothsome. [Obs. Eng. *gust ;* Lat. *gustus,* taste.]

gutcher, *n.* grandfather. [Older forms *gud-schir, gud-syr.*]

gutters, *n.* mud, mud puddles. [M.E. *gotere,* channel for water; O.Fr. *goutiere.*]

Ha', *n.* hall.

ha'-bible, *n.* family Bible kept in the hall or principal apartment.

had, *v.* see *haud.*

hae, *v.* have. Esp. used in proffering a thing, 'here.'

haet, *n.* whit.

haffets, *n.* sides of the head. [Older form *hevid* (Wyntoun) ; A.S. *hēafod,* the head.]

hafflin, *adj.* half-grown. [*half* and *-lin, -ling.*]

hafflins, *adv.* partly. [See *-lins.*]

ha-folk, *n.* hall-people; i.e., of the servants' hall.

haggis, *n.* kind of pudding. [M.E. *haggas, hakkys,* fr *hag,* hack, infl. by O.Fr. *hachis,* hash.]

hain, *v.* spare, economize, save; lit. to hedge in. [O.N. *hegna,* to hedge.]

hairst, *n.* harvest.

haith, *interj.* 'faith.'

haivers (havers), *n.* nonsense, 'blethers.'

hal', *n.* hold; *house an' hal'* = 'house and holding.'

hale, *n.* and *adj.* whole ; sound, robust. [A.S. *hāl.*]

halesome, *adj.* wholesome.

half-lang, *adj.* corruption of *hafflin.*

hallan, *n.* partition wall of a cottage; sometimes (see *C. S. N.*

85) it separated the dwelling apartments from the cow house.

hallowe'en, *n.* All Saints' Eve. [M.E. *halwe ;* A.S. *hālga.*]

hame, *n.* home: **hamely,** *adj.* homely.

han', haun', *n.* hand; capable person.

han'-daurg, *n.* single-handed day's labor. [See *daurg.*]

hand-waled, *adj.* chosen by hand; especial. [See *wale.*]

hansel, handsel, *n.* first money, or gift, bestowed on a particular occasion; an earnest; first use: also *adj.* and *v.* [O.N. *handsal;* cf. A.S. *hand-selen,* a giving into the hand.]

1. **hap** (short *a*), *n.* and *v.* cover, wrap.

2. **hap** (long *a*), *v.* hop.

happer, *n.* hopper of a mill.

happin, *ptc.* of *hap* 2.

harkit, past of *hark,* 'listened to.'

harn, *n.* coarse kind of linen. [Also *hardin,* from the material, *hards.* A.S. *heordan,* hards of flax.]

hash, *n.* fool, soft, useless fellow. [Also a wasteful, stupidly reckless person; prob. fr. *hash,* to cut up wastefully.]

haud, had, *v.* and *n.* hold. [Cf. *scaud,* scald.]

hauf, *n.* half.

haugh (pron. gutt.), *n.* meadow by a river side. [Prob. conn. w. A.S. *haga,* a place fenced in; cf. O.N. *hagi,* a pasture.]

haun, *n.* see *han'.*

haurl, *v.* drag roughly; scrape, peel.

havins, *n.* propriety; sense of propriety. [Perh. O.N. *hæfa,* to behoove, be meet ; *hæfinn,* aiming well; but cf. Eng. *havior,* behave.]

havrel, *n.* for *haver-el,* foolish person. [See *haivers.*]

hawkie, *n.* cow; strictly a cow with a white face. [Cf. *hawkit,* white-faced, spotted or streaked with white.]

heal, see *hale.*

hearse, *adj.* hoarse. [M.E. *hors ;* A.S. *hās;* cf. O.Du. *haersch.*]

heave, *v.* throw, pitch.

hecht, *v.* promise. [Orig. to name; A.S. *hātan, heht;* Eng. *hight* (be called).]

heckle, *n.* comb for dressing flax or hemp. [M.E. *hekele ;* Du. *hekel.*]

heeze, *v.* raise. [M.E. *hoise ;* O.Du. *hyssen.*]

heft, *n.* haft, handle.

heigh (gutt.), *adj.* high.

herryment, *n.* devastation; plunderers. [*herry,* to harry, plunder; A.S. *hergian.*]

het, *adj.* heated, warm.

heugh, *n.* lit. a crag, a ragged, steep hillside ; wh. a ravine, gully. [O.N. *haug-r;* cf. M.E. *hogh ;* Eng. *how,* hill.]

hich, see *heigh.*

hie, *adj.* high.

hilch, *v.* halt-limp, prance, curvet.

hing, *v.* hang.

hirple, *v.* limp.

hirsel, *n.* flock, herd. [Also *herdsel.*]

histie, *adj.* usu. given as = dry, parched. [Perh. it means 'autumnal'; cf. Dan. *höst,* autumn.]

hitch, *n.* loop, hook. [M.E. *hicchen.*]

hizzie, *n.* lass, without any derogatory sense. [Same as Eng. *hussy,* housewife.]

hoast, see *host.*

hoble, *v.* same as Eng. *hobble.*

hodden-gray, *n.* coarse gray cloth of undyed wool.

hoddin, *ptc.* jogging (the motion of a man on a heavy work horse).

hog-shouther, *v.* jostle. [Prob. fr. *hog* and *shoulder,* fr. the action of pigs at a trough ; prop. a boy's game of butting with the shoulders, in which the contestants have to hop on one foot.]

hoodock, *adj.* miserly.

hool, *n.* hull, shell, sheath. [A.S. *hulu.*]

hoolie, *adv.* gently, cautiously.

hoord, *n.* hoard; -et, *adj.* -ed.

hoosie, housie, *n.* dim. of house.

horn, *n.* ale-cup ; horn-spoon.

host, hoast, *n.* cough. [O.N. *hōsta,* to cough.]

hotch, *v.* move uneasily. [Cf. O.Du. *hotsen.*]

hough-ma-gandie, *n.* illicit intercourse.

houlet, *n.* owl. [Dim. of *owl,* A.S. *ūle,* infl. by *howl,* and perh. by Fr. *hulotte.*]

howdy, *n.* midwife.

howe, *n.* valley, hollow. [*holl,* to dig ; A.S. *hol,* a hole.]

howe-backit, *adj.* hollow-backed.

howk, *v.* dig. [M.E. *holken;* Sw. *holka ;* cf. A.S. *holc,* and *hol.*]

hoy't, *v.* past of *hoy,* call, incite.

hoyte, *v.* halt, amble clumsily.

huff, *v.* snub, bully. [Orig. to swell with insolence, to blow. Imit. word.]

hurcheon, *n.* hedgehog. [O.Fr. *hericon ;* cf. Eng. *urchin.*]

hurdies, *n.* hips.

hurl, *v.* wheel. [Same as *whirl.*]

I', *prep.* in.

icker, *n.* ear of grain. [Older form, *echer ;* Old Northumb. *æhher ;* O.H.G. *ehir ;* cf. A.S. *ĕar ;* Eng. *ear.*]

-ie, -y, dim. of familiarity or contempt.

ilk, ilka, *adj.* each, every. [M.E. *ilke ;* A.S. *ilca.*]

ill-willie, *adj.* malevolent, uncharitable.

indentin, *ptc.* of *indent,* bind by indenture.

ingine, *n.* genius, talent. [M.E. *engine ;* L. *ingenium.*]

ingle, *n.* chimney-corner, fireplace. [C. *aingeal.*]

ingle-cheek, *n.* fireside.

ither, *adj.* other. Cf. *brither, mither.*

Jad, *n.* lass, used in both good and bad sense; orig. a poor horse. [Also *yade, yaud ;* Eng. *jade.*]

jauk, *v.* and *n.* trifle.

jauner, *n.* gabble.

jaup, *n.* and *v.* splash. [Also *jalp.*]

jee, *v.* move slightly : *adv.* w. *gang,* — *gang jee,* open slightly. [Same as *gee.*]

jillet, *n.* longer form of *jilt.* [From *Jill.*]

jimp, *v.* modified form of *jump.*

jing, only in expletive, 'by jingo.'

jink, *v.* move rapidly aside and about, dodge (as a hare from a hound) : *n.* evasion, slip.

jinker, *n.* swift and agile mover, sprightly creature. [*jink.*]

jo, *n.* sweetheart, love.

jocteleg, *n.* pocketknife, jack-knife. [Said to be from Fr. *Jacques de Liège,* a maker whose name appeared on the blades.]

jorum, *n.* punch-bowl. [Perh. C. *jorram,* a boat song; wh. a social or convivial song; wh. the bottle which always accompanied the song.]

jouk, *v.* duck, stoop. [Same word as *dook, duck.* M.E. *duken;* Dan. *dukke;* the Sc. word *deuk* (the fowl) is in Angus pron. *jook.*]

jow, *v.* oscillate, swing (of a bell); wh. clang. [M.E. *jolle,* to knock about ; wh. *jolt.*]

jundie, *v.* push past another.

Kail, *n.* cabbage, colewort; wh. soup of which this is the chief ingredient, broth. [*kale,* var. of *cole.*]

kailrunt, *n.* cabbage-stem after the head is off.

kane, *n.* farm produce paid as rent. [Also *cane, cain,* C. *cain.*]

kebbuck, *n.* a cheese. [C. *cabag.*]

kebbuck-heel, *n.* last piece of the cheese.

keek, *v.* peep. [M.E. *kiken, keken;* O.N. *kikja* or Du. *kijken.*]

keepit, *v.* kept.

kelpie, *n.* a water-spirit. [C. *cailpeach,* a steer or colt. The spirit was supposed to appear in form of a horse.]

ken, *v.* know. [M.E. *kennen;* O.N. *kenna* (A.S. *cennan* ·is causal).]

ken'le, *v.* kindle.

kennin, *n.* something perceptible, a little bit, a shade. [*ken.*]

kep, *v.* catch as it falls, intercept. [M.E. *kippen;* O.N. *kippa,* to snatch.]

ket, *n.* fleece.

kiaugh, *n.* anxiety, fret.

kilt, *n.* kilt, Scotch Highlander's dress: *v.* tuck up. [Dan. *kilte,* to tuck up ; cf. O.N. *kilting,* skirt.]

kimmer, *n.* young woman, wench. [Also *cummer,* Fr. *commère,* a gossip.]

king's-hood, *n.* second stomach of a ruminating animal; said to be named from its fancied resemblance to a puckered headdress worn by persons of quality.

kirk, *n.* church. [M.E. *kirke;* A.S. *cyrice;* cf. O.N. *kirkja.*]

1. **kirn,** *n.* churn. [O.N. *kirna;* A.S. *cyren.*]

2. **kirn,** *n.* prop. the last handful of grain cut ; wh. harvest-home, a rustic feast given to the shearers when the 'stuff' was safely packed. [Etym. dub.]

kirsten, *v.* christen, baptize.

kitchen, *n.* relish : *v.* give a relish to.

1. kittle, *adj.* ticklish, difficult to handle.

2. kittle, *v.* tickle, stimulate, enliven. [M.E. *kitelen ;* A.S. *citelian.*]

kittlin, *n.* kitten. [M.E. *kitelinge,* dim. fr. *kit ;* cf. O.N. *ketling-r.*]

knaggie, *adj.* having protuberances, bony (of a horse). [*knag,* a protuberance ; C. *cnag.*]

knappin-hammers, *n.* stonebreaker's hammers. [Du. *knappen,* to crack.]

knowe, *n.* knoll, hillock. [M.E. *knol ;* A.S. *cnoll.*]

kye, pl. of *cow.* [A.S. *cȳ.*]

kyte, *n.* stomach, paunch. [A.S. *cwið,* matrix ; O.N. *kviðr,* belly.]

kythe, *v.* show, appear. [M.E. *cyðen ;* A.S. *cyðan.*]

Laddie, *n.* dim. of *lad.* [Also pron. *lathie ;* C. *lath.*]

lade, *n.* load. [M.E. *lode;* A.S. *hladan,* to load ; cf. O.N. *hlaða ;* Dan. *lade.*]

lag, *adj.* laggard, sluggish. [C. *lag,* faint.]

laggen, *n.* angle between the side and the bottom of a dish. [Cf. O.N. *lögg,* the ledge or rim at the bottom of a cask ; Sw. *lagg.*]

laigh (gutt.), *adj.* low. [M.E. *lah ;* O.N. *lāgr.*]

laik, *n.* lack. [Obs. Eng. *lak ;* cf. O.N. *lak-r,* defective ; Du. *lak,* stain.]

1. lair, see *lear.*

2. lair, *v.* to sink when wading through snow or mud. [M.E. *lair ;* O.N. *leir,* mud.]

laird, *n.* owner of land or houses, landlord. [M.E. *laverd ;* A.S. *hlāford,* lord.]

lairdship, *n.* property, estate. [*laird.*]

laith, laithfu, *adj.* loth, shy. [A.S. *lāð ;* O.N. *leiðr.*]

lallan, *adj.* lowland. [*law, low,* and *land.*]

lampit, *n.* limpet.

lan', *n.* land.

lane, *adj.* lone. [See Gram. Introd.]

lang, *adj.* long.

langsyne, *n.* long since, long ago.

1. lap, *v.* past of *lowp,* leap.

2. lap, *v.* for *lapped,* covered, wrapped.

lat, *v.* let. [M.E. *laten, leten ;* A.S. *lǣtan ;* cf. O.N. *lāta.*]

lave, *n.* what is left, remainder. [M.E. *laif, lave ;* A.S. *lāf ;* cf. O.N. *leif.*]

law, *n.* hill. [M.E. *hlāwe ;* A.S. *hlāw,* mound.]

lay, see *ley.*

leal, leil, *adj.* loyal, true, trusty. [O.Fr. *leial.*]

lear, lair, *n.* learning. [M.E. *lere, lare ;* A.S. *lār.*]

lea-rig, *n.* pasture-field.

learn, *v.* learn, teach. [M.E. *lernen ;* A.S. *leornian.*]

lee-lang, *adj.* livelong.

leeze, only in phrase *leeze me,* = 'my blessing on.' [*lief is me ;* earlier form *leuis me.*]

leister, *n.* a three-pronged fork, usu. for spearing fish. [O.N. *ljöstr;* Dan. *lyster.*]

leuk, *v.* and *n.* look.

ley, lay (pron. **ley**), *n.* lea. [M.E. *leye;* A.S. *lēah.*]

lien (pron. **ly'n**), *ptc.* lain.

1. **lift,** *n.* helping hand, share. [Eng. *lift,* to raise.]

2. **lift,** *n.* sky. [Same root as *lift* 1; A.S. *lyft.*]

lightly (gutt.), *v.* slight, disparage.

like, *adv.* as it were.

limmer, *n.* hussy. [O.Fr. *limier,* a hound; wh. a base person.]

lin, linn, *n.* waterfall with a pool below. [C. *linne,* pool; cf. A.S. *hlynn,* torrent.]

link, *v.* trip, skip; do actively.

-lins, *adv.* term. w. force of *-ways,* e.g., *sidelins, backlins.* [Orig. *-lings, lingis;* from suffix *-ling,* used for diminutives, and *-es,* adv. gen. ending.] The two term. are seen in *hafflin* = a half-grown man; and *hafflins* = partially.

lint, *n.* flax. [M.E. and A.S. *līn;* L. *linum.*]

lintwhite, *n.* linnet. [Early form, *lyntquhite;* A.S. *līnetwige: līn,* because it feeds among the lint.]

listen, *v.* hearken to.

loan, *n.* lane in the country between two hedge-rows. [M.E. *lone;* A.S. *lane, lone.*]

loe (pron. **lü** or **loo**), *v.* love.

loof (pron. **lüf**), *n.* palm. [O.N. *lōfi.*]

loon, see *loun.*

loot, past of *lat,* permitted; *loot on,* 'let on,' gave evidence.

loun, loon, *n.* rogue; young lad. [Akin to O.Du. *loen,* fool.]

lowe, *n.* and *v.* flame. [M.E. *lowe;* O.N. *log, logi;* cf. Dan. *lue.*]

lowp, *v.* leap. [O.N. *hlaupa.*]

1. **lowse** (sharp *s*), *adj.* loose. [O.N. *lauss;* cf. M.E. *loos.*]

2. **lowse** (pron. **lowz**), *v.* loosen. [*lowse* 1; cf. M.E. *losien.*]

luckie, *n.* mistress, usually with a shade of contempt, a designation given to an elderly woman. [Cf. *Goody.*]

lug, *n.* ear; *chimla lug,* side of the fireplace. [Perh. Sw. *lugg,* the forelock, and so conn. with *v. lug,* wh. orig. meant 'to pull by the forelock.']

lugget, *ptc.* having 'lugs,' or raised handles.

luggie, *n.* small tub with 'lugs' used for milking.

lum, *n.* chimney. [C. *llumon.*]

lunt, *n.* light, smoke, steam. [Dan. *lunte;* Du. *lont,* a match; wh. *luntin,* smoking.]

luve, *v.* and *n.* love. [Cf. *loe;* A.S. *lufian.*]

lyart, *adj.* gray. [Also *liart;* M.E. *liard;* O.Fr. *liard,* dapple-gray.]

Mae, *adj.* more. [A.S. *mā;* cf. M.E. *mo.*]

mailin, *n.* farm; land rented. [*mail,* rent; Fr. *maille,* a coin.]

mair, *adj.* more. [A.S. *māra;* O.N. *meiri.*]

maist, *adj.* most: *adv.* almost. [A.S. *mǣst.*]

mak, *v.* make.

mang, *prep.* among.

manteel, *n.* mantle. [O.Fr. *mantel.*]

mark, *n.* a sum of money = 13s. 4d. stg.; a mark Scots would be 1s. 1⅓d., or 26⅔⍧.

marled, *ptc.* mixed, mottled, checkered. [*marl,* a mixture of lime, clay, and sand, fr. O.Fr. *marle.*]

maukin, *n.* hare. [M.E. *malkin,* dim. of Maud, a general name for a kitchen girl; wh. applied to cats (cf. grimalkin) and to hares, like *puss.*]

maun, *v.* must. [O.N. *munu,* shall.]

maut, *n.* malt.

mavis, *n.* thrush. [Fr. *mauvis.*]

mebbie, *adv.* perhaps. [*May be.*]

meere, meare, mear, *n.* mare. [M.E. and A.S. *mere.*]

meikle, mickle, muckle, *adj.* much. [M.E. *mikel, mukel;* A.S. *micel;* cf. O.N. *mikill,* great.]

melder, *n.* quantity (indefinite) of grain sent to the mill to be ground. [O.N. *meldr.*]

mell, *v.* mix, associate. [M.E. *mellen;* Fr. *mêler.*]

melvie, *v.* soil (as with meal). [Prob. M.E. *mele,* meal; A.S. *melu.*]

men', *v.* mend.

mense, *n.* discretion, decorum. [Also *mensk;* M.E. and A.S. *mennisc,* humane; O.N. *mennsk-r,* fr. *man.*]

menseless, *adj.* void of discretion, 'misleared.' [*mense.*]

merle, *n.* blackbird. [Fr.]

messan, messin, *n.* cur.

midden, *n.* dungheap. [M.E. *midding;* Dan. *mögdynge.*]

midden-hole, a standing pool at the end of the dunghill.

midgie, *n.* midge, *dimin.* [M.E. *migge;* A.S. *mycg.*]

mill, *n.* snuffbox (said to be so called from the grinding of the tobacco leaves which used to be done in the box).

mim, *adj.* prim, affectedly precise. [Softer form of *mum,* demure.]

mind, *v.* remind, recollect, heed.

minnie, *n.* mother. [Cf. Du. *minne,* wet-nurse.]

mirk, *n.* murk, darkness. [A.S. *mierce.*]

misca, *v.* miscall, abuse.

mischanter, *n.* mischief, accident. [*mishanter, mis-* and *aunter,* O.Fr. *aventure.*]

misguide, *v.* squander (of money).

mislear't, *adj.* unmannerly, illbred; cf. *menseless.* [*mis-* and *lear't,* taught.]

moop, moup, *v.* mump, nibble. [Imit. word.]

moorlan, *adj.* belonging to the moors.

morn, *n.* morrow; *the morn,* to-morrow. [M.E. *morwein;* A.S. *morgen, mor(g)ne.*]

mottie, *adj.* full of motes.

mou, *n.* mouth.

moudiewart, *n.* mole. [M.E. *moldwerp;* A.S. *molde,* soil; *weorpan,* to throw up; cf. O.N. *moldvarpa.*]

muckle, *adj.* see *meikle.*

muslin-kail, *n.* very thin soup; barley-soup with scarcely any vegetables. [Perh. *maslin, mashlim,* mixed grain; wh. corrupted through assoc. with *muslin.*]

mutchkin, *n.* pint. [Dan. *mutsje,* quartern; lit. a cap; wh. Sc. *mutch,* cap; cf. the Scotch 'tappit hen.']

1. Na, *conj.* nor; see *nor.* [A.S. *ne, nā.*]

2. -na, termination = 'kind of,' *whatna, sicna.*

3. na, 1. nae, *adv.* not. [A.S. *nā, ne.*]

2. nae, *adj.* no, not any.

naething, *n.* nothing.

naig, naiggie, naggie, *n.* nag, horse. [M.E. *nagge;* O.Du. *negge.*]

nane, *adj.* none.

nappy, *n.* ale. [Prim. the *adj.* = 'strong,' 'heady' (of ale).]

near-hand, *adv.* nearly.

neibor, *n.* neighbor.

neist, see *niest.*

neive, neave (pron. nev), *n.* fist. [M.E. *nefe, hnefe;* O.N. *hnefi;* Dan. *næve.*]

neive-fu (pron. neffa), *n.* fistful, handful.

neuk, *n.* nook, corner. [C. *niuc.*]

1. Nick, *n.* auld Nick, the deil. [A.S. *nicor,* a water-goblin; cf. O.N. *nykr.*]

2. nick, *v.* cut. [Same root as *notch.*]

niest, *adj.* next. [A.S. *nīehst.*]

niffer, neifer, *v.* and *n.* exchange, 'swap.' [*neive.*]

nine, nines, in phr. 'to the nines' = perfection.

nit, *n.* nut. [The *i* is local.]

no, *adv.* not.

nor, *conj.* than; see *na.*

norwast, *n.* northwest wind.

nowte, *n.* cattle, neat. [O.N. *naut;* A.S. *nēat.*]

O', *prep.* of.

onie, ony, *adj.* any.

oo, also written woo (pron. oo). *n.* wool. [O.N. *ull;* A.S. *wull;* for loss of *ll* cf. *pu, fu.*]

or, *conj.* ere. [M.E. *or, ar,* var. of *er.* [A.S. *ǣr.*]

ourie, *adj.* dull, drooping. [Usu. given fr. O.N. *ūr,* rain; *ūrigr,* wet; prob. only a var. of *weary;* cf. *ook,* week, and *oo,* we.]

outler, *adj.* unhoused. [-*ler* is prob. a mere term. added to *out;* cf. *tinkler, pantler;* cf. also *outlin* = an alien.]

outowre, *prep.* out over, over. [Cf. *attour.*]

owrehip, *adv.* overhip, applied to the swing of the sledge-hammer.

owsen, *n.* oxen. [Cf. *neist.*]

Pack, *adj.* close, intimate; *pack an' thick,* very intimate, 'thrang.'

paidle, *v.* paddle; dabble in water; walk with short steps. [For *pattle,* freq. of *pat;* and cf. Fr. *patouiller.*]

painch, *n.* paunch, stomach; tripe. [O.Fr. *panche.*]

paitrick, *n.* partridge. [M.E. *pertriche;* O.Fr. *pertris.*]

pang, *v.* stuff, cram. [L. *pangere.*]

parritch, *n.* porridge (usu. oatmeal).

pat, past of *pit*, put.

pattle, *n.* plow-spade. [Same word as *paddle*, a small spade.]

paughty (gutt.), *adj.* haughty. [Cf. Du. *pochen*, to be proud.]

paukie, **pawkie**, *adj.* shrewd, cunning, 'slee.' [Sc. *pauk*, a wile; cf. A.S. *pǣcan*, to deceive.]

pechan, *n.* stomach.

penny-fee, *n.* money-wages.

penny-weep, *n.* small ale. [*wheep = whip*.]

pettle, see *pattle*.

philabeg, see *filabeg*.

phiz, *n.* physiognomy, face. [M.E. *fisnamie*; O.Fr. *phisonomie*.]

phraisin, *ptc.* flattering. [*phrase*, to make fine speeches.]

pickle, **puckle**, *n.* a grain of corn; a small quantity of anything. [*pickle*, to glean, to pick up grains; *pick*.]

pit, *v.* put.

plack, *n.* a small coin, two bodles, four pence Scots, one-third of an English penny, two-thirds of a cent. [O.Fr. *plaque*.]

plackless, *adj.* penniless, poor. [*plack*.]

plaid (pron. **play'd**), *n.* a long, narrow shawl worn by Highlanders. [C. *plaide*.]

plaister, *n.* plaster (also form. spelled *plaister*).

plea, **pley**, *n.* quarrel, disagreement: *v.* disagree. [M.E. *ple*, *plaid*; O.Fr. *plait*, a plea at law.]

plenish, *v.* furnish (a house); stock (a farm). [O.Fr. *plenir*.]

pleugh (gutt.), *n.* plow. [M.E. *ploh*; O.N. *plōg-r*. The A.S. *plōg* is a measure of land.]

pock, *n.* bag, sack. [M.E. *poke*; cf. C. *poca*; O.N. *poki*.]

poind, *v.* impound. [M.E. *punden*; A.S. *pyndan*, to shut up.]

poortith, *n.* poverty. [Older form *purtye*; O.Fr. *poureté*; the *-th* is an accretion.]

pou, *v.* see *pu'*.

pouch, *n.* pocket (in clothes). [O.Fr. *pouche*. It is a doublet of *pock*.]

pouk, *v.* poke. [M.E. *pukken*, *poken*, to thrust; C. *poc*, a blow.]

poussie, see *pussie*.

pouthery, *adj.* powdered. [Cf. *shouther*.]

pow, *n.* head, poll. [Cf. *knowe*.]

pownie, *n.* pony. [C. *ponaidh*.]

prank, *n.* act of mischief. [*prank*, to trick out.]

pree, *v.* taste. [For *preif*; M.E. *preven*; O.Fr. *prover*, to prove.]

preen, *n.* pin. [M.E. *pren*; A.S. *prēon*.]

preif, **prief**, *n.* proof. [M.E. *preef*; F. *preuve*.]

prig, *v.* entreat, insist upon; haggle (at a bargain). [A modification of *prick*.]

primsie, *adj.* demure. [Eng. *prim*; O. Fr. *prim*.]

propone, *v.* set forth, advance. [A law term.]

proves, *n.* provost, chief magistrate. [O.Fr. *provost*.]

pu', *v.* pull, pluck.

puir, *adj.* poor.

pund, *n.* pound. A pound Scots = 1*s.* 8*d.* stg., or 40 cents.

pussie, poussie, *n.* hare.

Quat, past of *quit.*

quaukin, *ptc.* quaking. [A.S. *cwacian.*]

quean, *n.* young woman, wench (used in both good and bad sense). [A.S. *cwene*, cf. A.S. *cwēn.*]

quey, *n.* heifer. [Cf. Dan. *kvie;* O.N. *kvīga.*]

quo', *v.* quoth.

Rab, *n.* Rob, Robert.

raible, *v.* rattle off nonsense: *n.* nonsensical talk. [Same as *rabble;* M.E. *rablen;* cf. O.Du. *rabelen*, to mutter.]

rair, *v.* roar (of ice breaking up, or the plow cutting through roots). [A.S. *rārian;* cf. O.Du. *reeren.*]

raize, *v.* madden, excite. [M.E. *reisen*, O.N. *reisa*, raise.]

ram-stam, *adj.* precipitate, headlong. [Prob. *ram*, to drive with violence, and *stam*, a riming syllable, intens.; cf. *hurly-burly.*]

rant, *v.* riot, live hilariously: *n.* noisy mirth, jollification. [Eng. *rant*, to be noisy or bombastic.]

rantin, *adj.* full of animal spirits; wh. *rantinly.*

rape, *n.* rope. [A.S. *rāp;* cf. O.N. *reip;* Du. *reep.*]

rase, past of *rise.* [M.E. pret. *ras.*]

rash, *n.* rush. [Cf. M.E. *resche;* A.S. *risce.*]

ratton, *n.* rat. [M.E. *raton;* O.Fr. *raton.*]

raught (gutt.), past of *rax*, q. v.

raw, *n.* row, line. [M.E. *rawe;* A.S. *rāw.*]

rax, *v.* reach; stretch. [M.E. *raxen*, *recchen*, pret. *rahte;* A.S. *rǣcan*, *rǣhte.*]

ream, *n.* cream, froth: *v.* mantle, froth. [M.E. *ream;* A.S. *rēam.*]

reave, reive, *v.* rob, plunder. [M.E. *reaven;* A.S. *rēafian;* cf. Eng. *bereave.*]

red, *v.* counsel, advise. [M.E. and A.S. *rǣd*, counsel.]

red-wat-shod, *adj.* walking in blood. [*red* (the color), and *wat-shod;* M.E. *wat-shod.*]

red-wud, *adj.* stark-mad. [*red*, intensive; M.E. and A.S. *wōd*, mad.]

reek, *n.* and *v.* smoke; steam. [M.E. *rek;* A.S. *rēc.*]

reestit, *ptc.* smoke-dried, singed. [O.N. *rist*, a gridiron; Dan. *riste*, to broil.]

reif, rief, *n.* theft. [M.E. and A.S. *rēaf*, spoil.]

reive, see *reave.*

rig, *n.* ridge, row; properly the raised portion between two furrows, about a rod in breadth. [Same as *ridge;* A.S. *hrycg;* cf. Dan. *ryg.*]

riggin, *n.* ridging, roof-timbers, rafters. [*rig.*]

rigwiddie, *n.* used as *adj.*, the rope (*widdie*) which crosses the back (*rig*) of the horse to support the shafts : wh. *adj.* ropy-looking, dried-up, tough.　[*rig* and *widdie*.]

rin, *v.* run.

ripp, *n.* handful of grain not threshed.　[M.E. and A.S. *rip*, reaping, a sheaf of corn.]

riskit, *ptc.* cracked (a word expr. of the noise made by tearing roots).　[A.S. **hrȳscan*, to creak.]

rive, *v.* burst, split open ; tear to pieces.　[M.E. *riven* ; O.N. *rīfa*.]

rock, *n.* distaff.　[M.E. *rocke* ; cf. Du. *rok* ; O.N. *rokkr*.]

roose, ruse, *v.* praise, extol. [M.E. *rosen* ; O.N. *hrōsa*.]

rousin', *ptc.* rousing, big.

rout, *n.* way.　[Fr. *route*.]

rovin, *ptc.* roving, 'stravagin.'

row, rowe, *v.* roll, wrap.　[Cf. *pow*.]

rowte, *v.* low, bellow.　[M.E. *routen* ; A.S. *hrūtan* ; cf. O.N. *rauta*.]

rowth, *n.* abundance.　[Perh. conn. w. *rough* (*roch*) as *sowth* w. *sough*.]

runkled, *ptc.* wrinkled.　[M.E. *runklen* ; M.Du. *wronkelen*.]

runt, *n.* stump, stalk with root attached, as in *kail-runt*.

ruse, see *roose*.

Sae, *adv.* so.

saft, *adj.* soft.

1. **sair,** *v.* serve.　[Cf. Fr. *je sers*.]

2. **sair,** *adj.* sore, heavy: *adv.* extremely.　[M.E. *ser, sar* ; A.S. *sār* ; cf. O.N. *sārr*.]

sang, *n.* song.

sark, serk, *n.* shirt.　[M.E. *serke* ; A.S. *serc* ; O.N. *serkr*.]

sarkit, *adj.* shirted ; *half-sarkit*, with poor underclothing.

saugh (gutt.), *n.* willow, sallow. [M.E. *salhe* ; A.S. *sealh*.]

saul, *n.* soul.　[M.E. *saule* ; A.S. *sāwl*.]

saumont, *n.* salmon.　[For the *t*, cf. *tyrant*.]

saunt, *n.* saint.　[*sanct* ; O.Fr. *sainct*.]

saut, *n.* salt.

sautit, *ptc.* salted.

1. **saw,** *v.* sow (seed).　[A.S. *sāwan*.]

2. **saw,** *n.* salve.　[M.E. *salfe* ; A.S. *sealf*.]

sax, *adj.* six.　[The *a* is unique.]

scaith, *n.* and *v.* harm, scathe.

scaud, *v.* scald.　[O.Fr. *eschalder*, later *eschauder*.]

1. **scaur,** *v.* scare: *adj.* timid. [Cf. O.N. *skjarr*.]

2. **scaur,** *n.* cliff, scar.　[M.E. *scarre*, rock ; cf. O.N. *sker*, a rocky islet.]

scawl, *n.* scold, scolding wife.

scho, *pron.* she.

scone (pron. **scon**), *n.* cake of flour or barley-meal, 'bannock.'

scower, *v.* scour, run precipitately.　[O.Fr. *escourre*.]

scraichin, *ptc.* screeching.　[Cf. O.N. *skrækja* ; C. *sgreach*.]

screed, *n.* rent, tear.　[M.E. *screde*, A.S. *scrĕad*, shred.]

scrievin, *ptc.* rushing.　[Cf. O.N. *skref*, Dan. *skrev*, pace.]

scrimp, *v.* stint.　[Akin to

shrimp and *shrink;* cf. Dan. *skrumpe,* shrivel.]

scrimply, *adv.* scarcely.

scroggie, *adj.* abounding in stunted bushes (*scrogs*). [C. *sgrogag,* stunted timber.]

scunner, sconner, *n.* disgust, loathing: *v.* to loathe. [M.E. *sconien;* A.S. *scunian,* shun.]

see'd, for *saw* (unusual).

seizin, *n.* possessions (a law term). [O.Fr. *saisine.*]

sel, *adj.* self.

sen', *v.* send; grant, bless you with.

1. **set,** *v.* send (*D. D. II.*).

2. **set,** *v.* become, suit. [Same as *sit.*]

shachl't, *adj.* splay, misshapen. [*shachle,* to walk clumsily in loose shoes; *schach,* distort; cf. O.N. *skakk-r.*]

shank, *n.* leg. [A.S. *scanca.*]

shaul, *adj.* shallow. [M.E. *schóld, schald.*]

shaver, *n.* wag, trickster. [*shavie.*]

shavie, *n.* trick, 'pliskie.' [Cf. O.N. *skeif-r,* Dan. *skjœv,* crooked; but perh. both words are from *shave,* to drive a close bargain, to cheat.]

shaw, *n.* wood, wooded dell. [M.E. *schawe;* A.S. *scaga,* copse.]

shear, *v.* clip; reap grain.

shearer, *n.* reaper.

sheepshank, *n.* leg-bone of a sheep; something thin and weak: *Nae sheepshank,* a person of importance.

sheugh (gutt.), *n.* furrow, ditch. [Also *seugh;* prob. M.E. *sough,*

trench, conn. w. A.S. *sulh,* L. *sulcus,* a furrow.]

shiel, *n.* hut, cottage. [Cf. O.N. *skjöl,* shelter.]

shift, *v.* exchange, shift places.

shill, *adj.* shrill, resounding. [M.E. *schil;* A.S. *scyl.*]

shog, *n.* a shake causing oscillation; shock. [M.E. *schoggen;* cf. F. *choc;* Du. *schok.*]

shool, *n.* shovel. [M.E. *schoule;* A.S. *scofl.*]

shoon, *n.* shoes. [M.E. *scho, schoon.*]

shore, *v.* offer; threaten. [*adj. schor,* sheer (of rocks) and so threatening.]

sic, *adj.* such; *siclike,* such-like.

siccan, *adj.* such kind of. [Also *sican a = sic kin' o';* cf. *whatna.*]

sicker, *adj.* steady; sure. [M.E. *siker;* A.S. *sicor;* L. *securus.*]

sidelins, *adv.* s i d e w a y s, obliquely. [See *-lins.*]

1. **siller,** *n.* money, riches. [*silver.*]

2. **siller,** *adj.* silvery, made of silver.

silly, *adj.* simple, weak. [M.E. *sely;* A.S. *sælig.*]

simmer, *n.* summer. [Cf. *kimmer.*]

sin, conj. since. [M.E. *sin,* for *siððen.*]

skaith, see *scathe.*

skeigh (gutt.), *adj.* shy and skittish, high-spirited. [M.E. *skey;* A.S. *sceoh;* Dan. *sky.*]

skellum, *n.* wretch, worthless fellow. [O.N. *skelmir,* a rogue; Sw. *skälm.*]

skelp, *n.* slap, blow with the open hand : *v.* to slap : wh. (from the ringing noise made by the feet) to run with alacrity. [C. *sgealp*, a slap.]

skelpie-limmer, *n.* young hussy. [See *limmer* ; *skelpie* in this conn. prob. = ' gadabout.']

skelvy, *adj.* shelving. [*skelf*, shelf ; A.S. *scylfe.*]

skinkin, *ptc.* thin, liquid. [A.S. *scencan*, to pour ; M.E. *schenchen* ; O.N. *skenkja.*]

skirl, *v.* and *n.* scream. [Cf. M.E. *schrillen* ; Norw. *skræla*, *skryla.*]

sklent, *v.* slant, direct with oblique intention : *n.* deviation, digression. [M.E. *slenten*, *sclenten* (cf. *sclendre*, slender) ; O.Sw. *slinta*, to slide.]

skouth, *n.* scope, liberty to range.

skreigh, *v.* screech. [M.E. *skrichen* ; O.N. *skríkja* (of suppressed laughter) ; cf. *scraich.*]

slade, past of *slide* = slipped.

slae, *n.* sloe. [A.S. *slā.*]

slap, *n.* opening in a fence or thicket or between hills. [Cf. Sc. *slack.*]

slee, *adj.* sly, knowing, ' pawky.' [M.E. *slie*, *sleh* ; O.N. *slœg-r.*]

sleekit, *adj.* sleek. [M.E. *sleke*, O.N. *slíkr*, smooth.]

slight (gutt.), trick, sleight ; skill. [O.N. *slægð* ; cf. *slee.*]

sloken, *v.* slake, quench. [M.E. *sloknen* ; O.N. *slökva*, to quench.]

sly, *adj.* see *slee* (good or bad sense).

slype, *v.* fall gently over, slip. [A.S. ** slīpan.*]

sma, *adj.* small.

smeek, *n.* and *v.* smoke. [Also *smook* ; A.S. *smēocan.*]

smiddie, *n.* smithy. [For *d*, cf. *widdie*, *stiddie* ; M.E. and A.S. *smiððe* ; cf. Dan. *smidse.*]

smoor, *v.* smother, choke. [M.E. *smoren* ; A.S. *smorian.*]

smoutie, *adj.* smutty, dirty.

smytrie, *n.* small number, smattering.

snapper, *v.* stumble. [Freq. of *snap.*]

snash, *n.* abusive language, insolence.

snaw, *n.* snow; wh. *snawie*, snowy.

snaw-broo, *n.* melted snow.

sneck, *n.* latch. [Akin to *snatch* ; M.E. *snekke.*]

sneck-drawin, *adj.* latch-lifting, sneaking.

sned, *v.* lop, cut off. [M.E. and A.S. *snǣdan*, to cut.]

sneesh, **sneeshin**, *n.* snuff. [Same as *sneeze* ; M.E. *snesen* or *fnesen* ; A.S. *fnēosan*, to sneeze ; for *sh*, cf. *creesh.*]

sneeshin-mill, *n.* snuffbox. [See *mill.*]

snell, *adj.* keen, piercing. [M.E. and A.S. *snel.*]

snool, *v.* snub, keep under ; submit tamely, cringe. [For *snovel* (cf. *shool*) ; M.E. *snuvelen* ; cf. Dan. *snövle*, to snivel.]

snoove, *v.: snoove awa*, take a breath and move on, move on with a sniff or snort. [M.E. *snuven*, to pant ; O.Du. *snuiven.*]

snowk, *v.* smell out, poke the nose into. [M.E. *snoken;* L.G. *snōken;* Sw. *snōka.*]

snuggit, *ptc.* snugged, made secure.

soger, *n.* soldier. [Cf. M.E. *sodiour.*]

something, *adv.* somewhat.

so'ns, *n.* sowens, flummery, a kind of porridge made of the juice of oat husks. [M.E. *seau,* A.S. *sēaw,* juice.]

sonsie, *adj.* plump and good-natured, buxom, well-conditioned. [*sons,* happiness; C. *sonas.*]

soom, *v.* swim. [Same as *swim;* cf. M.E. *sote,* sweet, and Sc. *soop,* sweep.]

sootie, *adj.* covered with soot.

sough, sugh (gutt.), *n.* the sound the wind makes in trees. [Imit. word; cf. O.N. *sūgr,* a rushing sound; M.E. *swogen,* A.S. *swōgan,* to moan.]

soupe, see *sowp.*

' souple, *adj.* supple, pliant. [Fr. *souple.*]

souter, *n.* cobbler, shoemaker. [M.E. *soutere;* A.S. *sūtere;* L. *sutor.*]

sowp, *n.* spoonful, sup, liquid food. [M.E. *soupen,* A.S. *sūpan,* to sup.

sowth, *v.* whistle softly. [Perh. conn. w. *sough.*]

sowther, *v.* solder. [Also *sowder;* O.Fr. *souder,* to cement; cf. *shouther.*]

spae, *v.* spell, foretell. [M.E. and O.N. *spā,* prophecy.]

spairge, *v.* scatter liquid, splash;

asperse. [Fr. *asperger;* L. *spargere.*]

spak, past of speak.

spate, *n.* flood. [C. *speid.*]

spaviet, *ptc.* spavined. [*spavin.*]

spean, *v.* wean. [M.E. *spanen,* A.S. *spanan,* to entice; cf. Du. *spenen,* to wean.]

speel, *v.* climb, mount.

spence, *n.* inner room; prop. the place where the provisions are kept, the buttery. [O.Fr. *despense;* L. *dispensorium.*]

spier, *v.* ask. [M.E. *spire,* A.S. *spyrian,* to track, inquire into.]

spleuchan, *n.* tobacco pouch. [C. *spliuchan.*]

splore, *n.* revel, jollification; long-winded talk.

spottin, *ptc.* discoloring with splashes of wet.

sprachle, *v.* scramble. [Cf. O.N. *spraukla.*]

sprattle, *v.* sprawl. [Cf. Sw. *sprattla.*]

spring, *n.* piece of dance music.

spritty, *adj.* full of tangled roots of bent, etc. [Also *sprotty;* A.S. *sprot,* a sprout; *spryttan.*]

spunk, *n.* spark; fire, mettle. [C. *sponc,* tinder.]

1. spunkie, *adj.* spirited. [*spunk.*]

2. spunkie, *n.* will-o'-the-wisp. [Do.]

squatter, *v.* a word expressive of the sound made by a duck rising from the water, a combination of flutter and splash. [Cf. O.N. *skvetta,* to squirt water.]

stacher, *v.* stagger as under a load. [M.E. *stakeren;* O.N. *stakra.*]

stack, *v.* past of *stick.*

staggie, *n.* colt. [Dim. of *staig*, a young unbroken horse, a stallion ; same word as Eng. *stag.*]

stan', *n.* and *v.* stand.

stane, *n.* stone. [A.S. *stán.*]

stank, *n.* ditch with stagnant water, a pool. [M.E. *stanc* ; O.Fr. *estanc* ; L. *stagnum.*]

stan't, *v.* p. p. of *stan'* = stood.

1. **stap**, *v.* stop.

2. **stap**, *n.* step. [A.S. *stæpe.*]

staukin, *ptc.* stalking.

staumrel, *adj.* applied to one whose action is of a stupid, stumbling kind; doltish. [Cf. Eng. *stammer, stumble.*]

1. **staw**, *v.* past of *steal* ; p. p. *stown.*

2. **staw**, *v.* surfeit. [Cf. Northumb. *stall*, to satiate; the idea is taken from the stall-feeding of cattle, i.e., feeding to satiety.]

stechin, *ptc.* of *stech*, pant with fatigue or repletion.

1. **steek**, *n.* stitch. [A.S. *stice.*]

2. **steek**, *v.* shut close. [M.E. *steken* ; same root as above.]

steer, *v.* stir; molest, hurt. [A.S. *styrian.*]

steeve, steive, *adj.* firm, well-knit (coupled with *buirdly*, which implies strong appearance, while *swank* adds a touch of elegance). [A.S. *stíf*, the vowel being shortened in *stiff* ; Dan. *stiv.*]

stell, *n.* still.

sten, *v.* and *n.* leap, bound. [For *stend* ; O.Fr. *estendre*, to stretch, take long elastic steps.]

stent, *n.* tax, levy. [M.E. *stent* ;

O.Fr. *estente*, a valuation for assessment; L. *extenta.*]

stey, *adj.* steep. [Obs. Eng. *sty* ; M.E. *stighen* ; A.S. *stígan*, to rise.]

stibble, *n.* stubble.

stibble-rig, *n.* leading reaper.

stile, *n.* gate: prop. a set of steps for climbing over a fence. [M.E. *stile* ; A.S. *stigol* ; cf. *stey.*]

stilt, *v.* lift the feet high ; prance.

stimpart, *n.* a measure, one-fourth of a peck ; the 'sixteenth part' of a bushel. [Erron. der. fr. *huitième part.*]

stirk, *n.* a one-year old steer. [M.E. *stirk* ; A.S. *styric.*]

stock, *n.* cabbage plant. [A.S. *stocc*, trunk.]

stook, *n.* shock of sheaves. [Cf. L.G. *stuke*, bundle.]

stookit, *ptc.* set up in shocks.

stoup, see *stowp.*

stour, *adj.* strong, harsh. [M.E. and A.S. *stór.*]

stoure, *n.* turmoil, struggle ; wh. dust in motion. [M.E. *stor* ; prob. O.Fr. *estour.*]

stowlins, *adv.* stealthily. [*stown*, stolen, and *-lins.*]

stowp, *n.* drinking vessel. [O.N. *stamp* ; cf. A.S. *stéap.*]

stoyte, *v.* stumble. [Du. *stuyten*, to bounce; M.E. *stoten*, to stutter.]

strae, *n.* straw. [M.E. *stre* ; A.S. *stréaw.*]

straik, *v.* stroke, smooth down. [M.E. *straken* ; A.S. *strácian.*]

strang, *adj.* strong. [M.E. and A.S. *strang.*]

strappin, *adj.* strapping; tall,

handsome, and well-built; cf. *strapper*.

straught (gutt.), *adj.* straight. [M.E. *straught*, A.S. *streht*, *ptc.* of *strecchen*, *streccan*; Sc. *streetch*, or *streek*.]

streekit, *ptc.* stretched. [*streek*, see above.]

striddle, *v.* freq. of *stride*.

stroan, *v.* urinate.

strunt, *n.* spirits.

studdie (for *stiddie*), *n.* stithy, anvil. [M.E. *stith*; O.N. *steði*.]

stuff, *n.* grain crops (these being 'material' for sustenance). [Cf. O.Fr. *estoffer*, to furnish with necessaries.]

stumpie, *n.* dim. of *stump*, a well-worn quill. [M.E. *stumpe*; O.N. *stump-r*.]

stumpin, *ptc.* walking stiffly and heavily.

sturt, *n.* trouble, turmoil, strife. [Cf. M.E. *sturte*, impetuosity.]

sturtin, *ptc.* troubled, frightened. [Same.]

style, see *stile*.

sucker, *n.* sugar. [Fr. *sucre*.]

sud, *v.* should. [Past of *sall*, shall; cf. M.E. *sulde*.]

sugh, see *sough*.

sumph, *n.* a dull soft fellow.

swaird, *n.* sward. [A.S. *sweard*, skin.]

swall, *v.* swell.

swank, *adj.* well-built and without spare flesh, supple, 'strappin.' [A.S. *swancor*, agile; cf. O.N. *svang-r*, slim.]

swankie, *n.* 'strappin chiel,' a 'swank' young man.

swap, *v.* and *n.* exchange. [Perh. M.E. *swappen*, to strike; cf. '*strike* a bargain.']

swat, *p.* of *swite*, sweat. [A.S. *swāt*, perspiration; cf. O.N. *sveiti*.]

swatch, *n.* sample. [Prop. a strip of cloth cut off; same word as Eng. *swath*.]

swats, *n.* ale. [A.S. *swātan* (pl.), ale.]

swirl, *v.* and *n.* curl, whirl. [Cf. Norw. *svirla*.]

swirlie, *adj.* full of twists, knotty. [*swirl*.]

swither, *n.* state of hesitation. [A.S. *swæðer*, whichever of two.]

swoor, past of *swear*. [M.E. and A.S. *swōr*, *swerian*.]

syne, *adv.* then, thereafter. [M.E. *sin*, *siððen*.]

Tae, *n.* toe; *tae'd*, toed. [M.E., A.S., and O.N. *tā*.]

taen, *ptc.* of *tak*, taken.

tak, *v.* take.

Tam, *n.* Thomas; dim. *Tammie*.

tangle, *n.* seaweed. [O.N. *þang*, *þöngull*; Dan. *tang*.]

tangs, *n.* tongs. [M.E. and A.S. *tange*.]

tap, *n.* top, head.

tapetless, *adj.* torpid, lifeless, numb (esp. with cold). [Sc. *tabets*, bodily sensation.]

tapsalteerie, *adv.* topsy-turvy.

tarrow, *v.* show lothness. [Another form of *tarry*; M.E. *targen*; O.Fr. *targier*.]

tassie, *n.* goblet. [Fr. *tasse*.]

tauld, past of *tell*. [Cf. M.E. *talde*.]

tawie, *adj.* tractable, tame. [*taw*, to handle much; M.E. *tawen;* A.S. *tāwian*, to treat, prepare.]

tawtet, *ptc.* matted, shaggy. [Cf. O.N. *tæta*, to tease wool; *tōt*, a flock of wool.]

teat, also **taet,** *n.* small quantity. [Perh. O.N. *tæta*, shreds.]

teen, *n.* vexation. [Obs. Eng. *teen;* M.E. *teone, tene;* A.S. *tēona*, injury.]

1. **tent,** *n.* box-pulpit, used in open-air preachings, with a covering stretched overhead. [L. *tendere.*]

2. **tent,** *n.* care, heed: *v.* take care of; heed. [M.E. *tent, atente;* Fr. *attendre.*] Wh. *tentie*, careful; *tentless*, heedless.

tester, *n.* small coin; sixpence. [For *testern* fr. O.Fr. *teste*, head (from the stamp).]

teughly, *adv.* toughly. [M.E. and A.S. *tōh*, tough.]

thack, *n.* thatch. [M.E. *thak;* A.S. *þæc*, a roof.]

thack an' rape, see *T. D.*, 78, note, and *B. A.*, 2, note.

thae, *pron.* those. [A.S. *þā.*]

thairm, *n.* gut; intestines of animals used for 'puddins,' also for fiddlestrings. [M.E. *tharm;* A.S. *þearm.*]

thairm-inspirin, *adj.* inspiring the fiddlestrings.

that, *adv.* so; *nae that fou*, not so very full.

thegither, *adv.* together.

the-morn, *adv.* to-morrow.

thick, *adj.* intimate; cf. *pack.*

thieveless, *adj.* without 'virtue,' ill-natured, cold, inactive, bootless. [Also *thowless;* M.E. and A.S. *þēaw*, virtue.]

thir, *pron.* these. [O.N. *þeir.*]

thirl, *v.* thrill. [M.E. *thurlen;* A.S. *þyrlian*, to pierce; cf. *dirl* and *drill.*]

thole, *v.* suffer, endure. [M.E. *tholen;* A.S. *þolian;* O.N. *þola.*]

thowe, *n.* thaw. [M.E. *thowe;* A.S. *þāwian.*]

thrang, *n.* throng, press: *adj.* busy, in great numbers. [M.E. and A.S. *þrang*, a crowd.]

thrave, *n.* two 'stooks' of cut grain, twenty-four sheaves. [M.E. *threve;* O.N. *þrefi.*]

thraw, *n.* and *v.* twist. [M.E. *thrawen;* A.S. *þrāwan.*]

thretteen, *adj.* thirteen. [M.E. *threottene;* A.S. *þrēotīene.*]

thrissle, *n.* thistle.

through, *v.* carry through, accomplish; *mak to through*, manage to finish.

throu' ther = *through ither*, through each other, indiscriminately, in confusion.

thrum, *v.* hum, 'birr'; strum. [O.N. *þrymr*, noise.]

thud, *v.* make a heavy booming sound.

tiend, *n.* tithe. [Dan. *tiende;* O.N. *tīund.*]

tight (gutt.), *adj.* well-knit and shapely, 'strappin.'

till, *prep.* to. [O.N. *til.*]

timmer, *n.* wood; timber.

tine, *v.* lose. [M.E. *tinen;* O.N. *tȳna.*]

tinkler, *n.* tinker, vagabond worker in tin; wh. vagabond. [*tink, tinkle.*]

tint, see *tine.*

tip, see *toop.* [The *i* is local.]

tippence, *n.* twopence.

tippenny, *n.* twopenny ale.

tirl, *v.* strip the roof off. [Freq. of *tirr*, to strip, pluck off.]

tither, *adj.* other: only with def. art. *the tither.* [Cf. *the tane* (the one); A.S. *þæt ān, þaet ōðer.*]

tittie, *n.* sister. [A corruption; cf. *sissy.*]

tittlin, *ptc.* chattering. [Cf. *tittle-tattle.*]

tocher, *n.* marriage portion. [C. *tochradh.*]

·tod, *n.* fox. [Prob. from *tod*, bush, on account of his tail; O.N. *toddi*, a tod of wool.]

toddy, *n.* whiskey punch.

todle, *v.* walk unsteadily, as a child.

toom, *adj.* empty. [M.E. and A.S. *tōm*, free from; O.N. *tōmr.*]

toon, see *toun.*

toop, tip, *n.* tup, ram.

toss, *n.* toast; belle (from the custom of toasting the reigning beauty).

toun, *n.* farm-stead. [A.S. and O.N. *tūn*, an enclosure, farmhouse and buildings.]

tousie, towsie, *adj.* shaggy, tumbled (of hair). [M.E. *tosen;* A.S. *tæsen*, to tease.]

tout (pron. **toot** with prolonged vowel), *v.* blow a blast of a trumpet. [Imit. word.]

tow (*ow* as in *cow*), *n.* rope, bell pull. [M.E. *towen;* A.S. *togian;* O.N. *toga*, to pull; *taug*, a rope.]

towmond, *n.* twelvemonth. [O.N. *tōlf;* Dan. *tolv*, twelve (w. *l* and *v* softened), and *month.*]

town, see *toun.*

towsie, see *tousie.*

toyte, *v.* totter, 'todle.'

transmugrified, *ptc.* metamorphosed.

trashtrie, *n.* trash [=*trashery.* For the *t* cf. *wastrie*].

trig, *adj.* neat, spruce. [Akin to Eng. *trick*, adorn.]

trouth, trowth, *adv.* troth, in truth.

tryste, *n.* agreement, appointment; wh. a hiring-market, fair. [M.E. *tryst*, trust; O.N. *treysta*, to rely on.]

trysted, *ptc.* agreed upon.

twa, *adj.* two.

twal, *adj.* twelve.

twin, *v.* divide in twain, separate; wh. deprive. [M.E. *twinnen;* cf. A. S. *getwinne.*]

tyke, *n.* dog, cur. [M.E. *tike;* O.N. *tīk.*]

Unco, *adj.* uncouth; strange, unusual: *adv.* very, uncommonly. [M.E. and A.S. *uncūð*, unknown.]

uncos, *n.* odds and ends of news.

unfauld, *v.* unfold.

unsicker, *adj.* unsteady, untrustworthy. [*sicker.*]

usquebae, *n.* whiskey. [C. *uisge beatha*, aqua vitae.]

Vauntie, *adj.* proud, boastful. [Fr. *vanter*, to boast.]

vera, *adv.* very. [Cf. obs. Eng. *veray;* O.Fr. *verai.*]

virl, *n.* ring, ferrule. [M.E. and O.Fr. *virole.*]

vogie (*g* hard), *adj.* vain, proud.

Wa', *n.* wall.

wabster, *n.* weaver. [M.E. *webstere;* A.S. *webbestre,* a female weaver.]

1. **wad,** *v.* would. [Cf. M.E. *walde.*]

2. **wad,** *v.* wed; wager, pledge. [M.E. and A.S. *wedd,* a pledge; cf. Sw. *vad.*]

wae, *n.* woe: *adj.* woful, vexed. [A.S. *wā, wǣ;* O.N. *vei.*]

waesucks, *interj.* alas.

wae worth, see *worth.*

waft, *n.* weft, woof. [M.E. and A.S. *weft.*]

wair, *v.* spend. [O.N. *verja,* to lay out money; A.S. *werian,* wear.]

wale, *n.* choice: *v.* choose, select. [M.E. *walen;* O.N. *velja.*]

walie, *adj.* goodly; powerful. [Prob. from *wale.*]

wallop, *v.* swing loosely: *n.* loose and unsteady movement. [M.E. *walop;* Fr. *galop;* O. Flem. *walop,* gallop.]

wame, *n.* belly, stomach. [M.E. *wambe;* A.S. *wamb.*]

wan, *v.* past of *win.*

wanchancie, *adj.* unlucky. [M.E. *wan-,* un-; A.S. *wan;* O.N. *van-r,* lacking, and *chance.*]

wanrestfu', *adj.* unrestful, restless. [See above.]

ware, *v.* worn. [Form not legitimate.]

wark, *n.* work.

warl', warld, *n.* world.

warlock, *n.* wizard. [M.E. *warloghe,* a deceiver (esp. the devil); A.S. *wǣr,* troth; *loga,* liar.]

warly, warldly, *adj.* worldly.

warsle, *v.* wrestle, struggle, twist. [M.E. *wrastlen.*]

warst, *adj.* worst.

wastrie, *n.* waste. [*wastery;* cf. *trashtrie.*]

1. **wat,** *adj.* wet.

2. **wat,** *v.* trow, know. [M.E. *witen;* A.S. *witan;* pres. ind. *wāt.*]

wattle, *n.* wand, flexible rod. [A.S. *watol,* a hurdle.]

wauble, *v.* wabble, reel, move unsteadily.

waught (gutt.), *n.* draught of liquor. [For *quaught,* fr. C. *cuach,* a beaker, bowl; Eng. *quaff* is cognate.]

1. **wauk, wauken,** *v.* wake, awaken.

2. **wauk, wauket,** *ptc.* thickened and hardened (through shrinking). [M.E. *walkien,* to full, fr. A.S. *wealcan,* to roll, toss; cf. the name *Walker,* and Dan. *valke,* to full cloth.]

waukrife, *adj.* sleepless, wakeful. [*wauk* 1. and *rife,* plentiful.]

waur, *adj.* worse: *v.* worst, get the better of. [M.E. *werre, worre;* O.N. *verri;* Dan. *værre.*]

wean, *n.* child; dim. *weanie.* [M.E. *wenen;* A.S. *wenian,* to wean; cf. Eng. *weanling.*]

weason, *n.* weasand, throat. [M.E. and A.S. *wāsend.*]

1. **wecht**, *n.* weight. [M.E. *weghen;* A.S. *wegan.*]

2. **wecht**, *n.* an instrument for winnowing grain, like a sieve without the holes, the bottom being of stretched sheepskin. [M.E. *weggen;* A.S. *wecgan,* to shake.]

wee, *adj.* little; *wee bit,* used as *adj.* slight; *wee thing, adv.* slightly. [Obs. Eng. *we,* as in *a little we,* a little bit, a short way; prob. fr. M.E. *wei;* A.S. *weg.*]

weed, *n.* array. [M.E. and A.S. *wǣde,* garment.]

weeder-clips, *n.* shears for cutting weeds.

weel, *n.* prosperity: *adv.* well; *weel I wat,* I 'm sure; *weel-won,* honorably earned, hard-worked-for.

weepers, *n.* mourning bands.

weet, *n.* and *v.* wet.

weil, *n.* eddy. [M.E. and A.S. *wǣl.*]

we'se, *v.* we shall.

westlin, *adj.* westerly.

wha, wham, whase, *pron.* who, whom, whose.

whaizle, *v.* wheeze. [A.S. *hwēsan.*]

whalpit, *ptc.* whelped.

whang, *n.* large thick slice. [Prob. conn. w. *whack;* cf. Sc. use of *dunt,* a blow, or a large piece.]

whare, whaur, *adv.* where. [M.E. and A.S. *hwǣr, hwǎr.*]

whatna, *adj.* what kind of.

wheep, *n.* see *penny-wheep.*

1. **whid**, *v.* whisk, move rapidly: *n.* rapid movement.

2. **whid**, *n.* fib, falsehood.

whigmaleerie, *n.* whimsies, crotchets. [The name of a ridiculous drinking-game.]

whiles, *adv.* sometimes. [Adv. gen. of *while* and the more primitive form of *whilst.*]

whin, whinstane, *n.* greenstone, trap. [Said to be for *whern-stone,* millstone, fr. *quern,* a mill.]

whins, *n.* gorse. [C. *chwyn,* weeds.]

whintle, see *wintle.*

whip, *v.* snatch.

whirligigum, *n.* fantastic ornament.

whirrin, *ptc.* word expressive of the flight of a partridge. [Imit. word; cf. Dan. *hvirre.*]

whisht, *n.* silence: prop. an *interj.*

whitter, *n.* dram, drink.

whittle, *n.* knife. [M.E. *thwitel;* A.S. *þwītan,* to pare; wh. Sc. *white,* to cut.]

whunstane, see *whin.*

wi', *prep.* with.

widdie, woodie, *n.* rope (prop. of *withes*), halter. [M.E. *wiði,* a willow; A.S. *wiðig.*]

wile, wyle, *n.* instinct, penetration; ruse, artifice: *v.* lure, entice. [M.E. *wile;* A.S. *wīl.*]

willyart, *adj.* wild, shy. [Same as *will,* astray, with term. *-art.*]

wily, *adj.* astute, shrewd. [*wile.*]

wimple, *v.* meander; ripple. [Prob. freq. of *wimp,* doublet of *wind,* twist.]

1. **win**, *v.* winnow. [*wind.*]

2. **win**, *v.* get; reach. [M.E. *winnen;* A.S. *winnan*, to toil, suffer.]

winna, *v.* will not.

winnock, *n.* window. [M.E. *windowe;* O.N. *vindauga*, lit. wind-eye.]

win't, past of *wind* = wound; cf. *stan't.*

wintle, *v.* stagger, reel. [Freq. of *wind;* A.S. *windan*, twist.]

winze, *n.* oath, curse. [Cf. Du. *verwenschen*, to curse.]

wiss, *v.* wish. [Cf. *buss*, bush.]

wistna, *v.* wist not, knew not. [Past of *wat.*]

wizened, *ptc.* dried up, wrinkled. [M.E. *wisenen;* A.S. *wisnian;* O.N. *visna.*]

wonner, *n.* wonder; scarecrow. [Cf. *hunner.*]

woodie, *n.* see *widdie.*

wooer-bab, *n.* lovers' knot. [See *bab.*]

1. **wordie**, *n.* dim. of *word.*

2. **wordie**, *adj.* worthy.

worset, *n.* and *adj.* worsted. [A corruption.]

worth, *v.* be, happen; *wae worth*, woe be to. [M.E. *wurthen;* A.S. *weorðan.*]

wow, *interj.* oh!

wrack, *v.* vex, torment.

wrang, *n.* and *adj.* wrong: *v.* injure. [M.E. and A.S. *wrang*, fr. *wringan*, to twist.]

writer, *n.* solicitor, lawyer. [W.S., *Writer to the Signet*, a title in Scots Law.]

wud, *adj.* mad, crazy. [Obs. Eng. *wood;* M.E. and A.S. *wōd.*]

wyle, see *wile.*

wyte, *n.* and *v.* blame. [M.E. and A.S. *wīte*, punishment.]

Yard, yaird, *n.* garden. [M.E. *yard;* A.S. *geard*, enclosure.]

yealins, *n.* things or persons of the same age. [Also *yeildins*, *eildins*, fr. *eild.*]

yell, *adj.* giving no milk. [Also *yeld;* M.E. *gelde;* O.N. *geld-r.*]

yerk, *v.* jerk, tug.

yestreen, *adv.* yester-even, last night.

yett, *n.* gate. [M.E. *yate;* A.S. *geat.*]

yeuk, *v.* itch. [Du. *jeuken;* cf. A.S. *giccan;* M.E. *yiken, yicchen;* Eng. *itch.*]

yill, *n.* ale. [*y* is local; cf. *yin* = *ane.*]

yill-caup, *n.* ale mug.

yird, *n.* earth.

yirr, *v.* gnar, snarl. [M.E. *yeorren;* A.S. *georran, girran.*]

yokin, *n.* yoking, half a day's work; wh. in general, a 'bout.' (See *Ep. Mrs. Scott*, 4, note.)

yont, *prep.* beyond. [Also *ayont;* cf. *ahint.*]

younker, *n.* youngster, young person. [Cf. Du. *jonker;* Dan. *junker.*]

yowe, *n.* ewe. [Dim. *yowie;* A.S. *ēow.*]

yule, *n.* Christmas. [M.E. *yol;* A.S. *gēol;* O.N. *jōl*, festival of the midwinter solstice.]

INDEX OF FIRST LINES.